I0723619

Adam, for every story you've ever made me believe in
Robert, for your unending support and encouragement
Sabrina and Christine, for inventing characters more
colourful than I could have imagined

Thank you.

This story is for all of us,
...so we never forget

Also by Justine Alley Dowsett:

Neo Central

Crimson Winter

Ruins of Sapphire
Lands of Jade
City of Ruby

With Murandy Damodred:

Mirror Worlds

Mirror's Hope
Mirror's Heart
Mirror's Deceit
Mirror's Despair

And coming soon... Mirror's Fate

Ismera

Unintended
Uncharted
Uncommon

CITY OF RUBY
CRIMSON WINTER
VOL.3

JUSTINE ALLEY DOWSETT

Ch. 1 – The Great Red Wave

"Yukari…"

The voice was distant and somewhat muted, but familiar. I fought through a red haze that threatened to engulf me.

"Yukari Namikoya!" the voice demanded again and I struggled to put a name to the speaker.

"…Sonoma-sensei?" The haze pulled back a little.

"That's more like it," he grumbled, the aged dwarf of a man coming into focus.

Sonoma-sensei taught science at Shinjuku High School…but I wasn't –

"Pay attention," he chided me, or perhaps the whole class. I could hear them now, chattering amongst themselves in a familiar fashion. "I have a new foreign exchange student to introduce…"

I struggled against the red haze, which filled my head like a fog. What was wrong with me?

"…now, take your seat," Sonoma-sensei instructed the new student.

I shook my head to clear it and glanced back over my shoulder to catch a glimpse of the exchange student, but all I saw was the back of his blonde head. Oh well, perhaps this new student would provide a challenge for me, but likely he wouldn't and things would remain as they always had.

Or had they…?

I had a vague recollection of a foreign exchange student coming to our class before, but I couldn't remember his name or even which country was from. The red haze began creeping again and I mentally forced it back – no, I was going to pay attention.

For the next few hours, I felt out of place. It was like I was having trouble shaking myself out of a dream, or like I was still half-asleep, though I didn't feel tired, but whenever I dwelt on it the red haze would return, filling my mind with its fog. I even considered making a trip to see the school nurse, but as the morning wore on the phenomenon grew less frequent and I started to settle back into my routine.

I filed into the cafeteria with everyone else and headed to my usual table overlooking the school yard through a wall of floor-to-ceiling windows. Taking my usual seat, I lifted my bag onto the table and reached into it for my bento box, but it wasn't there. Had I forgotten it?

I tried to think back to the morning, but all I got for my troubles was more red fog.

Even more than not paying attention in science class, forgetting my lunch was particularly unlike me. With a sigh, I pushed my chair back, fished some yen from my bag, and reluctantly joined the cafeteria line-up.

The sandwich cost me one hundred and fifty yen. The shrink-wrapped slices of white bread with the little bit of ham poking out in the middle were nothing particularly special. I sighed dejectedly – that would teach me not to forget my lunch again.

I felt eyes on my back. I stiffened, then forced myself to relax. It wasn't every day, but people often stared at my blue hair. I sighed and turned to see who it was this time, only to not recognize the blue eyes staring back at my own.

The foreign exchange student, it must be. He was tall and powerfully muscled with deeply tanned skin, golden blond hair, and light eyes. He stared at me in puzzlement, as if he was trying to figure out where he knew me from. I returned the stare from behind the shelter of my square-framed glasses, wondering myself at the aching familiarity I felt studying his features. Surely it wasn't possible we had encountered each other before if he was from out of the country, but nevertheless the feeling remained. We continued to study one another until a student passed between our two tables and the moment was broken. I forced myself to return my attention to my sad excuse of a lunch.

Fresh white bread, roughly cut, with a slice of meat and a leaf of lettuce; the sandwich before me lay innocently in its cloth wrapping. My hand hovered over it, unable to reach for it as I watched pink blotches blossom on the pristine white bread, marring it with the fluid leaking from my dead mount. That sandwich, soaked pink with discharged mount water and chunks of combined metal and flesh, was all that remained of the place where we had made camp and the sand around me was soaked with blood and tears.

Something was wrong. Something was missing and it ached that I couldn't remember what it was.

Red fog swirled in my mind, covering the strange vision until the fog was all I could see, all I could think. I forced my way past it and it was like swimming upstream against a powerful current, but then, all of sudden, I burst free of the haze.

I peeled the plastic wrap from my commercially produced sandwich and reconciled myself to taking a bite. It tasted just as synthetic as it looked, but what had I been expecting?

The afternoon sun was high in the sky as I exited through the main doors of Shinjuku High. Though it was well into fall now, the sun beamed down with a determined intensity, baking my skin with its dry heat. There was not a cloud anywhere to be found across the pale blue expanse and the harsh light gave no indication of dimming any time soon. I closed my eyes against the glare, but that only served to fill my vision with the red of light through my eyelids and I'd had enough of that colour for one day.

Shaking my head, I shrugged my way out of my unnecessary jacket and quickened my pace toward my mother's silver Toyota. Up ahead, I caught sight of my friend Yue boarding her father's bus after greeting him with an exuberant hug.

I smiled slightly, watching them. I would never admit it aloud, but I had always felt a little envious of the easy relationship Yue had with her parents. My family life had never been so simple, my father being a busy military lawyer and my mother made bitter by the fact that Father never seemed to have any time to spend with her. Unfortunately, that bitterness often spilled over onto me.

Mother smiled and waved as she caught sight of me. I froze, shocked – what could have made her so happy? Not wanting to ruin it for her, I quickened my pace further and practically darted to the rear passenger door of the little car, letting myself in and wondering what I could expect.

"Are you in a hurry, dear?" she asked with a bemused expression.

"No, Mother."

"Are you comfortable back there, Yukari, or did you want to move up here and sit with me?"

This was…different.

"I know you usually sit back there," she admitted, "but I realized we hardly ever talk, you and I, and I thought it might be good if we got to know each other a little better."

"All right, Mother," I answered tentatively and joined her in the front, leaving my school things behind.

"That's better, isn't it?"

I nodded but said nothing, worried my voice might betray how awkward I felt. It wasn't usual for my mother to treat me like an equal and I wondered what this could possibly be about. As she started up the car and pulled out onto the street I found myself studying her out of the corner of my eye.

"So," she said as she met my gaze with a sidelong one of her own, "any cute boys I should know about?"

"Mother!"

"What?" She grinned impishly. "It's just your father and I always sort of hoped that you would bring someone home to meet us, but you never did…not even any friends, except occasionally Hotaru."

"I don't like any boys, Mother," I answered, but as I spoke the words I knew in my heart they weren't true – there was someone…

"What about that boy…what was his name?" Mother continued, incorrigibly. "He was kind of cute. A little rougher around the edges than I would have expected…oh, what am I saying? I'm sure whomever you choose will be perfect."

My mind whirled, trying to understand what could have caused this change in my mother and what could have gotten her on the current subject, but along with my swirling thoughts came the red haze, blurring everything until I had no hope of unraveling it. I was lost in a maze of red and it wasn't until we reached our apartment complex, Hyuski Heights, that I became aware of my surroundings once more.

My mother never questioned my dazed state; remarkably, she left me alone and allowed me to retire to my room without so much as asking me if I had any homework. I closed the door with relief; I was used to being alone and more comfortable with it. My mother's strange behavior and my unexplained illness had me on edge.

My room was much as it always was, with the exception of a rather large box sitting atop my bed. It was more of a crate than a box, really, and it was unlabeled. Inexplicably, a crowbar lay next to it. Picking it up, I pried up the lid of the box and peered inside.

The red haze swirled ominously around an odd collection of objects. Reaching into the crate with both hands, I pulled out a stiff leather bag with a sturdy buckle and a silver badge in the shape of a lion's head affixed to the front. Placing the bag aside, I reached for an overly complex-looking longbow. I was in the archery club at school, was this meant to be a gift? And if so, from whom?

I reached in once more. Silken fabric rustled as I pulled a creamy white dress from the bottom of the box. It was in the Chinese style, with a high collar and a lengthy slit up one side. However, instead of being decorated with dragons or flowers as one might expect, there was a trail of white doves climbing from the hem to the neckline, as if in the midst of taking flight.

"It's beautiful," I whispered, despite myself, "but I don't have any krevels –"

Krevels…now where had I heard that before?

I felt suddenly dizzy as everything around me went red. I leaned on the bed, putting a hand to my head.

"Yukari!" Mother called from the other room and the fog cleared with her voice. "Dinner's ready!"

Leaving the red haze behind me, I headed out to join my mother and father around the long oval table in our dining room.

"How was your day, Yukari?" my father asked as we settled down to eat.

"Fine," I answered without thought, but as my blue eyes met his brown ones I suddenly had the feeling there was something I was supposed to tell him.

"What is it, Yukari?"

I struggled to remember what I wanted to tell him, but the red haze threatened again.

"Nothing, Daddy," I said quickly, cutting off that line of thought.

"You know you can tell me anything, right Yukari?"

There was something…something important I was supposed to tell him before it was too late…

Red fog enveloped me.

"You look very pretty today, Yukari," my mother said, her voice pulling me back to the dinner table. "I forgot to tell you earlier, but I like your hair down like that."

My hair was down? I brought a hand up to my head, and sure enough my hair was loose and tumbling about my head. Had I been so distracted that I hadn't even noticed until now I'd forgotten to wear it up like I always did?

"Oh, does it look okay, then? Usually it's a mess unless it's up."

"It's lovely," Father seconded, "and did you try those contacts I bought for you? It's a nice change to see you without your glasses."

I brought my hand down from my hair to feel about my face, and I also wasn't even wearing my glasses. Remarkably, I could see well enough, but as if in response to the realization I wasn't wearing my glasses, my sight began to blur visibly at the edges with the slightest hint of red.

"Oh no, I must have forgotten them at school…where I changed into my contacts…" I added the last bit to reassure my parents, even though it was false. "I guess I'll have to go back for them."

Mother frowned and I immediately regretted having dampened her rare good spirits.

"I'll go right after dinner," I assured them. "I know where they are," I lied, "and I was going to get some swimming practice in tonight anyways."

I hadn't intended that either, but with my mother's smile restored, I decided that was exactly what I would do with my evening. Perhaps swimming, something I loved, would help me to clear my head.

"You do that, Yukari," Mother agreed in a tone more characteristic of her, "and I don't want to hear that you've lost them. You know how much they cost…"

"Yes, Mother."

Lying wasn't like me, but neither was forgetting or misplacing things, and provisions had to be made for unusual circumstances. After helping to clean up, I poked around my room for my swimsuit, but when I couldn't immediately locate it I determined I must have left it at school as well. Perhaps my swimsuit and my glasses would conveniently be together in my locker or the girl's change room at the pool complex. With yet another sigh at the day I was having, I headed out, intent on reaching Shinjuku before dark.

Unfortunately, luck wasn't with me and it was almost fully dark before I even reached the entrance to the park across the street from Hyuski Heights. The sky was lit only by the oversized moon. The familiar notes from a common cell phone ring tone danced from the park, causing me to freeze with a sudden, unexplained feeling of terror.

The notes continued on, much longer than the average phone call could account for, and still I could not bring myself to break away from the park's entrance and continue on my way to the school.

Unbidden, my legs carried me closer to the sound.

No – I froze. I didn't want to go in there. There was something waiting for me in there, something I didn't want to see. The park was dangerous; I knew it in every fiber of my being, I just didn't know how I knew.

I recognized the ring tone, though I couldn't quite explain why it was familiar. It wasn't coming from my cell phone – I had the peculiar feeling I had lost my phone along with my glasses and my swimsuit – that particular ringtone belonged to…Kaji's girlfriend, Shuzhue.

If I followed that ringtone, would I find my friend's girlfriend waiting for me in the park? Was she there alone? Did she need my help?

Suddenly, I couldn't help but feel that finding Shuzhue and making sure she was okay was one of the most important things in the world. I took a step, then another. I couldn't leave her alone in there; if she was okay, she would have answered her phone by now, wouldn't she?

The eerie ringing stopped as soon as I crossed the threshold into the park, leaving only empty silence in its place. There were a few street lamps illuminating the park, but that was it. I seemed to be alone, but it was too dark to be completely certain.

"Hello?" I called out tentatively, hoping Shuzhue would be the one to answer, if anyone. I didn't feel safe here; I felt poised on a precipice, about to fall.

Motion caught my eye and I realized I wasn't alone after all. Yue was here, just out of reach of the light and swinging on one of the swings, her impossibly long brown hair trailing after her on the slight breeze created by her passage.

"Yue!" I called to get her attention, but she didn't respond.

Taking a few steps toward her as she entered her backswing, I realized she wasn't able to hear me; she had her earphones in and her head was bobbing in time to her music.

I hurried forward. "Yue, we have to get out of here, it's not safe!"

Yue had a habit of pretending to be listening to music when in reality she was paying attention, but she showed no sign of it if she could hear me. As if in defiance of my warning, she leapt suddenly from the swing and began to walk further into the park.

"Yue, wait!" I called again, but she was oblivious to my presence and kept on walking until she faded into the trees.

The red fog was back. I shook my head to try and clear it. Was I crazy? Had Yue been here with me or had I simply imagined her?

A scratching sound startled me out of the red haze and I spun, wary and alert, but the scene before me was a familiar one.

"Hotaru?" I questioned the two people digging in the sandbox at my feet. "Kaji?"

Kaji and Hotaru were both close friends of mine. My best friend, Hotaru, recognizable by her long and straight dark hair held back in a ponytail, was bent over double and digging furiously in the sand as if searching for something. Kaji beside her, usually so self-controlled, was doing much the same, only there were tears streaming down his face and I could tell that for him the act carried some deep emotional significance.

Shuzhue – I recognized what they were looking for immediately. Kaji's girlfriend was missing; of course they would be searching for clues to her whereabouts.

"Come on," I urged them. "We can't stay here. It's not safe."

"They'll never find me in there, you know." I flinched at the veiled accusation in her tone and my head snapped up at the sound of the familiar voice.

She came out of the deepest shadows between the trees. She was taller than I remembered but still short for her age, which looked to be about twenty-five or thirty, though in reality I knew her to be over eight hundred. Her hair was deep red, the colour of blood, and she wore her Shinjuku High school uniform as if it was a costume for her. Her eyes glowed like a ruby lit from within and there was a diamond-shaped mark upon her breast that glowed to match.

"Shuzhue, why –"

"Don't call me by that name!" she shrieked.

I struggled through the haze to remember what had changed about Shuzhue. The red fog was constant now. It felt as though I had to peer through it to even make out the scene before me. The fog swirled and coalesced around Shuzhue…no, Akuma; that was the name she wanted me to use. Lady Akuma had spent eight hundred years at the side of the Vile Emperor and she wasn't just Kaji's girlfriend anymore, but the Chosen of Rubia.

"Kaji!" I yelled. "She's here. She's right here, Kaji, you can stop looking for her now."

Kaji and Hotaru continued to dig as if I wasn't even there and perhaps, with all this fog between them and I, I wasn't.

Shuzhue – no, Akuma – laughed, her musical voice tinkling. "They can't hear you. They don't care about you. They only care about finding me. Should I lend them a hand?"

Shuzhue removed her bracelet from her wrist and dangled it between us. I reached for it, but before my hand closed around the intricate silver band she let it drop. As the bracelet struck the sand it suddenly became real in the scene before me and Kaji picked it up with a look of obvious horror on his features.

"Kaji, no, it's a trick!" I yelled, but to no avail; having found this clue to his missing girlfriend's whereabouts, Kaji resumed digging with a renewed vigor.

"I'll show you a trick." Shuzhue's voice deepened and took on a rougher quality.

Dreading what I would find, I raised my gaze to Akuma's waiting red eyes only to see her face had elongated slightly, taking on an almost canine appearance, and her skin had darkened, sprouting a sort of short, reddish-brown fur.

"Let's see what they think of this," she growled dangerously, using a now-clawed hand to tear free a ragged strip from the skirt of her school uniform.

The strip of plaid cloth fluttered down into the sandbox to land before Hotaru, who picked it up with a kind of reverence. "Kaji! I think we found Shuzhue's skirt!"

"No! Kaji, Hotaru, we have to go!" I screamed at them, despite knowing it would do no good.

Shuzhue's horrific transformation was nearly complete. She was on all fours now, claws digging into the ground. She was nearly eight feet tall at the shoulders and horn-like protrusions sprouted from her head and shoulders,and along her spine. The humanity Shuzhue had once possessed was now only barely evident in the intelligent eyes of the creature and the inquisitive tilt of its head, as if she – or it – was waiting to see what I would do next.

I had already proven to myself that Kaji and Hotaru could not hear me. I hoped for their sake whatever Shuzhue had become wouldn't hurt them, but I could not hold the same hope for myself. I took a cautious step backwards and was relieved when the fiendish creature did not follow.

Perhaps it wasn't as intelligent as it appeared; the animal before me certainly wasn't Shuzhue any longer. I put my hands out before me in a placating gesture and continued to back away from the massive beast, one step at a time.

I was halfway to the park entrance when I noticed yet someone else watching me. He stood beneath the glow of the street lamp, glaring hatred in my direction. His blond spiked hair, all-black clothing, and hateful expression were familiar to me and this time I was prepared for the wave of red fog that came as I remembered his name: Kai-Een, Talon of the Vile Emperor.

As if realizing I had recognized him for who and what he was, Kai-Een immediately dropped any pretense he had of simply being in this park by coincidence. Reaching behind himself, he pulled two slightly curved blades from sheaths at his back. In the light of the street lamp they glistened with freshly shed blood and, looking beyond Kai-Een, I was able to make out the crumpled forms of the two policemen he had already killed.

"No," I whispered, horrified. "This is impossible."

Kai-Een started forward and I broke and ran for the park's entrance.

"You can't outrun us!" Shuzhue's voice growled menacingly from the shadows. "We are relentless! We are eternal!"

I ignored her and kept running, the streets of the Shinjuku district speeding by in a red blur. The howls of the creature that was Shuzhue followed me, but I didn't look back.

The school's hallways were blissfully quiet and surprisingly bright. Even the red haze seemed to clear from my mind a bit as I caught my breath within the relative safety of Shinjuku High.

Had I imagined it? Perhaps the red haze was more troublesome than I had originally thought. It seemed as if my imagination was running away with me and creating horrors where there was nothing to fear. I took a deep breath to steady myself and determined I would make a doctor's appointment tomorrow – even my nightmares were not usually this horrible or vivid.

For now I had my glasses to find, and if I could also locate my swimsuit then a dip in the pool would certainly make me feel better. Reigning myself in, I strode with purpose toward the new swimming pool complex our school's student council president had raised the money last year to construct for us.

As expected, I found my swimsuit in my locker in the girl's change room, though my glasses were not in there. Changing quickly, I folded my uniform and placed it in the locker, grabbing a towel on my way out to the pool area. Considering the time, I figured that I would have the pool to myself, but surprisingly that wasn't the case.

He was waiting there for me, the blonde exchange student.

At least for a moment it seemed that way, as he looked up expectantly at the sound of my entrance. At first I was tempted to ignore him – being a student of Shinjuku High, he had just as much right to be here as I did – but after a moment I found myself studying him curiously. Why did he seem so very familiar?

Oddly, he wasn't wearing swim clothes, but rather he was still dressed in his school uniform from earlier in the day. Had he even gone home yet?

It occurred to me after a moment perhaps he wanted to swim, but hadn't yet been provided with a swimsuit from the school. However, the look on his face as he regarded the calm surface of the pool betrayed a deep aversion to water.

"What are you doing here?" The question escaped me before I even wondered if it would be rude of me to ask.

He looked startled, then immediately confused. "Me? Oh, I…" He stumbled over his words as if embarrassed and I noticed that though he was speaking Japanese, his accent was decidedly foreign, almost Scottish or Irish. "I suppose I just wanted to see it."

"See what?"

He turned his attention back to the pool and gestured vaguely at the clear blue water.

"Haven't you ever seen a pool before?" I asked, startled by his answer.

He shook his head, looking confused. "No, I don't think I have."

I found myself wondering where he had come from and wishing I had paid more attention to his introduction this morning. I opened my mouth to ask him when I was interrupted by the distant, yet unforgettable, sound of a chilling inhuman scream.

"What was that?!" I asked no one in particular, but he answered me regardless.

"Lillem."

The word brought up a sudden wall of red fog and I fought to see through it.

"There you are," a new voice spoke and the fog parted at the sound of it, revealing the face of someone who belonged in this setting, but I still hadn't expected to see. "Goji?"

Goji Nakamura, student council president of Shinjuku High, stood before me with a disapproving frown. He wasn't wearing swim clothes either, but his school uniform appeared uncharacteristically rumpled and his hair was unkempt.

"I've been looking all over for you," he informed me, his expression haggard.

"You have?"

Goji was my senior and considering I generally kept to myself, there was no reason for me to have drawn the attention of the student council president. He also didn't look much like himself at the moment. I was used to a more high profile president who always appeared confident and in control of his surroundings, not this disheveled creature with his long black coat, dark greasy hair, and sinister eyepatch.

Eyepatch? I did a double take, but sure enough Goji was wearing a worn eyepatch over his left eye. I stared, unable to look away, but before my very eyes the eyepatch seemed to fade into nothing more than red mist, which dissipated as it floated away.

Was this simply more of the red fog, creating nightmares to plague me while I was still awake? Real or not, the horrors were far from over. Beneath Goji's eyepatch was not the eye I expected to find, but only an empty socket containing a glowing red ruby, twirling rapidly in place as it pulsed with power.

Despite the revealed horrors of his face, Goji regarded me steadily and advanced slowly, as his appearance shifted from the enigmatic student council president of Shinjuku High to the sinister Fuzen, another Talon of the Vile Emperor.

"I see you managed to save one," Fuzen mocked in his thick European accent, gesturing beyond me to the foreign exchange student who no doubt still stood there, staring in shock much like I was. "What about the others you left behind to die?"

I took a step back from Fuzen's horrifying visage. Others? What others? I was alone, wasn't I?

I was nearly always alone, but yet I knew in my heart Fuzen's words were true. There were people I had forgotten, people and things missing from this nightmare I was stuck in. I couldn't deny it any more than I could deny the instinct screaming at me that I had left those people in grave danger and I had a duty to protect them.

"No," I said forcefully, denying Fuzen. "You can't have him. I won't let you kill him or anyone else."

I took a deliberate step to place myself between Fuzen and the foreign exchange student, prepared to do whatever it took to protect him from the Talon. Fuzen smiled wickedly, his mouth stretching at the corners in a menacing, unnatural fashion as he continued to advance.

I didn't hesitate. The red fog came and enveloped me, but I didn't let that stop me either; I knew what I had to do.

I formed an arrow with my mind.

It shone brightly with a cyan light more intense than the red fog. The arrow, like my will made manifest, appeared before me and shot out from between my outstretched hands to impale Fuzen with its glow. He fell, crumpling to the ground lifelessly, as if he had been nothing more than a puppet dancing on unseen strings.

The inhuman screams of the Lillem were repeated from various directions and I wasted no time, whirling to face the person I had just saved.

"Yukari?" The exchange student was regarding me wide-eyed, no doubt shocked by what he had just witnessed.

I took his reaction in stride at first, grabbing hold of his arm to pull him away from here, but then I realized what he had just said. He knew my name…

Perhaps he had heard it in the classroom this morning, but even if he had that still didn't explain the familiarity with which he had spoken it. That accent, so memorable, speaking my name; I was certain I had heard it before.

"Masaru," I responded and his name, who he was, and how much he meant to me came flooding back all at once, as if whatever had tried to keep the information from me hadn't been enough to contain it forever.

This was Masaru. My Knight, my Roughlander, and the love of my life – how could I ever have forgotten him? It just didn't seem possible, but then again none of this had made any sense since the beginning.

The red fog was swirling everywhere now, but it didn't leave me unable to function like it had before. It also didn't seem internal any longer, but instead it threatened to destroy the landscape before me, eating at the floor and the walls here and there, making them look less than solid.

Masaru was studying me curiously, as if he was battling his own inner fog. The expression on his face was so familiar to me and I realized I had seen it before. I had left Masaru behind once because he couldn't remember who he was back at the Roughlander

Sanctioned Outpost in Taiyou. I had left him there and it had resulted in him almost losing his life to Fuzen.

This time Fuzen lay dead on the floor behind me, but I could hear the Lillem scratching at the door now, trying to break it down to get to us – their prey. I wasn't going to leave him behind again, no matter what; I had promised I would always keep him safe.

"Masaru," I said his name once more as behind me I heard the door crash inwards to admit the hoard of Lillem.

He met my eyes, his expression muddled as he struggled to regain his own will and memories. I willed him to succeed, but I could hear the Lillem behind us now as they scrabbled across the room, their talons clacking ominously along the tiled floor. Memories flooding back to me steadily now, I did what I had done the last time to try and snap him out of his haze and kissed him full on the lips.

It worked; I could feel it as Masaru returned the kiss with feeling.

It lasted only a moment, which was all we had time for before the Lillem reached us. I pulled back from him and gave him a push forward. "Go!"

Hoping he would do as directed and flee, I whirled about to face the Lillem and do what I could to buy him the time to get away.

There were so many of them. The students of Shinjuku High, every one of them, had been infected with the curse of the Lillem and now they were after Masaru and I to make us just like them. Lillem talons, like scorpion tails, shot upwards from their shoulder blades and out from their hips to allow them to scuttle their way forward and to give them deadly weapons with which to infect anyone they came across. The Lillem were undead, in a way, and their animated corpses screeched unnaturally, contorting their expression beyond anything a human could have produced. I shied back from them involuntarily, but the situation was far worse than simply a horde of mindless Lillem intent on my death.

Shuzhue was there too, or at least the Hound Shuzhue had become, and alongside her stood Kai-Een, glaring balefully. Together they would act as the Lady Lilyth's generals and direct the Lillem that made up her army.

I spared a glance over my shoulder at Masaru to see how he was faring, only to realize he was climbing up the high diving board. Higher ground, yes. I needed to get to higher ground to defend us both.

Not having the time to hesitate, I whirled about and ran after Masaru to the base of the diving platform's ladder. Climbing faster than I ever thought possible, I raced the encroaching Lillem to reach the top before they could stop me, urging Masaru to climb more quickly.

We reached the top before the Lillem were more than halfway up the ladder. Lifting my arms, I fired off a few more of my cyan arrows to slow them down. "We have to find a way out of here," I told Masaru. "I can't hold them off forever. It's only a matter of time before they overwhelm us."

"I know," he responded solemnly, understanding the threat, "but Yukari, how do we go back?"

Tearing my gaze away from his in our final moments together, I looked about the room to see if there was any hope of escape from this situation. The red haze eddied and swirled about the room, blurring parts of the walls, the windows, the ceiling, and even the horde of Lillem below.

Curiously, Adel's words came back to me as I surveyed the scene: *No matter how real it seems, it could be a hallucination or what she wants you to see.*

The Lady Lilyth – more memories flooded into my mind. The Lillem were her creatures, her army; the Hounds, her Generals. I looked toward the Shuzhue-Hound. The Lady Lilyth saw through her Hounds. If a person was bitten or injured by a Hound, she could make them see or believe whatever she wanted them to, like the school being infested with Lillem, or like I was back on Earth in Japan instead of where I belonged.

The more I realized this place and the horrors within it weren't real, the more tendrils of red fog developed to help me to see through the illusions. The red infected everything, swirling about and through the visions my mind had created to help Lilyth control me.

I glanced back over at Masaru. Was he a figment of the hallucination also? Would he, too, turn into a Hound, or a Lillem, or something else, and reveal himself to be no more than one of her creatures?

No. The red swirled around him but never through him, like it did everything else. He remembered. She had tried everything to keep us from remembering each other because together we would be strong enough to break this illusion of hers. He had to be real.

And so was the water in the pool below us.

In fact, the water looked more real than anything else in this horrific dreamscape, only it didn't reflect the room but rather an endless desert – or Sand Lake, as Masaru would have called it. The desert showed rocky cliffs in the distance and a pale blue sky with not a single cloud to block the harsh light of the sun. As I watched, the sun lowered itself to the horizon, bounced, and then began its return journey through the sky.

Home.

"That's it, Masaru, look!" I directed his gaze downwards.

He looked into the pool, but his expression remained dubious.

"We have to go," I insisted. "It might be the only way out of here."

"Aye," he responded, "and it might kill us too."

"I'll keep you safe," I promised.

Remember fear, Yukari. I heard Sabien's voice in my mind and the Knight Commander's words stiffened my resolve. No matter how frightening taking that leap into the unknown would be, I knew it was the right thing to do.

You can do it, kiddo, Jeth's voice added, reassuring me.

I felt a hand on my shoulder offering me wordless support and I realized there was more here in my mind than just a nightmarish dreamscape. Lilyth could use my memories against me, but no matter how powerful she was she couldn't control me completely.

I was a Chosen of Sapphiros – I had access to just as much power as she did and I had the backing of my Knights, my friends, and my family, and I could feel all of them here with me.

Not wasting another minute with meaningless distractions, I summoned my power and created wings at my back made of cyan energy in the shape of a multitude of feathers. My cyan power glowed, obliterating the remaining images of the dreamscape and leaving only an empty red shell in its place. Taking Masaru into my arms, I leapt as the last of the diving board we were standing upon faded out of existence and back into the red fog it had been created from. Together, we dove into the reflection of the world where we belonged, leaving the false vision of Earth Lilyth had created to trap us behind forever.

CH. 2 – SACRIFICE

*P*ain.

The icy shock of suddenly being alive once more was almost too much to bear. In some ways the world of memories and illusions Lilyth had created for me was almost preferable; certainly it had been easier and simpler to believe I was back on Earth. The unforgiving cold stone beneath my aching body felt just a little too real.

I gasped, taking ragged breaths of air into unused lungs, trying to regulate my erratic heartbeat and gain control of myself – what had she done to me?

My mind, though no longer filled with haze of any kind, was as disoriented as my body, but my memories were all present and very much immediate. The last thing I remembered was turning Adel and I to mist to save us from…

The Lady Lilyth.

She had taken over her own daughter's body, but there was no denying who had been responsible for the fall of Taiyou.

My thoughts stumbled over one another, as if trying to make up for the time I had spent unaware of my circumstances. If Lilyth was back and Taiyou had fallen to her, then where was I now?

Wherever I was, it was pitch black and I couldn't see a thing. There was cold stone beneath me, and when I moved my right hand it brushed up against something jagged and sharp. There was a draft, but somehow I felt I was somewhere inside rather than out in the open. I heard someone panting to my left and someone else rustling in the dark behind me, so at least I wasn't alone here.

"Masaru?"

"No, it's me," a male voice answered. It wasn't Masaru, but I recognized the voice all the same.

"Kaji?"

"Yeah, and Hotaru's here too, beside me."

"What about Yue?"

"I think she was here before, but she's gone now. You know how fast she is."

I did know how fast Yue had become with the help of the power Sapphiros had granted us. Thinking about who we were and what we were capable of reminded me that I could see through this blackness if I chose. It took surprisingly more effort and concentration than I was used to, but before long the darkness began to lighten for me enough to be able to make out my surroundings.

The large, cavernous chamber around us seemed like a natural formation despite its roughly circular shape. The floor was relatively smooth stone like I had surmised, but the area around me was littered with shards of Ruby. The shards confused me at first, until my eyes adjusted enough to see what lay in the rest of the room: eggs. Large, oval egg-shaped Rubies covered the floor of the cavern.

I looked down once more, a horrid realization dawning. The pile of Ruby shards fanned out in a rough oval from where I sat in the center. Turning my head, I noted three more piles, one surrounding Hotaru, another where Kaji was slowly climbing to his feet, and a third, unoccupied, where I gathered Yue had awoken. There was no sign of Masaru and no other broken eggs. I scanned the room once more in horror as my understanding of the circumstance grew; there were people in each and every one of these eggs, each of them experiencing their own horror as I had done.

Was Masaru even here? Was he in an egg of his own or had he really just been a part of the dreamscape?

I clamped down hard on my rising panic. I could find him with my power, but for that I had to stay calm. I closed my eyes and relied on the otherworldly sense Sapphiros had gifted me with. *Masaru.* A glowing ball of light, though dimmer than I was used to, appeared in my mind and I could sense exactly where he was in relation to me.

Opening my eyes, I scrabbled in the direction where I had felt his presence, my legs not quite working well enough for me to stand, until I reached his egg. He was here, but why wasn't he free? I had taken him with me, hadn't I?

But perhaps it didn't work like that. Maybe Masaru needed to find his own way out. I stared at the Ruby egg before me, my ears straining for any indication it might be cracking open, but the room stayed silent other than the sounds of Kaji helping Hotaru to her feet behind me.

I took a moment to count the eggs in the room, barely noticing Kaji and Hotaru trying to fumble their way through the room in the darkness. There were a little over thirty eggs and only our four had cracked open, freeing us. My brain, logical as ever, provided me with reasons why this might be, as much as I wanted to deny it. Kaji, Hotaru, Yue, and I were the Chosen of Sapphiros and, like it or not, our powers made us different from everyone else. We had broken free of Lilyth's strange sort of prison, but perhaps it had been our power that had enabled us to do so.

Masaru, being a Knight, like Adel, Sabien, Jeth, and the others, had been given a certain measure of power as well. It was possible he could also find a way free of the egg as we had done, but there was no way of knowing how long that would take, if that even was the key to freedom.

"Kaji, Hotaru?" a lightly accented voice spoke from the cave's entrance. "Yukari?"

Aysel, newly-made Knight of Sapphiros, was her twin sister Adel's exact double in physical appearance, though vastly different in personality and experience. In the months I had known her, Aysel had been through as much as any of us, but in her case that had involved losing her arm and gaining a substitute one created by the power of her Knighting. Her right hand was now made of blue Sapphire and was connected to her shoulder by a field of cyan light. She held up a lit torch so she could see us. Her red hair reflected the torchlight brightly, but her expression looked haggard and there was a deep worry in her eyes. Yes, we had lost and things had gone very badly, but it was a small relief to see Aysel alive and well and walking about freely.

"...Yue said you'd all be out, but how did you do it?" Aysel sounded awed. "No one's ever gotten out of one of Lady Lilyth's eggs before, or so I've been told. It's not supposed to be possible."

"We're Chosen. Her power couldn't hold us forever," Kaji stated.

I'm just glad you're safe," Aysel responded, "and Ris will be happy to see you as well."

"Ris is okay?" I asked. "And Sabien?"

"What about everyone else?" Hotaru interjected. "What about Taiyou?"

Aysel's face fell. The relief at seeing the four of us must have been the only thing keeping her going. "We don't know about Sabien...or...almost anyone. We're in the Temple of Machalite. Fuun brought us here and he saved as many people as he could, though until now we didn't know who the eggs contained. We were pretty sure we had you four, but...Ris is upstairs with Sir Rama and Ao Kouen. Neither of them have been well for days –"

"How long, Aysel?" Kaji asked sharply, interrupting the flow of information.

"What?"

"How long has it been?"

"A week I think, or thereabouts," Aysel said. "A lot has changed. Come upstairs with me and I'll do my best to fill you in with what I know, though it isn't much."

Kaji helped Hotaru to the entrance by the light of Aysel's torch, but I didn't move from where I sat next to Masaru's egg.

"Yukari, are you coming?" Aysel asked. "I'm sure Ris would be glad to see you and your help with the wounded would be welcome."

"No..." I spoke quietly, my denial sounding strange even to my own ears, and then I repeated myself a little louder to make sure they heard me. "No, I'm staying here. I'm not leaving him. Maybe there's something I can do...to get them out."

Aysel nodded after a moment. "I understand. Just...be careful, all right? Sir Rama tried to put his hand into one of those eggs three days ago and he still hasn't recovered. They're dangerous if disturbed."

I nodded my understanding and the three of them left me in the darkened egg room. Alone, the truth of my circumstance finally began to sink in.

We had lost; Taiyou had fallen and somehow I had to assume Lilyth, or at least her innumerable forces, ruled there now, if they hadn't destroyed it completely. The four of us, Aysel, Rama, Ris, Ao Kouen, and these thirty odd Ruby eggs, were the survivors and now we hid licking our wounds in the Temple of Machalite.

It had been a week, Aysel said. A week ago, Taiyou and its defenders had stood strong against a horde of invaders protected by every means and every ally we could gather, and just like that it had all fallen apart, reducing us to no more than a few scattered refugees.

Masaru was imprisoned, but he was beside me and I knew where he was, at least. What about everyone else? My parents, my friends, the rest of the Knights – where were they? Aysel said they had no way of knowing who was in these eggs they had liberated from Taiyou, but maybe I did.

I unfolded my legs carefully from my tangled dress, trying to ignore the ragged state of the blue cloth. This dress had been a gift from Felice, my friend Mifa's sister, and I had hoped to be able to wear it at least more than once before ruining it. My legs felt stiff and sore from misuse, but other than a few yellowed bruises they appeared fine and I was able to get them under me, though I would need some help to stand. I reached out with my left arm to support myself when I felt a sharp stab of pain and realized something was wrong.

With the flare of pain came the memory of what happened, or rather the absence of it.

My arm had been broken during the time Lilyth had occupied my body, using it to help her reach the throne of Taiyou to defeat us all. Adel and Rama had valiantly tried to delay her and they had fought me, which resulted in my body taking the damage from their attacks. I remembered snapping back to awareness in my own skin feeling broken and battered; the Knights had done their job well.

Now it had been a week, or maybe a little longer, judging by how much my bone had mended while held immobile in the Ruby egg. Each of us was different, but with my powers as a Chosen I was able to alter my vision in different ways; one of those ways – or perhaps a combination of those ways – was to be able to see through or into objects and people like an x-ray. Doing so, I noted the bone in my arm would need to be reset. It had healed incorrectly and was nearly useless as it was. Unfortunately, the healing process would have to start all over again once I set it, but perhaps I had a solution for that.

Masaru had always chided me for not trusting the medical miracle the Roughlanders were so fond of, Flaqqers. With my other hand, I pulled my Flaqqer device from the medic kit I always wore strapped to my chest and proceeded to check it; three uses left.

Flaqqers caused a person to heal so much faster than what would be considered natural on Earth, but to use a Flaqqer on someone meant injecting them with the larvae of a sandcrawler, one of the massive beasts that roamed the Sand Lakes on this world. Masaru assured me the larvae died once their task of accelerating the healing process was complete and I had seen the evidence with my own eyes – thanks to my power – but still, the thought of injecting myself with bug larvae was not a comfortable one. Though, I supposed using a Flaqqer on myself was just something I would have to get used to if I wanted to be accepted as a Roughlander.

I could see clearly what I would have to do to reset the bone, but it meant re-breaking it; there was no other option. I set the Flaqqer device on the ground to my right and then, trying not to think too hard on what I was about to do, I took hold of my left wrist with my right hand and flung myself bodily at Masaru's egg.

I heard the sickening crunch before the pain caused me to cry out. It was nearly impossible to even think past the pain in my arm, but I forced myself to fumble around for the Flaqqer device and jab the pointed end of it into my arm, using my power to ensure it was now aligned properly.

I constructed a basic sling from the Roughlander belts I had left around my waist for sentimental value, but it still took some time before the pain began to dull enough that I could function. I stood and supported myself with my uninjured arm, realizing I had to do something to distract myself, both from the pain and from the uncomfortable thought of baby sandcrawlers worming themselves through my flesh.

Technically, I needn't have moved as I could just as easily adjust my vision to see things close up or far away, but I didn't yet know if the Ruby of the eggs would impede my powers, and chances were they would. I had already discovered that on this planet, where the five gem gods reigned, precious stones like Sapphire, Jade, and Ruby, usually bore some power or relation to the gem god they represented. Other than being a creative prison, I wouldn't be surprised if the Ruby eggs had some other special properties simply born of the material of their creation.

Staring at the egg before me, I twisted my vision to try and see who might be trapped within. I got deep enough within the egg to see a shoulder and some brown hair before the egg retaliated by filling my vision with a burning red.

Startled, I stopped trying to see into the egg and the sensation eased immediately. Unfortunately, I hadn't seen enough to identify the egg's occupant, beyond the fact it was likely female.

Were the eggs trapped? Aysel had said Rama was injured trying to reach into one; I could well imagine what Rama had tried. The particular power granted to him with his Knighting allowed him to pass through solid objects at will. Evidently, when he had tried to do so with these Ruby eggs, they had stopped him – and so violently that he was left too injured to try again.

Frowning, I lowered myself to the ground once more – it was getting easier as my legs got used to working again. I closed my eyes and forced myself to concentrate; there were other ways of finding out who was in the eggs. I felt the room with my power; fanning outwards with my mind from where I sat somewhere near the center. There were twenty-nine whole eggs left in the room – I had counted them – but I could feel twenty-nine and a half life forces present, two very near to each other. It came to me in a flash of insight as it was the only explanation: someone was pregnant.

I opened my eyes and pin-pointed which egg had the expectant mother. It was on the far side of the room, along the wall. As I tucked that information away, it struck me just how tragic it was. So many lives had been disrupted, people separated from one another. There were less than thirty people in this room and likely not many more than that had been brought here by Fuun; where were all the others?

I closed my eyes once more and I could feel tears beginning to form, but I had to concentrate. Our powers were linked to our emotions and too much would make me unable to be of use.

Sabien. There, he wasn't far at all. I opened my eyes to find myself staring at the egg nearest to the door and I breathed out in relief; we had him.

Steeling myself for the next name, I tried again. This method was slow, but it was the only way to be sure the people I loved were okay. *Dahlia.* The Roughlander Corporal and the woman Masaru saw as a sister was here too, in another egg. I let out another breath.

Razor. Dahlia's brother and another person in Masaru's pseudo-family. I searched and searched, holding my breath, but there was nothing, not a glimmer of his presence. The tears began; I couldn't stop them, but I had to go on.

Mifa, my friend from Taiyou, was in the egg I had first inspected. *Goji,* Shinjuku High's former student council president and the person closest to Mifa's heart, was missing, and so was Mifa's sister, *Felice,* whom I thought I felt, but was too distant to make out.

Jeth, nothing. *Pine,* another Knight of Sapphiros, was in the room, imprisoned, while *Adel,* was somewhere above me and far away – maybe Taiyou?

I had left the names I was most concerned about until the end, but I was crying fiercely now and it was only a matter of time before my power stopped working. I had to find them now, before I discovered anyone else was missing and broke down completely.

I took a deep breath. *Father.*

My mother and father, along with all of our parents, had followed the four of us to this planet once they had figured out where we had gone. I hadn't wanted them to stay, knowing how dangerous it was, but truthfully in my heart I had been glad when they had decided to remain anyway.

Now my worst nightmares were coming true. I could feel my father's presence and so I knew he was alive, but he was far away from here, somewhere near where I had felt Adel. His life force was much fainter than hers had been; was there something wrong with him? Was he dying?

I wanted to hold on to the sense of his presence and will him to stay strong until I could get to him. I was unbelievably tempted to simply use my power to send myself to him, but there was no way of knowing where I would appear and I was certainly in no condition to fight for myself or him, should I appear somewhere in Taiyou before Lilyth, or one of her innumerable agents. Regretfully,

I tore myself away from the thought and forced myself to return to reality as I still had one more person to try and find.

Mother. I let out a breath in relief. She was here; not in an egg, like most of the others I had sensed, but actually here in Machalite's Temple, wherever that was. Before I fully realized it, my power worked on my behalf and I sent myself to her.

"Yukari!" Mother dove at me and tried to pull me into an embrace before she realized I wasn't fully solid. "Is that you? Are you really here or am I just imagining you?"

"I'm really here, Mother," I assured her, feeling numb.

We were alone and it was rather dark; the small, empty room we were in was lit only by the glow of my astral form. Mother looked tired and sad, her eyes were red from crying. From what I could tell she wasn't hurt, but she showed signs of having lived through an ordeal. Her disheveled hair and the way she sat, huddled in on herself, betrayed how afraid she was.

"Are you all right?"

Tears fell down her face. "How can you even ask that? I was worried about you. You've been missing for days and no one knew what happened to you, only that the Chosen were gone and weren't coming back."

"Didn't Aysel tell you we were in the eggs?"

"I haven't seen Aysel," Mother admitted, "or any of your Knights. It's dark here and there's the danger of falling off the cliff. None of us have any lights. I've only spoken with some of the refugees, the other parents…Yukari, I haven't been able to find your father."

The way she choked over those words broke my heart. "I know, but he's alive," I reassured her. "I found him with my power. We'll get him back."

"Oh, Yukari!" My mother looked so grateful and it was obvious she wanted to hug me, but I couldn't stay here and I wouldn't leave Masaru to come here in person, not while he was still stuck in that egg and there might be something I could do to get him out.

"I have to go," I told her, regretfully. I didn't want to leave her alone now that I had found her, but I could sense distantly that someone or something was trying to get my attention back in the egg room. "I'm below you somewhere in the room with the Ruby eggs. I'll come back when I can, but that's where I am if you want to come find me, all right?"

Mother bit her lip worriedly, but she nodded. I left her and let myself become aware of my own body again, and the pain and discomfort that awaited me there, only to find I wasn't alone anymore. When she saw the glimmer of awareness return to my eyes, Ris darted in and caught me up in a hug, nuzzling her furred face against my cheek.

"Careful, Ris, my arm is broken," I warned her, though in truth the Kumori had been very gentle.

Ris was one of the Knights of Sapphiros, as well as being a very talented healer and a good friend, though she wasn't human. The slightly built, brown-furred woman was a Kumori, a race of silent bat-people who, from what I could gather, were rare, even on this world.

I'm so glad you are all right, Ris signed to me in the manner she used to communicate. Being mute, she was naturally very expressive, but through working with her on various patients I had come to understand her more readily than most people did. The exception, of course, was Sabien, who seemed to have a sort of mental connection with the woman he loved.

"I'm mostly fine Ris, but so many people are missing…"

Ris' face fell and I saw the strain she was under. I had seen the Kumori Knight tired before. I had seen her use her magic to heal everyone before tending to herself, but I had never seen her like this. The pain, the loss, and the worry was eating her alive.

"Oh, I'm sorry Ris…I didn't mean…Sabien is okay. He's in an egg, right over there," I said and pointed to show her which one I meant. Likely, Ris didn't have any way of knowing if Sabien was one of the people Fuun had rescued.

Ris scurried over to the egg I had indicated. *This one?* she signed, and at my confirming nod, she knelt down and wrapped her slender arms around the large Ruby.

I gave her the minute she needed and used the opportunity to relocate myself back next to Masaru's egg. I, better than most, knew exactly what Ris was feeling.

Soon enough, Ris was by my side again. *You're not going to come upstairs? I can fix your arm.*

"I can't leave him, Ris."

Forever, Ris signed with a frown. *The eggs are forever. They won't open. We tried.*

"I got out Ris, surely that proves it's possible."

She leaned in close, her soft breath warming my face in the cold room. With a deliberate motion, the Kumori pointed a delicate finger at the spot in the center of my chest, the place where the diamond-shaped mark of Sapphiros showed just above my dress' neckline.

Her meaning, once again, was clear: *You are a Chosen, for you, it is different. For a Chosen, anything is possible.*

Kaji's words came back to me as Ris started away, back over to the egg where Sabien was imprisoned. *We're Chosen. Her power couldn't hold us forever.* Ris placed a long-fingered hand longingly over Sabien's egg a moment before pulling herself away from the man she loved and forcing herself to walk from the cavernous room, back straight with determined pride.

Like she was walking away from his coffin after saying her goodbyes.

I was wrong; the eggs weren't prisons, they were tombs. Lilyth had sent Masaru and everyone else to their graves, and only my power had prevented me from joining them.

The tears began in earnest this time, and once started nothing was going to stop them until I cried myself out. Lilyth had taken nearly everything from me, but worst of all Sapphiros' power had made it so I still had to live with the knowledge of everything and everyone I had lost – and that life would last an eternity, since Chosen were immortal.

I cried and I raged for all the good it did me. I wasn't a religious person, and despite being one of the Chosen of the gem god Sapphiros, I had never spoken to him, nor had I asked him for much beyond the formal ritual requests of the Knighting ceremony. But for all his silence I couldn't deny he was real – I had his power in my veins as proof of that – and so I raged internally at him for not protecting anyone but his Chosen and for not letting me die when Lilyth took Masaru away from me.

It was all just useless words, though, and deep down I knew that. I loved Masaru deeply, but I had far too strong a conscience to give up on this world and its survivors. Even if there was nothing left here for me, I would keep on fighting and doing what I could to protect those who had been left behind, even if it meant living for years beyond counting. I couldn't allow myself to do anything else and it was also what Masaru would have expected me to do. Roughlanders didn't give into death; they bounced, like the sun rising on a new day, and kept on living.

I don't know how long I sat there for, the sounds of my sobbing interspersed with long painful silences, but there came a time when I realized I wasn't alone anymore.

"Hello?" I couldn't see anymore. In my distress my powers were no longer available to me. No one answered me and I didn't hear any footsteps, but I couldn't deny the feeling there was someone else in the room with me and it wasn't simply the silent eggs that lay all about me. "Who's there?"

"Why?" The response came as a whisper, but from no discernable direction.

"What?" I questioned, startled out of my despondent state by the oddness of the question.

"Why do you cry out so? Are you in pain?"

"Some," I answered truthfully. My arm still throbbed, but the Flaqqers had done their work and it was no longer a pressing concern, as long as I didn't try to move it. I felt tired and drained from all the crying, but at the same time strangely detached from the world around me. I found an uncharacteristic lack of curiosity as to the identity of this stranger, my only concern being why he wasn't leaving me alone when I so obviously wasn't looking for company.

"Ah," he responded knowingly. *"That is why you cry, then."*

"No," I answered, frustrated by his assumption, "the physical pain I feel is nothing compared to the pain in my heart. I cry because I lost someone very close to me."

"Pain in your heart? I do not understand this. Explain it to me."

I don't know why I humoured him. Perhaps deep down I needed to talk about what I had lost without receiving sympathy. I wasn't the only one who had lost someone dear to them and I didn't want to put my troubles onto anyone else's shoulders, knowing they had enough problems of their own to deal with. However, this stranger was different; he didn't seem sad in the slightest. It was almost as if he didn't understand what that emotion was.

"I'm sad," I told him, knowing how much of an understatement that was. "Someone I love is trapped inside this egg and I can't get them out. It's the same for everyone in here. They all have people who love and care about them who are feeling the same way I am and there's nothing I can do for them."

"Love? Is that the reason, then?"

"Yes, I suppose so," I answered, wishing now that this strange person would just go away and leave me alone. His questions prodded at the wounds in my heart and didn't seem to serve any real purpose.

"What is love?" The questioning continued, whispering from the very walls. *"I have heard of this, but I do not know it. You will explain it to me."*

"Who are you?" I asked, realizing suddenly just how odd this conversation was.

It occurred to me then why the toneless voice seemed so familiar even though it was no more than a whisper. Machalite's Temple, Machalite's presence...and Machalite's voice. I was speaking to a god, more specifically Fuun's god; the black god of order and chaos. I was suddenly more wary of my circumstance. If Fuun was anything to go by, I should be very careful in dealing with the gem god himself. And Machalite had just given me an order, whether I wanted to answer him or not.

"I can't explain love," I protested weakly. "I hardly understand it myself."

"You said you love the one caught in the egg. You will explain what that means, or I will take the egg away and study it myself."

"No, I –" I started, clutching Masaru's egg with my good hand, ready to defend it with my life if necessary. I had been told the situation was hopeless, but that still didn't mean I was ready to give up what slim chance I had of freeing him someday.

"Ah..." Machalite made that knowing sound once more. *"So love means you do not want to be separated."*

"It's not just that," I disagreed with his limited assessment, when perhaps I should have left it at that. "It's not that you can't live without that person but more that you don't want to imagine a world without them in it."

"You don't have to be alone," Machalite interjected in his dry whisper, *"there are many of your kind scattered about this place. Why this one? Why does this one matter so much?"*

36

"I told you – I love him." This gem god may not have ever been human and could not possibly understand human emotion, but for me loving Masaru was as easy and natural as breathing. "And it's not just one," I explained as patiently as possible, "there are many different kinds of love. Friendship and family are important to me as well, it's just that how I feel about Masaru is different."

"Different?" I could hear his interest growing. *"Different, how?"*

"I don't know. It's not that it's necessarily stronger, just different."

"Explain."

"Okay." I struggled with a way to explain it in terms that he could understand. "The gem gods each have their Chosen, right? Or at least they can all choose someone?"

"Yes."

"Well, Sapphiros once wrote in a letter to us that he loves us and considers the four of us as his children. Is it not the same for you?"

"Sapphiros chose to experience a mortal existence," Machalite countered. *"I choose to study mortality from a different perspective."*

"All right, but you do have a Chosen, don't you? Her name is Ku-Roi, isn't it?" I hesitated to remember the cloaked woman who had killed so many before disappearing to Earth, where I hoped she wasn't wreaking havoc. "For what reason did you choose her?"

"She interested me," he stated. *"I found her curious and at times fascinating to observe, as you are. I understand why Sapphiros chose you. That does not ignite my curiosity, but this emotion you call love, does."*

"Are you not concerned for her wellbeing when she is threatened?" I struggled to find a link I could use to continue my explanation. "Would you not do anything within your power to protect her and keep her alive so you can continue to…observe her? Is that not why you granted her your power and your immortality?"

"Is that love?" Machalite seemed genuinely curious.

"It can be," I replied, uncertain if he was grasping the right meaning from my words. "In my case I would give my life to see Masaru safe. In fact I would give almost anything to save him because I love him."

"Ah." He made that same sound again. *"So love is sacrifice."*

"Sometimes, yes," I admitted.

"So you would give anything?" Machalite's voice was suddenly much more real and immediate, more present than he had been before, and it was no longer a whisper.

I looked up and by now I was calm enough that my power supplied me with enough light to see by. Fuun stood before me, his tall form cloaked in shadows and his dark eyes even blacker than usual in his pale face, with no pupils or whites to speak of.

"Yes." I answered truthfully – what other answer could I give? Masaru meant everything to me; in even just the short time we had known each other, he had become my whole world.

"It would have to be something of equal value, though," Fuun spoke with his god's voice. "Another life, perhaps?"

"I already said that I would give my own life for his," I responded, not fully grasping where this was headed.

"No, that would be too simple," Machalite continued through Fuun. "It would have to be someone else. Who would you be willing to sacrifice for your one?"

I felt my jaw lock shut instinctively and it was this more than anything else in our conversation so far that alerted me I had blindly walked into dangerous territory.

"I would understand love," Machalite stated coldly, "so I must understand sacrifice. What is the value of love? What is this emotion worth to you?"

"I wouldn't sacrifice anyone," I stated, horrified. Though in the privacy of my thoughts I was torn – what if he was lost forever unless I gave someone else up? Would I? Could I sacrifice another for my own selfishness? Could Masaru forgive me if I did? "The lives of others are not mine to give."

"And if they were?" Machalite demanded coldly, speaking my guilt-ridden thoughts aloud. "If it was within my power to free him or take him away forever, which would you choose?"

The words tore out of me, "Free him."

"A life, then," he continued, relentless.

"I can't..." It was too cruel; hadn't I already lost enough? Hadn't we all? I couldn't name another to be taken away. Not even for this.

"You will name a life of equal value or I will take him."

I was sobbing pitifully now, my form a useless heap on the stone floor, but inside I was working furiously trying to think of a way out of this devil's bargain. Deep down I knew I had allowed myself to be manipulated and there was no safe way back out of this corner, which meant I had to name someone.

The unfortunate truth of the matter was even knowing how selfish and wrong it was, some part of me was tempted by Machalite's offer. Could this gem god free Masaru? Would he? Or was this all some kind of sick game he was playing because my suffering was of interest to him? I didn't know, but I could sense time was running out. If I didn't name someone and Machalite wasn't bluffing, he would take Masaru from me and then I would have no hope of ever getting him back.

So that left me to think of names. Each name that came to mind was like a stab of pain that left me gasping for air. I had already been forbidden from naming myself, but each person I thought of led to a chain of other people who would be devastated and I couldn't be responsible for that kind of pain. Even if it did bring Masaru back, I wouldn't be able to live with myself afterwards and I wouldn't expect him to be able to live with what I had done either.

There was only one possible answer to my problem. I would have to outwit Machalite.

"Razor."

Razor was Dahlia's brother and Masaru's close friend; all who knew him well would be devastated to learn he was dead, but he was also the one person I knew who would willingly give his life for Masaru's sake. Razor had risked his own life more than once before to save Masaru's and I knew Masaru had planned to ask him if he would stand for him at our Joining, which would essentially mean agreeing to care for me should something happen to Masaru. There was little doubt this scenario qualified, but the most important part about naming Razor is that my power hadn't been able to find him, which likely meant he was not able to be found.

I was wrong.

"Done." Razor appeared between Fuun and I, in the flesh, only he wasn't himself – he had been infected by the curse of the Lillem.

Fuun drew his lengthy, thin-bladed katana.

"No!" My conscience screamed out against what I was about to witness.

"No?" Machalite asked, Fuun's lips moving despite his intense concentration on the target before him. "You wish to go back upon our agreement? Choose the other option?"

"No..." I whispered, at a loss for how to save both their lives, though Machalite was right; I had spoken Razor's name knowing what the consequences were. "Just...I can't let him die like this. Please, I can restore him to himself. Let him at least go to his...death...knowing..." I took a deep breath. What I was trying to say, but couldn't, is I wanted him to know it was me who was asking this of him; for him to forgive me if he could. "Please, I would have it be his decision."

Fuun nodded and, struggling to my feet, I faced Razor squarely.

It hurt to see him like this. Razor's belted Roughlander clothes were in worse condition than usual, torn in places and stained with blood where other Lillem had stabbed him. His light brown hair was as scraggly as his rough facial hair and the customary patch he usually wore over his scarred left eye was dangling from a broken strap. He was a full Lillem, having presumably been infected a week ago during the fall of Taiyou, but despite that he stood warily, for the moment at least not moving more than his upper talons, twitching them intermittently.

I didn't flinch from the horrific monster my friend had become. If he would kill me for this as his altered nature dictated, then it would be no less than I deserved for what I was about to ask of him. Holding my hands out, I fought my unruly emotions for the power to do what was necessary.

Blue-white mist sprayed from my outstretched hands and the creature Razor had become shied back, though it would do him no good. The power I manifested would enter through Razor's pores, pass through his body, and destroy any foreign matter, thus cleansing him of the Lillem's taint. It would hurt, momentarily, but I had created this power knowing full well what I was doing; the particles would close up any holes and heal any damage they caused while searching out and destroying the infection.

It didn't take long. From one heartbeat to the next, Razor went from a near mindless creature back to his old self again. The Lillem talons that had adorned his back clattered to the ground, unexpectedly retaining the solidity of bone, but the ones that had jutted out of his hip bones turned to sand as they fell away from his body.

"Razor, I –" I began, but choked on my own words.

Razor didn't seem to notice my distress as he lunged forward to catch me in a hug. "Yukari! Oh, but it's good to see you."

Razor's enthusiasm only made me feel that much worse for having brought him here. As awful as the thought was, he might have been better off staying a Lillem if it would have meant staying far, far away from Machalite.

"Razor, I have something I have to ask you."

Pulling back and straining to see me in the darkened chamber, Razor noticed my tear-stained face for the first time. "Don't cry, Yukari, I'm fine now. See," he said as he passed his hands over his shoulder where the Lillem talons had been. "All better, so you don't have to worry."

"I know," I whispered, stricken. "It's not that. I —"

"Where's Masaru?" Razor interjected suddenly, catching on to the problem.

It was now or never, I knew that. "He's been imprisoned, Razor, by Lady Lilyth. Machalite said he'd free him, but…Razor…" I broke down crying, there was no use trying to hold it in. "We were going to be Joined. Dahlia was so excited…only we hadn't yet had a chance to tell anyone else about it. I wanted to tell my parents first, especially my father," I rambled, afraid to tell him the truth of why he was here, "only I didn't know how he would take it."

"Well, that's wonderful news, Yukari," Razor congratulated me, still not understanding. "I'm sure once we get him out of wherever she's got him, it will be a wonderful Joining, so don't you worry."

I sniffled, struggling to keep speaking, but knowing I had to get everything I wanted to say out now, before we ran out of time – before Razor ran out of time. "Masaru and Dahlia explained Roughlander customs to me, Razor. About the Joining? Before…before Taiyou fell, Masaru told me he wanted to ask you if you would stand for him, but he never got the chance…"

Realization seemed to dawn on Razor then. For Roughlanders, a Joining ceremony was like what we would call a wedding on Earth, and 'standing for someone' was similar to the role that a best man or maid of honour might play, only the role had quite a bit more significance after the ceremony. The two people Masaru and I chose to stand for us, if they accepted, were expected to support the couple should they go through hard times and if one of the Joined were to lose their lives, the person standing for that person would be expected to step in and care for the bereaved, sometimes even taking their place, romantically speaking.

"So you're asking me now, on his behalf..." Razor ventured, linking his eyes with mine and not letting me look away.

I nodded slowly. "Yes, but before I do, I want you to know what it means-"

"I know what it means." Razor's tone was deadly serious.

"Masaru's in trouble, Razor," I tried to explain. "Machalite asked me –"

"A life for a life," he whispered. "I know well what it means and if it's for Masaru, or you," he added, studying me, "I'll do it."

"Razor, no..." I cried, though I knew it was useless; the decision had already been made, the conditions of my unwilling agreement with Machalite met. "Please, don't. I...can't...it's too selfish...I have no right to ask...there are so many others..."

"On one condition, of course," Razor added, ignoring me for the moment and turning around to address Fuun, who still calmly held his sword at his side, Machalite patiently giving us the moment I had asked for.

"State your condition," Machalite stated tonelessly.

"I get to decide the terms."

"Terms?"

"The manner of death, and what it's worth," Razor responded. "How many lives will you free in exchange for mine? How many has she captured?"

"Thirty," Machalite answered. "You would sacrifice yourself for their lives? Is this love?"

"Yes," Razor answered simply, "and I would say goodbye to her first, if you'll let me."

Fuun nodded again and Razor turned to me, his expression tender as he cupped my face with the palm of his hand.

"I'm so sorry," I whispered, unable to think of what else to say.

"Don't be sorry," Razor replied gently, leaning his face into mine. "Just think of it as an early present for your Joining."

"Razor..." I wanted to tell him to change his mind, to not go through with this, that we could find some other way, but all that came out when I opened my mouth to speak was, "Thank you."

Razor's lips met mine and he kissed me with the passion of a man saying goodbye to the woman he loved. To my surprise, I found myself kissing him back just as passionately. I owed this last moment to him, but it was more than that; I realized in the midst of that kiss I had always had a special place in my heart for Razor. I loved him, just not in the same way that I loved Masaru. If circumstances had been different, I might have ended up falling for Razor, but either way I was thankful Masaru had chosen him to stand for us; there was no better choice.

With a satisfied sigh, Razor at last ended the moment between us and pulled away to face his own death.

"How would you like to die, then?" Machalite asked tonelessly, with only the barest hint of expectation in his voice.

Razor smiled, with just a smidgen of his roguish charm showing through the seriousness that had dampened his customary good spirits. "Well, I'd like to die of old age like the type of Rouglander nobody really gets to see any more. You know, grey hairs, aching bones, and all that, but I don't really think you'll let me get away with that."

"Done," Machalite stated and Fuun slumped, the gem god returning his stolen body with an unexpected suddenness.

"That's it?" I asked, startled, staring between Fuun and Razor with wide eyes.

"You are mine," the whispered voice from earlier returned, seemingly from everywhere at once. *"When you die, it will be at a time of my choosing, but you will live to see old age. I am patient, but the moment you gain immortality in any fashion, you will die. Understood?"*

Razor nodded, my power having returned enough to see that his face was ashen.

"Then we have a deal. Well played, mortal."

CH. 3 – BE CAREFUL WHERE YOU KEEP YOUR HEART

The room filled with the sounds of the Ruby eggs cracking open and, true to Machalite's word, Masaru's was the first to open. Masaru and all twenty-eight of the others were revealed in various states of physical health, though every single one remained unconscious.

Razor was fine and somehow, miraculously, still alive, but as Razor and I labored to sort the unconscious and clear away some of the shards of Ruby, I was lost in a sea of guilt and was hardly capable of doing much more than tormenting myself.

Did the end justify the means? When it comes right down to it, is it selfish to sacrifice one to save many? Or is it the other way around: would I, in my selfishness, have sacrificed many just to save one?

The questions swirled around in my mind and I knew whatever Machalite had intended to do, he had succeeded in pushing me very near to my limits. I had to admit there was a part of me that didn't know how much further I would have gone to save Masaru had it been necessary. That part, however small it was, scared me.

"Yukari, you can stop. We're done now. Rest a minute, would you?" Razor's voice startled me out of my thoughts.

"I…" I stumbled, looking him over and wondering how I would ever repay him. "Are you all right?"

"Just tired," he admitted, "and sore. How 'bout you? Is your arm broken?"

"Yeah." I nodded, shrugging my shoulder to indicate that it wasn't bothering me…much. "Is there anything I can do for you?"

"Now that you mention it," Razor said with a winning smiled, "I could really use someone to try and work the kinks out of my shoulders." He rolled his arms to show how stiff he was. "Those Lillem parts weren't exactly comfortable."

I smiled despite myself and started over to where he sat perched on a rather large hunk of Ruby, which had been too heavy for us to bother moving from the center of the room. "Sure. We've got some time to waste before they start waking up."

With my uninjured arm, I did my best to poke and prod Razor's shoulders for him. I fumbled slightly when I realized he still had an extra bit of bone from the limbs he had lost protruding from his shoulder blade, but I thought it best not to mention the abnormality to him, especially when I didn't think there was anything I could do about it.

I lost myself quickly in the simple task, and I found my conscience eased somewhat by the gentle, comforting sounds of Razor's breathing and the life I could feel beneath my fingertips. My mind drifting, I found myself thinking about a story Jeth had once told me. It had been while we had all been staying at the palace in Taiyou and during a rare and quiet moment when we had found ourselves alone in each other's company…

"Be careful where you keep your heart," Jeth warned, his tone uncharacteristically serious.

"What?" I questioned, surprised by his change in demeanor.

"You asked about Yuko Seig, didn't you?" Jeth asked, leaning forward across the small, round table.

We were in the Knights' room common area, Jeth with a half-eaten apple in his hands and me feeling uncharacteristically lost. I had been doing a lot of thinking about how a fate that stretched across almost a thousand years was now finally playing out, with us at its center. The tall, lanky Knight with his rumpled brown hair, deceptively lazy eyes, and slumped posture, was right in saying I had come in here looking for answers about the long dead Priestess of Sapphiros and the world in which she used to live. However, I hadn't been expecting those answers to come from the usually reticent Jeth.

"Well, that's the lesson, see?" Jeth continued, whether I was following along or not. "Every good story's gotta have a lesson and I like mine right up front where everyone can see it." He shrugged. "Makes the story better, knowing what to expect. S'why you can hear a story a hundred times and never get tired of it, if it's a good enough story."

"And the story about Yuko Seig?"

"Oh, that's a good one. It's got a sad ending, though."

I rolled my eyes in Jeth's direction – of course it had a sad ending; it was the story of how she died I was interested in, after all.

"Can I hear it, please? None of the others would tell me what happened to her."

"Well, I'm not too surprised that neither Adel nor Sabien would talk about it. Adel 'cause she doesn't know much and Sabien...well, he cared about her and he was pretty broken up, you know, afterwards.

"Yuko Seig saved Sabien's life. I guess you could say that's where it started or where, if someone was paying attention, they might've noticed the first signs of what was to come...

She found him bleeding to death, halfway along the road from the mountain settlement of the Blue Moon tribe to the Temple of Sapphire, which he had been trying to reach.

The dark-haired young man, though muscular and healthy looking other than his unfortunate state, was unconscious, and judging by the sluggish beat of his heart, the cold mountain air and the blood loss had nearly done him in.

The frosty wind was bitter cold this far into the southern mountains where winter reigned, and particularly in this exposed spot on the trail, but Yuko Seig didn't dare move him. He lay as he had fallen, half leaning against a rock outcrop which jutted out of the snow like a jagged tooth. Blood soaked the snowy ground in a pool around him – too much blood – but it was clear the rock wasn't what had impaled him.

This had been no accident.

The sword wound that was still trying its damndest to take his life had been caused by a long, thin blade travelling straight through his body in a smooth stroke, expertly inserted through the overlapping plates of his armour. Yuko Seig bit her lip, looking about herself with concern rapidly turning to alarm as she found herself wondering if the one responsible for this atrocity might still be nearby. It was a dangerous time and nowhere was truly safe from the war that gripped the world, but this place was supposed to be secret and therefore marginally safer than anywhere else. But if they had been found out…well, that didn't bear thinking about.

She studied the man before her. He was handsome in a rugged fashion and in the prime of his life. His clothes and armour bore the marks of someone from the Blue Moon tribe and so there was no doubt in her mind this was the man she had been sent to retrieve. He was supposed to accompany her back to the Temple where he would pass his final tests before the Knighting ceremony would be held, but those tests were a mere formality at this point as he had already been chosen for the honour.

Worrying her lip between her teeth, the conclusion was evident; she couldn't move him and she couldn't leave him. This left only saving him, and in order to save him she would have to Knight him here and now, tests or no tests, as she had no gift with healing and he wouldn't last the hour without a miracle.

Ris might've been better to send, Yuko Seig thought wistfully, *but I suppose I will just have to be enough.*

Sapphiros, my friend and benefactor, she began the ritual words fervently in her mind, knowing despite her outward silence, Sapphiros back at the Temple of Sapphire would hear her as clearly as if she were whispering in his ear.

Yuko Seig felt the gem god's power pass through her and into the young Knight, creating an irrevocable link between them. Now Sabien was hers in the same way she was Sapphiros', and provided that the god's power was enough to save him from the brink of death, he would be her Knight for as long as they both lived. It was a lot to commit to an almost complete stranger, but Yuko Seig trusted Sapphiros' will and judgment implicitly.

The newly-made Knight of Sapphiros took in a sudden gasp of air as his eyes snapped open. Yuko Seig let out a sigh of breath in relief, but before she could exhale completely he was gone.

She stared at the ground before her in disbelief. She had seen some strange and remarkable things in her lifetime, watching and training those blessed by a gem god's power, but never could she have predicted the dying man before her would simply disappear. But where Sabien had been lying a moment before was now only a puddle of water and bloody slush, which was rapidly seeping into the cracks in the rocky ground.

"Sabien had turned into a puddle for the first time, see?" Jeth interrupted his story to clarify.

"Yes, Jeth, I know this part already."

"Huh, well why didn't you say something?" He shook his head wonderingly. *"Well, as you probably also know, it took Sabien nearly a month to reform. In all that time Yuko Seig never did find out who had attacked him and if Sapphiros knew who it was he sure wasn't telling...*

Sabien proved himself to be an exemplary Knight and never gave Yuko Seig any reason to doubt Sapphiros' wisdom in choosing to Knight him. However, it was when the Oujou came that Sabien displayed his true worth.

The men and women of the Temple of Sapphire fought bravely trying to deny her access, but they were no match for someone who could kill or curse with a single touch. It didn't help that when the Oujou first arrived, no one had any idea what they were up against.

"Stand back and let her through if that's what she's after," Sabien called out to the other Knights atop the battlements of the city's high defensive wall, overlooking the snowy expanse beyond where the strange woman had been visible only a moment before, "and have someone send warning to everyone inside. Make sure no one gets in her way."

"She could kill us all," one of the Knights protested. "You saw what happened to Lorne!"

"I did and you'll follow my advice if you don't want the same to happen to you," Sabien responded stoically. "There are times when the obvious answer is not necessarily the correct one. If we fight her we will lose, so we stand back."

Sabien promptly followed his own advice and sheathed his sword, urging the others to do likewise with their various weapons and powers. No sooner had he done so than the mysterious woman appeared before him in a blink, forming herself on the battlements in a wisp of green smoke. She was tall and attractive in a too perfect sort of way and she oozed confidence in every aspect of her being, including the absent way she wore what little clothing was necessary to conceal herself for modesty's sake, even though it was the dead of winter and freezing cold this far south.

"A fool you are not," she noted professionally, studying him from a distance closer than was comfortable, even discounting her dangerous ability, "many would have died, had we fought."

Though Sabien was far from defenseless even without his weapon, he wisely kept silent, not wishing to provoke her and thankful she had decided to try civility over more wanton murder and casual destruction.

"Lives need not be lost," she continued, absently gesturing with long, claw-tipped black fingernails, softly implying menace, "if the one we seek will pay the cost. The chosen one be not you," she commented with a sniff in Sabien's direction, "nor are they in view. The Chosen we are here to see, you will bring them here to me -"

"That rhymes, but that's not how she would have said it," I noted critically, interrupting Jeth. "She always spoke in the plural because she was made up of many sentient particles, remember?"

"Who's telling the story here?"

"Yes, sorry, go ahead."

"Well, anyway, the Oujou demanded to see the Chosen – that was you four, of course," Jeth clarified unnecessarily, "only I don't think that you were more than a couple of months old yet, if you had even been born by this point…

"Sapphiros has not chosen." Sabien was glad this was true so he did not have to lie to this dangerous woman.

Following this pronouncement, there was a long, tense moment where the Oujou inspected Sabien as if waiting for him to flinch and give his words away as false. Sabien did not waver and in the end she had no choice but to accept his words, or murder everyone for no real purpose.

"A Chosen's life be more cursed than blessed," she noted, peering into Sabien's eyes to make sure he was listening carefully, "but the Oujou know curses best. Tell Sapphiros for now we wait, but when one is chosen our meeting is fate." With that warning, the Oujou left the Temple of Sapphire just as suddenly and inexplicably as she had arrived.

Exactly one week later, Lorne died. It was decided then that Sabien would take Lorne's place as the Knight Commander. Even still, the death of such an old and loyal Knight was a shocking blow to all who had known him, though no one took the loss harder than Sapphiros.

None knew for certain, but it seemed that being unable to stop or prevent the senseless death of one of his oldest companions took a toll on the aging gem god. Either way, following the death of Lorne, Sapphiros secluded himself in his quarters and would see or speak to no one save Yuko Seig. It seemed he had all but given up on experiencing life and was now preparing for the moment of his inevitable death…

"The last time anybody saw Sapphiros was when he formally chose the four of you," Jeth informed me. "He didn't look too good then, and he didn't last more than a week after that. Most people think he gave you guys the last of his power and that's what killed him, but the way I figure, it was just his time and he knew it."

"I thought this story was about Yuko Seig?"

"I'm getting there," Jeth insisted. "Don't get your pretty blue hair in a knot.

"As I was saying," he continued, without missing a beat, "when Sapphiros left this world he took a part of Yuko Seig with him. She wasn't the same after that, kinda empty inside, you know? She tried for a while, went through the motions of living, but she wasn't fooling anyone. It was obvious she wanted to follow after Sapphiros, you know, permanently.

"It got to the point where she was just asking to die. She even asked me if I would kill her, but it's just not in my nature to do something like that and I'm pretty sure Sabien would've had my head if I'd tried."

"Why didn't she just end her own life if she wanted to die that badly?" I asked, genuinely curious.

"She couldn't, any more than you could," Jeth replied. "The power wouldn't let her."

I was taken aback by this statement. "Surely, there must be a way."

"Nope," he said, shaking his head, "doesn't work like that. Your power responds to your instincts, right? Well you can't turn it off any more than you can stop yourself from breathing, or so I understand. I've never tried it myself."

"Okay." I accepted this as fact for the sake of the story, but I filed it away as something that would bear more thought in the future. "So she wanted to die, but couldn't. So what happened then?"

"Fuun came," Jeth answered with a troubled frown, "and we all worried that maybe he would do for her what the rest of us wouldn't...

It was time.

He had trained and trained, sacrificed, and been pushed to his limits time and again. If he was not ready now, he wasn't sure he ever would be. It was time to show them all what he was capable of, and if this time they would not admit his worth – well, he would not take no for an answer.

The path to the Temple of Sapphire was well familiar to him as he had traveled it many times thinking he was ready to face his destiny, each time only to turn back before he crested the rise that would allow him to see the mountain city. This time was different; there would be no turning back and he would claim the position that was his by right of training and birth.

At the top of the hill, Fuun felt his feet stop despite the mental commands he gave them to the contrary. It was as he had always imagined it, but somehow the snowy, high-walled city nestled in the mountains with its tall spires and open courtyards was both less and more than he had expected. More, because his arrival was so long anticipated and that small remnant of the boy he had once been rejoiced at finally laying eyes on the place he had always dreamed of reaching, but less because of the bitterness that welled up within him when he remembered being denied his dream so many times.

With that bitterness came the familiar feeling of anger barely controlled and determination sharply focused. The joint feelings washed over him like a wave and with them driving him, he was able to take that first step toward the temple and once begun, the would-be legendary Fuun was an unstoppable force. With his black cloak swirling in the wind behind him, he swooped down upon the unsuspecting Temple of Sapphire like a vengeful tempest bent on destruction.

Getting within the walls was no trouble for Fuun, but getting past Sabien was another story; his brother drew his sword at the sight of him.

"How dare you show your face here, of all places?" Sabien demanded coldly.

Fuun's inner rage boiled and he deliberately hardened his heart. "You are a Knight of Sapphiros," he stated, glancing around the empty courtyard in the center of the city. It was a cold day and no doubt the denizens of the mountain city were keeping warm in their homes and in their Temple.

It had not been a question, but Sabien answered regardless, "The Knight Commander."

So, not only had Sabien been made a Knight, but they had made him their leader. Why was it that his brother always managed to have everything handed to him on a silver platter? It was Fuun who had to work for every inch granted to him. Fuun who never received any honours for all the effort he applied time and again.

"I challenge you, then," Fuun stated, "for the right of Knighthood."

"It doesn't work that way, Fuun," Sabien denied him as he always had. "You can't just walk in here and demand to be made a Knight of Sapphiros, you have to earn it."

"I have earned it!" he growled. "I am just as worthy as you are, maybe more, and you know the truth of that, *brother*."

Sabien's expression darkened further and he looked fully prepared to deny Fuun yet again, when a feminine voice spoke from nearby, "Let him try, Sabien."

"Yuko Seig…" Sabien gave away the woman's identity with a half-hearted protest.

Yuko Seig, red eyes gleaming dully, said nothing as she met Sabien's eyes from beneath the hood of her thick, fur-lined blue cloak. After a moment, Sabien nodded his acquiescence, albeit still reluctant.

"Priestess?" Fuun questioned, studying the slight-built woman with her round features and bluish-white hair. Yuko Seig returned his stare, but there was no interest in it and Fuun recognized something in her eyes. This woman was dead inside; no matter how healthy her body, life had lost meaning for her. She was waiting to die. "It is an honour," he acknowledged her.

"What are your terms, then, Fuun?" Sabien asked, his usually calm voice betraying his own anger. "Let's end this once and for all."

"Certainly, brother," he agreed. "We duel to the death and the winner gets to be a Knight of Sapphiros."

"No, Fuun," Sabien scowled, "if you're to have any hope of being named one of us, you have to understand we are a team. We cannot accept losing anyone for such a petty reason."

"I'll summon the others," Yuko Seig interjected. "I will make sure to include Ris in that summons, so if either of you falls, she will do her best to see that you live. Sabien," she addressed him sharply, "if you will not accept your brother's challenge, then choose another to fight in your place or grant him his request and be done with it."

"Yes…Yuko Seig," Sabien responded, clearly startled.

"So they fought," Jeth concluded. "And under normal circumstances there'd be little chance of someone without powers overcoming a Knight of Sapphiros, much less the Knight Commander, but Fuun had a secret. He had already defeated Sabien once and they'd trained together when they were younger, so he knew his brother's style very well. But more importantly, Fuun was no longer just an average human. He had gone and gotten himself Knighted by someone else."

"Machalite," I supplied, "and later people thought he must be the Chosen of Machalite, so he must have been fairly powerful, even then."

"He was," Jeth admitted. "Still, Sabien held his own and the fight between them was very close. In the end, I think it was Fuun's ruthlessness that allowed him to strike the final blow. No matter how angry Sabien was at his younger brother, it was obvious he still didn't want to hurt him, let alone kill him."

"But Fuun wouldn't have held back. So he won?"

"Yeah, he did, but it's possible Sabien let him, knowing he was going to win anyway and not wanting Fuun to do something he would learn to regret as a Knight of Sapphiros."

"And then?" I asked, fully engaged in the story now.

"Yuko Seig Knighted him like she said she would. And then she asked him to kill her." Jeth paused for dramatic effect.

"Did he do it?" I asked because I knew he wanted me to.

"No." I rolled my eyes and Jeth laughed before continuing. "He wouldn't. It seemed, at that point, that having won what he was after, Fuun wasn't in a killing mood. Maybe he wanted to turn over a new leaf or something now that he was a Knight of Sapphiros."

"But if he didn't kill her, who did?"

"Did I say somebody killed her at the end of this story?" Jeth questioned and I narrowed my eyes at him. "All right," he admitted, "the Vile Emperor killed her, but it's not what you think. You see, even now, she isn't really dead and yet she is, you know?"

"No, I don't."

"Well nobody really knows what happened in this part of the story," Jeth admitted, sounding somewhat frustrated, "but, having tried every other option, Yuko Seig journeyed to the Ruby City where she thought she might find the one person who would finally grant her request...

"Kill me," Yuko Seig pleaded with the man she once loved.

Verasheen, the man more commonly known as the Vile Emperor, sat upon his massive throne of flawless black obsidian, his expression hidden by the intimidating visage of his ruby-visored helmet. From head to toe, the man beneath and any feelings he might claim were concealed beneath the impassive posture of his deeply purple spiked armour. He gave nothing away, not even a hint of compassion for this woman who had come to his throne room asking to die.

She prostrated herself before him on the red velvet carpet that guided petitioners from the double doors to the throne itself. The room, lit archaically by torchlight and the walls roughly hewn as if to give the illusion of being a natural formation, was as uninviting an atmosphere as could be designed, indicating that none were expected to be comfortable here in the domain of their ruler. Yet Yuko Seig showed no fear as she attempted to peer past the spiked helmet to the man beneath.

"Please, I beg you, Verasheen," she continued, "I do not wish to live any longer. Grant me one last favour and let me die."

"No." When the Vile Emperor spoke it was with the deep rumble of his voice reverberating through his helmet, yet the one word was as clear as a death sentence, even if it meant quite the opposite.

Yuko Seig slumped, all hope draining out of her, and her gaze returned to the vacant expression she had worn since Sapphiros' death. "I'm sorry to take up your time, Emperor," she spoke in an empty monotone. "I'll be leaving now."

"I won't kill you," Verasheen amended, "but I can make certain that you die…"

"So the Vile Emperor put Yuko Seig in the Splitter?" I asked, piecing it all together from what I already knew.

"The way I understand it is the Vile Emperor split her soul somehow, leaving part of her in the Splitter for eternity where she would never be fully alive, but always within reach."

"So her body is dead, but her soul lives forever in the Splitter?"

"And on Earth," Jeth added.

"Earth?"

"Yeah, the end of the story says that the other half of Yuko Seig's soul will be reborn on Earth. So he didn't kill her, but he made sure she got to die."

"That's cruel."

"Would it have been any kinder to just kill her, or to let her live?" Jeth asked cryptically. "Yuko Seig loved Sapphiros so much she gave him her heart, so when he left that piece of her went with him and left her as only a shell of her former self."

"But the Vile Emperor, if he loved her, how could he do such a thing to her? He made her suffer for eternity."

"Well, you might say that his heart was with her," Jeth replied, referring to the lesson he had been trying to impart. "People do some strange things for love, kiddo."

I smiled a little ruefully remembering his tone, but as offhand as the comment may have seemed at the time, Jeth had been right on the mark. Each of us had someone who made us vulnerable, and in my case my heart was irrevocably with Masaru. Recalling the lesson Jeth had taught me – and the meandering story he had used to get there – made me feel a little better. Soon I was prepared to face the world again, and not long after the people Razor had saved began to awaken.

"Everyone, try to stay calm," I called out to the darkened room over the general sounds of confusion and distress. "I know it's dark and cold, but I assure you that you are safe and I'll be coming around to see to your injuries if you have any. Everything will be all right."

"Yukari?" Masaru called out.

"Yes, it's me," I answered and with my broken arm strapped to my side I awkwardly formed an arrow of cyan light, then fired it so that it split into five beams of light that struck the walls at various points, digging in so we could have some illumination. A few people in the room gasped; I wasn't sure whether this was because of the sudden illumination, my display of power, or their revealed circumstances, but I ignored them all in favour of hurrying to Masaru's side.

"You're all right?" I asked, looking him over.

"I'm all right," he confirmed, taking me into his arms, "just a little confused. Where are we?"

"The Temple of Machalite. I'll explain more in a bit, but I know there are quite a few injuries."

He let go of me. "Go on then, do what ye need to. I'll still be here afterwards."

I nodded and stood, stepping back from him reluctantly.

"Yukari, yer arm," he noted my Roughlander-style sling with a frown.

"I know," I grimaced down at it. "It hurts, but I Flaqqered it, so it's only a matter of time now."

I watched the corner of Masaru's mouth twitch upward in a smile and, despite everything that had happened, I returned it.

The first thing I did was send a message arrow to Ris to let her know the good news about Sabien. The Knight Commander was groggy, but otherwise unhurt, so I left him alone in favour of those who needed medical attention. Recalling there was a pregnant mother somewhere in the room, my next priority was to ensure she was not injured in any way that could endanger her baby. I repeated my earlier method of sensing the life forces of those in the room until I identified which body contained not one life force, but two.

Neva?

Neva was a Roughlander and the only female member of Razor's gang. Studying Neva from across the room, I watched as Razor helped her gently to her feet with concern in his eyes. "I'm fine, Razor, honestly," Neva protested in her soft Roughlander accent as Razor tried to get her to take a seat on the broken Ruby egg he had been using earlier.

Watching them, I recalled the few times recently when I had observed Neva putting herself in dangerous situations and her general lack of regard for her own personal safety. Before I knew it, I was weaving my way toward them through disoriented groupings of people.

"Neva, can I talk to you for a moment?"

"Yukari, is that you there?" Neva peered through what, to her, was a dimly lit room.

"Yes," I responded, suddenly self-conscious – I had certainly never given Neva any reason to desire my company.

"All right," Neva answered cautiously, separating herself from Razor and making her way over to me. "What is it ye wanted?"

"I know you and I have never really gotten along," I began, figuring I best get everything I had to say to her out at once, "and I'm not asking you to do anything for my sake, but Razor means a lot to me and I can see he really cares for you –"

"Razor?" Neva interrupted in a sharp whisper, sounding surprised, but I also noted a hint of a blush cross her fair cheeks. "Ye think Razor has a thing for me?"

"You mean Razor's not...?"

"Not what?"

"Not the father," I choked out.

"What?!" Neva's eyes bulged and I instantly regretted my method of delivery until she grabbed hold of my good arm in sudden excitement. "I'm going to have a baby?"

I nodded, weakly; it was the truth after all.

"How do ye know?"

"I can see it," I answered. "Well, I sensed it anyways and I could see it if I looked. Did you want me to?"

She nodded, her mood shifting once again so she was biting her lip in uncertainty. "Ye better do so, just to make sure."

"All right, but Neva, if Razor's not the father, may I ask who is?"

She smiled shyly, colour rising in her cheeks. "Well the only person I've, ye know, been with…is Yuge." I tried to stop my mouth from falling open in shock, but I fell just short of containing my surprise at this revelation. Thankfully, Neva didn't seem to notice my reaction. "Oh, Yukari, d'ye think he's all right? Now that I know there's going to be a baby involved…well, I was hoping maybe he might, ye know, Join with me?"

I frowned, thinking of all the people I hadn't been able to locate. "I can try to find him for you, but I'll warn you that Taiyou fell and those of us here in the Temple of Machalite were the lucky ones as far as I've been able to discover." I tried to consider Neva's situation from a Roughlander perspective. "If I can't find Yuge, can you please promise me you'll at least let Razor try to take care of you and the baby?"

"As if he was standin' for me and Yuge, ye mean? D'ye think he would if I asked him?"

I glanced over at Razor only to see him peering through the darkness at us with a concerned expression. "I don't doubt he would, but if you're going to let him down like that Neva," I warned her, speaking from experience and knowing how much Razor had been through first with Masaru's sister Tira, then myself, and now Neva, "I would do it gently."

"Thank ye, Yukari," Neva said, letting go of my hand, "I will. And you're sure?"

Using my power, I twisted my vision to see past the layers of her clothing and skin until I could see within her body and sure enough what I found there matched what I had seen of pregnancy in biology textbooks back on Earth.

"I'm sure."

Neva beamed and with a slight bounce in her step, turned to head back over to Razor. Feeling overwhelmed, but glad our discussion had not gone badly, I turned to the nearest person to see how they were faring and quickly lost myself in the varied tasks associated with tending the wounded.

Ris came, and after making sure I had everything under control she left again, taking Sabien with her and promising she would send down what torches and food they had to spare. I knew a handful of the people that had been in the eggs, but not many. With those I did know, there were tearful reunions as they came to terms with what I could tell them about who was present and accounted for and who was still missing.

Remarkably, one of the life forces I had sensed belonged to a Roughlander mount, those half organic, half robotic horses they used to cross the Sand Lakes. Dahlia had been in one of the eggs as well, and, ever one to adapt to any given situation, once briefed with what I knew, she was the first to offer to venture out and see what else she could discover about our shared circumstance.

"It's pitch dark out there and I hear there is a dangerous unmarked cliff edge," I warned Dahlia, repeating to her what my mother had told me about trying to wander about the Temple of Machalite.

Fiery, red-headed Dahlia confidently patted the neck of the mount she had appropriated for herself. "That's what the mount is for. They've got lights built into them, so I should have little trouble out there. I'll come back shortly with whatever I can find out."

"I'll go with her," Pine, the Croatin Knight of Sapphiros, added in his usual whispered voice, coming up on the other side of Dahlia's mount. He was still wearing his customary dark cloak with the hood drawn up to conceal his alien features and odd markings. "I can see well enough in the dark."

"Dahlia," I said with a nod to Pine and took a deep breath before I gave her the bad news, "I can find people, with my power, but I wasn't able to locate Krox." I was referring to her mate, the Croatin Head-taker. "I'm not sure what that means."

Dahlia swallowed hard, but she nodded. "Thank ye for trying, Yukari, but Krox'll be all right. He's a tough brute and no matter what trouble he gets himself into, he always comes back to me."

I took comfort in Dahlia's strength and having seen to everyone else, last, but certainly not least, I was able to make my way back over to Masaru. He sat speaking softly to the first friend I had ever made in Taiyou, Mifa.

Mifa looked up at my approach, her brown eyes red and puffy. Dropping to my knees beside her, I offered her a one-handed hug, which was about all I could manage with my arm still strapped tightly to my chest. After a moment, Mifa pulled back from me and she met my eyes searchingly.

"I told her ye might be able to help, with yer arrows," Masaru clarified. "I did warn her what happens when yer arrows can't find the person they're meant for."

"I don't need the arrows anymore," I explained, "but Mifa, I'm sorry…I couldn't find Goji or Felice, I've already tried." Her tears began again, but by Masaru's expression I gathered it was better she knew I had tried. "It doesn't mean anything for sure," I added, trying to salvage what I could for her. "Razor was missing too, when I first tried, but it turned out he had turned into a Lillem and that's something that can be cured, now. The same might be true for them." I could tell the thought was not a comforting one, but certainly it was better than the alternative.

"We'll find them," I assured her, internally adding up their names to the list of people I would have to find.

"But Kaji's okay?" Mifa choked out, looking for assurance.

"Yeah," I answered her, glad I knew how to answer that question at least. "Kaji, Yue, Hotaru, and I all managed to break out of the eggs first. The rest of them left with Ris the first time. They should all be somewhere within the temple, but as I understand it's not a good idea to go wandering about."

"But you can go, can't ye?" Masaru asked. "Ye can see in the dark just fine and ye can get to just about anyone ye choose, right?"

I nodded. "Yes, I can, and I did promise my mother I would go back and see her. Will you both be all right if I go?"

"I would feel better knowing what was out there waiting for us, if ye know what I mean," Masaru admitted as Mifa nodded in agreement.

"All right then." I fitted myself under Masaru's arm and closed my eyes to send myself back to my mother. "Don't be alarmed if I just disappear," I warned them. "I'll come back as soon as I can."

Ch. 4 – Temple of Machalite

"**Y**ukari!"

I was as relieved to see my mother as she was to see me, even though her circumstances had not changed since I had last sent myself to her. My heart went out to her, sitting alone and huddled in the dark, and without consciously deciding to do so I brought myself fully to her, leaving nothing but mist back where I had been in the egg room.

As soon as I was fully solid, the room lost what little illumination my faintly glowing astral from had provided, plunging the two of us into darkness. My eyes adjusted quickly, but not before my mother pulled me into a tight embrace.

"Careful, Mother," I cautioned, "my arm's broken."

"That answers my question of whether or not you're fully here," Mother responded with a grimace.

"I'm here," I stated unnecessarily, simultaneously firing off a handful of glowing cyan arrows to offer her some light to see by.

"Oh, that's much better, Dear, thank you."

"I have something I need to tell you."

The thoughts of the things left unsaid between my parents and I weighed heavily on my conscience. It was important I speak to them both, but as my mother was here and my father was not, I supposed I would have to tell them one at a time. Thinking of how best to begin, I tried to open my mouth and I immediately felt my jaw clench shut as panic overtook me.

"What is it, Dear?" Mother watched the shifts in my facial expressions with some concern, all things considered. "Has something else happened? Is that Masaru of yours missing?"

"No, nothing else is wrong and Masaru is fine now," I assured her, immediately feeling guilty for causing her additional anxiety. "It's good news, actually."

"I could certainly use some of that," Mother responded before narrowing her eyes. "If it's good news, why are you so worried about telling me? Oh my god, you're not pregnant, are you?"

I shook my head quickly, too nerve-wracked to protest more vigorously at her assumption as I might once have done.

"What is it then, Yukari? Don't draw it out."

"Masaru asked me to marry him," I blurted, blushing furiously.

Mother's expression gave away nothing following my pronouncement and I marveled at her control. "And?"

"Well it's not marriage, exactly," I clarified. "It's a Roughlander custom called Joining that's very similar." Mother's mouth twitched at the corners, betraying amusement. "Dahlia could explain it better than I could..."

"Yukari," she interrupted my floundering after a moment, smiling now, "so Masaru asked you to 'join' with him, do I have the terminology correct?"

"Yes."

"And what did you say, Dear?"

"Oh," I stated, startled. Had I missed that part entirely? "Well, yes, of course."

Mother's expression turned from smiling to stern in an instant. "You know he's a little old for you, Yukari."

"I know how old he is, Mother," I interjected a little tartly, having expected this objection to be raised, "but we're both supposed to live forever, so I hardly see how a few years one way or the other will make a difference."

"Yukari, Chosen or not, you are still only fifteen That's hardly old enough to –"

"We're not on Earth anymore," I countered. "The cultural expectations here are different and let's face it, Chosen or not, I face the threat of dying every day here and so does Masaru, even more so since I Knighted him. It's equally as likely that one of us will die tomorrow as both of us living for thousands of years. I've already faced the thought of losing him more than once and it made me realize I don't want to live in a world without him in it."

"You're sure, Honey? Forever is a long time, especially in your case, and this is the first boyfriend you've ever had. I just want to make sure you've thought this through. I don't want you to be unhappy."

"I'm sure, Mother," I answered honestly, recognizing what she left unsaid: *I don't want you to be unhappy like I was.*

My mother, being originally from this world – the Blue Moon tribe specifically – had left it for my father and me. She had spent the last fifteen years on an alien world, feeling bereft and isolated from everything and everyone she had known. In my case, though, I wasn't giving anything up by choosing to be with Masaru. I was gaining a whole lot more instead.

"Believe me when I say I haven't made this decision lightly."

"I know that, Honey, it's just..." Mother sighed and then emotion abruptly overwhelmed her and the tears came. "I just wish your father were here."

I accepted her hug wordlessly, knowing she just wanted to feel that she was holding onto the part of her family she could for the time being, and also knowing there really wasn't anything I could say to lessen her pain, or my own for that matter.

"Come on," I said after a moment, standing and urging her to do the same. "Let's get you out of here."

"I'm proud of you, Yukari." Mother's words stopped me in my tracks, my hand on the partially open door. "You know what you want and you go for it. You must have gotten that from your father," she added ruefully, "I was never like that."

I found that there was nothing I could say to that either, but thankfully I was saved from having to think of a response by a familiar accented voice coming from just outside the door.

"Hello?" Dahlia called out questioningly as I opened the door the rest of the way. "Oh, is that you, Yukari? I thought I saw a bit of a glow coming from in there. Oh, and Yukari's mum, isn't that a nice surprise?"

"You and I have a bit of planning to do, haven't we?" Mother spoke past me to Dahlia, sounding exactly like her old self again, as if she had not just been crying pitifully a moment before.

Dahlia's answering smile widened across her whole face. "That we do! I was wondering when yer daughter would get around to tellin' ye."

"Who else knows, then?" Mother asked, brows furrowing in disapproval – she never appreciated being left in the dark about anything.

"Oh…just about everybody," Dahlia responded shamelessly, with a sly wink in my direction. "The ones I've had a chance to talk to anyways. We can't keep happy news like this to ourselves, after all."

"I promised Masaru and Mifa I would return as quickly as possible," I interjected before Dahlia could get me into any further trouble. "Can I leave my mother with you, Dahlia? I'll just be going back to the egg room."

"Oh, certainly ye can," Dahlia replied, her eyes lighting up at the prospect and her grin never faltering. "I'm sure yer mum and I have a lot we can amuse ourselves with."

"You'll be okay, Mother?"

"Hmm? Yes, Honey, go back to your man, I'll be fine," Mother assured me absently, clearly distracted by the prospect of conspiring with Dahlia on my wedding.

I tried not to think about that too closely.

"All right, I'll be going then. You know where to find me."

Closing my eyes, I sent myself back to Masaru in the same fashion I had left him, but the dark and somber egg room I had left was nothing like the bright and noisy place I found on my return. My arrows had long since faded out of existence, but torches had been brought in and mounted on the wall to replace them with a brighter and more stable light source. The room was also much cheerier than it had been before, for which I no doubt had the Roughlanders among the refugees to thank. Every Roughlander present, and some others as well, were gathered around and exclaiming over Neva and the news she must have shared.

"And Razor," Neva was saying to the enrapt attention of her audience, "I want you to be there for the baby, especially if Yuge can't."

I watched Razor carefully for the hurt I expected to find in his expression, but I saw only a proud smile and a happy light in his eyes. "You mean I'm going to be an uncle?" he asked with pleased disbelief.

"Aye," Neva agreed, laughing. "That is, if ye want to be."

"Of course I do!"

My mother had it right; what we all needed right now was a dose of good news. Feeling a slight smile cross my own face, I took a step forward and became solid, joining them and putting a hand on Masaru's shoulder.

"Oh, ye're back. Did ye hear the news?" he asked with a smile. "Neva's going to have a baby."

I nodded. "I was the one who told her about it."

"So that's what ye were talking about back there, I'd wondered."

"Masaru, I'd like to talk to you for a minute, if that's okay."

Masaru stood and nodded his agreement, then offered Neva one last congratulations of his own before he began following me from the room.

"Yukari, wait," Neva called out and I turned to see her hurrying to catch up to us. "Ye know what ye said about getting off on the wrong foot? Well, ye're right about that and it isn't fair to either of us. I'd like to start over, if ye don't mind."

I was a little taken aback by her offer, but pleased nonetheless. "No, of course I don't mind. That's a wonderful idea."

"Good," Neva pronounced. "Well then, I also have one more thing to ask ye. I want ye to be there, ye know, when the baby is born."

I smiled. "I'll do one better than that. I'll be your midwife, if you'll let me. That is, if you don't already know of somebody more qualified or experienced."

"You will? Ye mean it, Yukari? You won't be too busy bein' a Chosen and all that?"

"I can't say I won't be busy," I admitted, recalling how intense my life had become since taking up the mantle of my new position, "but I will make time to check in on you and the baby, and I will be there when you are ready to deliver."

"Thank ye!" Neva exclaimed. "And thank ye as well," she repeated unnecessarily to Masaru before rushing back to the others to fill them in on this new development.

"I'm glad you and Neva have decided to get along," Masaru noted once we were standing just outside the lit open arch of the egg room, a few steps away from venturing into the dark and cavernous unknown that was the Temple of Machalite. "She means quite a bit to Razor, or so I've gathered."

"Speaking of Razor, Masaru, that's kind of what I wanted to talk to you about."

"Oh?"

"Razor was the real hero today," I began a little awkwardly. "You were all stuck in those eggs and I didn't have any way of saving you, but Razor he…"

"Hey there, it's all right. We all seem to be fine now," Masaru noted.

I nodded to the truth of his words and decided to try facing a topic that was a little easier. "I know you wanted to talk to Razor about the Joining yourself, but I had to tell him before…" I stopped, realizing that this line of dialogue was headed down the same path as the one I had already abandoned.

"I take it Razor had to fulfill some of his duties of standing for me a little before the fact?"

I nodded, biting my lower lip self-consciously.

"I'll have to thank him then," he added.

"Razor kissed me."

"Or maybe I won't then," Masaru amended with a frown.

"We both thought he was going to die and –"

"So it was a farewell?" Masaru asked gently, cupping the side of my face with his hand. "I understand, Yukari, it's nothing to be worried about." His expression abruptly shifted to a lopsided smile and he continued, "Just as long as outside of the Joining ceremony it doesn't happen again. Did I mention you'll have to kiss him during the Joining? Ye'd better warn Hotaru about that also. We could take that part out I guess, if she's, ye know, got someone else, but it'll be expected."

This statement broke the tension I had been feeling as nothing else could have and I found myself laughing at the thought of telling Hotaru that she would have to kiss Masaru.

"Oh no," I commented, realizing something, "I told my mother, but I haven't yet talked to Hotaru."

"Ye better think about doing so before Dahlia tells every person she lays eyes on. I know we told her to keep quiet, but ye know with Dahlia that's not likely to happen. She's too excited about it."

"Tell me about it." I rolled my eyes and remembered how Dahlia had acted with my mother. "Okay, I will. Did you happen to learn where she and the others went?"

"Aysel came down a little bit ago with the food and the torches. She said they're staying up in the small lit house at the top of the ramp and to be extra careful about the ledge, if that makes any sense to ye."

"All right. Did you want to come with me?"

"I think I'll stay here where there's light, if ye don't mind. Besides, I have to talk to Razor now, don't I?" he added with a wink.

Smiling and shaking my head at Masaru's unfailing good humour, I turned to leave when he stopped me with a hand on my wrist, "Oh, Yukari, one more thing."

Unexpectedly, Masaru pulled me into an embrace and kissed me soundly and passionately, as if to remind me who I had actually chosen. When he was done, he left me red in the face and out of breath, but infinitely happier than I had been until now.

"There," Masaru pronounced, smiling smugly, "go on now. I'll be here when ye get back."

The little house at the top of the ramp was clearly marked by being both illuminated and the first building one came across when following the path that meandered up from the egg room. Turning towards it, I gave silent thanks to the fact that my power allowed me to see effortlessly in any light as the steadily inclining path followed dangerously close to a gaping ravine so vast that even I was unable to make out either the ground below or anything on the far side. Shuddering at the thought of what could possibly await the unfortunate below, I opened the only visible door to the little house and let myself into the well-lit room, shutting the darkness out behind me.

The interior of the house was not large; the main level barely big enough for the two beds and the small square table between them. Hotaru was sitting in the only chair within sight, a rickety old thing propped up against one of the beds upon which lay Sir Rama, writhing in agony.

Aysel was there too, looking exhausted, but hovering over Rama, repeatedly dousing his left arm with water from a bucket placed at his bedside. I took a step forward to get a closer look at what sort of ghastly wound Aysel was administering to.

I did a double-take. Visually, Rama's arm was fine, yet it was obviously causing him a great deal of pain and Aysel's concerned expression betrayed how serious she believed it to be. Thinking I must be missing something, I twisted my vision to see what lay beneath the surface of skin, but I still found nothing unusual.

"What's wrong with him?"

Aysel turned at the sound of my voice, noticing me for the first time. "That's just it – we don't know," she admitted, sounding tired and somewhat frustrated. "He just keeps insisting, when he's got breath enough to speak between sleeping and screaming, that his arm is on fire. I'm sure it feels that way to him, but…"

"I take it there is nothing Ris can do for him?" Aysel nodded. "Why don't you just put his whole arm in the bucket?"

"We've tried that. The water only boils and then it's of no use to him."

"So it's not just in his mind, then. Something is causing this."

Aysel nodded, but it was Hotaru who answered in a voice hoarse from crying. "It's because he stuck his hand through one of the Ruby eggs trying to get us out. He told me…before he passed out."

"We thought we had figured out which eggs were yours," Aysel elaborated. "Sir Rama thought he'd use his power to try and get you out. He put his arm through the egg and then he started to scream. He's been like this ever since, and that was maybe three or four days ago now."

"Has he been able to eat or drink anything?" the medic in me asked.

"A little," Aysel replied. "There are times when his pain is less. He was actually doing much better a bit ago when Hotaru first arrived."

I considered the problem a moment. The symptoms were strange, but the cause of them was not. Lilyth had clearly demonstrated the ability to possess others and then manipulate their minds and bodies; there was no doubt in my mind that making someone suffer with the belief that their arm was on fire was a simple task for her.

"The eggs were trapped. Has anyone thought to check for possession?"

As soon as I spoke the words, I regretted them. Aysel's expression fell and it was clear to me what the dilemma was: Adel was not here.

Lady Adel Kusabana had trained under Lilyth during her reign more than eight hundred years ago, and though she was a Knight of Sapphiros now and by her own choice no longer one of Lilyth's supporters, she was very knowledgeable about the Lady's methods. Unfortunately, Adel was one of those still unaccounted for and undoubtedly that fact was tearing her twin sister, Aysel, apart.

"Aysel, did you ever learn to do what your sister can, the blood ritual?"

"No," Aysel said, shaking her head, "but I've watched her do it a number of times. I may be able to give it a try."

I had watched Adel perform the ritual a number of times myself, but when I had asked the Knight how she did what she did, she had told me it involved pitting the strength of her will against that of the possessor. I wondered if Aysel knew that aspect of it. I opened my mouth to share what I knew when Hotaru interrupted with an unexpected offer.

"I'll do it," she stated with a decided expression. "I've also seen Adel do it before and I was there when she was teaching Shuzhue how to do it."

Ordinarily, I would have sided with Aysel being the more knowledgeable of the two, but as I considered Hotaru's words I realized she was nearly the most willfully stubborn person I knew, second only to Yue. "All right, but it's all or nothing, Hotaru. We can't have you end up like Rama, or worse."

She swallowed apprehensively, glancing over to Rama, who was still twitching and writhing fitfully in his shallow sleep, but when her gaze locked once more with mine all I saw was her resolve.

"Aysel, can I borrow your sword?"

I held up a hand, forestalling Aysel, as I reached into my medic kit and drew out a surgical knife. "Here, use this," I instructed, holding out the knife, "it's more sanitary. And be careful with it, you don't need a gaping wound for this, Hotaru."

It was a measure of the seriousness with which she viewed the situation that she didn't argue, but held out her hand instead. "Can you do it?"

I made a shallow cut across the face of her open palm with a quick swipe before fishing out a sanitary napkin to clean the blade.

Hotaru studied Rama for a moment, her bloodied hand poised in the air above him. "You'll help me," she asked with her gaze focused on the task before her, "the way you help Adel?"

"If necessary, yes," I agreed.

"Concentrate, Hotaru," Aysel cautioned, "you'll need all of your attention for this."

With her determined expression returning in full force, Hotaru worked from her memories and, as far as I could tell, accurately copied the motions Adel used for this purpose, touching her bloodied hand to each of Rama's shoulders in turn before placing it flat on his forehead. Then she set her jaw and drew her hand back, clenching her fist with the motion.

"I won't lose anyone else!"

I was used to watching Adel's fist clench tighter as it was wracked with pain, but with Hotaru it wasn't just her arm but her whole body that convulsed with the effort of holding onto the power that would set Sir Rama free of his torment, if she could just hold on long enough to master it. I could tell immediately that Hotaru's will wasn't going to be enough; even exhausted, it had never been this bad for Adel. Not waiting for any further indication that my help was needed, I did the only thing I thought might have any effect: I formed an arrow with my mind and let it loose.

The arrow exploded as soon as I let it go, expanding outwards until it had created a glowing net of cyan energy that covered Hotaru from head to toe, and even draped across some of Rama's bed.

The effect was immediate; the tension in Rama's body seemed to ease as the net touched him and Hotaru wilted, drained by the power of my net. Fortunately, whatever Adel's ritual was allowing her to hold on to also slackened like a rope no longer held taut on the other end. Feeling the change, her eyes widened with sudden understanding and Hotaru renewed her effort, pouncing on whatever advantage my power had lent her.

On and on it went, Hotaru suffering and Rama's freedom hanging in the balance, but she refused to give Lilyth – if that was indeed who she was fighting – the upper hand. She held on tight through whatever was thrown at her, while my nets slowly drained her strength and the horrible power that had latched onto Rama.

Finally, it was done. Aysel caught Hotaru as she swayed and held her until she was certain she wasn't going to topple out of the chair. Hotaru looked worn, but she remained conscious and showed no signs of being in pain. Rama also looked peaceful, but I couldn't help but check on his arm to be certain; it was cool to the touch.

"Can I have some water, Aysel?" Hotaru asked weakly.

Aysel nodded and picked up the bucket she had emptied wetting Rama's arm earlier. "I was just going to get some more anyways. I'll be right back."

"Yukari," Hotaru began once Aysel had left, "did I do it? Is he going to be all right?"

I nodded. "It seems that way. His arm is cool to the touch and just by looking at him you can see he is not in pain any longer."

The last bit of tension seemed to seep from Hotaru's frame in relief and I realized my friend had been doing everything in her power to keep herself together until now. At a loss for what to do, I crouched down to offer Hotaru a hug. "Shh, it's all right now. I knew you could do it."

"It's not that." She sniffled, pulling back from me. "It's just that I couldn't lose him too…not after learning about Harford-san."

Tim Harford? I remembered our class' foreign exchange student with a bit of a start – Lilyth's vivid dreamscape was still causing me to confuse some aspects of reality. Tim Harford, along with Goji Nakamura and two other students, had been taken from Earth and turned into the Vile Emperor's Talons. Goji had been stuck in the identity of Lord Fuzen until we freed him, but Tim had been the Talon Kai-Een until he was returned to us by the Ruby City as an 'act of good faith'.

The last time I had seen Tim was when I had brought him to my operating room in the palace of Taiyou. Had Tim somehow become one of the many casualties of the fall of Taiyou? Had Hotaru heard some word of what had become of him, or any of the rest of the people who were unaccounted for – like my father?

"What do you know, Hotaru? Is he dead? Was he in Taiyou with the others?"

"He's not in Taiyou, he's here," she explained. "The thing is, he's not exactly dead either. Tim Harford is mostly gone, but Kai-Een is still here."

I stiffened immediately. Kai-Een? Here? The nefarious Talon was the first of the four of them I had ever encountered and I felt my anger boil upon hearing he still lived, never mind that he had also stolen the body of a friend.

"Where?"

"With the Rubians. There are a number of refugees here from the Ruby City, mainly Lady Mikura's Deathsquad."

I was halfway to my feet before I remembered I had a reason for coming here and no matter my desire for answers or revenge – or whatever it was I actually wanted from Kai-Een – that came first.

"Hotaru, that aside, I have something I came up here to tell you," I began, taking in a breath to ready myself to say the words one more time and realizing that they were getting easier, "Masaru and I are getting married."

"Oh, you mean the Joining? Dahlia told me about it and I meant to congratulate you –"

"When did you see Dahlia?"

"Oh, well, she found me just after I talked to Tim – I mean Kai-Een. She told me I had to keep going, that Tim would never really be gone if I carried his memory with me, and that I should focus on the good things whenever I can. I've been trying and I'm really happy for you and Masaru," she insisted through the tears still on her face, "you know that, right?"

"I know that. I just wanted to tell you myself, but it seems like everyone already knows."

"I didn't," Rama spoke unexpectedly in as jovial a tone as he could manage, his bed creaking as he painstakingly rearranged himself into a seated position, "and I think it is wonderful news! Congratulations to you both."

"Sir Rama, are you all right?" I asked, concerned that he might strain himself.

"Much better, thank you for asking," he replied, sounding pretty much like his old self again. "I suppose I'll be a little tender for a while, but to be honest with you I'm just happy to see you all free of those eggs, even if I wasn't the one to free you. Who was the one to manage it, if I might ask?"

"Razor," I answered to Hotaru's confused expression – she knew we had gotten free, but she didn't know how the others had managed it and I wasn't quite ready to talk about it, if I ever would be. However, at the mention of Razor's name I abruptly recalled the rest of what I had come here for. "Hotaru, there's one other thing. I wanted to ask you if you would stand for me – It's a little like being a maid of honour, only with a Roughlander twist to it."

"Really? You mean it, Yukari?"

"Even if it means that you might have to kiss Razor?" I teased her.

"What?!"

"I don't know exactly what you're talking about, but it sounds lovely," Rama interjected, closing his eyes and leaning back on the bed's headboard. "Except that last bit, of course," he added, cracking one eye open to regard me with a strange expression. "Judging by her reaction, I take it that's a Roughlander custom and not an Earth one?"

I spent the next while explaining Roughlander Joinings to Hotaru and Earth weddings to a bemused Rama. The conversation was happy and lighthearted, and allowed the three of us and Aysel, when she returned with the water, some much needed escape from the depressing nature of our shared circumstance.

But for all the light inside that little house, the silent darkness outside hit me like a wall of bricks, never mind that my eyes automatically adjusted to allow me to see. As I stepped fully into the dark, reality returned with the force of a slamming door and I immediately latched on to the one unresolved issue I thought I could do something about – Kai-Een. I wanted answers, and Kai-Een was going to share, whether he felt like it or not, even if I had to truss him up in an energy net to prove I was serious. I started deeper into the Temple of Machalite when I was startled by a light ahead as the source of it rounded a corner. The light was held low to the ground as if carried by a child or…a Seventh Spawn Croatin – Ticket!

It was Ticket, one of the first Croatins I had ever met back at Masaru's outpost, before we had all been forced to flee. The frog-person's green skin was more vibrant than it had been in the desert when I first met him, as Ticket had spent the last few months in a lush tropical paradise – that is, until he too had to flee to Taiyou and then to this hidden underground temple.

"Ticket, what's going on?"

Beyond Ticket stood a sizeable group of disoriented and war-torn refugees in a ragged cluster. They carried and supported a number of wounded between them, but all bore signs of a battle and wore outfits they last would have been wearing a week ago in

Taiyou. I recognized a few people in the group, which mainly consisted of Taiyoun Legionnaires, but notably among them were both Kaji and Hotaru's parents, the Zukatoros and the Hatsumuyas, respectively, and Yue's father, Noh-san. I was glad to see them of course, but I couldn't help the pang I felt upon realizing my father was not with them.

"Yue saved us – all of us," Ticket told me, his lisped, nasal voice sounding awed. "We all had those spiky things." The Croatin raised his arms above his head in imitation of Lillem talons. "But she fixed us and they just fell off."

"Where is Yue now?"

"Last I saw her, she left the guardians in charge of the rooms where all the Lillem – I mean where we – were kept. I think she plans on making all the Lillem parts," he said, raising his arms again to show what he meant, "disappear."

That made sense; Yue's power allowed her to vanish objects. Though it still didn't explain why she wasn't with these people, helping them. The discarded Lillem pieces, unnerving as they were, could wait until the surviving humans were cared for.

"Come on, I'll help you all down to the egg room and we'll see what can be done to make you a little more comfortable."

With Kai-Een forgotten about for the moment, I made nets for the able bodied to use as litters to make carrying the seriously wounded a little easier and fired off a group of glowing arrows to light our path back the way I had come. Once the procession was back underway, I selected the few who most urgently needed my help – of which thankfully there weren't many, although Noh-san was unfortunately among them – and I turned the smaller group of us to mist to get us to the egg room more quickly.

I found Ris there and along with the help of the others, we began preparing the room for the new arrivals. Noh-san I left to Ris and her miraculous healing abilities, but for the rest I attended to each of them one at a time, doing for them whatever I could, even if it was just a few words of comfort or support in the wake of the trauma they had lived through.

"No, go on, I'm fine – there are others who need you more than I!" I stopped at the sound of a familiar protest and was startled to realize I knew the speaker – I had treated this man before.

"You!" I exclaimed, whirling to face him.

"You remember me?" He grinned somewhat sheepishly. "I'm flattered."

"Don't be," I responded wryly, remembering the last time this particular member of Sir Rama's Lion Brigade had been under my care and I'd had to force him to submit to the healing of his mangled arm. "I wouldn't have recognized you without your helmet if it wasn't for your stubbornness. How's your arm?"

He shrugged one shoulder lopsidedly and I noticed his right side that had been injured before didn't move at all, though by all appearances it should have healed to be almost as good as new by now. "How's yours?" he retorted, eyeing my makeshift sling.

I returned the one-sided shrug with a hint of a smile. "I'll do, there are people hurting more than I am. The question is, what can I do for you?"

He opened his mouth ready to protest, but my quelling look made him think better of it. "It's just that my right shoulder is unbelievably stiff and I can't seem to move it much."

"Let me see it."

Pulling aside the tattered remains of his clothing, he adjusted his position so I could get a better look. It wasn't pretty; protruding out of the man's shoulder was a nub of bone like Razor had, only in this man's case it was much worse, extending about six inches out from his shoulder blade and the flesh healed all around it as if it had always been there.

"Being what you were for so long, it must have begun to alter you permanently," I spoke softly and with as much delicacy as I could manage.

"Lillem, you mean. You can say it. I remember it, or at least the latter part of it. I suspect we all do."

I grimaced. "Yes, well the extra limbs, they didn't all fall off. It's perhaps possible one day it can be removed, you know, surgically, but unfortunately we don't have the proper tools here and I wouldn't know how to go about it."

"That's all right, go on. I wasn't lying when I said there were people who need you more than I do."

Nodding to the truth of this, I stood and bid him goodbye. The next patient awaiting me was a slight-built boy no older than ten with dark hair that fell in his eyes as he huddled in a ball on the floor of the egg room, trying to make himself as small as possible to avoid notice. I didn't yet know if anything else was wrong with him, besides the obvious, but my heart went out to him, knowing how alone and scared he must feel.

"Hey," I said gently to get his attention as I kneeled down beside him, "my name's Yukari, what's yours?"

The boy's head came up sharply and he regarded me with eyes red from crying. "Jem."

"Well, Jem, I'm a medic," I said, showing him my medic kit, "and I'm just checking up on everyone to make sure they're okay. Is there anything I can do for you?"

The boy sniffled, wiping his face on his sleeve, but remained huddled. "I'm not hurt," he answered, shaking his head, "so you don't need to worry."

"You're from Taiyou?" He nodded. "Have you seen anyone here that you know?"

Jem shook his head slowly and I saw the tears welling up in his eyes again.

"Well, there're lots of people who fled Taiyou and came here," I assured him, "but they're all scattered about this place, just as lost and confused as we are. I'm sure we'll find someone you know eventually…" I cut off as I noticed Jem's expression had turned to one of horror. "Jem, what's wrong?"

"I don't want them to find me!" he wailed, distressed. "They can't see me like this!"

"What is it, Jem? What don't you want them to see?"

"I'll show you, because you're a medic…but you can't tell anyone else, okay?"

I nodded my agreement and with deliberate caution, Jem unfolded himself enough to let me see what he was hiding – his hand.

It simply didn't look human any longer. Jem's right hand was perfectly normal, but his left was curved; the three fingers, instead of the usual four, elongated and ended in unnaturally sharp points, with wicked looking clawed tips that were sharpened bone, not fingernails. The thumb was altered with sharp ridges, making the entire hand more of a pincer or claw than anything else. The only thing still human about it was the colour of the flesh it had grown from.

Jem was looking at me, anticipating my revulsion or fear. He expected me to draw back from what he had become in horror, or perhaps offer, as a doctor, to have it removed or fixed somehow. I forced myself to smile at him and made sure it was the sincerest thing I'd ever done.

"I think it's kind of cool."

"What?" Jem asked, surprised. "You do?"

"Yeah," I affirmed. "I mean, now you're different. No one else is going to have a hand like that."

Jem regarded his new hand dubiously. "What if I don't want to be different? What if I want to be like everybody else?"

"Well, you won't be the only one who's different now. Lots of people were changed by what happened and when this is all over there are going to be things that everyone's going to have to get used to seeing," I told him, thinking of all the changes that had occurred from what Lilyth had done, to the changes the planet itself was undergoing. We would have to adapt and that was the honest truth.

"Look, Jem, you see that person over there?" I indicated my friend from the Lion Brigade. "He's got extra bone sticking out of his shoulder blade, and that person over there, he's got an extra rib bone inside of him." I pointed to show him where I meant.

"Yeah, so?"

"What I'm trying to say is, we're all different," I said, giving his hand a squeeze, "and I think yours is the coolest."

"Really, you think so?"

"I think your hand is much 'cooler' than my shoulder," the man I had been attending to earlier added, having been paying attention to our conversation from where he sat only a few feet away. "Come here and let me get a closer look."

Jem scooted over to make a new friend and I stood. The Lion Brigade soldier met my eyes above the boy's head and smiled. I mouthed a thank you to him before leaving the two of them to get acquainted.

I scanned the room, trying to decide where to head next, when I heard what sounded like an explosion coming from outside the egg room. The underground Temple of Machalite shook with the sudden deafening sound, and without a thought my wings appeared at my back as I shot out of the arch-shaped entrance as fast as I was able.

CH. 5 – FIRST STEPS ARE ALWAYS THE HARDEST

Spurts of supernatural green fire lit up the vast cavern intermittently as explosions continued to go off far below the ledge I had believed marked the edge of Machalite's domain. Flying over the edge, I realized there was a ground level. The flashes of green light revealed the floor was littered with bones of all shapes and sizes, like a long-forgotten graveyard..

The scene below me as I descended rapidly on wings created by my power was so strange it took me a moment to really take in what I was seeing. Ao Kouen, the former Roughlander who was now both King of Taiyou and Chosen of Jedeite, stood before a thing out of nightmares. It towered over him, a massive beast molded from the shadows themselves, with dark wispy tendril-like wings writhing in a non-existent wind. It had a long, sinuous tail, which lay unmoving on the ground, but from above like I was it was clear that the creature had used its tail to surround Ao Kouen, cutting off any means of escape.

Ao Kouen seemed to pay the menacing creature no mind and instead bore a look of intense concentration, his eyes glowing green with the light of Jedeite's power. His arms shot out and another burst of green flame shot from them, followed by another round of smaller explosions. My eyes followed the line of explosions, wondering why Ao Kouen was firing off into the darkness instead of fighting the monster beside him, when I realized what the explosions were doing.

Every clearing puff of green smoke revealed a small cluster of people. Peering closer into the aftermath of their unorthodox arrival, I made out hundreds of confused and frightened individuals, along with various carts and beasts of burden. Their clothes and the presence of cattle marked them as Taiyoun, but where exactly they had come from and how Ao Kouen had managed to bring them here remained a mystery to me.

"Yue, please, I need more power," Ao Kouen called weakly. "They're frightened and they just keep coming."

Yue?

"I'm not sure how much more I have to spare," the demonic creature spoke in a dark, otherworldly voice. "I must keep you alive."

"If I die saving what's left of my people, then at least it would mean something."

"I will keep you alive," it answered and lowering its head on a sinuously curved neck, the creature placed its chin on Ao Kouen's shoulder as it kept him upright with its tail.

"Yue?" I questioned.

The creature raised its head and nodded to me but said nothing, its expression unreadable on such alien features. I decided simple was best. "What's going on here?"

Yue, as was her policy of late, declined to answer me, but Ao Kouen, despite his distraction, spoke, "My people. I can feel them when they cross the Leyins of Taiyou. They're fleeing to me."

I had the feeling Ao Kouen's people were simply fleeing, having no way of knowing their King would be ready and able to save them, but here was likely the safest place for them if out in the countryside, where the Leyins were located, was now threatened by the forces of Lady Lilyth. Having said that, Ao Kouen raised his arms once more and fired off another blast of green power in a different direction from before, so as not to injure the people he had already saved.

"And you're using the power of the Leyins to bring them to you?"

The Leyins, magical lines of power that fanned across Taiyou and connected to the Temple of Jade in the center of the land, existed to keep Taiyou safe. They were extremely powerful. If Ao Kouen was in some way still connected to them from here – however distant we actually were from Taiyou now – it would explain how he was able to summon and control so much power.

"Yes, but I wouldn't have been able to do it without Yue's help. She's figured out a way to share her power with me…" He paused as he fired off another blast, bringing hundreds more people to the dubious safety of Machalite's boneyard. "Without it…I…"

I abruptly recalled the conversation I had briefly overheard before. "I understand. I'll stop distracting you and see what I can do for these people."

I repeated everything I had done for the other refugees, quickly losing track of time and my own feelings of exhaustion with these important tasks. The most important thing I accomplished was spreading the word of where we were and what had happened to the many displaced people who had trouble understanding that this dark and foreboding place represented safety.

I was so caught up with the refugees that I hardly noticed when the explosions stopped and I was surprised when a familiar voice called my name. "Yukari!" The impossibly loud call could only have been made by the one person who had the power to project his own voice at whatever volume he pleased – Kaji. Using my own power, I quickly located him by sensing his life force and made my way to him, flying over the crowd so as not to have to wade through all the settling refugees.

"What is it?" I landed before Kaji who was standing with Hotaru. "How did you two get down here, anyway?"

"We've been down here for a while, helping people," Kaji informed me. "Hotaru's making water and I've been getting some numbers and organizing people to distribute supplies."

"I got us down as water," Hotaru added, "but I don't know how we're going to get back up again."

"That's not a problem," I told them. "Now that I know you are here, I can take you back up."

"I can get myself up," Kaji noted. "I left a clone up there, which is kind of related to what I wanted to tell you. Yue's up there now and so are representatives from the Ruby City."

"What?!"

"They came through Machalite's Splitter, here in the Temple," Kaji explained. "Akuma's here."

I caught his meaning immediately. Kaji's girlfriend, Shuzhue, from Shinjuku, now known as Lady Akuma after spending nearly eight centuries on this world, was once again in the role of official ambassador from the Ruby City.

"All right," I agreed, with mixed feelings. "I've done what I can here for now, anyway. Hotaru and I will follow after you."

The Kaji before me splashed to a puddle at my feet like he had never really been there and, shaking my head a little over how much our lives had changed since leaving Tokyo, I willed Hotaru to turn to mist, as with my arm weakened there was no chance of me carrying her. My wings appeared once more at my back and I took off, swirling around the cavern to gain some height and make it back up to the ledge above, watched by awed refugees on the cavern floor.

Lady Akuma and her escorts were in the little house by the time we reached it, but the situation turned out to be not quite what I was expecting. Rama was nowhere to be seen, but in his place on the bed lay Shuzhue, looking pale and drawn and somehow more like the young girl I remembered from Earth, rather than the powerful Chosen she had become.

Yue was also in the room, looking like her old self again, with her long hair still dyed white from her latest hairstyle change in Taiyou. Aysel was present also, as was a stoic looking Deathsquad soldier in their signature black armour and featureless helmet, and finally Kaji was by Shuzhue's side, despite the disapproving stare of Bastion, Akuma's Knight.

"What's wrong with her?" Hotaru asked.

"This place seems to drain her the same way it does Ao Kouen," Aysel explained. "It's curious, it doesn't seem to do the same to the four of you."

It was curious, yes, but I was fairly certain I understood why. This was Machalite's Temple and clearly this was his way of saying he didn't like the Chosen of other gem gods in his domain. Perhaps Sapphiros, being a god of balance, was exempt from this disdain, or perhaps it was just the insatiably curious gem god found us particularly interesting. Either way, it was clear now why Ao Kouen had needed Yue's power in addition to his Leyins.

"Yeah," Yue agreed, "but that's why I've got Ao Kouen in here." She waved her arms around her head to indicate the nebulous space where she kept the things she stored with her power – apparently it was also possible for her to store people, though how she discovered that in the first place was more of an experiment than I would have attempted.

"You shouldn't have come," Bastion stated in his thick European-sounding accent, his muscular arms folded over his dark, hairy chest, exposed by the open red robe he wore tucked into his black hide pants.

"I had to come, Bastion," Akuma replied patiently. "It was the last place to try, we had looked everywhere else." She turned to address the rest of us. "You did a good job of going to ground. I dare say the Lady Lilyth has no way of knowing where you are, let alone of getting here. We only had an idea after Lady Mikura finally woke up." She frowned. "She was in a bad way."

"How is she now?" Hotaru asked.

"She is doing…better," Akuma replied evasively. "It was you we were worried about. I see now that you have a hiding place, but how are you for supplies? Do you have food? Water?"

"There are many more of us than we anticipated," I answered with diplomatic caution, wary of Akuma's intentions and knowing the woman she was now was far removed from the student I had once known. "I don't know how long our supplies will last, even with the more recent additions," I added, thinking of all the supplies that had come in with the people Ao Kouen had rescued.

"We can help with that. Food, at least. Water might be trickier, but we could bring some through the Splitter."

"Water shouldn't be a problem. We have Hotaru for that, but what would we have to give in return for your help?" I asked the question, knowing that only I was likely to, and that it needed to be asked. As much as Shuzhue was in some ways like us, with ties to

Shinjuku, she had much stronger ties to her nation, and it was ruled by the Vile Emperor who was no friend of ours – or Taiyou's.

"Nothing," Akuma answered. "I only ask that you keep an open mind. As I see it, we are on the same side now. Lady Lilyth threatens all of us and I know you would be reluctant to accept our hospitality, but know that the Ruby City is available to you should you need to seek other accommodations."

I nodded slowly, accepting this. She was right in saying I would be reluctant to accept her offer, but none of us could deny a possible ally at this time and we would be fools to turn away a helping hand, even if that hand came ultimately from the Vile Emperor.

"Food, then," Lady Akuma said. "Bastion?"

Bastion nodded and looked over his shoulder at the Deathsquad soldier who had been standing unobtrusively in the corner until now. At this cue, the soldier stepped forward and stood at attention. "You know what to do," Bastion stated gruffly, and then he elaborated after seeing our collective puzzled stare. "This Deathsquad soldier is special." I raised my brow at this; I would need more of an explanation than that before I even considered letting this Deathsquad soldier wander about in the Temple of Machalite amidst scared refugees. "He has ability. He makes food, see?"

I didn't see, but as Akuma was nodding, I had little choice but to accept this information as fact. Breaking his statuesque pose, the Deathsquad soldier took a step forward and I realized he had brought no weapon or shield. Uncertain if this made me feel more at ease or not, I nodded to the Deathsquad soldier and he gestured in the Kumori fashion as if to say, *Where would you like the food?*

Was this Deathsquad soldier a Kumori? I stared at him curiously a moment, trying to look behind him, but seeing no sign of wings. "Below," I answered, to break the tense silence. "I will take you."

"Can I come too?" Hotaru asked. "I wasn't finished making water."

I nodded my assent and feeling very strange indeed, I turned them both to mist and led Hotaru and the Deathsquad soldier out of the little house after me, calling back to Kaji and the others from the doorway, "Look after her. We'll be back as quickly as possible."

"Take your time!" Yue called. "I can always stick Akuma in my Noh-space."

"Thank you, but no," I heard Akuma protest as I shut the door behind my misty passengers and took to the air once more.

I reformed both Hotaru and the Deathsquad soldier in the most secluded spot I could find on the ground floor, leaving my wings out to give them enough light to see by.

"I'm going to find a bucket!" Hotaru announced immediately upon reforming, being used to travelling as mist by now, and took off, leaving me alone with our potentially dangerous ally.

I stood poised, watching the Deathsquad soldier closely as he regained his stoic composure after flying as mist for the first time. His dark helmet and ruby visor were identical to every other Deathsquad soldier I had ever encountered and there was no way of reading his expression – or was there?

Nodding to me, as if asking my permission to begin, the Deathsquad soldier turned from me and took a firm-footed stance, then began waving his arms before him as if physically gathering some form of power. Continuing to watch him, I held myself poised in case this should turn out to be some sort of ploy by the Ruby City and I should need to act quickly, but internally my curiosity grew.

Who was this Deathsquad soldier? I didn't know too much about the enemy ranks, but from my understanding, only the Generals, who were also Knights had access to powers and abilities like ours. Regardless, before my eyes the soldier finished gathering his power into a tight red ball between his hands and in a motion that tugged at my memory he released it, firing it off before him with his palms directed outwards.

It was a miracle. A row of foodstuffs of all kinds appeared as if growing out of thin air in a rough line nearly twenty feet beyond where the Deathsquad soldier stood. There were fruits, vegetables, sides of meat, and loaves of bread. There were foods I recognized and those I didn't, but all of it was fresh and plentiful.

"Whoa!" Hotaru called out, returning with a bucket held in her hand and staring in wonder at the sudden appearance of such a bounty. "How'd you do that?"

The Deathsquad soldier didn't answer her. He merely shrugged and turned to begin gathering his power for another blast. His silence intrigued me and apparently Hotaru was wondering the same thing I was.

"Are you a Kumori?" she asked without preamble. "Without wings, I mean."

The soldier gave no indication he had heard her or intended to answer, instead firing off another line of food.

"Can you hear me, or are you deaf too?" Hotaru continued, trying to catch the soldier's eye.

Hotaru brought up an interesting point, no matter her lack of tact in addressing it, but while studying the Deathsquad soldier and his odd ability out of the corner of my eye I realized if he was a wingless Kumori the situation might make a little more sense. Ris was a Kumori and she had a miraculous way with healing, perhaps this food creation power was similar in some way and related to his race – since he wasn't answering, there was only one way to find out.

I twisted my vision to see past the layers of the Deathsquad soldier's armour. He had long dark hair tied back, with a square jaw and eyes tinted red by the reflection of light through his ruby visor – I was surprised to discover he was human, albeit a silent one. I was tempted to x-ray further and see if I could discover if his muteness was by choice or affliction, when my concentration was interrupted by Hotaru's exclamation, "Wow, thanks!"

Vision abruptly refocusing back to normal, I took in the sight of Hotaru holding her bucket before her filled to the brim with cooked white rice instead of the water she was supposed to have been making.

"Hotaru," I reprimanded her sharply, "don't you have something you're supposed to be doing?"

"Can you teach me?" she asked the Deathsquad soldier, ignoring me.

He looked up at me instead of giving Hotaru any form of answer and I gathered from his quick gesturing in the Kumori style that he was done and ready to go back up.

"You are a Kumori!" Hotaru decided, misinterpreting his gesturing and the reason behind it entirely. "So you'll teach me, then? Now?"

"Another time, Hotaru," I interrupted. "Lady Akuma is suffering. They have to go."

We had been told that Splitters were necessary for traversing the distance between planets without physically crossing the intervening space. Regardless of the truth of that statement, I had never before seen a Splitter, active or inactive, yet I had obviously somehow crossed the unimaginable distance to this world. Granted, it had apparently taken us eight hundred years to do so, but it hadn't felt nearly so long for those of us who experienced the process.

The device was formed entirely of precious black stone and took up an entire hollowed out space in the temple approximately the size of the egg room. The smooth black Machalite of the floor and walls gleamed dully and seemed to slope inwards toward a smooth, tapered pillar in the center, which looked like a stalagmite, and it had a matching counterpoint above it coming down from the ceiling.

Akuma lay draped in Bastion's arms, but her presence was such that she managed to appear regal despite her position. At her direction, Bastion took a deliberate step to place them both upon the Splitter platform and Akuma fished a slender diamond-shaped Ruby out of a pouch at her waist when the mysteriously mute Deathsquad soldier joined them.

"What's that?" Hotaru asked, insatiably curious by nature.

"Access key," Akuma answered, handing the object in question to the Deathsquad soldier as Bastion's arms were currently occupied. "Don't you have one of your own?"

Hotaru met this question with puzzlement, but I kept silent, my thoughts turning to the scroll case I kept hidden in the medic kit that was strapped to my chest. Sapphiros had left a message that the key to operating the Splitters was contained within the Blue Moon scroll – perhaps now I finally knew what that meant.

"Then how did you –?"

"Get here?" I finished Akuma's question for her. "We'd like to know that ourselves."

"Ah. Well, I have to go, but please remember my offer. I hope you will also keep in mind where the help you received came from," she stated with added diplomatic significance. "We could all use allies right now."

Her meaning was clear to me also. Whether we liked it or not, we were indebted to the Ruby City now and it was best we did not forget it.

"Allies, then," Kaji stated in response before I had a chance to think of a suitable reply, and just like that the agreement to ally with our former enemies was made.

"Oh, I almost forgot," Akuma noted. "Bastion, give him a mirror."

"Are you sure, my Lady?"

"Yes, Bastion," she answered patiently. "They may have need to contact us and Kaji is familiar with its use." Her eyes flickered inexplicably to the Deathsquad soldier behind her before returning to Bastion. "Please, Bastion, give it to him so we can leave this place."

"You'll have to come here," Bastion noted gruffly to Kaji. "I cannot reach it just now."

With a little bit of maneuvering, Bastion had Kaji remove a plate-sized disk of flat Ruby from his oversized pocket. "Thank you," Kaji spoke to Bastion, but it was clear his words were meant for Lady Akuma. "I will use it wisely."

"See that you do," Akuma noted, giving Kaji a meaningful stare. "Bastion?"

Bastion seemed to instinctively know what his mistress wanted and carried her over to the center of the Splitter platform. Once there, Akuma extended her slender arm, holding out the narrow diamond-shaped Ruby before her until it was poised in the exact center between the two pillars. Satisfied with its position, she let it go and it simply hovered there, impossibly suspended.

Bastion stepped back and the Ruby began to twirl in place, slowly at first, but with increasing speed. A whirring noise filled our ears and a wind picked up from nowhere, whipping our hair about but leaving Bastion and Akuma's eerily still. We watched with bated breath for the moment that visitors from the Ruby City would simply disappear, but with a suddenness that startled everyone present the Ruby access key clattered to the ground and all went silent.

"I gather that wasn't supposed to happen?" Yue enquired blithely.

"No," Fuun answered, coming into the room behind us. "What are you all doing in here?" he questioned and then noticed Lady Akuma, whom he had tried to kill the last time he had encountered her. "You," he stated accusingly, "are not welcome here."

"I've gathered that," Lady Akuma answered with poise, but a disapproving frown. "We were just trying to leave."

Fuun, usually so stoic and emotionless, frowned worriedly.

"What is it, Fuun?" I asked.

"There has not been this many here for a long time," Fuun answered, his gaze centering on me with intensity, and I could see that his eyes were black with no hint of the blue that marked him as also a Knight of Sapphiros – here, in this temple, there was only Machalite in him.

"Is that a problem?" I pressed.

"Long before I came here for the first time, there were people here. Followers of Machalite, his priests and their families. There is a village here because they lived here. Then one day they all simply vanished. No one was left alive to tell why, but as you may have seen their bones litter the floor of the cavern. I believe they all leapt to their deaths, though only Machalite knows why."

I sharply remembered my own dealings with Machalite and felt guilt weigh down upon me. "Yes," I whispered, "we must go then, and not…wear out our welcome."

Fuun nodded, but it was Akuma who spoke, "Where will you all go, then? Will you come to the Ruby City, provided we can get the Splitter working?"

"What are our options?" I questioned, looking about the room for input. "We will be hunted no matter where we go. I know none of us wants to think of it, but we have the Splitters here, we might consider taking the refugees to Earth. It would certainly be a safer place with plenty of resources."

"And admit defeat?" Kaji countered. "We're not beaten yet. Besides, I don't think we'd receive a warm welcome in Japan. I've been talking with my father and it seems the Japanese government would love to get their hands on us, to use as a secret weapon."

"We could take them to America," Hotaru suggested. "We don't have to stay in Japan."

As much as I didn't want to admit it, Kaji was right. Back in Taiyou my father had hinted at much the same thing. "No, Kaji's right. It's not such a great idea, but we should still probably keep it in mind in case it becomes our only option."

"Well, I already thought of this," Yue spoke up, "I asked Fuun to take a look around and find out what is going on out there, so we'd know where we should go next, and I think we should go to the Mountains of Sapphire. Fuun?"

"I went to my former home at Yue's request, though I have not been back there since I left it. I found it abandoned. It is much like the village here, like the inhabitants simply vanished, leaving no indication of the reason or method."

It was an option, I supposed, which I felt qualified more than taking shelter in the home of the Vile Emperor. "Though, that puts us in much the same boat we are in now. Provided we can take all the food and supplies with us, we will be far out of the way and still cut off from everyone else."

"What else can we do?" Hotaru questioned.

"Lady Akuma is right," Kaji pointed out, "we need allies right now. We have no hope of getting stronger if we just keep hiding and dwindling our resources until there's nothing left. At best, the southern mountains can only be a temporary measure."

"So that leaves the Ruby City, then," Yue noted, "or Espearia."

"Espearia still stands," Fuun stated. "They would not let me within the gates, and for the sake of your alliance with them I did not insist, but the city seems to have withstood the Lillem until now."

"Of course!" Hotaru exclaimed. "Chikara! I hope she's doing all right."

Yue seemed to consider this. "I still think the Mountains are the best place to go, so we don't draw trouble to Espearia, but I suppose we really should check how they are faring and offer our help."

"Espearia, then?" I looked to Kaji for his opinion and, with a glance down at the Ruby mirror in his hands, he nodded. "All right, it's decided. Akuma, we thank you for your offer of hospitality."

"I understand your reasons," she answered, "but we are not allied with Espearia as you are. You have the mirror should you need to contact us, however."

"We'll just have to see about changing that," Yue noted with a stubborn set to her features. "We're all in this together now."

"I wish you luck," Akuma added, "but I'm afraid there's too much bad blood between us and Espearia."

"If your decisions are made, then it is best we begin departing," Fuun interjected.

"Yes," Akuma agreed. "Will your Splitter work for us now or must we attempt contacting the Ruby City for transport?"

Fuun's gaze took on a far away look as his pupils darkened and then all of a sudden he was back, not as himself, but Machalite. "You all may leave," his dark voice whispered emotionlessly. "I will not detain Chosen, but the others will remain. They have been most interesting and it has been some time since I have had humans to study."

The others, having presumably not encountered Machalite before, appeared startled at Fuun's sudden change in demeanor, but I knew exactly who I was dealing with. At the sound of his voice, something inside me snapped and I decided right then and there that I was not going to be trapped in a deal with Machalite again – this ended now.

"You can't keep us here. We had an agreement for the freedom of those people, one life for many, remember?"

There was no warning. Between one breath and the next, thirty people appeared in the room, looking startled. Every single person who had been in an egg was now in the Splitter room, including Masaru, who seemed to take his strange transportation reasonably in stride and make his way over to my side.

"Done," Machalite stated coldly and I felt my panic begin to rise at the single word. It was just like before; he was manipulating me and lives were in the balance.

"No," I protested, my breathing coming faster now as my brain rushed through the implications of Machalite's actions. "Not done. What about Razor? You granted him his freedom, you can't take it away now."

Razor appeared. "Oh, that's where everyone went to," he commented, getting his bearings. "What's going on here?"

"And the others?" I questioned, feeling fear wash over me like a wave. "My mother, the rest of our parents, Ris…for every single person you are letting free, there is someone down there whom they love and would give anything not to leave behind. I thought I taught you something about love. Did I suffer for nothing?! Would you take them all away from me all over again?"

"Stop it." Razor spoke sharply and it took me a moment to realize that he wasn't speaking to me, but to Machalite. "I've already offered my life, but if you need me to do it again, I will. Take it now and let everyone go."

I felt Masaru's hand on my shoulder and I realized how badly I was crying. I wouldn't go through it again, I wouldn't. Razor's almost sacrifice on my behalf had been too much to bear. I wasn't going to lose anyone else for no better reason than Machalite's idle curiosity.

"These have been paid for. I have no reason to release the others," Machalite stated, our impassioned words having no effect on the unfeeling gem god. "I would require something of equal value."

"You want to understand human emotion, to study us?" Yue spoke unexpectedly. "I offer my memories in exchange for everyone's freedom."

"The life of one human –" Machalite began.

"Not just one," Yue interrupted him. "My power has allowed me to see the memories of countless humans and even a few Croatins. I can show you all of it – if we have a deal?"

"Deal."

Machalite left Fuun's body in a rush and he sagged with the sudden shock of the gem god's departure, then Yue stiffened, her eyes went black, and the symbol of Sapphiros on her chest came to life with a cyan glow. It took longer than it ever had before for Yue to transfer memories to someone else, but then I suppose Machalite was being particularly thorough. In the meantime, the now populated room waited in a tense silence with only the occasional whisper breaking out amongst the worried group.

"I take it I missed a fair bit," Masaru spoke softly in my ear.

I shook my head slightly to indicate that no, he hadn't. "We're leaving," I replied, just as softly, "and going to Espearia where we have allies."

"That's the best idea I've heard all day," he pronounced. "This place is dark and it gives me the creeps."

When it was done, Sabien caught Yue in his arms as she sagged limply and he gestured to Akuma to try the Splitter again. Her Deathsquad escort picked the Ruby up and inserted it into the space it was intended for, and within moments the Rubians and their access key were gone.

It would have taken the rest of us much longer to leave the temple had not Machalite, being true to his side of his bargain with Yue, transported us all instantly to a ridge overlooking Espearia, proving in one single instant just how much power a gem god was able to manifest without even straining himself.

The abrupt transition from dark to light was not as debilitating to me as it was to everyone else, save perhaps Fuun, and my vision adjusted automatically. I took in the view of the open desert hungrily and for the briefest moment I let the warm sun and clean air lift my spirits – then I saw Espearia and felt my hopes come crashing down. From it rose a column of thick, black smoke and looking closer as only I could, it was evident that a good portion of the city was aflame.

"No," I stated, willing what I saw to be untrue, "not here too."

"What is it?" Masaru asked from beside me, blinking his eyes against the brightness of the sun.

"We have to go, now. We have to help them. Dahlia, Razor!" I lighted on the Roughlanders first, knowing the two of them were good in a crisis and used to leading others. "Get everyone organized as best you can and start them walking in the direction of the city, but don't get too close – we don't want them to think us a threat. Kaji, Yue, Hotaru, the city is on fire. We need to get down there quickly. Knights –"

"We'll be right behind you," Sabien answered. "Go!"

Yue reached for the nearest person to her – Kaji – and slung him onto her back, taking off in a flash and disappearing by running more quickly than most eyes could follow. Following her example, I willed Hotaru and Masaru to mist and took off into the air.

As we got nearer to the city's walls, I realized the fire wasn't nearly as widespread as it had appeared. From an overhead view the city was circular, with each of the five sections visibly divided into wedge-shaped pieces, and a circular courtyard in the center where they all met up. Due to the city's segmented construction, the disaster seemed to be localized in one section, though the fire would spread if it was not stopped soon, consuming and destroying everything in its path.

Having met a number of the Priestesses of Espearia, I half-expected to see the winged women soaring about the damaged section of the city, making use of their timeless magic to help the citizens of Espearia, but as I swooped down to land on the outer wall I remembered the Priestesses of Air had been with us in Taiyou when it fell.

There were people scurrying about with frantic haste, of course, some with buckets or just personal belongings, but nowhere did I see the familiar robes of the Priestesses of Espearia. Had they all been lost in Taiyou? But no, I recalled the Head Priestess, Arashi, mentioning she had left two of the five orders of Priestesses behind to defend their homeland and look after her daughter, Chikara. But if they were here, what could be keeping them from saving a portion of their city and their people?

As my feet touched down, I reformed Masaru and Hotaru to either side of me on the battlements. Without waiting for further instruction, Hotaru used her power to form jets of water beneath her hands as she leapt into the city of Espearia to begin doing whatever she could.

Trusting Hotaru could take care of herself, I turned to Masaru. "There seems to be a way down there." I pointed to where I had seen a staircase heading down from the battlements on my way in. "See if you can search for survivors and promise me you'll stay safe, all right?"

"You as well," Masaru commented, his expression grim, before taking off at a run.

Taking a deep breath to prepare myself for what I was about to face, I leapt to take flight again when a sudden rush of wind stopped me and I whirled about, hovering in the air. "Fuun," I commented, a little surprised to see he had followed me, but more surprised at the person he had brought with him.

I recognized the short, rounded man from a few of the council meetings held in Taiyou before its untimely fall. He was not Taiyoun, however, but one of our allies. Looking the unlikely warrior in his bulky metal suit of armour and with his Japanese features for the moment unhelmeted, I recalled this man was one of the Espearians who had arrived with Arashi and the others.

"You're one o' them Chosen types, aren't you?" The man spoke with a thick southern drawl, much stronger than I remembered Arashi's accent to have been. "I'm The Head. I rule this here city and I could sure use your help in savin' it."

"I brought him because he said he knew what he was doing," Fuun commented emotionlessly. "I will leave him to you now."

Fuun didn't give me a chance to protest at having this 'The Head' dumped in my lap, but instead disappeared in a way reminiscent of Yue.

"If y'all wouldn't mind takin' me down there," The Head spoke again, regarding me expectantly, "I'm sure we'll have no trouble at all getting this here fire under control."

I regarded The Head dubiously for a moment, but knowing there was no time to waste I humoured him and turned him to mist for the short trip down to the ground where he had asked to go.

There was no reason that once there I couldn't leave him to his own devices and get started finding people who needed help evacuating. However, once reformed back on solid ground The Head had another task for me.

"D'you mind just holding the end of this here nozzle?" he asked, shoving the device in question into my hands before I could take off again. Turning from me, The Head began turning a massive crank stuck into the wall with all the force the little man could muster, talking to me all the while. "Now you'll just want to take that up there with your purdy little wings and see if you can't get some better distance with that than the system I've already got in place."

I had no idea what the man was talking about, but moments after he had turned the crank all the way to one side, I became aware of the familiar rushing sound of water and a rumbling in the walls and in my hands. Looking down at the nozzle I held, I realized belatedly it was attached to a pile of lengthy hose at the base of the wall, as all at once water jetted out forcefully, knocking me off balance and forcing my wings to shoot out instinctively to compensate.

"Go on, girl, we don't have all day!" The Head called, waving his arms at me to fly up, before he scurried away to yet another crank I could see a ways down the wall. How many of these things did he have and where was all the water coming from?

"What about the Priestesses of Espearia, shouldn't they be out here helping you?" I called after him.

"We'd lose more than half the city if we sat around waiting for them," he called back over his shoulder, not slowing in the slightest. "Those witches help no one but themselves and they certainly aren't coming out here to help the 'makers of the heretical machines!'"

Not sure I was following along entirely with the man's rant, I left the issue alone for now and proceeded to do as requested, taking to the air and carrying the hose with me. I made good headway against the flames nearest to the outer wall, but before I had even really begun to make a difference, The Head opened another of the valves and from a point high on the wall another nozzle began spraying water, dousing any flames it could reach.

Seeing The Head had this area covered, I flew quickly and took my hose with me as far up and out as it could reach in order to do as much as I could against the fire. In the distance I watched rain clouds gather from this world's customary clear skies and I smiled as it began to rain in a localized area about the radius of a few city blocks where the worst of the fire was. It appeared Hotaru had things well in hand. From another direction I noted buildings that had become no more than pillars of flame wink out as Yue or Kaji, or perhaps both, lent their power to the task of combating this fire.

Soon I was able to leave things to them and start seeing to the wounded.

And they just kept coming.

The Knights had long since arrived and everyone present was doing whatever they could to help. The wet cobblestone street I first cleared with the hose became an area for the survivors to gather, and Ris and I had our hands full sorting out those who could be helped from those who couldn't.

At long last, Hotaru and Kaji returned under their own power, but reduced to a state that I almost had to consider them among the wounded. I called Ris over to see to them as I looked about for Rama whom had been in no better shape when last I had seen him.

My power located him more quickly than my eyes could have through the smoke and soot, and when I saw the state he was in I didn't hesitate in turning him to mist and letting him drift over to me where I could see to him.

Exhausted, I continued doing what I could to help, tending to both friends and strangers and in my preoccupied state I didn't think to wonder what had become of Yue or the strange little man who called himself 'The Head.'

CH. 6 – SPIRIT OF ESPEARIA

I awoke sometime later in one of two warehouses requisitioned by someone – I had no idea who – for the sake of the displaced survivors. Being covered in soot, my blue hair was effectively muted and I looked much like everyone else, and for the first time in what seemed like forever I found myself anonymous as local volunteers passed me by, intent on helping their fellows.

Sitting up and stretching out the kinks in my muscles, I noticed Masaru was stretched out on another cot near to my head, and at the other end by my feet Hotaru lay curled on a cot of her own, looking peaceful. I couldn't remember much about how we had all gotten here or where exactly we were, but I was grateful for the accommodations, regardless.

"Here you go, honey," I blinked in confusion as my Mother stepped into my field of vision and handed me a chipped bowl filled with a cooked grain of some kind. "Don't worry, I didn't make it," she noted with a grimace – my mother was known for having little patience with most domestic tasks. "Corporal Zukatoro's wife did. You're okay, though?" she added when I hesitated to take the bowl from her.

"Fine." I coughed, my throat feeling still thick with smoke.

"I brought you a drink, too," she added, reaching behind her for another of the many bowls on the cart she had brought with her. This one was filled with water. "All we had were bowls."

"Thanks." I sipped at the water gratefully.

"Eat and make sure you keep your strength up," she commanded, pushing a bowl in Masaru's direction as well.

"Thank ye," he responded, sitting up quickly to accept the bowl from her.

"My name's Hana, but you can call me Mother, if you'd like."

"Thank ye...mum. I've never called anyone 'mum' before."

"Isn't he just the sweetest thing?" she commented before continuing to wheel her cart down the row, handing out bowls to those who were awake enough to take them and leaving me to stare after her in disbelief.

"Does that mean she likes me, then?" Masaru asked, pulling my attention back to him.

"It must," I answered, just as taken aback by my mother's fluctuating personality. She had gone through some miraculous transformations since her return to this – her home – world. I kept expecting her to return to being the cold and distant woman I had grown up knowing, but even in the face of adversity it didn't seem as if that was going to be the case.

"Aren't ye hungry, then?" Masaru asked, eyeing my bowl and I noted his was already empty.

"No," I answered and abruptly I realized I wasn't, though by all the time that had passed and all the effort I had expended I should be ravenous. In fact, I couldn't remember when I had last eaten, or even felt the pangs of hunger. Had it been before the Ruby eggs, then, back in Taiyou? Was that even possible?

I didn't feel hungry, but neither did the thought of eating turn my stomach, so I wasn't sick. Just to prove the point, I took a deliberate mouthful of the porridge my mother had brought me. It tasted fine, delicious even, and yet I didn't want it, nor did a taste of it spur me to wanting more.

"You can have it," I told Masaru, handing him the bowl, "but tell me something, Masaru, are you actually hungry?"

"Well, no, not really," he replied with a curious expression, pausing to examine the food for a moment as I had done, "but it's good and there's no sense letting it go to waste."

It was just as I thought. I glanced over in the direction my mother had gone once more, just to make sure, and sure enough, Mifa, someone else who had been in an egg, was wolfing down her bowl's contents like she was starving.

"Masaru, have you considered that we might not need to eat anymore?" I had, in fact, never seen Fuun eat anything and I had once heard him remark the power was what sustained him. Fuun, although with the reputation of a Chosen, was only a Knight, but if he didn't eat then it would follow Masaru wouldn't have to and neither would I.

"You know, ye might be right," he agreed, "but I like food personally, and if ye don't mind I don't think I'm quite ready to give it up just yet."

"No one said you had to." I smiled, taking another drink from my bowl of water – that, my parched throat seemed to want. "It was just a thought."

"Where's mine?" Hotaru asked, waking up and causing us both to laugh.

"Yukari," someone called my name, interrupting the rare peaceful moment and I was surprised to note it was Yue's mother. "It's Yue, she's asking for you."

This was even more surprising as Yue and I hadn't exactly been communicating much – if at all – lately. We had been thick as thieves on Earth, but we'd been estranged since some point during our stay in Taiyou and if I was being honest about it I would still have a hard time pinning down exactly when and how we had drifted apart – we had simply stopped seeing eye to eye.

"Go on," Masaru encouraged. "She wouldn't ask for ye if it wasn't important."

He was right. Curious about what could possibly await me, I hopped off my cot and followed Yue's mother back the way she had come. She led me to the far end of the crowded warehouse and into a curtained-off area. There I came across Hotaru's parents and Kaji's mother. Beyond them, Yue's mother led me to a door and opened it

"No, I won't just relax," Yue protested to her father, as she stood atop her cot, waving her arms in as dramatic a way as possible. "I'm possibly irradiated and I might've done the same or worse to Ao Kouen, not to mention The Head and Pine. Though Pine's probably okay, considering," she added, calming immediately and tilting her head to one side as she considered the facts, "and I guess The Head would have been worse off without me."

"See, it's not all your fault, Honey," Noh-san noted with an encouraging smile.

"Yeah, but it could have been," Yue replied, waspishly, "if Chikara hadn't – where is Chikara anyway?"

"She's gone to Adel's house," Yue's mother answered. "She said you would know where that is. Anyway, I brought Yukari, just like you asked."

"Yukari, perfect," Yue noted, taking in my presence for the first time, "I need you to help me with The Head, though I'm not sure if he's still alive, or if he's even safe to be near. You may want to get Ris back in here for this too."

"Safe to be near? Yue, what are you talking about?"

"Well, I kinda sorta found The Head near the radioactive core of the reactor the Espearians had hidden underground. I think he was trying to shut it down before the fire caused an even bigger problem, but –"

"Radioactive core?" I interrupted her, wondering how in the world she was alive to tell me about this if her story was true.

"Yeah, they had a reactor to power the city, but not anymore." Yue waved her arms about her head the way she did when she was referring to the way she could vanish things with her power. "Anyway, The Head was down there and when I took his helmet off to see if he was still alive his skin started to boil, which I didn't figure was a good sign. So do you think you can handle it or should we get Ris?"

Without needing to think too hard about it, I sent Ris a message arrow anyway. I didn't know if there was anything either she or I could do, but it would be better to have the both of us present, regardless. In short order Ris arrived, accompanied by Sabien, and I briefly filled them in.

"I remember well my own experience with this radiation and it was less than pleasant," Sabien noted. "Are you all right, Yue?"

"Never better," Yue replied, sounding impatient. "Can I let them out yet?"

"Them?" Sabien asked, confused, having missed Yue's earlier rant.

"Pine, The Head and Ao Kouen," she clarified for his sake. "I'd really rather let them out as soon as possible."

"I understand that Yue," Sabien commiserated with her, "but if they have been affected by this radiation as you say then we will have to be very careful not to expose ourselves by attempting to treat them."

"I don't know how Yue's – what did you call it, Dear? No-space?"

"*Noh*-space, Mom, like our family name."

"Right," she acknowledged, "well I don't know how my daughter's 'Noh-space' works, but I scanned Yue when Chikara brought her in, after she told me where she'd found her. She's not giving off any traces of radiation."

"How is that possible?" I asked.

"I'm immune?" Yue asked, shrugging her shoulders and giving the rest of us a sheepish smile before her face took on a surprised expression. "Oh, that probably means Pine's okay too!"

And before any of us could think to stop her, Pine appeared in the flesh – so to speak – before us. I had seen him without his cloak before, but it had not been for some time and evidently now he was different. I had thought he seemed taller, and I had noticed he no longer quite moved the same way most Croatins did, but without his cloak to cover him the Pine I recognized ended somewhere around the chest. His upper third was the same neon-green poisonous frog-person I remembered, with his smooth skin and features and blotchy purple markings, but the rest of him, including one arm, was now robotic and therefore more reminiscent of a Binoid than a Croatin. While I adjusted to Pine's new appearance and mentally tried to work out when the change had occurred, Yue's mother cautiously approached with a device in her hands that let out a persistent beeping.

"What's it at?" Yue enquired, jumping down from the cot and bounding over to her mother's side to check the device. "Oh, three? That's normal for him, nothing to worry about."

Yue's mother looked like she wasn't so certain, but I remembered well the warning Yue had first given us concerning the Second Spawn; their touch was poison. Now it seemed that fact had an explanation; they were radioactive, which was simply wonderful. Still, it was a relief to know that Pine was no more dangerous to us now than he had ever been.

"All right," Yue announced. "Who's next?"

At Ris' suggestion, translated by Sabien, we summoned Kaji and with the help of his power we transformed Yue's cot into a bed of ice, after questioning Yue on every last detail of how she had found The Head to get some idea of the state in which he would appear. When we were as prepared as we could be, which meant leaving only Pine and Yue in the room with Yue's mother's Geiger counter to test for radiation, Yue caused The Head to appear on the bed of ice. What resulted was a sudden cloud of steam and a sharp hiss as his overheated suit of armour made contact with the bed. Over the hissing, however, the frantic beeping of the Geiger counter could be heard clearly, until it abruptly went silent without explanation.

"It's okay now!" Yue called to the rest of us. "You can come in."

Ris was the first to enter, taking Yue's words at face value, while the rest of us followed more hesitantly. Checking the device as we filed in, I learned Yue was correct; the Geiger counter still appeared to be working and the only thing radioactive in the room was Pine.

"What'd you do?" I asked, genuinely curious.

"I just used the same power that lets me not be affected by Pine. It's the same way I cleansed the sand of Lillem before," she explained. "Your power should be able to do the same."

We moved The Head to a dry cot where Ris could tend to his burns, and while our backs were turned Yue released Ao Kouen from her Noh-space where he had been held until now.

"Ahh! Why is it so cold?!" he exclaimed sharply, the shock of the ice water he landed in being enough to spur him to leap out of the soggy cot. "What was that for?"

The Geiger counter stayed silent despite his arrival, and although he may have appeared somewhat drawn at first, being out of the Temple of Machalite did wonders for Ao Kouen and he seemed his old self again within minutes.

I returned to find Masaru with Sir Rama.

"Are you coming to the Kusabana residence for the meeting?" Rama asked as I approached. "I was just telling Masaru I've been there and back a few times now running errands, and I can take you if you'd like. Chikara plans to fill us all in on how things have been here in Espearia these past few weeks."

I hadn't been aware that Adel owned property in Espearia, but the Kusabana House was a thick-walled stone building that stood in a courtyard next to what Rama identified as The Head's manor house. Adel's house was not large when compared to the manor, but it had two stories and a walled-in garden behind, where the forces of Sapphiros gathered to meet the young-seeming but supposedly ancient Chosen of Damos.

As the tale went, the land we were now on was a piece of the planet of Espearia, which had crash landed here to save them from extinction. I had also been told the person single-handedly responsible for saving that small piece and propelling it across the vastness of space was Chikara herself.

Given all that, the girl who greeted me as I filed into Adel's backyard was not what I expected. She appeared no more than twelve years of age and only her impossibly long silver-white hair – much longer than even Yue's, which nearly reached the floor – betrayed otherwise.

"Oh, you must be Yukari!" Chikara exclaimed in a sweet-sounding southern drawl, her face lighting up with an innocent, dimpled smile. "I've heard so much about you and Kaji also. Neither of you have heard any news about my mama, have you?"

Arashi – I winced slightly, realizing I hadn't even thought to check for the High Priestess' whereabouts before coming here.

"That's all right," Chikara said optimistically, but I could hear the sadness behind the words and I understood it well. "She'll come back, she promised that she would."

I tried to smile in what I thought was a reassuring fashion, while inside my heart cried out for this little girl. No matter how much power she may have, she was still powerless in this and it wasn't fair. Silently I vowed that I would apply my own powers to the search for Arashi and do whatever I could to help return her to her daughter.

"Chikara, why didn't the Priestesses help with the fire?" Yue asked suddenly.

"Well that's sort of why I wanted to talk to y'all," Chikara clarified, speaking to everyone. "You see, things haven't quite been right in Espearia since my mama left it. She took the Orders of Air,

Fire, and Water with her and left the Orders of Metal and Bone here with me. It's not like I haven't tried, but the Priestesses just won't listen to me the way they did my mama.

"The Priestesses of Water and Fire are all real nice, and Air's my mama's own element so they've always considered me like one o' their own, but with the Orders of Metal and Bone it's different. Metal's very black and white, they don't see shades of grey, so when my mama told them to look after me, they took it real seriously. And the Sisters of Bone..." Chikara trailed off, looking distressed.

"What is it, Chikara?" Yue asked. "What'd those harpies do to you?"

"It's not exactly their fault," Chikara explained. "All the Sisters, and all the Espearians in general, have never really thought well of Chosen. On Espearia it wasn't like it is here. There were many kingdoms always fighting against each other and since Espearians aren't allowed to use their powers on each other, they would use the Chosen as weapons. I tried to tell them I'm not like that, and even my mama tried to tell them, but they can't see it any other way.

"They're simply trying to keep me quiet for now," she continued, "like they don't want me makin' any trouble for them, but I'm afraid it isn't safe in Espearia for y'all. Espearians don't like Chosen they can't control and there's so many of you, I'm afraid they'll think you're a threat and try to hurt you."

"They would provoke a fight with four Chosen and their Knights even when we're supposed to be their allies?" I asked, taken aback.

"The thing is, I don't think they see it that way," Chikara replied, "and there's so many of them I think they'd try. Also, I should probably warn you the Sisters of Bone have special ways of dealing with people like us. They can stop our powers. Their bone magic is like a poison against us and it hurts real bad, bad enough to stop even the Vile Emperor if they got close enough to use it on him, past all his spiky armour, that is."

"Well, that's a problem, then," Kaji noted.

"Does that mean we have to leave?" Hotaru asked.

"Well it certainly means we have to re-examine our options," I agreed.

"To the mountains of Sapphire, then?" Yue chimed in with her earlier suggestion.

"If we go, Chikara, you should come with us," Hotaru noted. "You shouldn't stay here if it's dangerous for Chosen."

"Oh, I can't leave Espearia," Chikara answered, her expression worried. "My mama wanted me to stay here."

"I don't think that'll be necessary," Kaji stated. "If Chikara believes she's safe enough here, then she should stay. Espearia needs her powers and we don't want to place its citizens in any more danger than they are already in. What we need is a way to convince the Priestesses that we're on their side and here to stay. Chikara," he addressed her, "who would you say, other than Arashi, that the Orders of Bone and Metal would listen to?"

"Well, I don't know," Chikara replied. "I never thought much about it. My mama's always been there and she left me in charge since she left…but I suppose before that the royal line would've had control over all the Espearians. So if we had someone of the royal line here, that person could certainly help us out."

"Well, is there anyone descended from the royal line on this planet?" Kaji asked dubiously.

"Well, of course there is," Chikara replied, "there's uncle Jeth! His brother was King of Espearia before we all left. Did he come to Espearia with y'all or…" She trailed off, her smile dropping from her face as she took notice of our various expressions. "He's missing too, isn't he?"

"We don't know where Jeth is." Sabien was the one to break the tense silence that followed Chikara's question. "But knowing Jeth, he can take care of himself and I don't doubt your mother can as well."

Hotaru, who had been uncharacteristically quiet throughout much of the conversation, now wore a decidedly guilty expression and was squirming uncomfortably on the rock she had chosen as a makeshift seat.

"What is it, Hotaru?" I questioned. "If you know something that could be of use…"

"It's all my fault," she wailed somewhat unexpectedly. "Arashi and Jeth are in trouble because of me. I'm so sorry Chikara, I didn't mean for it to happen."

"For what to happen, Hotaru?" Sabien asked.

"Arashi tried to save me from a Hound but she got taken instead, and then Jeth went after her and wouldn't let me help," Hotaru said between sniffles. "I wanted to go after them but the ground closed up behind them and then everything went red, and that's the last thing I remember…after that, we were in those awful eggs."

"So Arashi and Jeth might well be together, wherever they are," Kaji noted.

"And since I can't seem to locate either of them," I added, "they're likely well hidden."

Yue looked murderous, but she surprisingly didn't lash out at anyone. "We'll keep looking for them, but for now what else have we got?"

Blank stares and an uncomfortable silence greeted this question also until Chikara hesitantly raised her hand. "There's more, I'm afraid."

"Go on, Chikara," Sabien instructed. "Let's hear all of it so we can make an informed decision."

"Well, I heard from Yue you've brought survivors from the Ruby City with you," Chikara began.

"Lady Mikura and her squad were instrumental to us in the defense of Taiyou," Sabien noted, "and now they are our responsibility to look after in the absence of their General."

"Well, I don't have a problem with it myself," Chikara replied. "I trust y'all know what you're doin', but I can tell you that none of the rest of the Espearians will take kindly to the Vile Emperor's troops seekin' our hospitality, no matter what the reason or circumstance. And as I've already said, they're not likely to listen to my opinion or yours.

"Now, I know you've been real careful and I'm fairly certain they don't know about the Rubians yet, but it's only a matter of time before they find out, and I'd be surprised if they let any of y'all leave alive if they learn that y'all are helping Espearia's enemies."

"So what you're saying is we need to leave now, regardless," Kaji stated. "Or at the very least we need to get the Rubians out of here. I should call Akuma, maybe there is some way she can help."

"Now, Kaji, don't be doin' that," Chikara warned. "If you try and contact the Ruby City from here, the Priestesses will be able to detect it. That'd be worse than announcin' that you're a Talon yourself."

"Kaji, approximately how many of them are there that we would have to move?" I asked.

Kaji frowned, considering the problem. "No more than four hundred, including Lady Kichigai and Kai-Een, maybe even a little less than that."

Four hundred might be a strain, but one I could probably handle over a short distance. "I can turn them all to mist and take them over the wall and out of city limits," I suggested.

"I'm afraid that getting them out of the city would only be the first step," Chikara pointed out. "Y'all are in the heart of Espearia, but the land of Espearia has very definite borders and the Priestesses won't be satisfied until you're well clear of them."

"How far would we have to take them?"

"I've never been myself, but you'll need to go at least until the land changes before you can say for sure that you're out of Espearia," Chikara answered.

Hotaru frowned. "If that's where I think it is, then Adel and I saw it on our way into Espearia before, and it's more than a day's walk from here."

Another tense silence fell as the group of us considered the problems facing us and unhappily weighed our options.

"I guess there's nothing for it, then," Kaji said at last. "We'll have to do everything within our power to see the Rubians out of here safely."

"Where do we take them?" Yue asked. "To the mountains with us?"

"The Ruby City," I answered. "We take them home, or at least to a point where Lady Akuma can take them off our hands."

"And what about everyone else?" Hotaru asked. "And us? Like Chikara said, it won't be safe here if the Priestesses of Bone and Metal find out about the Rubians, or if they decide they don't want more Chosen in Espearia."

I didn't want to have to say it – no one did. "We split up. No matter where we go we'd have to walk with so many people, but the mountains make sense as a last resort, so south seems the best way to go. What I'd like to know is if there are any Roughlander outposts left standing between here and there, especially hidden ones where we could take shelter on the way, or maybe help those left stranded out there."

"According to the map Dahlia gave me," Kaji said, unfolding the map in question from his pocket, "the nearest outpost to here is to the south, maybe a two-day journey."

"Aye," Masaru agreed, "that's the nearest, but it's not the one ye want. The Children's Outpost is south of here and if, like I hope, it hasn't been found out, it should be one of the safest places left to us."

With the decision made, all that was left to do was make what preparations we could. The Rubians would go west along the mountain range separating Espearia from the lands controlled by the Vile Emperor and the remainder of the refugees would leave soon after, heading south. Yue, often contrary to the rest of us, made it clear she was taking Fuun back to the Mountains of Sapphire to investigate them more thoroughly in case we should need a backup plan.

"Would you mind terribly if I came with you?" Rama asked once he, Kaji, and I were headed back to the warehouses where the Rubians were temporarily being housed to inform them of the dilemma they faced and the plan we had made to deal with the situation. "I'd like to see if Lady Akuma will let me join her, as I can very much see that this might be Taiyou's best opportunity to parley officially with the Ruby City, and on behalf of my father and the King I'd like to try and see if a mutual understanding can be reached."

"You can go wherever you'd like, Sir Rama," I answered him, not really envying him the task that he seemed so inexplicably keen to undertake.

"Well, the reason I'm asking the both of you, and I'll speak to Hotaru and Yue about it also," Rama elaborated, "is that I would like your permission – no, your blessing, if possible – to speak to the Vile Emperor on your behalf."

I felt my mouth settle into a grim line as it often did whenever our enemy, the Vile Emperor, was mentioned. "You can speak for Taiyou and for yourself, Sir Rama, and even as a Knight of Sapphiros, if you'd like," I informed him tersely, "but if the Vile Emperor has anything he would like to say to me, then I would rather it be said to me directly."

My abrupt refusal seemed to make everyone a little uncomfortable, but I was not about to take my words back. From my standpoint, the Vile Emperor had made his case clear enough and there was nothing more to be said about it, unless he was going to offer us an explanation for why he had attacked us back in Shinjuku and so drastically altered our lives in the process. Barring that revelation, we had nothing further to discuss.

"It's not that I don't trust you to speak for us, Leon, but I'm coming with you," Kaji stated somewhat unexpectedly in answer to Rama's proposal. "Hotaru can go south with everyone else. She won't need me to help her, having Ao Kouen and the rest of the Knights with her, and I feel I need to see the Ruby City for myself."

"I understand, Kaji," Rama replied sincerely, "and I'll be glad to have you with me as long as I know you are going for the right reasons."

Kaji grimaced. "I'm working on that part, but trust me, I won't disrupt your peace talks."

"Very good," Rama said with a smile, "that's what I was looking for."

The second warehouse was guarded by Noh-san, who sat innocuously with his back to the door, lounging and munching on a strip of dried meat. Upon closer inspection, he had a Japanese-style gun propped beside him, covered loosely with rags, and was very much prepared to reach for it. Seeing who was approaching, Noh-san wriggled himself out of the way and let us pass with a smile and a nod. Rama entered the building on my heels, but Kaji remained outside a moment. I could hear him begin to relay the situation to Noh-san as the door shut once more, cutting him off from view.

"Yukari," Rama said and I turned to face him, realizing it was just the two of us within an entryway to the warehouse, which was stacked floor to ceiling with crates, giving the feeling of privacy. "You do realize where you're going, don't you? I know you can turn these people to mist to get them out of the city, but if you really want to help them you'll have to put aside your prejudices concerning the Ruby City and their Emperor."

"I know what I'm doing, Sir Rama."

"Really? Because the way I see it, you have passed judgment on the Vile Emperor based on his reputation alone and without considering that there may be a reason for it. We have an opportunity here to start mending the breach between the people of this world and I would hope that is something you would support."

"I do support it," I snapped. "I've told you as much before. An alliance between Taiyou and the Ruby City, and even likewise with the Roughlanders and the Espearians, is what we need right now, especially in the wake of Lady Lilyth's return, but do not presume to know anything about my reasons for not trusting the Vile Emperor or his remaining Talon, for that matter."

"Tell me then," Rama urged.

I narrowed my eyes at him, feeling my anger rise, but at the same time I was remembering in horrific detail the night the Vile Emperor had come for us. There was no escaping him as we were surrounded by a force field created by his Talons to trap us.

Without warning, Kai-Een unsheathed two slightly curved blades, longer than his forearms. They glinted in the glow of the barrier as he raised them high and then drove them into the necks of the two unsuspecting policemen. They never got the chance to raise an alarm. The dead men crumpled to the ground and the blonde teenager wiped his blades clean on their backs with a sickening nonchalance.

I froze in fear. In my mind's eye all I could see was the sudden death of the two policemen over and over again. I was the only witness to how they had fallen and I couldn't even scream for help.

A clawed metal foot stepped out from a pillar of light within the center of the force field the Talons had created. The thing that emerged, one deep purple spike at a time, was shaped vaguely like a man, only covered in armour so deeply purple it might have appeared black, except for the otherworldly red light that bathed it. The armour was pointed and spiked on the arms, knees, and shoulders, and each spike ended in a wickedly sharp point. The helmet was the most grotesque and frightening of all. It had great curving metal tusks and an alien cast to what features there were. Not an inch of what might lie beneath the armour showed, not even in the eyes of the helmet, which glowed a sinister red, exactly like the glowing crimson rubies used by his followers to trap us.

Facing us, the Vile Emperor paused in his advance, gathering power, intent on striking us all down, perhaps in one blow. Lava formed from within his hands and began to grow between them. I could see the heat rippling from it in the still air.

We stood powerless before him and if he unleashed this power on us, there would be nothing left to save...

"'In Rubia's name – Die' was the first and only thing he ever said to us," I said as I finished recounting the events of that night to Rama in a subdued tone. "You tell me what you think that means."

"That's just it, Yukari," Rama interjected, "clearly the four of you are alive and well today. Maybe it did have some sort of hidden meaning."

"Die means die to me, Sir Rama," I replied bitterly. "He threatened us with death and the only reason I'm still alive to tell you about it today is because Yuko Seig saved us by bringing us here. I can't see how he could have meant anything else when he followed up on his threat by trying to kill us with his power. We weren't as we are now, Sir Rama. We had no means of defending ourselves from him!"

I realized I was yelling when Rama opened his mouth to reply in kind, his face flushed with anger, but before he could lay into me further for disagreeing with him Kaji stopped him, having entered the warehouse at some point during our passionate discussion. "Leon, Yukari, that's enough. We have work to do."

Kaji was right, but that didn't make what we had to do any easier to swallow, which was first proven by the tense expressions of the Rubians who awaited our news.

"Why would you help us?" Kai-Een asked, sour-faced after Kaji's explanation of the plan to evacuate the Rubian survivors.

I could tell the question was directed mainly at me, but it was the Deathsquad General, Lady Kichigai, who was the unlikely one to answer it. "Because we're on the same side, you dolt, and if you hadn't noticed their necks are already on the line for having helped us this far."

"Let's get something straight," I directed my words to Kai-Een, "I will use my powers to help make your escape from Espearia easier, but I don't owe you anything and if you don't want to take me up on my offer then you can find your own way to flee the Priestesses of Metal and Bone. Either way, I claim no responsibility for you or your actions. Do we have an understanding?"

"Fine," Kai-Een replied, glaring murderously in my direction. "Your way seems easiest for now."

Nodding, I faced the rest of the group including what I assumed to be a few higher-ranking Deathsquad, including Lady Mikura's captain, Grinkin. "We leave in an hour. Get everyone gathered in the courtyard and have them hold hands so I can take them all. Lady Kichigai, will you see that everyone is ready?"

Having her agreement, I turned on my heels and left them to it, storming back out into the sunny courtyard. I was right, wasn't I? Kai-Een was a bully and a murderer, no matter that he eerily resembled the body of the friend he had stolen, and I was certain his master was no better – and likely worse. I couldn't deny the benefits of doing whatever we could to seek an alliance with the Ruby City against Lilyth, but I was still certain that the Vile Emperor didn't intend to do any of us any favours and I wasn't prepared, nor did I feel it necessary, to seek his help.

Yet still I felt uncertain and unsettled after facing Rama's anger. Leon Rama had a good head on his shoulders, and if his opinion differed from mine there had to be a reason for it. I found myself unable to believe he was simply misinformed. Rama had lived on this planet with the Vile Emperor a lot longer than I had and in that time he was bound to have accumulated quite a bit of knowledge on such an infamous person. Perhaps I needed another opinion.

"Oh, there ye are," Masaru called, catching up with me on the quiet street. I had been wandering toward the burnt out portion of Espearia without really realizing where I was heading. "I've been looking for ye. Hotaru's trying to talk to ye, but ye don't have yer canteen with you."

"Huh?" I questioned as Masaru thrust his drinking water at me.

"Yukari, is that you?" Hotaru's voice spoke from inside the bottle.

"Yes, what is it, Hotaru?"

"I'm at The Head's house. I'm helping him get his things together. He's coming south with us because he figures the Priestesses will lump him in with the Taiyoun refugees and be mad at him too for helping the Rubians."

"Shh, Hotaru, keep it down," Masaru admonished her. "Ye never know who might be listening."

"Sorry," Hotaru apologized, lowering her voice as she realized her error. "Anyway, I wanted to wish you luck, Yukari, and tell you I wish I could come with you. I don't like the idea of the four of us being separated again, especially now after all that's happened. I don't want to lose anyone else."

"You won't lose me, Hotaru," I told her. "I'm just taking them as far as I need to and then Masaru and I will join back up with you as soon as we can. I'll probably be back with you long before you reach the outpost."

"All right," she answered dubiously. "At least I'll have Kaji and the Knights."

"Actually, you'll have Ao Kouen and most of the Knights," I corrected her. "Kaji and Sir Rama are going to the Ruby City to negotiate an alliance. Can you do me a favour, though?"

"What is it?"

"Look after Razor and Dahlia for me, along with everyone else, including my mother. I promised I would look after Razor and I don't want to start out by just leaving him to fend for himself at a time like this, and my mother could use the company. Can you do that, Hotaru?"

"I guess so," she answered. "I'd really rather being going with you, but with Yue running off to the mountains with Fuun I guess somebody has to stay with everyone else."

"Thank you, Hotaru, what you're doing is important."

Saying our goodbyes, Masaru replaced the cap on his canteen and effectively 'hung up' on Hotaru.

"Masaru, what do you think…about helping the Rubians, I mean?" I asked, whispering the question for caution's sake.

"I think it's the right thing to do."

I smiled at his easy confidence, feeling reassured.

The Rubians had all gathered in the courtyard like I'd asked, but seeing them all together like this made me realize what it looked like we were doing – fielding an enemy force in the center of Espearia.

The Rubian survivors were by and large Deathsquad soldiers, belonging mainly to Mikura's squad, and almost all of them had retained their armour if not uniformly their shields, swords, or helmets. At Kichigai's – or perhaps Captain Grinkin's – command they had formed traditional ranks to await us at the appointed meeting place for departure.

The appearance of a few hundred Deathsquad soldiers had not failed to catch the attention of the Priestesses of Espearia, and true to Chikara's predictions they had shown up to surround the enemy troops unlawfully present in their city.

Kaji had used his power to replicate himself and there were at least a dozen of him standing between a dozen grey-robed Priestesses of Espearia. The Priestesses all carried blades of various descriptions and some wore armour. I could only assume by the collective glint of them that these were the uncompromising Sisters of Metal, which still begged the question of where the Sisters of Bone were hiding.

Approaching the standoff cautiously, I could see one of the Kaji-clones talking with one of the assembled priestesses, a matronly woman with graying hair tied back into a tight bun. All the Kajis stood in exactly the same way with their arms held behind them, but only one of them held Akuma's Ruby mirror carefully out of view.

"You want them out of Espearia and so do we. Arashi made an alliance with the Chosen of Sapphiros and we do not want to see that alliance damaged, but I'm certain that *Akuma*," Kaji said her name with just enough emphasis that I was certain he was activating the mirror he held between his hands, in much the same way as I directed my message arrows or Hotaru found the person she wished to communicate with through water, "would want to know her people are safe, so she could send an escort out to meet them on the western border of Espearia along the mountain range."

"Arashi, in her wisdom, may have trusted you, but I am uncertain she would continue to do so if she knew you had not only brought, but attempted to conceal, Deathsquad soldiers within Espearia's borders," the priestess pointed out with a frown.

"Still," she conceded, "an arrangement has been made and I would rather not be the one to dishonour it. The Rubians are our enemies and, for now, the Chosen of Sapphiros our allies. If you would like to continue your stay in Espearia, you may hand over every single Rubian to us as prisoners. If you do not, you may have one day to remove yourselves, the Rubians, and every person and article you brought with you into Espearia. There will be no middle ground and no compromise, and should you not adhere to either option, know we will consider it as a breach of your alliance with

Arashi and the Priestesses of Metal will not be lenient with you, is that understood?"

"Perfectly," Kaji answered. "We will be just outside of Espearia's borders in one day's time, along the mountain range to the west, where we will await pickup."

"We agree to no such arrangement." Without any warning, a half-dozen Sisters of Bone, their order marked by their dark green robes, appeared as if from nowhere to join the mix.

The Sisters of Bone were a varied lot, but even though the Priestesses of Metal had largely ignored the arrival of Masaru and myself, it seemed that the Priestesses of Bone were not prepared to do the same and one of their number had appeared closer to the pair of us than I would have liked.

"Arashi has deemed the Chosen our allies and we will abide by her will," the Priestess of Metal began in a lecturing tone, but as she spoke I took notice of the real Kaji, alone out of all the clones, turning his head ever so slightly to make eye contact with me.

I needed no more prompting than that – it was time to go.

There were nearly twenty Priestesses present – that we could see – and not one of them could have predicted that as one, every non-Espearian in that courtyard would be touched by my power and turned to mist.

I didn't need physical contact anymore; I could feel every single person around me and choose which to take and which to leave behind. Before the Priestesses had a chance to even process what had happened, all three hundred and seventy-two of us were drifting away on a strong westerly wind, being carried away from the City of Espearia.

CH. 7 – WHERE YOU'RE NEEDED MOST

My fog rose higher and higher over the walls of Espearia and the Priestesses simply watched us leave, their ageless faces upturned to the otherwise cloudless pale blue sky. The wind carried us west, much faster than I could have managed without it. Soon we were well clear of the City of Espearia – if not the land – and I was exhausted from the strain of holding my power over so many.

I held on as long as I could to get everyone just that little bit further, but I could tell I was very rapidly reaching my limits.. Angling the cloud downward, I slowly let go of my hold over those I carried, like unclenching my fists after holding them tight far longer than I should have, and one by one the Rubians reformed as their feet made contact with the sand below.

Kaji, Masaru, Rama, and I were the last to reform, and as we drifted the rest of the distance down to the ground it was a daunting sight to take in the ranks upon ranks of Deathsquad soldiers, faceless and impersonal in their black armour, as they formed up at Kichigai's command. It was not lost on me that these were the ranks of my enemy, but this particular squad belonged to Mikura, who had helped defend Taiyou because she had believed in it, and now it was only right I get her soldiers back home in return for how she had helped us – even if that home was the Vile Emperor's seat of power.

I staggered on my feet a little as I landed, but Masaru caught and steadied me.

"We'll have to walk from here and I don't know how much further it is to the border," I informed everyone.

"Further than we'd like, I'm sure." Kichigai pointed westward. "Besides the sand, it's all Espearian rock as far as I can see."

The differences between the rocky outcroppings around us from those found elsewhere on this world were obvious now that I knew to look for them. Still, peering off into the distance as far as I was able, all I could make out were grayish rock formations that were decidedly Espearian when compared to the brown and dun-coloured rocks I remembered from elsewhere on this planet.

I frowned but didn't share my findings with anyone else as they would be of help to no one. "Let's get going, then."

The Deathsquads were efficient, orderly, and well-trained – I had to give them that much – and right now those traits would serve them well, as much as I didn't envy them the overbearing heat in their heavy black suits of armour. Still, the Deathsquad soldiers alternated walking with running while staying in formation, and very quickly it was evident they were no strangers to crossing this sort of terrain, heat or no heat.

Kaji and Rama tried to keep up with the Deathsquad soldiers, but with their heads uncovered it was easy to see the pace they set was a struggle, even for how fit the two of them had become in recent months. On the other hand, Masaru chose to keep well ahead of the soldiers and did not seem bothered in the least by the necessity of running across the open sand.

I knew my own capabilities well, so instead of running I kept myself aloft with power-borne wings, allowing them to do the work of propelling me forward. It wasn't exactly restful and the heat was still draining in its intensity, but I was better off than those below me, even if I didn't know how long I could keep it up.

As I soared above, I took notice that Masaru had developed an odd pattern of movement in contrast to the ordered motion of the

Deathsquad behind him. He ran as they walked, and before they sped up he would kneel to the ground and place his hand or head to the ground, then get back up again as they picked up the pace. Curious, I dropped down beside him. "Is something the matter?"

"Well, no…maybe…" he answered, looking puzzled. "I mean, I'm not really sure."

"I'm not following."

Masaru shrugged. "Before I was Knighted, I could sometimes feel a Sandcrawler coming, ye know, with the rumble they make in the sand and all that, but now it's like I can feel what's down there and there's somethin' real big beneath us, but it's so far down I'm havin' trouble making it out."

"But you think it might be a Sandcrawler, or at least alive?"

"Oh, it's alive all right," he answered, "but it's much larger than any Sandcrawler I've ever come across."

"Well, we'd better stay clear of it, then."

"Why have we stopped?" Kaji asked as he walked up to us and I glanced over my shoulder to discover that the rest of the soldiers were taking a break while they waited to see if we would have them stop or continue.

"Possible Sandcrawler," I informed him, "or something else we don't want to attract the notice of."

"That's just it, Yukari," Masaru clarified. "I don't think we can avoid it. It's big, very big, and I'm afraid if we head closer to the mountains to try and go around and it decides that it's hungry, we'd just get hemmed in."

"We don't have time for that anyway," Kaji noted, eyeing the sun warily. "When the Priestesses said we had a day we don't know if they meant a full cycle or until the sun sets, and there wasn't exactly time to find out the particulars."

"So we keep going forward, then?" Rama asked, joining the conversation with Kichigai at his side.

"You plan to outrun a Sandcrawler?" I asked, remembering the speed of the only one I had ever witnessed, which according to Masaru had only been a juvenile.

"Do we have any other choices?" Kichigai asked grimly.

"No, not really," Masaru answered. "Not any good ones."

"All right, it's decided," Kaji stated. "Resume a steady pace, so if we need to break out into a run we can do so. If the Sandcrawler shows itself, scatter the Deathsquad and we'll try to hold it off."

Kichigai nodded and turned around, presumably to inform the Deathsquad soldiers of the plan, and Kaji turned to Masaru. "You noticed it, can you give us any kind of warning if it's going to surface and where?"

"Aye, I can try," Masaru agreed.

"Good enough," I said, "let's keep moving."

I reluctantly left Masaru and the others on the ground while I took to the air once more. As it was, I didn't have the necessary energy to turn everyone to mist again to avoid the threat of the Sandcrawler – if that was even what it was – and as much as I might want to carry Masaru up into the air where it couldn't reach him, I knew he needed to be on the sand where his power would let him feel what lay beneath it. I kept a watchful eye on him regardless – if that Sandcrawler decided it was going to eat him, I was determined it would get no more than a mouthful of mist on the wind.

Masaru was jogging now and keeping ahead of the Deathsquad soldiers who resumed the pace they had been keeping before. I watched a look of concentration cross his face as he ran and before the group of them had even gone very far at all Masaru pointed with a shout "Over there!"

Sure enough as he spoke the words the sand began to rumble and shake moments before a dark fin broke the surface. At first I thought my eyes were playing tricks on me after so long in the sun's heat, but then I recognized the particular sand shark as its head broke the sand and I remembered Masaru's somewhat peculiar power. The sand continued to rumble as Masaru's sand shark skimmed along the surface like it was water, maneuvering with its fins and driving itself forward on its powerful hind legs, when in the space it had just vacated the ground suddenly began to give way.

At first the sinkhole was no larger than the body of the sand shark, but before long the hole had widened in a perfect circle until it was nearly the size of a city block, with Masaru and the others scattered around it and running hard to maintain some distance from whatever might emerge from the dark depths. I felt uncertain as I climbed higher in the sky, but I hung back in case Masaru needed me.

The head of the beast that emerged had a ridged, dun-coloured carapace thicker than any armour, and antennae the size and thickness of flagpoles. The beast didn't rise up out of the ground and expose itself like the other one had done; instead the colossal head stayed half-in, half-out of view as it devoured sand to reach the nearest prey to it – Masaru's sand shark.

As a diversion, creating the sand shark had no doubt been a good, if short-lived, idea. Moments before the impossibly large mandibles would have crushed his creation, however, I watched it dissolve into a mouthful of sand as Masaru let his control of it go.

Displeased it had been cheated out of its prey, the Sandcrawler let out a deafening roar I could feel on the wind as it swiveled its massive head around to search for its next victim. Faster than anything that large had a right to move, the creature settled on Masaru and dove after him with mindless intensity.

"Yukari!" Masaru called to me, but I didn't need prompting; before the Sandcrawler could close the distance to him, I had already turned him to mist.

Taking my chances, I quickly swooped downwards to catch Masaru's cloud of mist and allowed him to reform in my arms before righting my course once more, but the decision cost me. Perhaps it was the glow of my wings or the wind of my passage – who knew how a creature such as this one hunted – but either way, once robbed of its second choice of prey the very large and irate Sandcrawler fixated on me and it was all I could do to keep out of reach of its mandibles.

"That's a bull Sandcrawler!" Masaru yelled to me as I flew for all I was worth with the sand whizzing by below and the hot breath of the creature close behind us. "Go up, if ye can manage it. We'll need to draw it out!"

I was impressed at his level-headedness under the current circumstance, but I didn't share it. I flew upwards because it was the only direction available to me, the Sandcrawler's gaping maw being too large to avoid by angling sharply left or right. Unfortunately, the harder I flew the faster the Sandcrawler rose out of the ground and I began to worry about our chances.

"All right, ye've got just enough room. Go up and over it," Masaru instructed at a shout.

I hardly knew what he was talking about – the Sandcrawler was right behind us now – but trusting Masaru's judgment, I dove backwards abruptly, aiming to arc over the thing's head.

Time seemed to slow as I looked down through the blue feathers of my wings at the Sandcrawler beneath me and realized I had just narrowly avoided the thing's mandibles. I was now clearing its reach, as it couldn't seem to adjust its course quickly enough once this far up out of the ground. I felt a momentary surge of hope – we were going to make it.

"Okay, now let me go!" Masaru commanded.

"What?!" I responded, horrified, realizing if I did as he wanted me to he would fall onto the Sandcrawler's head, if not into its mouth. "No, I can't…"

"Do it, Yukari, now!"

I told my limbs to do as he commanded, but they simply wouldn't listen. In the end I don't know if Masaru wriggled free of my grasp or if I was somehow able to drop him, but breathing hard from both panic and exertion, I watched him fall and use his power to summon his blue energy knives.

Unbidden, my wings continued to keep me aloft as Masaru plummeted downwards, but it soon became clear his intention was not to feed himself to the beast. Instead, as his feet made contact with the Sandcrawler's armoured head, he used the momentum of his fall to propel himself backwards to slide down the creature's back. Digging both his knives in, he used them to help control his rapid descent, meanwhile filling the air with a horrible screeching as he scored the tough exoskeleton on his way down, thanks to the unmatched strength and durability of his power-wrought knives.

Before I knew it, Masaru's plan, whatever it was, began to take effect as the massive Sandcrawler continued to arc backwards in an attempt to reach him, putting itself in the most awkward of positions. From my vantage point up above, I could see now what Masaru intended. The Sandcrawler's plated exoskeleton would only allow it to go so far back, and if pushed beyond that point it would become very difficult for the Sandcrawler to right itself – almost like a turtle flipped onto its shell – only in this case, the Sandcrawler would need a little extra force to lock it into place.

Understanding what needed to be done, I raised my arms and took aim, designating with my mind the target I wanted to hit and forming a handful of arrows with my power. One after another I loosed them upon the Sandcrawler's less protected underbelly, striking in a line heading upwards toward the beast's chin, if it could even be said to have one. Each specially-crafted arrow struck exactly where I intended it to and exploded on impact, driving the Sandcrawler further and further back into an arc it couldn't escape from and using its own powerfully built body against it.

"Yukari!" Masaru called my name once more and my eyes followed the sound until I located him most of the way down the Sandcrawler now, dangling from one arm with the knife in his hand wedged in between two armoured plates and the other arm gesturing to me somewhat frantically.

Taking this to mean that he had completed the dangerous task he had set for himself, I obliged his implied request and turned him to mist, circling downward on the wind to meet him halfway as he drifted to me, and taking a good look at our combined handiwork now that the threat had largely passed.

The bull Sandcrawler – once exposed and relatively immobile – was a sight to behold. The scale of it was unimaginable, the visible body of the creature approximately the height and width of a high-rise building in Tokyo. Its pincer-like mandibles continued to claw at the air as its faceted bug-eyes whirled and its multitude of little legs wriggled along its length uselessly, indicating its distressed state. Some very small part of me felt a little bit of pity for what we had done to what was, in essence, nothing more than an oversized animal, but the feeling evaporated when I had Masaru – who was only one of the people it might have eaten – back in my arms once more.

"You all right?" I asked him, looking him over quickly as I flew, giving the Sandcrawler a wide berth.

"We did all right, didn't we, the two of us?" he replied, flushed after the excitement of wrestling with a bull Sandcrawler.

"Please don't ever do that again," I requested, frowning. "I didn't think I could let you go."

"Aye, but ye did and it turned out, didn't it?"

There was nothing I could say to that, so I brought us down to the ground only to find our troubles were far from over. Kaji, Rama, and Kichigai were deep in discussion by the time we reached them, the Deathsquad soldiers reforming their ranks nearby as directed by Captain Grinkin. As we landed, the group fell silent and Kaji merely pointed to indicate what the trouble was.

We were much closer to the northern mountain range now, after our encounter with the bull Sandcrawler, and even without adjusting my vision I could just make out people along the base of the mountains directly north of our position. Looking more closely – as only I could – I confirmed my suspicions; the people gathered were all Espearians, specifically the Priestesses of Bone, and there were many more of them than had seen us off in the city.

"Is that really them?" Masaru asked, shielding his eyes from the sun in an attempt to make them out.

"Yes, it's them," I confirmed, "but they just seem to be watching us."

"The agreement," Kaji stated. "They're abiding by it by the thinnest margin possible. We'll be lucky if they give us until dark. Come on."

"Aye, Kaji's right," Masaru seconded. "We'd better get a move on anyways before that bull Sandcrawler figures out how to straighten itself out. We don't want to be here when it gets loose, I can tell ye that much."

We quickly got the Deathsquad moving again and we pressed harder than we had before, racing against the setting sun, and though freedom was visible on the horizon – at least with my enhanced vision – it soon became evident that we would never reach it in time if the Priestesses were determined to stop us. At Kichigai's request, we called a halt before the sun could vanish completely.

"I refuse to let them pick us off at their leisure," she stated. "We will stand and fight. We may be a small and ragtag army, but we are still a Deathsquad."

As one, the Deathsquad soldiers rapped their fists against their shields in agreement and acquiescing to their will, the group of us formed a tight circle facing outwards to await the Priestesses or the darkness, whichever came to kill us first.

The Priestesses of Bone arrived very soon after, surrounding us with their superior numbers, though they hardly needed that advantage if what was said about Espearian magic was true. Fortunately, or unfortunately depending on one's perspective, an instant after the Priestesses of Bone arrived, they were themselves surrounded by the even more numerous Sisters of Metal, their various blades drawn and held at the ready.

"*Akuma,*" Kaji said loudly.

Before either group of Priestesses could engage us, or each other, the entire gathering was surrounded once again, this time by Akuma, Bastion, and an entire Deathsquad.

"You wouldn't dare attack Espearians within their own borders, would you?" one of the Priestesses of Metal asked.

"You wouldn't withhold our citizens from us, would you?" Akuma retorted. "I will have no need to retaliate if you let us depart. Otherwise this could escalate and I promise you this is but a fraction of the strength the Ruby City could bring to bear against you."

The silence weighed heavily as each group waited to see what the other would do until the matronly Sister of Bone finally stated, "You have made your point, Chosen. This will not be forgotten."

With her words, every single Priestess disappeared from view in the same manner they had arrived.

"I'm sure it won't," Akuma replied with a frown. "Bastion, keep a lookout. I would like a word with the Chosen of Sapphiros before we depart."

"Yes, my Lady."

Akuma approached us quickly, her red floor-length skirt swishing against the sand as she walked. "Thank you for bringing our soldiers home. It was a show of good faith and it is not unappreciated."

"It was the least we could do after what Lady Mikura's Deathsquad did for Taiyou," Rama responded. "Where is Mikura, anyway? I was hoping to see her expression when her squad was returned to her. The way she treated them was like family."

Akuma frowned. "Mikura is unwell. She...well, you'll see for yourselves. That is, if you are coming with us to the Ruby City?"

"Kaji and I would like to join you if possible," Rama replied. "I was hoping I might get to speak to the Emperor on behalf of my King and concerning the possibility of an alliance with Taiyou."

"And you?" Akuma asked, meeting my eyes directly.

I had set out on this mission, intending to see the Rubians on their way and then to take Masaru and I back to Hotaru by way of my power, but now I hardly felt I had the strength to take myself anywhere. If I couldn't succeed, it would mean a possible rough night for the two of us in hostile territory on the border of Espearia, but more than that I was no longer certain rejoining Hotaru and the others was the right decision. I had said it myself; Hotaru was with Ao Kouen, the rest of the Knights, and the very capable Roughlanders, not to mention our parents, who were well-armed and trained Japanese military personnel. Where I was really needed was the place where all this had begun and where I might be able to find the answers I had been seeking.

If I returned to the others, I would be hiding from this war and trying to survive another day, but going to the Ruby City might mean discovering if there was any way to turn the tables against Lilyth and win back this world for the people who lived on it. I couldn't make this monumental decision alone and I wouldn't go somewhere as potentially dangerous as the Ruby City without Masaru – it would have to be his decision, too.

I turned my head to look at him and gauge his reaction. Our eyes met and with no further communication necessary, I turned back to Akuma. "We'll come."

If Kaji or Rama were surprised by my decision, neither of them mentioned it, and faster than the blink of an eye we traveled on Akuma's – or perhaps it was Bastion's – red beam of light and were brought to the city of our enemy. We landed on a large platform made of white-flecked obsidian, which was constructed for the purpose of being a landing pad for Deathsquads going to and from the Ruby City.

Out of all the alien cities I had visited, this one seemed to be the best established and gave the impression of a long history as a seat of power. The city was nestled in the valley of an active volcano, with centuries-old buildings and cobblestone walkways taking up every inch of available space with dark volcanic rock. The streets themselves were devoid of people as we walked them, but pride in the Ruby City's heritage showed in every window and on every store front in the form of red pennants and strips of cloth. Here and there were other groups of Deathsquad soldiers patrolling the streets, who each paused and saluted Akuma as she passed by, rapping their fists against their shields once before resuming their tasks. In turn, Akuma nodded to each one and we continued on at a silent, brisk pace, headed directly for the volcano on the northwestern side of the city.

The palace was more in mind of a stone military keep, but was majestic nonetheless for being built into the side of the imposing volcano. The winding path up to the front gate was a long one and made it quite obvious why this castle would likely never be breached. We marched single file along narrow stone steps and were quite exposed within view of the turrets and arrow slits. Nevertheless, we made it to the top in one piece and before long, we were brought before the infamous Vile Emperor himself.

"You may call me as my enemies have called me," he said, his impossibly deep voice reverberating impersonally through the menacing helmet he wore.

Even now, hours later, I was still stewing over the Vile Emperor's response to our long anticipated arrival in his throne room. Truthfully, as strange as it seems, I had always anticipated our first meeting with the Vile Emperor would somehow be a struggle of epic proportions. After so long spent both dreading and anticipating the moment, the reality had been a bit of a letdown.

The throne room, a long rectangle of black and white tiled marble, led up to an imposing obsidian throne on a raised dais at the far end. The room was lit archaically, as much of the palace had been, with oil burning torches set into the walls at intervals. They gave dim illumination, simultaneously drawing attention to the flickering shadows beyond the red woven tapestries and causing me to wonder what secrets they might conceal.

Akuma entered the double doors first, flanked by Bastion and followed by Kichigai, leaving the four of us to follow along in their wake and try to appear as confident as possible despite the uncertainty of our welcome. Akuma took up what seemed to be her customary position to the right of the throne and Kichigai surprised us all by prostrating herself before her armour-clad Emperor.

"I failed you, Master," *she stated, her face to the floor.*

The Vile Emperor studied her for a time, his deep purple armoured form unmoving, before he finally gestured for her to stand with only the slightest motion of his left hand. *"Your squad is greatly reduced now, which is a punishment in itself,"* *he replied tonelessly.* *"However, there is honour in your return, so you will keep your position while I consider what is to be done with you."*

"Thank you, Master," *Lady Kichigai answered.*

The helmeted head then turned in our direction expectantly, but the infamous ruler of the Ruby City and Chosen of Rubia said nothing – not a greeting or a condemnation.

"Greetings, Emperor," *Rama began, stepping forward.* *"I am Sir Leon Rama of Taiyou, Knight of Sapphiros, here on behalf of my father, Lord Rama of the Raman province, and my King, Ao Kouen, Chosen of Jedeite. I am here to…"*

Rama trailed off, the Vile Emperor's impassive visage shifting past him to where I stood, as if waiting for me to make my introduction. Fine – if this was how this was expected to go, I could play along.

I met him stare for stare. "Yukari Namikoya, Chosen of Sapphiros."

He turned to Masaru next, but Masaru said nothing. Shifting my gaze to him, I saw that he was shaking with barely controlled rage, having come so close to the enemy of his people. I understood his emotion, but curiously found that at the moment I did not share it. Perhaps it was this farce of an audience we had been brought to, but having finally come face to face with him, all I felt for the man concealed beneath the spiked purple suit of armour was contempt.

Kaji was next, but after taking a step forward his only words were a tightly controlled, albeit loaded, statement, "I believe the Emperor knows who I am."

"You may call me as my enemies have called me," the Vile Emperor instructed once the introductions were complete. "We have a strict schedule in the Ruby City at present and you will abide by it during your stay. You have been provided with accommodations and a guide will be sent to you to explain the regulations that apply to you in more detail.

"For now, it suffices that you understand that the Ruby City is under martial law. In the morning we rest, and at night the army fights and the citizens are under lockdown." He regarded us all balefully for a moment, then continued, "You will have free access to the city during daylight, but there will be serious repercussions should you leave the company of your guide or harm any citizens.

"You are dismissed."

We now found ourselves in a nicely appointed room, similar in size to the room the Knights of Sapphiros had occupied in the palace of Taiyou, but at the same time it was decidedly more opulent. We had seen no hint of any guide, and had been left to cool our heels and be impressed by the amenities the Ruby City's palace had to offer. The room had no windows but there were a handful of comfortable beds with red velvet covers all in a row along the back wall. There was an abundance of fresh, hot food and chilled beverages on a table before the double doors, and the room even contained growing potted flowers displayed on the bed stands.

Around a corner, the remarkable sound of running water could be heard from a water closet, where Rama was happily taking a shower, and the steam from the warmth of it could be felt even where I stood, contemplating a painting of the city displayed on the wall.

I would have thought the enforced inactivity of our circumstance would have grated on me, but I felt strangely at peace with myself. While Masaru was busy enjoying the spread behind me and Kaji was taking a nap in the farthest bed along the row, I found myself contemplating why that might be. The simple answer to the question was that I was where I felt I needed to be. The Ruby City had the strongest army on this world – there was little use in debating that – yet, even though I knew the Vile Emperor had summoned all his troops home since the Lillem attacks had begun, there were signs the city's defenses were strained to the limit. There were marks of battles fought in the streets, the Vile Emperor's admission concerning martial law, his insistence on a strict rest schedule, and the need to lock the populace indoors at night. Not to mention Akuma's tense expression whenever asked how the Rubians were faring during the dark of night.

This city was enduring a war and there was little doubt in my mind as to whom they were facing. There was only one person who could pose such a threat to them and it wasn't any Roughlander, Espearian, or any of us. Having claimed Taiyou, no doubt Lilyth was now focusing her attentions on the city she once ruled, and if I wanted to make a stand against her then the place she wanted the most was the best one to defend from her.

Although that wasn't entirely my reason. To be honest, I could think of so many reasons why I should despair, my father's still unknown whereabouts being foremost among them. But I knew in my heart if I wanted to make any headway helping him, and everyone else, I had to keep looking to what I could affect and not dwell on what I couldn't. That meant finding out what had really happened here to end Lady Lilyth's reign the first time and seeing if we couldn't learn how to do it again – only more permanently this time.

Lilyth needed to be stopped and the odds were not in our favour. We needed to tip the scales and a good first step was finding a way to eliminate the threat of the Lillem. If I was correct in my assumptions about how they spread themselves across the world, then it stood to reason they would be most concentrated here, at the volcano, which had been the source of their original creation. If I could somehow find the answer to defeating the Lillem once and for all, then the result would be the removal of the largest part of Lilyth's army. I didn't know if it could be done, but this was the place to do my research.

The double doors opened suddenly. "Hi guys!" Mikura announced jovially, bouncing into the room, her blond ponytail swooshing from side to side. "I heard you had come to visit. That's wonderful news." She ran forward and immediately attached herself to Kaji and gave him a hug before stepping back to beam at the rest of us.

"She insisted on accompanying me, though officially I'm your guide," Kichigai announced, following the young and exuberant Deathsquad General into the room and gesturing for the two ordinarily armoured, non-Deathsquad guards stationed outside to leave the double doors open behind them.

"So is there anywhere in particular you would like to visit?" she asked, looking around at the four of us. "I've been instructed to take you wherever you want to go. Lady Akuma thought it best and I agree, since I have no other duties at present and am on the same schedule as you are, rest wise."

"Is there a library we could visit, or some other place that might have local history. A museum, perhaps?" I asked.

"There are both within the city. Is that acceptable to everyone?"

"Sounds good enough to me," Kaji answered. "I'm interested in seeing more of the city in general, but I assume we'll get to see some of it on the way, regardless."

The library consisted of two floors, the topmost of which was a wrap-around balcony, leaving the beautifully sculpted arched ceiling exposed to view from the bottom level. The librarian was an aged Kumori with dark fur and white markings, who communicated with us silently, as all her kind did.

I had the Kumori point us in the right direction and before long we were standing before an intricately crafted stained glass window depicting what the Kumori identified as Lilyth herself. The remarkably life-like representation stood over seven feet tall and filled the arched window with the horrific and powerful visage of the woman who had seized Taiyou from us with her horde of nightmarish creatures. By her depiction, she was only barely reminiscent of human in that her form was identifiably female, but the rest of her appeared a melding of many alien creatures, like some sort of ancient goddess of a foreign religion. Her feet were clawed, like those of a large bird of prey, and from her shoulders and hips protruded extra limbs, fanning outward like fleshless wings in the shape of talons reminiscent of those of the Lillem which she had modeled in her own image.

On her chest, or perhaps a part of it, was a large faceted Ruby heart, which with the help of the sun through the window seemed to glow with an inner light. Her hair, if indeed it was hair, consisted of thick strands like snakes, giving credence to the wickedness of her nature. Despite all of that, her face was a perfect oval. Overall, she possessed a terrifying beauty and sense of presence – and this was only an artist's rendition portrayed in coloured glass.

Forcing myself to look away from the haunting image, I turned to inspect the rows of shelves lining the walls to either side of the window and was sorely disappointed to discover the books were in yet another alien script.

"Sir Rama, can you read this?"

"No, I'm afraid not."

"That's what I was afraid of." I frowned.

"I can," Kichigai mentioned. "At least the more modern Rubian. The ancient texts are in a different dialect."

"…And this is the tower where the Kumori used to live within the city," Mikura was reading to Kaji a little ways away, balancing an oversized book on her lap.

"What can you tell me about the teachers you mentioned once before in Taiyou?" I asked Kichigai, realizing I had a valuable resource standing right in front of me. "Did they teach much about the past of this world?"

"Of course," she answered a little stiffly and I remembered abruptly the way we had stepped on each other's toes the last time we attempted to discuss this particular topic. "Why are you so interested all of a sudden?"

"It's not so 'all of a sudden'," I replied, pursing my lips. I didn't know much about the red-headed Deathsquad General, other than she had once been a Roughlander once. I tried to smile and soften my expression. "If you ever got to know me, you'd realize I have an insatiable curiosity. I also happen to believe that understanding what happened in the past will be the key to repairing the way things are now."

"You're right, and that's kind of why I came to the Ruby City in the first place," she admitted. "I wanted to understand the enemy. We're not so different you and I."

"No, I suppose not," I agreed.

"All right, I'll tell you what I know, but I have a question for you first, if you don't mind."

"Sure, what is it?"

"About Kaji...who is he to the Empress?"

Empress? "Oh, you mean the Lady Akuma, don't you?" She nodded. "Oh no," I whispered, covering my mouth with one hand. "Oh, Kaji..."

"So it is as it appears, then?"

"Yes and no," I answered finally. "Your Lady Akuma wasn't always who she is now. She came to this world much as we did, only she arrived when she was supposed to, I guess. Back on Earth, she and Kaji were involved with each other, and in his mind I suppose they still are."

"I'm beginning to see the dilemma," Kichigai noted wryly. "Well, you answered my question, so I'll answer yours."

"...And that's the Kumori Lord, and that one's the Lava Lord, and next to him is Yuko Seig..." Mikura's voice could be heard clearly in the open library.

"Hold on a minute," I instructed Kichigai, heading over to join the others who had gathered around Mikura and the book in her lap. "Can you repeat that?"

"This one?" Mikura put a slender finger on the page, pointing to a familiar red-eyed figure. "That's Yuko Seig," she repeated. "Oh, that's right, she was the Provincial Lord of Sapphiros' territory."

Mikura was not mistaken; the woman in the picture was indeed Yuko Seig. Her short bob of white-blue hair, petite stature, and haunting red eyes were unforgettable. And here in this ancient painting of a scene in the Ruby Palace's throne room, she was standing between a wildly orange-haired individual with a prideful expression and the Vile Emperor himself, in full armour.

"Provincial Lord?" I questioned, examining the rest of the painting and almost gasping in shock at who was seated upon the throne.

It could be no one else – Adel Kusabana sat upon the obsidian throne the Vile Emperor now called his own. She was leaning forward, her chin resting on her hand and her expression filled with vast contempt for all she saw before her.

I quickly scanned the rest of the picture for anyone else I might recognize, but other than Lilyth, hovering menacingly over the throne through what appeared to be a waterfall of lava, there was only the muscular-looking male Kumori, a brutish First Spawn Croatin, and a tall woman with long, blond hair.

Adel, Yuko Seig, and the Vile Emperor, all arrayed in the Ruby Palace's throne room and overseen by the Lady Lilyth. The image I was looking at hardly fit with any of the facts I had been presented with before now. "How is this possible? Adel said she worked under Lady Lilyth and trained Deathsquad soldiers, but this…"

"That's what I was just wondering," Kaji seconded.

"I think perhaps Adel was holding out on us," Rama noted. "She seems to have been quite a bit more to the Lady Lilyth than she led us to believe."

"Adel was the Lady's favourite, I thought everybody knew that," Mikura stated.

"Perhaps eight hundred years ago when this painting was made," I noted, "but certainly not now."

"Favourite?" Masaru asked. "What exactly does that mean?"

"Um," Mikura considered the question a moment. "Well, she, you know, ruled for her. She wasn't necessarily in charge of the other Provincial Lords, but they had to respect her or the Lady would get mad at them."

"You were there, then, weren't you, Mikura?" I asked.

"Yeah, of course," she answered. "The Lava Lord is my father."

I had Mikura flip through the rest of the book quickly for me to see if there were any other noteworthy paintings or descriptions that might explain the disparities causing me to question my prior knowledge, but nothing else in the book caught my eye as much as that one painting had.

"Hey, I found a book in Japanese," Kaji called over. *"Technical Requirements for Interlocking Door Mechanisms."*

"Open it," I instructed.

The first few pages contained only diagrams and complicated formulas, but three pages in the text suddenly stopped and the rest of the book was hollowed out to contain a palm-sized rectangular disk, reminiscent of a piece of hardware from the inside of a computer.

"What is that?" Masaru asked, joining us.

"I don't know," Kaji admitted, pocketing the device, "but you never know what we might need."

I might once have protested, but I remembered well a time I had acted similarly in Taiyou and my actions had proven to be both necessary and beneficial, so I let it be. We left the library then to make our way over to the museum, which was a tower in the rough center of the city that ended jaggedly about half-way up its length.

"What happened here?" Rama questioned, gesturing upwards.

"The Kumori Lord destroyed it during the civil war to keep it from the rebels and what's left has been turned into a museum." Despite Mikura's words, the guards at the front gate were both Kumori and when we approached they made it very clear in their own silent fashion that the museum was not open to the public.

"The Emperor has given these guests full access to the city and they wish to view the museum," Kichigai stated.

The powerfully muscled Kumori – the first males of the species I had ever come across, with the exception of the Kumori Lord of the past depicted in the painting – seemed to consider her words for a moment, conferring amongst themselves before one of them turned to us, hand-signing, *You have until the sun passes the mountain tops. Do not disturb what lies within.*

Agreeing to their terms, we filed past them into the darkened entranceway. "Thank you," I whispered to Kichigai.

"I owed you one," she replied in an offhand manner, never suspecting that my eyes didn't need time to adjust to the darker interior and that I would catch the pleased smile that crossed her lips.

The first few levels of the museum were fairly tame for being so well guarded; it wasn't until the fourth level that we came across the reason why people didn't just walk in and out as they pleased. She would have been nearly seven feet tall had she been standing, but as it was she rested on the many legs of her spider-like lower half and regarded us warily from her nest on the far side of the room. Her upper half was bare, her grey tinted skin and exposed chest only barely covered by a long mane of silky black hair. Somehow – even including the monstrous Lillem and the green-skinned Croatins – she still struck me as the most alien being I had seen yet.

"Ssshhhshhpshhhpshhphshhh," Mikura spoke unexpectedly, an unnatural hissing whisper emerging from her lips.

"Ssshhsssshhhppsshhpshh," the creature responded, tilting her teardrop-shaped face to the side and regarding us with a questioning expression.

"What is she?" Rama whispered tentatively to Kichigai, so as not to offend the creature if indeed she could understand our language.

"It's a Stirr," she answered, awed, "one of the original Teachers, but I had thought they were all extinct. This is amazing."

The hissing continued as Mikura communicated with the Stirr. I didn't want to seem impolite by staring at her, and truthfully, seeing as she was half spider, she kind of gave me the creeps, so as we waited for them to finish I found myself examining the room from where I stood. It was long and rectangular with the Stirr situated at the far end in a bed of what I could only presume was her own webbing, but the walls to either side and even the floor and ceiling were tiled with ancient stone, every inch covered in alien pictograms. They were interesting to look at, but no matter how hard I tried I couldn't make heads or tails of them.

"Mikura," I began when she had finished, "do you know what the walls mean?"

"Not really," she answered, "but I know it's written in Stirr."

Taking our leave of the mysterious Stirr so as not to disturb her further, we continued on to the next level and I nearly turned myself to mist on instinct when I came face to face with a full-sized Hound, until I realized that the lifelike display before me was merely a stuffed replica of one of the deadly creatures. In fact, the room we found ourselves in was filled with stuffed replicas of all sorts of different species, each with a little wooden stand before them describing what they were in Rubian script.

The rust coloured hound was followed by an example of a male Stirr, with a spider's hindquarters and the torso and face of a grey-skinned man. Beyond that a large First Spawn Croatin, a Kumori, and most disturbingly perhaps – from my cultural perspective, at least – a human.

It was the stand beneath the human that gave me my first clue on how to decipher the antiquated version of Rubian script. The word in the largest print on the stand was evidently supposed to mean 'human' and when I envisioned each character turned on its side, it was a simple process to see the commonalities this alphabet shared with what I had come to call 'Taiyoun'.

"Sir Rama, come here for a moment, would you?" I called him over and explained my findings.

"I believe you're right," he noted, a little awed. "Well that makes it much simpler, doesn't it?"

Armed with our newly found knowledge, we set about quickly translating the descriptions of the displays and realized nearly immediately that though the script was different, the language itself had not much changed.

"Human," it said and a brief description of average heights and weights followed, but then came the interesting part. *"Native region unknown. Potential: nonexistent.* 'Potential nonexistent,'" I questioned. "What is that supposed to mean?"

"I don't know," Rama answered, "but listen to this one: *Hound: native region plains. Potential: Knight."*

"Do you think Lilyth categorized these?" I questioned, thinking aloud.

"It's possible," Rama answered, moving down the row. *"Stirr: native region underground. Potential: servant."*

"She calls the Kumori 'great' and the Croatins 'warriors'," I read, quickly scanning the other displays. "I wonder why she bothered."

"I don't know, but humans seem to be the only race she didn't much like," he noted.

"Hey, you two," Masaru's voice called suddenly from the stairwell, "we think we found something up here."

"What is it?" I asked, coming up the stairs into a room filled with uncategorized junk and dusty storage containers.

"More like 'who is it?'" Kaji corrected me; looking beyond where he stood, I saw a Ruby egg.

With the amount of dust coating the egg, it had been here for some time. We couldn't move or see inside of it, and we all knew the folly of trying to bypass the shell with any of our varied powers. We spent some time debating about who the egg might possibly contain or why it was up here, but there was no real way to know. In the end we had to give it up as a mystery we might never solve.

I gave up somewhat sooner than the others did, feeling sorry for the poor soul trapped within but accepting there was nothing at this time that could be done for them. I found myself wandering through the dusty space, looking at what other mysteries this room might conceal. While absently rifling through the room, my eyes caught upon a dusty, tattered cloth and the hint of colour beneath. Without really knowing the reason why, I reached for it and pulled the cloth aside to reveal an ancient but well-preserved painting.

It was a portrait of a handsome man with strong features and a square jaw, framed with black hair. His eyes were a telltale red and I was shocked to realize I had seen this man before. A horrible suspicion began to dawn on me and looking down, I read the engraved gold plaque inset into the frame, *Verasheen, Emperor of the Ruby City.*

This was the man Yuko Seig called Verasheen and this was the face he kept hidden from the world. It was also the face of the nameless and mute Deathsquad soldier who had magically provided us with food in the Temple of Machalite.

This was the face of my enemy, the tyrant known as the Vile Emperor.

CH. 8 – TEMPLE OF RUBY

"Hotaru?" I questioned, as we returned to our room in the palace and the double doors opened to reveal her sitting anxiously on the edge of one of the beds.

"Why are you here?" Kaji's weighty question followed quickly after.

"Yue came back with Fuun and she offered to bring me here to help you guys. It's not like I just disappeared either," Hotaru insisted, "I told Sabien where I was going."

"It hasn't been more than a few days, Hotaru," I pointed out, trying desperately to keep my temper under control. "Did everyone at least make it where they were going, or did you just abandon them out in the Sand Lake?"

"It wasn't like that, really it wasn't," she assured us. "They didn't get so far as the Children's Outpost –"

"This is unacceptable, Hotaru," Kaji interjected. "You should have stayed with everyone else. You aren't needed here."

"Kaji has a point, Hotaru," I agreed, "but more than that, you promised me you would stay with the others and keep them safe."

"Should I just go, then?" Hotaru looked crestfallen.

"It's not that simple, I'm sure," Rama noted wryly. "It seems that unless we can convince the Emperor of our intentions, none of us are going anywhere."

"Not only that," I added, "but the Ruby City has a defensive barrier around it that blocks even our powers from crossing, or I would have contacted you myself much sooner to let you know where I was. Speaking of which, how exactly did you get in here? The Ruby City's barrier should have prevented you from entering."

"I don't know," Hotaru answered. "Yue put me in her Noh-space and brought the both of us in. After she let me out, Shuzhue had some guards lead me here."

I shuddered internally at the thought of travelling via Yue's extra-dimensional space; by her own admission she didn't know where things – or people, for that matter – went when she caused them to vanish. But Yue's Noh-space aside, that still didn't explain how Yue had gotten within the city's defensive barrier, as I was under the impression it was just as restrictive, if not more so, than the one that had protected Taiyou until Lilyth's full assault.

"So we're stuck here, then?" Hotaru asked.

Rama nodded. "It sure seems that way."

"Meaning what's done is done, so maybe instead of yelling at each other maybe we can all try to get some rest?" Masaru suggested. "The Lillem are still out there along with everything else and there's no way of tellin' if we're going to be needed to defend the city once it gets dark."

◊

"Kichigai's back." Masaru shook me awake some time later. "It seems we have been given an audience and *he* wants us in the throne room, now."

"All right," I conceded, sitting. "I'm up."

Clothes in various sizes had been provided along with everything else. I selected a simple, blue dress of fine quality, but Masaru declined. A small part of me was glad; Masaru's Roughlander attire was much a part of him and I couldn't imagine him trading in his worn leather belts for Rubian finery.

The five of us trooped down to the throne room behind Kichigai as I noted that the sun was nearing the horizon through the palace windows. If I had been mad or upset upon seeing Hotaru, then it was nothing when compared to what I felt upon seeing who – besides the Vile Emperor – awaited us in the Ruby Palace's throne room.

"Yue?"

"Hey guys," Yue responded, shrugging nonchalantly.

"What are you doing here?" Kaji demanded sharply, an echo of his earlier displeasure at Hotaru's unexpected appearance.

"She is here for the same reason all of you are here," the Vile Emperor rumbled in answer to Kaji's question, forcefully reminding us who's domain we were in. Having gotten our full attention, he continued, "I have been informed you wish to be of assistance. You will accompany me within the Temple of Ruby to seal a breach in the city's defenses."

"I came into the city by way of the Temple," Yue informed us. "I found a hole in the barrier that protects this place, and if I can get through it then Lady Lilyth might be able to."

"There is not much time before nightfall," the Vile Emperor stated, getting to his feet. "We must begin."

He turned his back to us, raising one arm in a commanding gesture to the wall behind the throne. The wall itself gave way before the Vile Emperor's power and began to melt and flow into the substance that had birthed it. As the lava dripped down like a waterfall it revealed a doorway, just like the one depicted in the book of paintings Mikura had shown us in the library.

Yue, Kichigai, and Rama went ahead at the Vile Emperor's behest, but the rest of us hesitated. I could not help but feel unsettled by recent events. For good or for ill, all four of the Chosen of Sapphiros had been reunited here in the Ruby City and were about to embark on a task assigned to us by our enemy. Preparing myself for whatever was to come, I took a deep breath and a deliberate step forward.

"Let's go," Kaji said darkly, stepping past me.

It grew increasingly hotter as we journeyed deeper into the active volcano. Thankfully one of us had a power that could help. It wasn't clear what Hotaru did, but some use of her power enabled us to resist the heat to the point where the inside of the volcano felt no warmer than the desert sun we had all grown accustomed to during our travels. And we were lucky it did; before long we were traversing rocky bridges over boiling pools of molten lava. Still, we followed after the impassive form of spiked armour as the Vile

Emperor led us deeper into his stronghold. When he finally came to a stop, he regarded us for a moment through his Ruby visor before gesturing for us to look over the ledge where he had brought us.

Far below us was another wider ledge, and below that there was a sizeable pool of lava fed from a constant flow along the far wall. The molten rock boiled, blasting us with heat and steam that was nearly unbearable, even with Hotaru's power shielding us. More worrisome than the lava, however, were the creatures that lay on the ledge nearest to it – Lilyth's Hounds.

There were nearly a dozen of them, most dozing peacefully. Oversized dogs with tusk-like teeth and bone protrusions down their spines, the Hounds were intimidating even at rest. This time they were not expecting an attack, but we were certainly outnumbered.

"So what's our plan?" Kaji whispered, breaking the tense silence.

I tore my eyes away from watching the Hounds below to realize we all were crouched near enough to each other that, as long as we were very quiet, we could speak without fear of being overheard down below – all of us, except Yue. Contrary as always, she was not attempting to plan our next move with the rest of us; she was conversing with the Vile Emperor a ways away.

Beyond them, the walls were covered in Lillem. Ornately carved, or perhaps fossilized there, the Lillem covered every inch of space along the walls. They looked as if they could spring to life at any moment and infect us all with their curse.

I shuddered with the thought as Yue joined us, speaking in a low voice, "He wants us to make a path for him and distract the Hounds. He needs to get to the lava below and drain it to get to the breach."

"We can't take on that many Hounds, Yue," I pointed out. "You remember what happened the last time we faced them."

"We don't need to kill them," Kaji countered, "just keep them busy."

"So I'll stay up here to keep an eye on everything," I clarified once the plan had been formed. "Masaru, can I borrow one of your knives? I don't have any weapons that will work on the Hounds otherwise."

"I suppose," he answered dubiously, handing me his black-bladed combat knife,, "but what if I have need of it? Two knives are better than one…"

I took the knife hilt from him and held it tightly in one hand, willing my power to work on it, then I threw it at the ground. Five knives thudded into the rock with the force of my power behind them.

"Whoa." Masaru reached for the hilt of one of the knives, surprised at finding it solid. "I suppose five knives would be even better than two."

I smiled at him – truthfully, I hadn't known if that was going to work before I made the attempt.

"All right," Kaji spoke. "Let's get going."

We stood as one, then Rama placed a hand on Kaji's shoulder and activated his power to allow the two of them to sink into the stone floor beneath. Yue, on the other hand, used her power to transform herself once more into the demonic creature I had encountered in the Temple of Machalite. Her long white hair fanned out and turned black, fading into writhing, tendril-like wings, and her features elongated, warping her visage until it was deeply terrifying to behold. Then she grew until she was a winged beast more than large enough to carry both Masaru and Kichigai upon her back.

Hotaru waited until the others were in position before she leapt from the cliff edge, trusting on her powers to help her safely land, and before long I was left alone on the ledge with the Vile Emperor until he leapt downwards, diving headfirst into the lava below. I watched him a moment, awed despite myself, as he splashed into the surface, causing the Hounds to start in surprise. Moments later, the lava pool was covered by a shimmer of blue.

Hotaru had shielded the Vile Emperor's passage so the Hounds could not follow after him and now it was time for the distraction. I picked up two of the four remaining knives and charged them with my power before throwing them downwards. As the two knives fell they became ten, seeking out the five targets I had designated for them, two to each Hound. The knives each struck their intended targets without fail and from there more knives were created, duplicating outwards until each of those ten knives had struck five more targets, fanning outwards at odd angles and striking each Hound below multiple times.

My strike was the cue for the others, and then five humans and one massive demonic creature leapt into the fray. I had two more knives and I used them to great effect, dropping them into the chaos below and using my power to strike only the targets I designated, keeping my friends safe.

I had just thrown my last knife when I took notice of movement out of the corner of my eye. I whirled about to catch sight of a Stirr, a male decorated with red markings and tattooed designs. The alien-looking Stirr regarded me watchfully from near to the tunnel where we had entered the chamber, one of its human arms poised and ready to touch the wall beside it where a Lillem carving seemed to await its chance to lash out.

The Stirr's spider-like bottom remained as still as the rest of it, but beyond him in the tunnel I could make out several more of them. I raised my arms to fire an arrow but the Stirr was faster. He slapped his hand on the wall beside him and the fossilized Lillem surged to life, clawing its way out of the wall itself.

My eyes met his; I didn't understand the Stirr, but in that instant I realized he was going to wake every Lillem in the place to protect it if he felt it necessary.

I couldn't let that happen.

I let my arrows fly, pinning the Stirr and the re-animated Lillem together with a net formed of energy and closing off the tunnel entrance to the others, at least temporarily.

Swooping in closer, I sent a spray of mist out from my outstretched hands to eliminate the Lillem while the Stirr regarded me with curiosity. I acknowledged his stare with a nod. He nodded in turn, and it seemed we had come to some form of agreement. Hoping our newfound understanding would mean the Stirr wouldn't try to release any more Lillem, I took a moment to look down and see how everyone else was faring.

It wasn't good.

Rama was down for the count and Hotaru wasn't much better off – one of her legs was bleeding and she was barely able to stand on it – but, even still, she was defending Rama's unconscious form against two Hounds who had her surrounded. Kaji, on the other hand, was in a dozen places at once. For every clone of his that went down, two more would appear and pick up one of the duplicated knives. Masaru and Kichigai fought back to back, Masaru throwing every knife he found lying at his feet and Kichigai trying to make headway with her double-bladed axe, while Yue seemed to have little trouble bashing the heads of the creatures together thanks to her greater size and strength.

There were too many Hounds, though, even considering the handful that had already been defeated. Kichigai missed a swing and a Hound caught her axe in his teeth before lifting a massive paw to swipe at her. She went down hard and the Hound was already picking the General up with its mouth before Masaru realized the danger his partner was in.

Masaru slashed at the enemy with both knives and the beast tossed its head, launching Kichigai into the air like a limp rag doll before sliding along the shield's shimmery blue surface. Masaru vaulted over its head, scored it on the way with a knife, and landed on the far side, causing it to whirl about to face him.

Meanwhile, Kichigai struggled to her feet out on Hotaru's shield and started determinedly forward to rejoin the fight. Something about Kichigai's jerky movements seemed off to me. The Hounds! I remembered Adel's warning from long before we had first encountered Lilyth's dread generals. *If a person is struck by a Hound's fire, or its saliva, they may also be in danger of possession by Lady Lilyth.*

But was she under the Hound's influence? Kichigai stalked forward, intent on Hotaru and Rama before her, but it wasn't clear whether she meant to help or harm them. Hotaru was losing ground and tiring quickly; soon she and Rama would be overcome. I had two choices: either find a way to help Hotaru or stop Kichigai.

I was torn and hesitated, but a red glint in Kichigai's eye made my decision for me. I let another energy net fly to pin Kichigai, but in that moment Hotaru took a devastating blow from a Hound's paw and she crumpled. The shield she was maintaining over the lava disappeared as she lost consciousness. A wave of heat blasted upwards, pushing me back with the very force of it, but the change was enough to alert the others that something was wrong.

The Hounds surged forward, intent on the three humans they believed to be defeated, when at last the lava in the pool below began to drain. I drifted downward slightly, thinking perhaps this ordeal was finally at an end, but what the sinking lava revealed was a far worse sight than the sinister visor of the Vile Emperor. Its body, if it could be called that, took up the length of the lava pit. I had seen Lillem of this shape before, only then they had been made out of sand and no larger than a house, but this one was massive and constructed purely of Ruby. All around it surged smaller Lillem of various sizes, mostly humanoid as I was used to seeing, but also some of the spider-like variety.

The Lillem from the Sand Lakes had been no more than animated sand and old bones, covered in illusion to look like the corpses they had once been. Surging from the depths of the Temple of Ruby were Lillem visibly made of stone, metal, lava, smoke, and also Ruby. Lilyth's army was here and perhaps had been here all along. Was this the trap I feared, or simply an unlucky coincidence? There was no time to decide. We had to fight or flee, and either way we chose, it was still likely that none of us would make it out of this temple alive –

"– that's better. So, as I was saying, I'd recommend closing that place up for a while," Yue stated, looking like herself once more. "You certainly don't want to go in there, but at least we stopped more of her army from getting in that way."

I looked about myself, feeling more than a little disoriented. The Vile Emperor, Kaji, Masaru, Rama, Hotaru, and I were all in the throne room, standing behind the throne and facing Akuma, who looked about as overwhelmed as I felt.

"You said Kichigai was possessed by a Hound?" Akuma questioned Yue. "Do you have her stored away like you had the others? In your Noh-space?"

Yue's Noh-space – was that where we had been? It would explain the gap in my memory.

"Let me see her, then," Akuma commanded.

"You're the boss," Yue replied and Kichigai joined the rest of us in the throne room, still held within my energy net and struggling to break free with a near mindless ferocity.

"See to your wounds," the Vile Emperor interjected tonelessly as he stalked from the room. "I expect to see you all with the army at nightfall."

Lost in my own thoughts, I watched as Akuma expertly performed the ritual taught to her by Adel before Taiyou had been lost. Halfway through, I fired an energy net to help ease the pain in her arm as I had done for Adel countless times, before attempting to pull myself together to see what else needed to be done. I could dwell upon the nature of Yue's Noh-space later and there was nothing at this instant I could do about the threat I had seen within the temple.

"Sir Rama, are you all right?" I questioned, realizing that other than Hotaru, who was still unconscious, he was the worst off.

"I'll keep," he answered wryly, setting Hotaru down so I could examine her.

The cut on her leg went down to the bone – wait a minute…I peered closer, but my power couldn't see past Hotaru's bones, and to my vision they appeared blue, like they were made of Sapphire. Nothing appeared broken, but I couldn't be sure.

Shaking my head, I turned my friend to mist. "Let's get her somewhere I can see to her."

"I'll send our healer," Akuma offered. "I know you are skilled, Yukari, but you should be resting if you are to be prepared to help us defend this night."

I frowned and nodded, thinking of what we might have to face once darkness fell and the hordes of Lillem we had seen would surge out of the temple, no longer being held out of the Ruby City by the light of the sun. Akuma was right, all of us would need to be prepared and even that might not be enough to save us.

But having got Hotaru back to the room where we were staying, I couldn't simply leave her in a state of agony, with her flesh torn and the bone in her leg exposed. Knowing my power could help cleanse the wound better than water could hope to, I held my hands above her wounds and sprayed her with the same mist I used to cleanse the infection of the Lillem. As my mist did its work I found myself thinking of Flaqqers and how the sandcrawler larvae in the innocuous devices wormed their way through human flesh, mending it as they passed through it. Couldn't my power perhaps achieve the same effect without having to inject my patient with the larvae of another living creature?

I shifted my concentration just slightly and watched as Hotaru's flesh slowly began to knit together as if she had been Flaqqered. With The healing process successfully accelerated, I twisted my vision to see into Hotaru and satisfy my curiosity concerning what I had noticed in the throne room. Hotaru's bones were indeed made of Sapphire and it wasn't just her limbs but her entire skeleton. Sapphire, being one of the five precious stones on this planet, was indestructible – or so we had been told – and the only possible explanation for what I was seeing was that Hotaru's power had made her this way.

Stranger than even the bones was that the Sapphire seemed to continue and elongate past the tips of Hotaru's fingers and toes. Returning my vision to normal, I picked up my friend's hand and noted that in some cases her nails were in the process of falling off, only to be replaced with pointed Sapphire claws.

I carefully pried the loose fingernails off and placed them on the bedside table to get rid of later, before doing the same for her toenails, trying not to shudder as I did so. I had my theories that none of us were fully human any longer, but what were we becoming?

"So you're the Chosen of Sapphiros, are you?" a new, almost nasal sounding voice questioned, breaking my focus.

"Yukari," I introduced myself. "You're the healer?"

"General Oka," the spindly man in a pristine lab coat responded, sizing me up in a clinical fashion. "You seem fine," he stated after a moment, "but your friend, on the other hand, could use some work."

"Yes, but she's healing," I noted, getting out of his way.

"She heals fast, doesn't she?" he commented with a slight smile and an almost acquisitive gleam in his eye. "Impressive regenerative properties."

"Actually that's my doing," I clarified.

He stopped and looked at me once more, as if really noticing me for the first time, and I caught a hint of respect. "Impressive," he repeated, and then turned his attention back to Hotaru "Nevertheless, there are still a few things I can do to speed the process along."

Having completed his initial examination, General Oka dove right in, almost literally. He rolled up the sleeves of his lab coat and inserted his left hand into the gash on Hotaru's leg. She didn't cry out or even so much as twitch in her sleep, so I didn't protest. And I was glad I stayed my tongue, as what Oka did next was even more miraculous than watching a Flaqqer do its work. With one hand within the wound and the other on top of the broken skin, Oka pinched the two sides of the gash together like he was preparing to stitch it, only the skin mended perfectly wherever his fingers touched.

"That's one way of getting the job done," I commented, a little awed as General Oka was washing his hands.

"Indeed, but it seems that whatever you did will be necessary to complete the job. I couldn't get through her bones for some reason and the flesh around them will have to heal on its own."

"Her bones are made of Sapphire. I'm not sure when that happened."

"Really? Well, isn't that different? You wouldn't by any chance let me take her to my lab to examine her further, would you?"

I gathered by his tone that Oka was a scientist first and a healer second, so when he said 'examine' he meant exactly that – it would be for furthering his knowledge of Chosen and how they worked, not necessarily for Hotaru's benefit.

"I suppose you'll have to ask her when she awakens," I answered diplomatically.

"I figured you'd say as much," he responded wryly. "Oh well, no matter. I should be getting back to the lab, anyways. It was…uh…nice meeting you all."

Oka turned about and made for the door, but the guilt in his step alerted me that something was amiss. My eyes snapped to the bedside table and sure enough, the toenails and fingernails I had pried off of Hotaru were missing – the scientist had taken his sample.

"He's an odd one," Masaru noted quietly to Rama. "Kinda creepy, don't ye think?"

"I don't know about that, but that thing he did with his hands was disgusting," he replied.

"Aye, I'm grateful I've got Yukari to fix me up if I need it."

"Masaru," Rama said, "I'd rather have you inject me with one of your Flaqqers than let him put his hands under my skin."

"What have ye got against Flaqqers?"

I tuned them out and took a seat on an empty bed, propping myself up against the headboard to rest now while I had the chance. It wouldn't be long before the Ruby City was shrouded in darkness and we would be called to war with everyone else – it was going to be another long and difficult night.

Hotaru still had not awoken by the time we were summoned, and considering the possible weakness of her leg I thought it best to leave her be no matter what the Vile Emperor wanted. The rest of us were divided and assigned to work with various Generals. I was paired with General Oka and his squad of healers, Kaji with Bastion, and Yue with Akuma.

Rama was paired with Kichigai, whose wounds had been seen to once she had been liberated from Lilyth's control, but by far the most surprising of the assignments was Masaru's.

"They've asked me to command Lady Mikura's squad – or what's left of it anyways."

"What about Lady Mikura?" I questioned.

"Ye know how she's been staying in the palace at night, aye? Well, they've been keeping her locked up for her own good. Lady Akuma told me that something about Mikura makes her an easy target for Lady Lilyth. She's been possessed a time too many, and if not contained she turns against them while it's dark out."

"That's terrible." I couldn't help but think of the devastation that magical little girl could wreak, but at the same time how awful she would feel afterwards.

"Aye," Masaru agreed, "but should I accept?"

I could see immediately why he was torn. On the one hand, even though she was a Deathsquad General, Lady Mikura had managed to worm her way into each of our hearts and being asked to lead her Deathsquad – brave soldiers who had been with us since surviving the fall of Taiyou – was a great honour. On the other hand, Deathsquad soldiers and other agents of the Ruby City had killed Masaru's family, and by heading a Deathsquad himself he might feel as if he were betraying their memory and his own morals.

"I don't think anyone but you can make this decision, Masaru," I told him honestly.

"Aye, you're right about that," he agreed, frowning. "It's just, I've come to see the Deathsquad as people. They're just soldiers like any other and they're in as much danger now as we all were in Taiyou."

"Then lead them, Masaru. Just because you lead them in battle doesn't mean you become one of them. You're a Knight of Sapphiros, I think everyone here knows which side you're on."

"Thank ye, Yukari." He smiled suddenly, giving me a quick kiss on the forehead. "I think I'll go find Akuma now. Stay safe."

"You too, don't give me a reason to worry."

"Oh, I'll be fine," he commented blithely, "I'll have a whole Deathsquad to look after me."

I rolled my eyes – it never ceased to amaze me how easily Masaru could bounce – and turned back to locate Oka, his white lab coat standing out amongst his black-robed squad. We were in the city, furthest back from those gathered on the ramp leading to the massive double door entrance to the Temple of Ruby.

"I'm looking forward to getting to see one of the Chosen of Sapphiros in action," Oka commented as I reached his side.

"I've discovered a way to cleanse the Lillem infection, so if anyone falls to it, bring them to my attention and I'll restore them."

"Well, that sure beats killing them. What else have you got?"

"I can fly and keep lookout, and I can also bring the wounded to me safely."

"Oh, my squad can get the wounded. You'll be needed here with me to look after them. But flying? Do you use wings? Float by magic?"

I didn't see any harm in showing him, since,y wings were always present, though usually invisible, so I spread the glowing cyan feathers out behind me. Oka was suitably impressed and had me twirl around so he could get a better look at them. I hardly thought it was the appropriate time to show off, but I obliged him.

I turned away from him for only a moment and my eyes caught movement between two nearby buildings in a city that should be empty, save for the army gathered in the opposite direction. One second it was there and the next it was gone. I lifted my arms and summoned an arrow, waiting for whatever it was, Hound or Lillem, to show itself again and instinct warned me just in time as the creature appeared before me.

"Hound!" I called out, but it was too late. Instead of engaging the group of us the Hound simply let out a jet of flames.

I took to the air instinctively and the blast missed me, but Oka had been standing directly behind me and by saving myself I had put him directly in the line of fire. "Oka!" I looked down, but all that remained of the spindly General was a charred and smoking corpse. "No!"

I searched the city, but the Hound was nowhere to be seen. I started back down to the ground where Oka's squad had surrounded his body.

"He's dead," one announced.

"You're next," another said, speaking to a third.

The third squad member stepped forward to kneel beside Oka's corpse. I watched confused and somewhat horrified as he took a set of pliers from his medic kit and used them to pry loose one of his molars. Blood streaming from his mouth, he took the tooth in his right hand and slammed the bloody mess onto the cobblestones. There was a flash of green light and the squad member simply crumpled. I didn't think, I simply rushed to the man's side, but I needn't have bothered – he was already dead.

It was one shock after another as I looked up to find the impassive helmet of the Vile Emperor himself staring down at me. "What happened here?"

I stood. "There was a Hound here a moment ago. The blast was meant for me –"

"Yeah, but I took the brunt of it," Oka's memorable nasal voice interjected. "That stuff's awful and it stings too."

I blinked a few moments in shock, looking from Oka's burnt corpse beyond to Oka himself standing before me.

"I lose more members of my squad that way," he commented, following my gaze. "Hard to find men willing to die for you, but I've got a couple lined up just in case."

"Where is the Hound now?" the Vile Emperor demanded, nonplussed.

"It disappeared," I responded, trying to collect myself. "I lost sight of it, but I believe I can find it again."

"Do so."

I didn't appreciate his tone but I activated my power regardless, trying to feel for that fleeting sense of a life force that did not belong to a human, a Kumori, or a Croatin, but a Hound – there had to be a different feel to the creatures Lilyth had altered; I should be able to sense her power.

"There!" I pointed. "And there as well, there are two of them nearby."

The Hounds leapt when they heard me, but Yue was faster. She appeared out of nowhere to leapt on the first, pinning it to the ground with the strength of her new form and tearing at its thick hide with her claws. The second one nearly made it to us, but it was no match for the Vile Emperor. He locked the beast's jaws shut in his armoured hands, using no more than brute strength to force it to the ground and slice its throat open on a sharp spike of his deep purple armour.

It was over in seconds; the threat of the two lone Hounds was taken care of, but it only served to remind me there were many more where those two came from, and soon we would have to face them in droves, backed by the multitude of savage and bloodthirsty Lillem.

CH. 9 – THERE WILL BE NO SURVIVORS

"Each night the Ruby City is called to war and each night we are victorious in our efforts, despite our losses," the Vile Emperor's voice reverberated through his helmet but was perfectly clear and loud enough to be heard even where I stood, far from the barricaded temple doors. "We have held our lines and we have survived, despite every unnatural creature that emerges to threaten us from where it dwells in the darkness. But this has gone on too long. It is no longer enough to simply fight to survive. In order to be free of this curse that plagues us we must take action.

"Tonight we no longer simply defend or hold the line. Tonight we storm the temple and take back what is ours with all the force that the Ruby City can muster. We will cleanse the taint that has festered within our very home and eradicate it once and for all. When the temple doors open this night, we will not simply keep the monsters at bay. We are the citizens of the Ruby City. We will take the fight to our enemies!

"Enter the temple! Kill every Lillem! Kill every Hound! Kill every Stirr and anything else that moves! There will be no survivors!"

The echoing cheer was deafening, the army's collective voice thundering loudly in support of the Vile Emperor. "No survivors!"

I felt like I was going to be sick.

I understood The Lillem and the Hounds; they were Lilyth's creations – her army – and though they were technically living beings, this was war and it was us or them. The Stirr, however, were an ancient race; I had seen their writings and their history displayed in the museum. They were a people of their own, not slaves to Lilyth.

The exhibition continued up at the top of the ramp near the temple's large double doors. Two unlucky soldiers were chosen by Akuma for the dubious honour of opening the doors, and as soon as the waiting horde was revealed the Vile Emperor launched a powerful blast of molten rock from his hands, destroying everything before him and pushing the enemy back far enough for the first wave of troops to advance.

I had to warn the Stirr. It was not a choice, but a necessity. Only I knew of the threat the Stirr faced and only I could warn them in time. I formed an arrow between my hands to carry a message of warning to the Stirr I had met before. But could the Stirr read Japanese, English, Taiyoun, or even Rubian? I almost dismissed my arrow, before I realized there might indeed be a way to communicate with the Stirr - pictures.

I thought up the simplest series of images I could to show the Rubian army was coming and that the Stirr should run and hide, away from the temple if possible. It wasn't art, but I hoped it would get my message across.

The message arrow flew over the heads of the army waiting eagerly for their chance to surge into the temple and begin the killing. The arrow whizzed past the Vile Emperor and Akuma, past Yue and the enemy host, and into the temple itself where I lost sight of it.

"Yukari, was it? If you're not too busy," Oka commented wryly, "I could use a little help here." It seemed Oka's squad members shared a unique ability. Be it by their own magic, or some means granted to them by Oka or someone else, they could flit about short distances without crossing the intervening space, which made them very efficient at retrieving the wounded and bringing them to where Oka – and I – could treat them. "Now would be nice!" The man Oka was dealing with turned on him, Lillem talons protruding out of his back with a dangerous suddenness, while at the same time another of Oka's squad appeared before me, locked in a deadly struggle with another half-turned soldier.

I let go of my form, fanned out into a cloud of mist, and exploding outwards until I enveloped both of the infected soldiers. My mist passed through them, the particles of my power seeking out and destroying the foreign matter of the Lillem curse.

I reformed just as quickly as I had expanded outwards, my two patients restored to themselves and healing faster than they would have without my interference. But it wasn't over yet; no sooner had I reformed than yet another of Oka's squad members appeared, this time with a man whose arm had been torn off.

"Stone Lillem," Oka commented, "or metal, they're both equally nasty. Hard to kill and they don't bother to infect, they just kill or maim."

"How do you fight something like that?"

"The Deathsquad's sword blast can destroy the stone and the Emperor can melt the metal with his lava. It's the Ruby ones that are particularly deadly. They're practically indestructible and they don't infect so much as kill instantly with no more than a touch."

"Some kind of poison?" I questioned, looking out over the army to where the battle was being fought and catching sight of a Lillem made entirely of Ruby, just like Oka was describing. Most of the soldiers were staying well clear of it, but as I watched Akuma put herself directly in its path.

"Not exactly," Oka replied. "I've dissected the corpses of the victims afterward and they don't have the Lillem infection in their blood. The blood simply crystallizes and turns to Ruby."

The Ruby Lillem lunged at Akuma and she dove to the side, rolling out of its way, but it corrected its course to follow after her with its talons faster than I expected. From here it looked like the strike had connected, but in that moment the creature froze and Akuma stood.

"Bastion!" I heard Akuma cry over the din of battle, and at her command Bastion appeared on his beam of red light to smash the creature before her into shards.

"So they can be destroyed, then," I noted.

"Hmm?" Oka turned his attention back to me from the patient he was treating. "Yes, Akuma can immobilize them and for some reason they aren't quite as sturdy as pure Ruby, which in this case is a good thing."

"Yukari, fix it." I was surprised to hear Akuma's controlled tones and I whirled about to see that she and Bastion had appeared, likely on his beam of red light, and she was gripping her arm fiercely. The arm had been punctured but no blood pooled there and she was still alive, despite the information Oka had just given me. "The Ruby is spreading," she stated by way of explanation. "I've taken control of the flow of my own blood to slow it, but I cannot hold it back forever."

I didn't know if this affliction was the same as the Lillem curse or something else entirely, but I tried the method I knew first, spraying mist over Lady Akuma's arm. Seeing into her arm, I noted the blood in her veins had indeed crystallized. Had this happened to anyone else but Akuma, who could control the flow of her own blood at will, that person would already be dead.

"Better," Akuma spoke through gritted teeth. "It's no longer fighting me, but the Ruby is still there and I'd much rather keep my arm, thank you."

"Not to worry," Oka stated, handing off a man he had just patched up to a squad member. "I've done this before – of course then my subjects were already dead, but the principle should be the same."

"Just do it, Oka," she commanded.

Oka ran his index finger along the length of Akuma's forearm, splitting the skin with his magic as he went. To her credit Akuma did not make a sound, but the pain was visible in her eyes as Oka reached into her arm, splitting her veins open with his fingernails and pulling out strings of solid Ruby.

"Almost done," he noted after a few tense moments. "I won't be able to get all of it out, but whatever Yukari did seems to be breaking it down."

"Thank you," Akuma said sincerely, slowly releasing her hold on her arm, "both of you," she added, meeting my eyes. "I'll have to get going. I might be needed to face more of them, but I'll try not to let that happen again."

"See that it doesn't," Bastion stated. "You're not invincible, my Lady."

"I know that Bastion," she responded with a smile. "That's why I have you."

"Guys?" Hotaru called out, looking about the empty and otherwise silent room with confusion and a growing sense of unease. "Is anybody here?"

Her head hurt and she felt a little dizzy as she swung her legs over the side of the bed, then she almost fell the rest of the distance to the floor when she realized her left leg couldn't support her weight without causing her pain. "That's right. I broke it, before…where is everyone?"

"Gone," a young female voice answered.

"Who's there?" Hotaru questioned, looking around but seeing no one. "Mikura, is that you?"

"Aww, you guessed," Mikura said, appearing in the center of the room.

"Don't scare me like that," Hotaru admonished.

Mikura grinned and Hotaru caught the wicked gleam in the girl's eyes before she was hoisted off the ground by the young General's magic.

"Mikura, this isn't funny," Hotaru complained, bobbing weightlessly in the air. "Put me down, I'll find them myself." Hotaru caught a glimpse of what the girl was concealing behind her back. Between Mikura's hands crackled a growing ball of red and black energy, which swirled in place, hovering only a few inches from her skin. "Mikura, what are you doing?"

"What I should have done before," the voice that came out of Mikura wasn't the one Hotaru expected to hear and the menace in it didn't sound like her friend at all, "eliminate the Chosen of Sapphiros!"

The little General pulled back her arm to throw her deadly ball of energy and Hotaru did the only thing she could think of, she erected a shimmering blue dome around Mikura. "Don't do this, Mikura. You'll kill us both!"

"You think I care about this body or what happens to it?" Lilyth responded through the body she had stolen, eyeing the ball of crackling magic appreciatively.

"Let Mikura go," Hotaru ordered, finally realizing who she was really dealing with.

"Or what? You'll kill me?" Lilyth asked sweetly. "Here, I'll save you the trouble. This tool, like so many others, has outlived its usefulness."

Lilyth brought the ball of energy closer to Mikura's face, until Hotaru could smell her friend's hair burning and could see her skin blistering.

"No! Stop it!" Another blue bubble of a shield formed within the first, surrounding the hand that held the deadly magic weapon. "I won't let you hurt her!"

"Oh? And just how are you going to stop me?"

"Yukari!" Hotaru yelled, activating her power to communicate through the water in the canteen attached to her Roughlander belts. "Yue, Kaji, anyone! Help me!"

A sneer crossed Mikura's face, and then shockingly the ball of magic Mikura had been holding suddenly went off inside Hotaru's blue bubble. A piercing scream filled the room, as Mikura clutched at the now charred stump of her arm, falling to her knees and writhing in agony.

◊

The bowl of water filled with blood-soaked bandages screamed at me with Hotaru's voice, followed by the sound of an explosion and a blood-curdling scream.

"Oka, I have to go, but I'll be back as soon as I can." I locked onto Hotaru's life force and I was gone before Oka could formulate a response.

I became solid immediately, bringing my entire being into the room with Hotaru. On one side Hotaru was getting awkwardly to her feet and to the other lay Mikura, sprawled awkwardly and cradling her right arm, which ended abruptly in a still-smoking stump. They were the only people in the room where I had left Hotaru and both were crying.

"Keep her away from me!" Mikura cried shrilly.

"Mikura, I –" Hotaru began and then stopped, seemingly at a loss for words.

"What happened here?" I questioned.

"She...attacked me..." Mikura sobbed, shaking her head forcefully. "She's not herself! It's like what Adel said might happen. I think a Hound got to her..."

I abruptly recalled the gash on Hotaru's leg and the other injuries I had noted on her; had there been any teeth marks? Even if there hadn't been, Adel had said that it was the saliva of the Hound that was dangerous, perhaps some had gotten into Hotaru's open wound?

On the other hand, I looked to Mikura; Masaru had told me why she was kept confined at night and it was full dark now.

"Shh, Mikura, it's all right," I spoke gently. "I'm here now, it's going to be okay."

"Don't go near her, Yukari!" Hotaru yelled, surging forward. "It's not Mikura, it's Lady Lilyth!"

I formed two arrows and let them fly, one to either side, targeting them both. I pinned both Mikura and Hotaru on opposite walls with nets formed of cyan energy.

"Yukari, what is this?!" Hotaru demanded. "I didn't do anything wrong and your net won't be enough to stop her when she tries to kill us both!"

"Be quiet, Hotaru," I ordered her. "Just let me think."

With the facts I had at my disposal either one of them could be possessed, or neither, or perhaps even both – though if that were the case they had me outnumbered. I was lost in an internal debate when the double doors to the room slammed open, startling all three of us.

"I thought you might be in here," Oka stated. "Verasheen's going to kill me for real this time if he finds out that I've left my post, but right now this is more important." He turned to Mikura. "I told you this was the last time, Mikura. Initiate self destruct sequence. Activation code: three-four-oh-seven-one..."

"What are you doing?" I looked from Oka to Mikura and back again, noting a snarl on the little girl's features that hadn't been there before – so she really was the one possessed.

"What we should have done before," Oka replied. "She's too vulnerable to the enemy and too dangerous a weapon to have pointed at us."

As if to prove Oka's statement, Mikura sprung into action, using her own power to counter mine and incinerating the net I had covering her with red-black flames. Once freed she launched herself at Oka, flying through the air with her face contorted in rage and her fingernails out before her like claws. I formed another arrow, uncertain of what I was going to do with it; but Oka's posture remained relaxed even in the face of Mikura's charge.

"Password: snowflake," he stated calmly and Mikura's advance simply stopped as she crumpled to the ground and lay there unmoving.

"Is she going to be okay?" Hotaru asked from where my net kept her against the wall.

"She's dead," Oka stated, kneeling beside the body.

"What?!" Hotaru exclaimed. "But why? We can get rid of possession! Why would you do such a thing?!"

"It wouldn't have done any good," Oka explained. "Removing the Lady's influence again would be nothing more than prolonging the inevitable. She's been taken over nearly every night since this all began and there's not enough of her left to save at this point."

Hotaru broke down crying and I dismissed my net to let her stand on her own two feet. I was in a state of shock myself, not yet able to feel the grief of having lost someone or even rage at how it had come about.

"You're sure, Oka?" I pressed.

"I'm sure," he answered, sincere, and for a moment I could see beyond his usual standoffish demeanor to the man beneath. "I've known Mikura a very long time and she was suffering more than she let show. It's better this way, trust me. Come on, we have to get back."

"You're just going to leave after that?" Hotaru demanded. "And you're going to let him walk away after what he's done?!"

"After what Lady Lilyth did," I told Hotaru tiredly. "Oka didn't do anything wrong."

"But she's dead!"

"And so many more people will be if there aren't healers to treat them. We have to go, Hotaru."

"It just doesn't make any sense," Masaru muttered, inspecting the obsidian wall by the glow of his blue energy knives. "We've seen Hounds and every type of Lillem ye can think of infesting every inch of this place, but this one room is completely empty. I just don't get it."

"And we still have not seen any sign of the Stirr," Bastion noted. "I presume this room is their nest, and if they are not here then I do not know where they might be."

The cavern that Masaru and Bastion with their respective squads had fought long and hard to reach was vast and silent. The walls were pitted with larger than man-sized openings, like holes made by a Sandcrawler passing through, only more regular, giving the impression the caves weren't exactly natural formations.

"Hold on a minute, would you?" Masaru asked and then dug one knife into the wall to hoist himself upward without waiting for a response.

The knives created by his power as a Knight made quick work of climbing the sheer surface of the wall, and before long Masaru was pulling himself into one of the lower caverns where he thought he had spotted movement for a second.

The cave he found himself in was as dark and silent as the larger cavern had been, but there, on the floor of the cavern amidst what looked to be cobwebs, was a familiar looking combat knife. In fact, as he reached for it he felt the notch in the wooden handle he had constructed himself.

He abruptly recalled how Yukari had thrown and multiplied his knife when last they had been inside the temple. All the other duplicate knives had disappeared some time after the fighting was done, but if this one still remained then it must be the original.

"The Stirr, was it?" Masaru asked, thinking aloud, and then he froze with the sudden feeling he wasn't as alone as he had first thought. He thought he heard a whispering hiss, but looking about for the source of the noise he found only a small spider amidst all the webbing. "You're just a wee one, aren't ye? Nothin' to get worked up over."

"Shphhsshhhh?"

He froze again, falling silent. He hadn't imagined it this time; there really was someone in here with him. The whispered hissing came from deep in the shadows and he thought he could just make out the silhouette of a vaguely human shape from the glow of the energy knife he still held in his hand.

Masaru faced the darkened silhouette, whispering in kind, "I've got no way of understandin' ye and maybe ye can't understand me either, but I mean ye no harm."

"*Shphssshhhh...*" The hissing could have meant anything, but to Masaru it sounded almost grateful.

"Well, I'll be going now," he said, backing up to show what he meant. "Ye've got nothin' to worry about from me, but I'd recommend ye stay hidden a bit longer, for what it's worth."

Taking his leave of the Stirr, Masaru sheathed his reclaimed knife and swung his legs over the side to begin the return journey to the cavern floor.

"Did you find anything?" Bastion questioned when he joined him.

"Not a thing," Masaru lied easily. "This place is empty. I'm not sure how long the Stirr have been gone for, if they ever were here at all."

"Let's keep going, then," Bastion said. "While you were investigating, the Emperor passed through here with Yue. He says he will need us to clear the way ahead, it seems he has a destination in mind."

Masaru frowned, unable to help his reaction every time he was reminded of whom he was technically working for at present. "All right, lead the way."

"Hand me those bandages," I ordered a member of Oka's squad, reaching out my hand without taking my eyes off the patient before me.

"You needn't bother with that one," Oka noted critically, "he's a lost cause. Get him outside with the others and focus on the ones we can send back into the fight."

"No. This one is going to make it, and provided I bandage him tight enough he'll be able to fight, too."

"What're the odds?"

"What?"

"The odds that your imperial soldier will make it through this fight with one arm pinned to his chest like that? What do you wager that he'll live?"

"I'm not going to wager against a man's chances in circumstances like this," I replied, not only appalled by the suggestion, but also the fact Oka was discussing it within earshot of the soldier in question. "It is his decision should he choose to keep fighting and I believe I have given him a chance to live through it."

"I'm going back in," the soldier stated. "My thanks to you for patching me up, but I'm not through yet."

"I'll bet five krevels he won't last an hour," one of the other healers announced.

"An hour?" an arriving squad member asked, looking the soldier in question up and down. "I'd give him fifteen minutes, tops. You haven't seen what it's like out there."

"There you have it," Oka said, smiling a tad smugly, "his odds aren't very good."

"Fine," I countered, "have it your way, but I'll match five krevels to each of you that this man not only lives through the hour but makes it out of this temple alive. And if he does, you have to ensure he is recognized for it, promote him or something."

"A shrewd bargainer. Very well, I'll put a word in for him with the Emperor if he lives. Maybe he can even join my squad." Oka gave me a toothy grin, reminding me of the price a soldier paid for entering his squad – one day he might have to lay down his life for his General to be reborn. "I'm down a member today anyways."

The soldier in question stood, saluting Oka and myself with his good arm. "Thank you, my Lady," he said to me before turning to Oka. "I'll do you proud, General Oka, you'll see."

"Off with you, then," Oka ordered and the wounded soldier headed off at a run to rejoin the rest of the army, full of renewed zeal.

I tried to look confident but internally I cringed – I hadn't had a krevel to my name since arriving on this world. Where did I get off betting money I didn't have, or didn't really know the value of? Well, the soldier would just have to live, that was all; there was nothing else for it.

I stood to look around for my next patient when a shout from the soldier I had just sent off into battle just barely warned me in time. "Look out!"

My power reacted instinctively, turning me to mist as a glob of lava whizzed by the place I had been standing. As mist it was impossible for me to scream, but every fiber of my being felt the heat of the lava's passage. I reformed immediately, shocked by the pain and crumpled to the floor, able to do no more than watch as our force of wounded soldiers attempted to defend us.

Never mind the soldier I had wagered would live, none of our chances looked very good against the threat of a being made of lava. The creature advanced with flowing movements, the molten rock within it constantly in motion and heat visibly coming off of it in waves. I had thought until now the Lillem infection was something to worry about, the strength of the stone and metal Lillem daunting, and the poisonous nature of the Ruby Lillem something to fear, but this was something else entirely. How could mere soldiers, or even someone with powers like myself, fight an element incarnate? Unless of course that someone was the master of that element, like the Vile Emperor was with lava, or master of the opposite element, like Kaji with ice.

A spike of ice formed impossibly on the cavern floor, reaching upwards and through the lava Lillem. Immediately following the first, another spike of ice formed, thicker than a man, to impale the lava Lillem through the middle. On and on the spikes formed, replacing those that melted, and slowly but surely the lava hardened until the Lillem turned to solid stone, which was then attacked in force by Deathsquad soldiers until the lifeless rubble was no longer a threat.

"Kaji?" I questioned, struggling to my feet.

"Yeah," a Kaji-clone appeared by my side to help me to my feet. "I seem to have gotten separated from Bastion, but I have a good bunch of soldiers with me from his squad and others, and we'd be happy to guard the group of you if you'd like to move further in."

"What is Lady Lilyth?" Yue asked, walking quickly to keep up with the Vile Emperor's steady pace. "Is she a Chosen, like us?"

They were climbing a steep and narrow path, coiling around the inside of somewhere deep inside the volcano. The Lillem still came before them, but the Vile Emperor made quick work of the creatures, and behind them the Deathsquad soldiers led by Masaru and Bastion continued to hold the rest of the monsters at bay. Yue had found she hadn't needed to use her much larger and fiercer demon form in some time, being so well guarded from either side, and so she figured it was time she spent her energy on getting much needed answers.

"Well?" she pressed.

"She is more than a Chosen and at the same time less than that," the Vile Emperor stated cryptically.

"You defeated her the first time, didn't you? What happened? How is it she's still alive now?"

Stony silence greeted her as the Vile Emperor tossed an approaching metal Lillem off their ledge. Yue watched it fall several stories into the lava pit far below. Perhaps it was a trick of the light, but from here the lava gleamed dully red as it pulsed and boiled, looking more like liquid Ruby than molten rock.

"You have to give me something. I can tell you don't want to share, but if we're facing what I fear we are then I need to know."

"Ask your question, then." The Vile Emperor stopped suddenly and turned his helmeted head to face her.

"Is she Rubia?" Yue whispered, despite herself. "Are we facing a gem god?"

"Would my answer change what we have to do?" The Vile Emperor gave away nothing, not a single hint. If it were true, Yue would never know. "I will return when the body and soul are reunited."

"What? What do you mean, 'return'?"

The Vile Emperor leapt from the ledge upon which they stood. In mid-air, he changed his leap into a dive and began plummeting head-first toward the roiling lava far below.

"Bastion's squad, to me!" I heard Masaru's voice over the din of battle and the savage screams of the Lillem. "We clear this ramp and hold the line!"

The small relief I felt at knowing he was nearby and still holding strong was almost taken away by the shock of having Bastion arrive as one of the wounded brought in by Oka's squad members.

"I don't think I need to stress that this one has to survive," the man said, lowering Bastion before me. The Ruby City had lost enough Generals this night and likely during this whole affair. This Deathsquad – for that's what he was, even if he didn't wear the armour – didn't want to see yet another of their leaders lost to this war.

"I'll see what I can do."

"Nooo!" Akuma's screams split the air, bringing the battle to a screeching halt. "No, you can't do this!"

She dove from the ledge and I looked up in time to see Kaji dive after her. I stood, forming wings to get some height, and watched them both fall toward the boiling ruby-coloured lava below.

Before they could reach it, however, the boiling lava fell impossibly still, and Kaji formed a clone of himself on its surface to catch Akuma and break her fall. She landed in his arms, the lava beneath now miraculously transformed into a solid lake of Ruby.

Fighting her way free of Kaji's grasp, Akuma threw herself at the precious stone and rammed it repeatedly with her fists.

All around me, and on each and every level of the temple, the Lillem froze and then fell, crumbling immediately into the base materials that formed them, as if Akuma had somehow disabled them all with her voice. We would all later learn, however, that the Lillem had been vanquished by some feat of the Vile Emperor's as he dove into what would come to be known as the 'Lillem Heart'.

Though, as providential as the destruction of the Lillem Heart and the subsequent eradication of the Lillem forces was, from my perspective the miracle came just a moment too late.

"Somebody help me!" I screamed at the top of my lungs, diving to reach Rama's side nearly at the instant of the Ruby Lillem's final attack, before it, too, fell with the rest. My power activated, causing my hands to glow with a cyan light as I willed him to hold on just a little bit longer. "I won't let you die like this!"

CH. 10 – You Will Be Missed

It had been a grueling night of using my power to try and keep Rama alive while Oka picked Ruby out of his veins, one piece at a time. Regardless, all of us were expected to attend the memorial service.

I had never seen so many people gathered in such silence. People from all walks of life in the Ruby City gathered respectfully and so did those of us who had formerly been considered enemies. Such differences seemed negligible in the face of the trials we had overcome together and the losses we shared, and we all came together to watch the sun set peacefully for the first time in nearly eight hundred years.

"Lady Mikura was well loved," Akuma spoke from the raised platform, hastily erected on one end of the courtyard. "For over eight hundred years she lived among us, protecting us with her power, entertaining us with her endless optimism, and making us feel as if we, too, could stay young forever.

"But the truth is that we can't. All things must one day come to an end and even those of us who have been termed 'immortal' aren't really – our time will come and all we can hope is that we've made a difference and we will be remembered. I believe that Mikura, as a friend, a General, and a leader, has made a difference in all of us and there is no one who did not benefit in some way from having known her.

"Mikura would have been proud of what we accomplished last night and she would have celebrated our victory in high spirits. It saddens me greatly that she is not here today to share in the freedom we have won for ourselves, but in her memory and in the memory of all who fell in the fight for freedom, I declare a day of rest. Until this time tomorrow, the Ruby City will celebrate what we have accomplished and we will remember the sacrifices that have been made on our behalf!"

I half-expected a cheer to break out, but that wasn't how things were done in the Ruby City. Instead, each and every person, whether they were a part of the army or not, gave the salute I was used to seeing from Deathsquad soldiers, rapping their fists just once against their chests or shields, if they had them.

I had only recently begun to accept Mikura as a friend, but the pain of losing her settled itself into my heart and I could only imagine what those who had known her better must be feeling. Especially Akuma and the remaining Generals, of which there were not many, who had known her for presumably hundreds of years.

"There is one other matter we must see to," Akuma added. "Bastion?"

"It is time we publicly thank the Chosen of Sapphiros for returning Lady Mikura's squad to the Ruby City after the incident in Taiyou," Bastion spoke formally. "We are grateful for the service you have done us and because of this we are able to see that Captain Grinkin and his men are not left without leadership at this sad time. Captain Grinkin, would you join me?"

The Deathsquad Captain separated from where the rest of Mikura's squad stood and climbed up onto the raised platform, his helmet carried under one arm and tears flowing unabashedly down his scarred face.

"And Lady Kichigai," Bastion continued, "would you join me also?"

With solemn steps, Kichigai made her way to stand at Bastion's side.

"The Lady Kichigai lost the majority of her squad while defending against our enemies," Bastion announced, "and Captain

Grinkin's squad has been left without a General. It is the will of the Empress that Lady Kichigai is presented to Captain Grinkin for his approval and, should he agree, the two squads will become one under Lady Kichigai's leadership."

"It won't bring her back," Kichigai murmured, "but we can fight Lilyth and avenge Lady Mikura, together."

"You would do that for us?" Grinkin asked.

Kichigai nodded. "Mikura was my friend, too. With your permission, Captain Grinkin? Squad! Form up and find your partners."

"Buddy up!" Captain Grinkin seconded and Mikura's Deathsquad – now Kichigai's, I supposed – paired off into groups of two as they once had done under Mikura's 'buddy-system'.

"And those of you who are missing your 'buddy,' I'm sure there are some in my squad who can fill that gap in our ranks," Kichigai continued. "Deathsquad, you are dismissed. I'll see you for training immediately following the rest day."

The soldiers saluted her before doing as she had commanded and dispersing. Their leaving seemed to be the signal for everyone else to depart; the day of rest had begun.

"You can go back to your own room now, you know," Oka commented dryly as we reached the doors to his laboratory and he hesitated to place his hand on the panel that would cause them to whoosh open.

"You're right," I agreed. "I'd just like to be there when he wakes up so I can prove it to myself that he's going to be fine."

"Suit yourself, but the same rules apply: no visitors allowed. You can come in because for the time being you're technically an honorary member of my squad, but no one else – unless they're dying, or coming in to be dissected."

I smiled slightly despite myself. "Understood."

The double doors whooshed aside at Oka's command; the scientist's lab was very similar in construction to the military base that was the Temple of Sapphire far to the south, but here in the Ruby Palace everything seemed at the same time more advanced and more archaic. The walls were rough stone and some of the medical treatments almost primitive, but Oka's science experiments and the larger portion of his machinery were beyond anything I'd ever heard of.

"I'm sure you know where to find him," Oka commented, heading toward an off-shoot hallway away from the main lab. "I have something I need to see to."

Of course I knew where to find Leon; he was exactly where I had left him on Oka's operating table in the center of the lab's main room, but upon seeing him again I realized something was wrong. His limbs were twitching erratically, their motions only growing more frantic by the minute, and there was something achingly familiar about the unconscious spasms that tugged at my memory – where had I seen this before?

"Oka!"

"What is it?" Oka hadn't gotten far in the moments it took me to piece my fears together, but he stopped dead when he took in what I was witnessing. "Oh, dear," he murmured, almost contemplative, despite my distress, "that's not good."

"What's happening to him?"

"Arocoth, or Zai-Aku," Oka confirmed my suspicions with a frown of displeasure, "I knew they'd come home eventually, but they're supposed to get permission before selecting a host. This is against the rules and they know it."

"Can you stop them?" I asked, believing Oka had to know more about the Talons than I did – they were a creation of the Vile Emperor after all; it was even possible that they were created in this very lab.

"Stop them? No, I don't think that's possible." Oka pursed his lips. "Once they take hold there's no going back."

"That's not true," I told him, feeling my panic rise as I watched Leon continue to thrash about – I hadn't spent all night saving him just to have his body stolen by one of Talons. "The Vile Emperor released our friends from Earth, which is how both Zai-Aku and Arocoth are bodiless now. It has to be possible."

"If it is, I don't know about it. The Talons were always Verasheen's pet project. I hardly ever had anything to do with them, beyond occasionally helping to store their spirits between bodies. It might be possible to coerce them to give up on this body before they take hold completely, but I would need a container to trap them in. Otherwise, once they were freed they might just try for the nearest warm-blooded individual, which could very much end up being me or you."

"A container? You said you've stored them before, don't you have one?"

"As a matter of fact I don't. Verasheen always took them away afterwards and don't even think of asking me where he hid them, because I have no idea. What I do know is that I'd need a sizeable chunk of Ruby and it's gotta be the good stuff, not like the crap those Ruby Lillem were made out of."

"Where would I get that?"

"Well, that's the issue now, isn't it?" he answered absently, partially ignoring me in favour of examining Leon and strapping him down to the table in an effort to make him be still. "The other way of dealing with this is to simply let your friend become a Talon. There are worse fates, and he would gain access to great power and several lifetimes of knowledge."

"No," I stated forcefully. "I won't let it happen."

"Suit yourself. Either way, I'll need the Ruby sooner rather than later if there is to be a chance of succeeding in this. Normally, I'd suggest Akuma – she's got a way with the stuff and might be able to find you some – but she's got her hands full at the moment and I wouldn't recommend bothering her."

"I think I can do better. I'll come back with the Ruby you need, just do what you can to buy us some time."

I didn't bother waiting for Oka's response before sending myself to Masaru as mist. I arrived, becoming fully solid in our room, to find that Masaru, Kaji, and Hotaru were all present and awake, though much like me they looked as if they hadn't slept since the night before.

"I'm sure he's going to be all right, Kaji," Masaru was saying. "Yukari knows what she's doing and she wouldn't still be up there if she didn't think she could save him."

"He is going to be all right," I answered, startling all three of them.

"Can I see him?" Hotaru asked.

I grimaced, remembering Leon thrashing about on the operating table, his body subconsciously trying to fight off possession by one of the Talons. "Not just yet, no. Besides, Oka doesn't allow visitors into his lab."

"But you're allowed in there," Hotaru pointed out.

"Yes, but right now he needs me to help Sir Rama, and speaking of which, there's something I need you all to help me with. Leon's life depends on it."

Somewhat reluctantly, I explained the current dilemma as briefly as possible. "So I need to bring Oka that Ruby egg we found in the museum. If he can get it open, he can use the Ruby shell to trap the Talon once he gets it out of Leon."

"That's a lot of ifs," Masaru pointed out. "Isn't there something else Oka can use? We know how difficult those eggs are to get open."

"What about Sapphire?" Kaji questioned.

"It's one of the precious stones, so it might be the same," I answered. "Why? Do you have access to a store of Sapphire I don't know about?"

"I have some," Kaji responded, pulling the sword at his side out of its sheathe and showing me the thin Sapphire blade.

"Where did you get that?"

"I made it," Kaji answered, "but it took quite a bit of effort and I don't know if I could make it in the quantity Oka would need. I certainly can't make something the size of that egg yet."

"Well, we can keep that in mind if Oka can't get the egg open, but for now would you mind helping me get it back to the lab?"

Masaru and Kaji nodded, but as we turned to leave I realized Hotaru had given no indication that she was coming with us. "What about you, Hotaru?"

Hotaru's face settled into a particularly mulish expression. "I'm going to go see Rama. Oka can't keep me out forever."

I shook my head, but I didn't have the time to waste in persuading her; that was up to Oka now.

We made quick time getting to the museum, and by waving my arms about in polite Kumori I was able to convince the guard that I had permission from the Empress to enter. The fifth floor was as I remembered it, with not a thing out of place except for what we had moved and our footprints in the thick dust on the floor.

"You've got to be kidding me," Masaru spoke from over where I knew the Ruby egg to be hidden, "this thing weighs a ton."

Kaji frowned. "How did you expect us to get this all the way back to Oka's lab, exactly?"

"Not a problem, I just need you to be able to lift it and I'll handle getting us back to the lab."

I had discovered inadvertently that it was possible for me to take others along with me when I projected myself as mist, and considering that whatever articles they had on their person also seemed to come with them also, then it stood to reason I should be able to take this with me as well. The only problem was I had never tried something like this and if should I fail it would be a long walk back to the museum to try again.

I would just have to get it right the first time. "Okay, pick up the egg between you and I'll mist us out of here."

I concentrated, feeling for the life forces before me. Masaru's was known to me, as was Kaji's, but I distinctly felt there was another present; it was weaker than the first two, but still decidedly human. So the person in the egg was still alive, preserved for who knows how long. Perhaps, if we were lucky, we would soon find out who had been imprisoned and tucked away for safekeeping.

I willed the four of us to return to Oka and was pleased to note when I opened my eyes that we were back in the lab before a confused-looking Oka and the Ruby egg with its unknown prisoner was still very much with us. Kaji and Masaru gratefully lowered the massive egg to the floor.

"I thought I said no visitors," Oka complained and I realized I had caused us to appear in one of the other, smaller labs, one I hadn't yet seen and which contained something I hadn't been expecting.

"Is that Mikura?" Kaji questioned, looking at the glass tube embedded into the wall.

In fact, this room was lined with tubes, much like the cryogenics bay in the Temple of Sapphire, but in this case only one of the tubes seemed to be in use. The floor to ceiling glass structure was lit up and had thick wires coming from it that draped across the floor to various terminals on the opposite wall. Within it floated a familiar face attached to a perfectly formed young body.

"Not exactly," Oka replied. "It's her body, I'm attempting to make repairs to see if I can revive her. Unfortunately, there's a lot of ancient script to muddle through and even if I am successful she'd never be exactly who she was, but I'll do what I can."

"Not to sound rude or anything," Masaru began, "but why bother? If it wouldn't be her, anyways, I mean. Would it not be better to let her go in peace?"

"Not only was Mikura well loved by nearly everyone who knew her, but she was also a very powerful ally. If I can bring some semblance of her back, I will."

"About the egg, Oka," I said, bringing us back on topic, "do you think you can open it?"

Oka's eyes widened, taking in the egg for the first time. "Where did you get that?"

"The museum," Kaji responded. "By the amount of dust in that place I gather it's been there for quite some time."

"Likely since Lady Lilyth's reign," I pointed out. "Is it enough Ruby for your purposes?"

"More than enough," Oka answered, "but I haven't seen one of these in centuries, and from what I remember they're supposed to be impenetrable. They're the Lady's perfect storage system. She puts someone in there and they stay there until she's ready to dispose of them."

"We got out of them," Kaji pointed out, "and so did thirty or so others, so it's not impossible."

"Oh yeah?" Oka asked. "How did you do it? If I can recreate the conditions then we might be talking."

"Well, we're pretty sure we got out because the eggs can't hold Chosen indefinitely," I answered, "but the others were sort of Machalite's doing."

"A gem god?" Oka questioned. "Oh that's great. I'll just get right on that and ask Rubia for a favor. No, I'm sorry, but there's nothing I can do, your friend is going to become a Talon."

"Who's going to become a Talon?" Yue asked, appearing suddenly in our midst with no rational explanation for how she had accomplished it or how she had known to find us here.

"No one, provided we can get this egg open," I answered.

"Another one?" Oka commented. "How did you get in here when I've kept the doors sealed to keep that other girl out?"

"Oh, that reminds me," Yue said and Hotaru appeared beside her. "I told Hotaru I'd get her in here."

"Chosen." Oka rolled his eyes.

Hotaru got her footing remarkably quickly following her sudden appearance in the lab, and ignoring us all, she strode between Kaji and Masaru, intent on the doorway through which Leon could be seen. Turning my head to watch her, I realized that Leon was now still and I found myself wondering if that was a good sign or a bad one, and then I decided I didn't exactly want to know.

"So, this is the egg you want opened?" Yue asked. "Any idea who's inside of it? Yuko Seig, perhaps?"

"Yuko Seig's in the Splitter," I answered tiredly, beginning to really feel the exhaustion that should have knocked me down hours ago. "Can you help us or not, Yue?"

"As a matter of fact, I think I can," Yue answered cryptically, folding herself into a cross-legged position on the floor before the egg. "Stand back, everyone."

Kaji and Masaru did as they were told, while Oka and I simply watched from where we stood with similar skeptical expressions. Yue closed her eyes and her head slumped onto her shoulders as a glowing bird made of cyan light like my arrows appeared in front of her.

It was the approximate size and shape of a raven and despite the obvious fact it was born of the power of a Chosen, it looked and moved in a very lifelike fashion, preening its wings with its beak before facing the rest of us with an intense expression. The bird tilted its head toward the egg as if to say 'watch this', before flapping its wings just once to hop onto the oval-shaped Ruby.

I was at a loss to guess what Yue intended to do with her bird that would help us get the egg open, but the bird didn't seem to hesitate, stepping carefully and pecking at the surface of the Ruby, almost as if looking for weak spots. Then it stopped and looked at us, before diving its beak downwards in a sudden motion. Its head passed through the Ruby like it was simply ducking under water. The bird's dive lasted no more than a moment, but as it disappeared I abruptly recalled what had happened to Leon when he had tried similarly passing through a Ruby egg to get to the person within.

"Yue!" Yue's entire body went limp and she crumpled to the floor before I could catch her, but while I was focused on Yue, with my back to the Ruby egg, I was surprised to hear a definite cracking sound. Whatever Yue had done, she had managed to split the egg in two. Masaru, Kaji, Oka, and I found ourselves staring at two perfect halves of a Ruby shell laying open on the floor in the center of the room.

"Where's the body?" Oka asked. "Isn't there usually a body inside these things?"

The egg lay empty – Yue must have…

"Ugh." Yue began to stir in my arms. "I'm certainly not going to try that again anytime soon. That was awful."

"Yue, did you –?" Kaji began.

"Yep, I got him…or her, whoever it was," Yue stated. "I have them in my Noh-space. Where do you want 'em?"

"Are you all right?" I asked.

"Yeah, I've just got a massive headache, that's all," she answered, getting to her feet. "I'll do better next time."

"I thought ye said ye weren't going to try that again soon?" Masaru asked.

"Yeah, well with all the eggs out there, I'm probably going to have to, you know?"

There was nothing to be said to that. If Yue had indeed found a reliable way to free the victims of the eggs, then she was sure going to have to use it. She could only hope that with practice it might become easier on her.

Oka directed Yue to yet another room in his lab, one that had a proper bed onto which she could dump the egg's mystery occupant. We all followed along behind, eager to get a look at who it might be, but were quickly ushered out by Oka once we learned he was unconscious and likely to stay that way for a while, similar to how the others had been when they were freed in the Temple of Machalite. All I managed to glimpse of the egg's occupant was fiery red-orange hair and strong facial features with a square jaw. It was no one I knew and for decency's sake we left him alone as he had come out of the egg without any clothes.

Whoever it was and whatever their story, it was time to get to work. Oka's plan was rash and highly unscientific, but it was the only one we had and time was running out, if it hadn't already done so.

Hotaru was crying fiercely by the time we reached her side, with Oka ordering Kaji and Masaru to move the egg halves into the main room.

"I'm going to use them as they are," he informed us. "There's no time to fashion them into anything else, and if you two are quick enough we shouldn't have any problems. Now, I'm only going to say this once and I expect everyone to obey: if the Talon should happen to decide to possess one of us, the rest of us will ensure that person is subdued if they can't immediately fight it off. Do I make myself clear?"

One by one we nodded; we knew what was at stake here.

"Good, then let us begin."

At first, my task seemed the simplest one, but once I had settled myself into position, Leon's eyes snapped open to look at me and my will faltered, leaving me wondering if I could do what Oka had asked of me.

His left eye was a startling red and there was a menace in it, but his right eye, blue and clear, was still his own. When he spoke it was with an eerie double voice, one layer belonging to Leon and the other female.

"Yukari?"

"I'm here," I told him, realizing that Zai-Aku or Arocoth, whichever Talon that female voice belonged to, hadn't completely won yet. Leon was still fighting and I was going to fight with him. "We'll get you through this, I promise."

"You can't stop us, Chosen." Leon's face contorted. "We want this one, he is ours!"

"Never," I replied defiantly and then nodded to Oka, activating my power to keep Leon alive – I wasn't about to give up now. "I'm ready."

Oka made quick work of hooking Leon up to a machine that would send electric pulses through his body, causing the Talon inside of him much discomfort while I kept Leon alive, despite the shocks to his weakened system. Oka hoped it would be enough to drive the Talon out of its chosen body, at which point we had a chance of containing it within the Ruby egg. When the process began, Leon's body rocked and bucked in a most unsettling fashion, but it became immediately clear it wasn't going to be enough to drive the Talon out.

"I need more power!" Oka called out over the clanging of the metal table shaking with the motion atop it.

"I'm on it!" Yue replied, bounding across the room to the far side and ripping a thick live wire in half with her bare hands, causing it to spark dangerously. "Where do you want it?"

Oka's jaw dropped, but he pointed mutely at the machine he was using. Taking hold of the live wire in one hand, Yue seemed miraculously unaffected by the electric current as she used her power to channel it through herself and into the air. I could tell by the arc of the electricity that Yue was aiming the current where Oka had requested, but electricity tended to react strangely around Leon Rama since he had been Knighted, almost like it was drawn to him.

He was the only person I had ever heard of who had been struck by lightning not once, but three times in rapid succession, and was perfectly fine afterwards. He had said to me once that he swore the lightning had sought him out; even while he had discarded his metal armour and had been under complete cover; it had altered its path in order to reach him – and this airborne electrical current was about to do the same.

Out of an instinct of self-preservation, I had no choice but to cease the use of my power and dive out of the way as the current struck Leon. There was a blinding flash and when my vision cleared he was no longer on the table, but standing next to Yue on the far wall, and floating above the operating table, where Leon had been no more than a second ago, were instead two familiar ghostly female forms – the Talons, Zai-Aku and Arocoth.

Recovering quickly, the spirit-forms of the two Talons rushed forward, gliding through the air toward where Kaji and Masaru waited. As Arocoth closed in on Masaru, I had an awful vision of what it might be like to lose Masaru to the Talon's permanent kind of possession, but thankfully Masaru was strong enough to raise the Ruby egg shard in his hands in time to act as a shield against her.

Kaji, on the other hand, simply activated his power, his eyes glowing cyan as he punched the incorporeal Zai-Aku and sent her spirit reeling after Arocoth into the Ruby egg half that Masaru held. A Kaji-clone then quickly picked up the other half of the egg to join the two together once more, sealing the Talons within.

"Well, I'd say that experiment was a success. Though, it was a surprise to see two of the Talons fighting over the same body. Your friend must have seemed quite a prize to them," Oka noted with only the barest hint of sarcasm as he looked about the room at the damage that had been wrought. "Now – all of you, get out my lab."

It wasn't as simple as all that, but one by one we did eventually leave Oka's lab. Yue was first, disappearing at her usual speed as soon as she was no longer needed, while Kaji and a few of his clones stayed behind to help Oka seal the Ruby egg back together, in order to ensure the Talons would not escape their makeshift prison.

My attention was focused on Leon, however. He appeared alert and in control of himself, but I could see the exhaustion in the way he stood and the sweat on his brow. There was also something in his expression that said he wouldn't just be able to laugh off this near-death experience as easily as he had laughed off some injuries in the past.

"Leon, I –" Hotaru began.

"Not now, Hotaru," he responded, his eyes dark.

"Come on, Hotaru, I'll walk back with ye," Masaru offered. "Yukari, you'll be all right?"

I nodded. "Go on, I'll follow after you in a bit."

Once they were gone, it was just Leon and I in the room, though I could hear Oka ordering Kaji about down one of the halls.

"Can we get out of here, please?" Leon spoke suddenly. "I feel like I've seen enough of these walls, but I know I've never been in this room before."

I smiled despite myself. "I can understand the sentiment. Sure, where would you like to go?"

"Anywhere but here or back to the room," he answered ruefully. "Some air would be lovely."

I had only gone a few steps when I realized that Leon was not as strong as he was making it appear by being on his feet, so I crossed the distance to him and fit myself under his arm.

"Thank you."

"Don't mention it."

We meandered at a leisurely pace through the palace hallways, having no real destination in mind and neither of us knowing the palace layout well enough to think of one.

"There," Leon said as he pointed to a curtained alcove ahead. "I've gone about as far as I'm going to for now."

"All right, hold on," I told him, letting my wings fan out behind me to give me the strength to carry us both.

The alcove in question was more of a balcony and with the red velvet curtains parted, the open-concept pillared area offered a splendid view of the city blanketed by a starry night sky. The city below was well lit, and even from way up here on the mountainside we could hear the revelers taking full advantage of the rest day. Leon and I sat wordlessly, leaning up against one of the pillars in silent companionship, for once able to appreciate the beauty of a peaceful night sky without fear that disaster would strike if we weren't alert to danger at all times.

"Are you all right?" I asked, speaking softly.

"Never better," he replied in his usual offhand manner.

"No, I mean really. How are you feeling?"

"I suppose I should thank you," he said instead. "I know what you did for me and I'm grateful. I know you could say we haven't always gotten along, you and I, but you mean a great deal to me, regardless."

He was right in saying we hadn't always seen eye to eye – we had certainly butted heads on more than one occasion – but there had never been a doubt in my mind that I would do almost anything to save his life, should it be necessary. Not just for Kaji's sake, or anyone else's, but for my own and for his. Sir Rama…no, Leon, was one of the most honest individuals I had ever met and this world would be missing something important if it were to lose him.

"I suppose all I can say to that is, you're welcome," I said after a moment. "I should probably tell you, Lady Mikura died."

"I know. I overheard Oka in the lab. She will be greatly missed."

"There's been no further sign of the Vile Emperor either," I informed him, "not since he jumped into that pool of liquid Ruby or whatever it truly was."

"I can't say I am personally too upset about that," Leon noted, "but I'm sure his people will feel the loss of his leadership."

I nodded. "It's certainly different here than we expected, isn't it?"

"I'd say."

"Leon –" I began.

"You know, you've never called me that before," he interrupted, smiling suddenly.

"I'm sorry," I apologized. "I didn't mean to presume."

"No, of course, it's fine," he replied. "My friends call me Leon. And since we're friends," he added, his smile widening, "may I get your opinion on a personal matter?"

"Go ahead."

"Well, you see, I could use a bit of advice. It's about Hotaru. You see, I've noticed certain feelings..." he started a little awkwardly, "and I was wondering...as an expert, how would you suggest I approach the matter?"

"What would give you that idea?"

"Well it's just that you and Masaru, you seem so perfect for one another and you seem genuinely happy together. How do you do it?"

"Do it?" I laughed. "It's not like that. Believe me, I was more surprised than anyone to discover how I felt about Masaru. It was nothing I did that brought us together, I just realized how I felt, finally found the courage to tell him, and was relieved to find out he felt the same way. Did you consider simply talking to Hotaru about it?"

"Of course I've thought about it, but I was hoping you might give me some indications of her feelings before I actually spoke to her. To see if she'd even consider me."

"Well, I can certainly speak to her about it on your behalf. Honestly, I'm not sure how she feels. She's been through a hard time recently – we all have."

"And that's my other issue," Leon admitted, "I *think* I have feelings for Hotaru, but I need some time to figure it all out. While everything has been keeping us so busy, there hasn't been any time. If you speak to her, can you see that she understands that and maybe when this is all over, she and I can speak about it in more detail."

"I can try," I told him. "Hotaru's not exactly the easiest person to explain things to."

"Just saying you will try means a lot," he replied, leaning his head back on the pillar behind him and turning his head to face me. "Thank you."

"So that means we're friends, then?" I asked, with a hint of a smile.

"Friends," he agreed.

"Well if that's the case, I could use some advice of my own."

"Really?" he asked, sitting up once more. "But you always seem so confident, so sure of yourself."

"Often that's simply to cover up how uncertain I feel," I admitted, "especially with regards to the kinds of decisions I've had to make lately. Tell me, what do you think we should do now? Are we still needed here or is there something else we should be doing? I mean something that might help us to feel as if we're really accomplishing something and not simply defending what's left.

"My father is still missing," I continued, wanting to explain myself and finding myself telling Leon all the worries that I'd kept inside until now. "I've been checking every day, even though I know it's not doing me any good from inside the ruby City's barrier. I can't feel him, and I worry that even out there I won't be able to sense him and know that he's alive. It eats at me."

"Yukari, I'm so sorry. I had no idea…"

"I just want to be able to find him," I confided, "not just for me, but for my mother. And the way we've just left everyone else at the Children's Outpost isn't sitting well with me, either. I know they've got the Knights and the Roughlanders to keep them safe, but it's not the same as us being there. If we're not needed in the Ruby City anymore, then perhaps it is time we returned to them."

"I hear what you're saying, and you may be right, but for now my place is here. If the Vile Emperor isn't intending to return any time soon, or can't for whatever reason, then Lady Akuma is going to need all the help she can get, and just maybe I will be able to negotiate on behalf of Taiyou and finally accomplish what I came here to do."

"So we separate, then?"

"It looks like it, but we must each make our own decisions and if you feel that you are not needed here, then you should go to where you feel you are needed most. Go, find your father. You won't forgive yourself if you don't do what your heart is telling you to."

"You're right. Thanks for the advice, Leon."

"You're welcome," he answered, his humour returning. "Now, is there any chance we can find ourselves a place to sleep?"

Acquiescing to his request, I took hold of the both of us with my power and located Masaru, then I sent us both as mist to our room in the Ruby Palace and made us both become solid so we could climb gratefully onto soft mattresses. With any luck I would speak to Akuma and the others when I awoke. Our time in the Ruby City was nearing an end.

CH. 11 – LIES AND TRUTHS

"We're leaving the Ruby City," I informed Akuma when we had gathered in the throne room the next day. "There is so much to do and we can't do any of it sealed away in here."

"I wish you luck and I would go with you if I could, but my place is here," she replied. "Do you know where you will go?"

That was the one missing element of my plan, which is to say that I didn't exactly have a plan. I was still hoping one might present itself.

"The Children's Outpost with the others, I expect," I answered hesitantly.

"Can't," Yue stated. "Ao Kouen's got the barrier up and from the outside there's no way to tell him to let us in. They're sealed off, just like they were in Taiyou."

"Has it been that bad there that they need it to stay safe?" Kaji asked.

"Don't know," she answered, "but from what I can tell the Hounds know exactly where they are, only they haven't made any move to attack yet. It's like as long as Ao Kouen and the others are penned in, they don't care enough to attack them."

"That doesn't sound very promising," Masaru noted. "It could only be a matter of time before they change their minds."

"So they need us, then," Hotaru said, "and we should go there."

"How are we supposed to do that if we can't get in?" I said. "If Ao Kouen brings the barrier down to let us in, that might be the opportunity they're waiting for."

"To the mountains of Sapphire, then?" Yue suggested. "It's close enough to the outpost and I can't see anyone guessing we'd head there. Hotaru can contact Ao Kouen through water once we're out of the Ruby City's barrier and we can lay low until we figure out our next move."

"Why is it that ye want to visit the place so bad, Yue?" Masaru asked the question I'd been pondering.

"There's something odd about that place. I'd like to get a better look at it and maybe get a second opinion while I'm at it," she answered. "Fuun wasn't exactly the best tour guide while we were there before."

"It's decided, then," Kaji determined. "We'll be leaving shortly."

"Except for me, Kaji," Leon announced. "I'll be staying to keep Lady Akuma company. That is, of course, if she'll have me."

"You are more than welcome, Sir Rama, and maybe we can finally get those negotiations underway."

"My thoughts exactly," Leon agreed with a winning smile.

When Yue let us out of her Noh-space, we discovered that the southernmost mountains were relatively cool compared to desert terrain we had grown accustomed to. It was still summer, however, as it was all over this world – or at least the side of it that had until recently seen constant sun. Most of the vegetation had long since died, with the exception of a few hardier plants and shrubs; their roots dug into clefts in the rocky ground, reaching downward for what moisture they could find.

And then, like witnessing a miracle, we came across a fountain.

"Would ye look at that," Masaru commented. "It's a wonder there're no Roughlanders who've settled here. I thought we knew where all of the sources of water were."

Although it was run down, somewhat dirty, and cracked in places, it was still running, water trickling from the stack of stones in the center as if the stone pool had simply been built around a natural spring that was still plentiful, even hundreds of years later.

"Looks like you missed one," Hotaru stated the obvious, "because this place looks deserted."

We were on the edge of what appeared to be a simple but long-abandoned village. The structures were all built of sturdy mountain stone and it was difficult to tell how long the village had stood empty. Either way, it seemed as if the villagers, whoever they had been or whenever they had lived, had left in somewhat of a hurry. There were signs everywhere of their hasty departure, including furniture and pottery simply left behind to rot.

"I'm going to go take another look around," Yue announced. "I wouldn't touch anything if I were you. Things in this village have a way of moving around when you least expect them to."

Yue disappeared after giving her somewhat cryptic warning, flashing off as usual, and the rest of us settled in around the fountain as Hotaru worked to get a hold of Ao Kouen.

"Hotaru, is that you?" Ao Kouen's voice came from the fountain's basin and his reflection could be seen on the water's surface. The King of Taiyou looked and sounded utterly exhausted.

"Yeah, it's me, and I'm here with Yukari, Kaji, and Masaru," Hotaru answered. "Well, Masaru's keeping a lookout and Yue's here too, she's just gone off to explore."

"Are you all right?" Ao Kouen asked.

"Yeah, we're fine. We were worried about you."

"We're holding," he answered vaguely. "Where are you – the Ruby City?"

"No, the mountains of Sapphire, so we're close by if you need us," Hotaru informed him. "Would it be better if we came there?"

"No, as awful as it sounds, it might be best if you stay away for the time being. The Hounds are keeping a fairly tight watch and we don't want to provoke them."

"It's all right, Ao Kouen," I told him. "We have some things we need to take care of out here for the time being, but we'll check in again –"

"Uh, Yukari, Hotaru," Masaru called our names, "I don't mean to interrupt or anything, but ye may want to turn around."

"Shhhpthhsshh..."

"It's all right, we don't mean you any harm." Yue's back was to us as she tried to placate the Stirr that was herding her back toward the fountain.

"Uh, Ao Kouen, we'll call you back later." Hotaru ended the connection with the Children's Outpost.

There were five Stirr altogether and they didn't look pleased to find us trespassing in what must be their territory. Once Yue reached us, the Stirr had us completely surrounded and it was then I noticed the difference between these Stirr and the ones I had seen before in the Ruby City – these five were unmarked. They had the same spider-like lower halves and human-looking torsos, their grayish skin darker below than on their upper halves, but these Stirr had no tattooed markings decorating them like the others I had seen.

"Shpthhsshhh shhhpphhhshh shhh..." All five Stirr spoke at once, their whispered hissing speech overlapping in a way that made it nearly impossible to separate one voice among the rest.

"We can't understand you," I told them, hoping that the communication barrier didn't go both ways.

Of the Stirr surrounding us, one stepped forward and raised his hands to silence his companions. Three of their number were women, I noticed. The fourth was an older male with black hair silvered at the temples and the one that had silenced the others seemed to be a male still in his prime.

"Shhphhhshhh..." the younger male spoke, taking the lead and holding one hand out to us.

"I'm sorry, I don't –" I began, but Yue stepped forward.

"I'm Yue," she introduced herself, "and this is Kaji, Hotaru, and Yukari. The four of us are the Chosen of Sapphiros and Masaru is our Knight."

"Shhphhhshhh..." the Stirr repeated with the exact same inflection, his hand still held out.

Yue copied the Stirr's motion, reaching out. The Stirr leaned forward until their hands were almost touching, and there on the Stirr's arm was a tiny spider, now making a beeline for Yue.

"Yue," I warned her.

"It's okay, I see it," she answered, her eyes still intent on the Stirr. "I don't think he means to harm me."

I was less assured of the fact, but nevertheless I watched as the tiny spider crossed the distance from one hand to the other, before scurrying along the length of Yue's arm while the Stirr regarded her impassively.

"*Shhpthhshh shphhthhhshhh...*" the Stirr spoke again as I lost track of the little creature in Yue's long white hair.

"Wait, what was that?" she asked, looking up at the Stirr before her with a startled expression.

"*Shhpthh shhh sphhphhth?*" the Stirr asked, raising its voice in question as it tilted its head to the side.

"Yes, I can," Yue answered it. "How is that possible?"

"*Shhhshhhthh thhhshhphhh shhh shpthhh...*"

"What's going on, Yue?" Hotaru asked.

"I can understand them," Yue replied. "It's the little spider, it's sitting in my ear and telling me what they say."

I shuddered involuntarily at the thought, even as I marveled over how it might be possible.

Hotaru, however, didn't share my aversion to such a discovery. "Really? Can I have one?"

I would have thought the Stirr would ignore her request, but one of the female Stirr stepped forward and offered her hand, and a similarly tiny spider, to Hotaru. Hotaru stepped forward to accept the offer gladly, as one of the other women offered another to me and the third to Kaji.

"No, thank you anyway," I said as I waved my hand and shook my head, "that won't be necessary."

Kaji accepted the offering stoically and Masaru only shrugged before sticking a spider to his ear – I shuddered once more.

"*Shhphhthhh shhhshhhshthhhphh shh...*" the Stirr continued. In fact, they had been speaking all along, but the whispered nature of their speech allowed it to easily fade into the background.

"But we're not like that," Hotaru protested. "We would never harm the Stirr."

"*Shh shhns Shhnd thhr shhhsts...*" I strained to follow the words of the Stirr even if I couldn't understand their meaning.

"*Thhh thhsthhphh phht thhy phhhr...*" Somewhere, deep down I knew that I was being stubborn and that accepting the tiny spider they had offered to the other was the right answer, but I simply could not bring myself to do it. "*Thhy phhhr phht thhy shhnnot unthhrshhnd.*"

"She thhr shor shmphhion is the shme." The Stirr may not have had the vocal cords to speak Japanese or English, but neither did Ris and yet somehow I could understand her; there had to be a way I could do the same for them. *"She chooses not to communicate with us because she fears that which is different from her own kind."*

"No, I don't," I responded, turning my head toward the one who had spoken. "I do not fear you or the other races I have met. One of our Knights is a Croatin, another a Kumori. I have met Stirr before you and communicated with them. Your spider is not necessary."

And it wasn't, I realized. "Humans fear what they cannot understand," I repeated the Stirr's words back to him, realizing that at some point I had begun to understand what was being said and likely I had my power to thank for it. "That's true, but they do not always destroy that which they do not understand, only what causes them to fear."

"That is the same."

"No, it isn't," Kaji spoke. "Yukari's right, fear is caused by ignorance and what is different can come to be understood. It doesn't always need to be destroyed."

"That is not what the Stirr have observed. Humans are violent, destructive, and untrustworthy. It is these traits which will lead to their eventual extinction, as they cannot co-exist with the other tribes of this world."

"That's not true of us," Hotaru argued. "We get along just fine with the Croatins, the Espearians, and the Kumori. Not all humans are like that."

"The humans burned our nests because they feared the differences between human and Stirr," he stated.

"And when was that?" Yue demanded. "Hundreds of years ago? What humans have you interacted with since then? Do you ever leave your nests and try to get to know any humans?"

"The humans that were here fled long ago and now we are diligent in keeping away any who come here. There is no need to present the Stirr to humankind. Humans cannot be trusted, your kind would say anything not to incur the wrath of the Stirr."

"And the Stirr don't lie?" Kaji asked.

"No," the Stirr stated. *"We have never seen the necessity. All Stirr are one and the same. What one Stirr knows, all Stirr know."*

"But we've never even seen the Stirr, apart from that one in the Ruby City's museum," Masaru noted. "So it seems like maybe the Stirr have based their opinions on a few small groups of people from a long time ago. Ye may be different, but ye're not all that scary, if ye don't mind me sayin' so. There's a lot scarier things out in the Sand Lakes that the Roughlanders deal with everyday. I'm fairly certain that most Roughlanders wouldn't mind havin' ye around after they had a chance to get used to ye."

"That is not what the Stirr have been told, but we find your words interesting."

"Told by whom?" I questioned, realizing that something wasn't exactly adding up here.

"The Lady Lilyth has warned us against the tribes of man," he answered. *"Her studies of humankind have been of great use to the Stirr. It has kept us from unpleasant encounters with the humans, as we have learned your habits in this way."*

"And you would trust her word rather than make observations of your own?" Yue asked. "She can lie just as easily as any human could."

"The Lady Lilyth would not lie to the Stirr."

I frowned. If we weren't careful, this could get out of hand very easily. I didn't know how I had missed it, but I hadn't considered that the Stirr could be more agents of the Lady Lilyth. They felt too neutral. I didn't feel as if they were malevolent, but I had to face the fact that they knew who they were talking to thanks to Yue's introduction, and they could bring Lady Lilyth right to us if they wanted to – or decide to destroy us themselves.

"We apologize for unwittingly trespassing on the Stirr's lands," I stated diplomatically, thinking fast. "We were simply looking for a safe place to bring refugees and we didn't know this mountain was inhabited."

"But we'd still like to stay, if you'd let us," Yue said unexpectedly. "I know that you are not inclined to trust us, but relations between humans and Stirr will never improve if you don't give us a chance."

"You speak sense," the Stirr admitted after a moment, *"and have shown no hostility in our presence, even though you are a human. Perhaps humankind can turn itself back from the brink of extinction if given the opportunity."*

"So you'll let us stay, then?" Hotaru asked.

"You may inhabit this once-human village and bring others of your tribe," the Stirr continued, *"but the Stirr will not be fooled by human tricks. No human will venture into the mountain at any time. Should a human venture beyond the light of any cavern's entrance, it will be seen as a breaking of our agreement. In addition, should any human kill any Stirr we will give humankind no more chances and do whatever it takes to eradicate humans once and for all."*

"We cannot control the action of every human," I protested. "The best we can do is inform those we bring here and those of our 'tribe', as you put it. Humans are not like the Stirr, We are individuals first and foremost, and each one of us makes our own decisions."

"You are leaders among your kind. The Stirr have heard of Chosen," he replied. *"So we will restrict the agreement to the tribe of Sapphiros at this time, but when all humans have been informed then all humans will be held to this agreement with the Stirr."*

"How did ye do that?" Masaru asked me as the Stirr were departing, heading back to the caverns that would take them to their underground homes.

"Understand the Stirr? I didn't at first, but then they suddenly became clear–"

"No, though I'd like to know how ye did that also," Masaru interjected. "How did ye talk like them?"

I'd been speaking Stirr? I tried to remember doing so, but couldn't.

"I mean, I could understand ye and all because of my little spider friend, but it was real strange to hear those sounds come out of ye, seeing as ye're a person and all."

"The Stirr are people," I pointed out.

"Ye know what I mean," he countered.

"Yes, and to answer your question I don't know how I did it, other than to say that my power provided what I needed. I wanted some way to understand the Stirr and now I have it."

"Aye, I suppose ye do," Masaru commented, shaking his head.

"Well, now that we have their permission," Yue announced, "how about we get some people to take shelter here?"

"Who do you mean, Yue?" Hotaru asked. "Ao Kouen and the others at the Children's outpost?"

"No," she answered. "I say we go to Taiyou."

"Isn't that a little dangerous?" Masaru questioned. "That place has got to be crawling with Hounds and I don't like the thought of what Lady Lilyth might do if she got her hands on any of ye."

"No, Yue's right," I said, startling everyone by agreeing with her. "As much as none of us want to face the prospect right now, Taiyou is where we are needed most. However, we don't need to just go in there blindly. I can locate anyone we might think to rescue and then send myself there as mist –"

"And alert her to your presence?" Kaji asked. "She controls Taiyou and I wouldn't be surprised if she, or one of the creatures at her disposal, had the ability to sense a Chosen's power within a certain range."

"If I find someone, I'm willing to take that chance. We can't hide forever."

Hotaru nodded, her expression grim, and eventually Kaji did as well.

"Let's do this, then," Yue decided.

"Masaru, will you watch over us and shake me awake if something appears to go wrong?" I asked, and he nodded. "Everyone sit down and hold hands. It'll make it simpler that way for me to take us all at once."

I sat and held my hands out to either side, as Hotaru, Kaji, and Yue quickly did as I instructed while Masaru turned his back to us to keep a lookout. He wasn't pleased with this plan, I could tell by his posture, but I'm sure he understood its necessity.

I started at the top of my mental list, perhaps somewhat selfishly, and I sent my thoughts out searching for my father.

There – I felt him. He seemed very far away, though undeniably in the direction of Taiyou, far to the northwest of here. He was still alive, though I couldn't quite feel the relief of that knowledge yet, not while I was so close to knowing one way or the other if I wasn't going to be too late to get him back.

I reached out and took hold of the others, then used my powers to send the four of us to Taiyou. When I opened my eyes on the other side, it was to a silent, deserted stone-walled room filled with Ruby eggs.

One of these eggs – likely the one I was nearest to – contained my father and as soon as the knowledge struck me, I made the group of us solid, bringing us fully into the room so we could be of some use.

Once fully present, I was struck with a sense of familiarity. It was not that I had been in this room before, but that I had visited many just like it. This round room, curiously without windows or openings to the outside except the one closed door, belonged in a Roughlander outpost.

The room was barren other than the Ruby eggs, and gave no indication of its prior occupants, but if this was indeed Taiyou then it was not an outpost I had ever heard of. There was only one outpost in Taiyou – or so I had been told – the Roughlander Sanctioned outpost, which any of us would have recognized on sight, having spent quite a bit of time there.

It was possible that this outpost was yet another hidden one, or that we were not quite in Taiyou but only nearby. Either way the eggs were here, including my father's, and however they had gotten here I was glad we had found them unguarded, even if only for the moment.

"Whoa," Hotaru exclaimed and I immediately shushed her. Even if we were alone with the eggs now, there was no way of knowing if someone was within earshot. Gesturing to her, I indicated she should put her ear to the door.

Yue, on the other hand, was already inspecting the eggs, seemingly counting them while Kaji made his way over to me.

"It seems we've stumbled across a storage facility," he whispered, "but we can't possibly carry so many eggs back and it would take too long to go back and forth to get them all. Do you have a better idea?"

"Well, I'm not leaving without this one," I answered, whispering in kind.

"There are twenty-two here," Yue interjected, having appeared beside Kaji in a flash, "and the eggs don't go in my Noh-space, I've tried. So unless we can figure out a way to carry them, we're going to have to free the people inside now, before we leave this place. "

"Can you do that?" I asked her. "The last time really seemed to take it out of you."

"I can do it," she answered with a mulish expression. "Only I can't take them all, I don't think. Maybe half, if I'm lucky."

"I can take three more with us," I responded, "if you three can lift one each –"

"Um, guys," Hotaru called from the doorway, "we're not alone. I hear footsteps…"

I altered my vision to see through the door, but whoever it was hadn't yet rounded the corner to be visible on the top floor's landing.

"We don't have much time," I warned the others. "Yue, get the eggs."

"Yeah, but which ones?"

And then came the hard decision: with twenty-two eggs and half to leave behind, which did we take? It was certainly a big possibility that this place wouldn't be here the next time we tried to find it; we had to decide now if we were going to free any of these people.

I closed my eyes and let my power supply me with more information. Of the life forces within the eggs, there were two that I recognized. "This one, and that one over there," I said, indicating the egg that contained my father and another across the room.

Yue abruptly plunked down, her head slumping against her shoulders as the cyan bird rose from her.

While Yue was doing her part, I continued to do mine. Of the remaining eggs, one was a strange life force signature that I didn't recognize as anything that I had yet encountered, two more were Espearian, and the rest human; I could tell no more than that.

"Yue –" I began to let her know what I had discovered, when the door burst open.

We were too late – Fuzen had arrived.

I did a double take – Fuzen? But there was no mistaking what my eyes were telling me. Lord Fuzen, Talon of the Vile Emperor, with his eye-patch over his left eye, was standing in the open doorway with his sword in his hand and a surprised expression on his face. I felt a momentary spike of fear, seeing him there and remembering all the times that his face had haunted my nightmares, but this was no nightmare and the four of us now were more than enough to handle any of the Talons now.

His hair was cut short from the time he had spent as Goji, but like Tim Harford had once again become Kai-Een, the red wave must have caused Fuzen to resurface, despite our belief that he had been defeated once and for all. It wasn't fair, but for now we had to deal with the person before us and not the friend he used to be.

"Yue, get as many eggs as you can," I ordered, not taking my eyes off of Fuzen. "Hotaru, Kaji – we're leaving, now."

"Wait," Fuzen called, his expression softening rather than settling into the sneer I expected. "I'm not here to stop you – we only hoped, but did not know that you lived."

I heard the faint but unmistakable whine of a Skyraider overhead. So, Fuzen was trying to stall and wait for reinforcements; how typical.

I narrowed my eyes suspiciously but kept quiet. Hotaru was backing up towards me and I could feel Kaji's presence behind me; all I was waiting on was Yue's go ahead and I would take us far from this place without a backwards glance.

"I've been guarding these eggs on behalf of the Resistance in Taiyou," Fuzen continued. "I know you have no reason to believe me, but I would appreciate it if you gave me the chance to explain – things are different now."

The whining sound of the Skyraider overhead was repeated, only much closer and louder now, and after a moment a second whine indicated that another had passed by.

"You're just stalling, aren't you?" I demanded and then my argument fell flat as I took note of the genuine surprise on Fuzen's usually stern features. He hadn't been expecting to hear that sound. "They aren't yours?"

"No. The Skyraiders that were in Taiyou have both been missing since the fall. I thought perhaps that they had been destroyed."

"Get down!" Kaji yelled and I became aware of a booming sound, reminiscent of gunfire.

I dropped to the floor as the room filled with light and sound, then the roof above our heads exploded in a shower of debris.

"Yue!" I screamed over the sudden increase in noise and wind. "The eggs!"

"I've got as many as I'm going to!"

That was all I needed to hear. Closing my eyes to shut out the chaos around me, I felt for the life forces in the room and took hold of them all – Fuzen included – there being no time to pick and choose which ones I wanted.

I had half-hoped that somehow my power would allow me to take all of those still imprisoned within the eggs, but I quickly discovered that that wasn't the case when we materialized back with Masaru by the trickling fountain. The four of us and Fuzen found ourselves arrayed about a bewildered-looking Masaru.

As for the eggs we had left behind, we could only hope that their indestructible nature would keep the people within unharmed until we could locate them again.

"What's he doing here?" Masaru asked, gesturing to Fuzen.

"It's a long story," I answered, "but we're just going to have to keep an eye on him."

"I assure you there will be no need for that," Goji's voice spoke inexplicably from behind me and I whirled about to find that Fuzen's features had softened into those of the much younger looking school student council president.

"Goji?" Kaji questioned. "Is that really you?"

"I'm in here," Goji answered, "but so is Fuzen. It's complicated, I know, but it's true."

I wasn't convinced, and I'm sure my expression said as much.

"Yukari, hear me out okay?" he asked and I gestured for him to go on. "Fuzen saved me and this isn't the first time, either. Even after I became myself again, he was still there in the background, even if I wasn't ready to admit it before. I never told any of you this, but when Hotaru was trying to bring me back to this world from Earth I wouldn't have made it if it wasn't for Fuzen.

"I was in a bathroom," he continued, "and there was water everywhere because Hotaru had me turn on the sink for her powers to work. A member of the Yakuza showed up and came at me with a knife. I needed something to defend myself with, and I swear I wouldn't have been able to see it myself because of my missing eye, but Fuzen in the mirror pointed it out to me. He gave me the hint I needed to reach for the live wire to my left," Goji said as he reached out with his left hand, "and when I came through to this world, it was Fuzen that pulled me through. Hotaru, I know you were trying, but I don't think that your power was enough to do it. I already had a link to this place though – through Fuzen – and I took it. I wanted to come back here pretty badly."

I frowned, considering this. I had learned since coming here not to discount anything as impossible, especially where magic and a person's spirit were concerned, but it didn't seem likely to me that Fuzen would have helped Goji here out of the goodness of his heart, if that was indeed what had happened.

"And that was enough to make you trust him?" I questioned, genuinely curious.

"Not exactly, no," he answered. "We've come to an understanding, Fuzen and I. You see, we're both in a peculiar circumstance now, his consciousness and mine being stuck in the same body. I can't exactly kick him out and he can't just leave, unless of course I die, but I would prefer that didn't happen."

"And I don't know if that would kill me now, as well," Fuzen added, his thick European accent indicating the switch. "I've never experienced anything like this before."

Goji grimaced. "Yes, he can do that and I can do the same to him. It's taken some getting used to. But as I was saying, Fuzen woke up again as the red wave hit Taiyou, and for the past few weeks we've been hiding and helping smuggle eggs out from under Lady Lilyth's nose. Fuzen couldn't have done it without me. He needed me to stay under her radar. Fuzen is detectable by her power, but Goji isn't," Goji somewhat confusingly referred to himself in the third person, "so we made a deal, and so far we've both managed to stay alive."

However it had come about, or whatever Fuzen's intentions, I couldn't deny the evidence before me. Fuzen and Goji were one now, sharing the same body at the same time, like they hadn't been before.

"How are things in Taiyou?" Kaji asked, changing the subject. "We haven't really heard anything."

"I can't tell you much," Goji answered. "We've spent most of our time hiding, but I can tell you that as far as I know Lady Lilyth is still very much present. Her Hounds and Lillem infect the city, and from all accounts she has seated herself upon the throne of Taiyou and does not leave the palace.

"There is a resistance force. They're mostly underground, but they have numbers. Other than her army terrorizing the people with their presence, we've been fortunate so far that the citizens are largely left alone. It seems that she's content to simply rule the city, but from what I hear it's not nearly so civilized out in the countryside. She's got the Hounds ranging out to try and take control of the outlying provinces. And before you ask, the only one I've really heard anything about is Rama. They're holding their borders, but it's only a matter of time before she concentrates her efforts there and they will be overrun."

"So that's what you were doing, then?" Hotaru asked. "Working with the resistance?"

"I was guarding the eggs. We didn't have any way of opening them to see what they contained, but the way the Hounds were hoarding them indicated that they were pretty important."

"They're people," Yue answered. "People with magic in them, mostly, and speaking of which, I'm going to let the ones I grabbed from that outpost out now."

"So you got what ye went for, then?" Masaru asked. "I was beginning to wonder."

Yue made the people she carried in her Noh-space appear more or less all at once and in as dramatic a way as possible, flourishing her arms to either side. One moment there was only the group of us and the next there were twelve unconscious forms scattered around us on the rocky ground.

I examined each of them quickly, making them as comfortable as possible, but internally my mind was churning through the facts I had at my disposal and by the time my task was complete I had come to a decision of sorts. I didn't have to like the new Goji/Fuzen arrangement, but I was sure as hell going to make use of it.

"Fuzen," I began.

"Yes, Yukari," the accented voice responded as Fuzen's eye locked with mine. "You have questions?"

"Yes, I do," I answered firmly, "and I think you understand that if I am to believe your change of heart, then I will expect them to be answered."

"Let me first begin by explaining that I have not exactly had a 'change of heart', as you put it. It is simply that it is in my best interests at this time to 'change sides', as it were. I hold no ill will towards Goji and since he sides with you, then so will I."

"Fine," I agreed. "I only really have one thing that I must know and I think that you might agree that you owe us all an explanation: what really happened that night? More accurately, why did all of this happen? Were you simply following the Vile Emperor's orders when you cornered us in that park, or did you have some other reason for the things you did on Earth?"

"Ah," Fuzen said as he nodded slowly, showing that he understood exactly what I was asking him, "I can tell you what I know of Earth, but I must warn you that it is likely not what you were looking to hear."

"Tell me."

"Very well," he agreed, taking a deep breath. "As Talons, we have the unique ability to travel vast distances. As long as we are not tied to a body, we can go almost anywhere in search of one. Even with only one Splitter it is a simple matter to journey to your world, and so because of this the Emperor chose us for a very important task. We were to go to Earth, find the Chosen of Rubia there, and taking hosts near to her, so she would be more willing to trust us. However, we quickly found that there were…complications…

"There is more than one Chosen here," Arocoth noted, the thin and androgynous black -haired Talon coming up behind the other three who had already gathered on the rooftop of Shinjuku district's hospital. "I detect five."

"What are the odds of that?" Kai-Een demanded, narrowing his eyes in displeasure.

"I'd say that the reason we were sent here is starting to make just a little more sense," busty, red-haired Zai-Aku commented, her focus less on the others and more on the people passing by far below as they went about their business.

"It is none of our concern as long as they do not interfere," Fuzen told the rest of them in a tone that brooked no discussion. "We have located the one that matches the description that we were given and none of the others have the feel of Rubia's power."

"But we'll have to make sure that they can't interfere, won't we?" Kai-Een asked. "We don't want those other Chosen getting in our way."

"We'll take care of the Chosen when the time comes," Fuzen replied. "If they are who I think they are, then our master will no doubt want to hear about them. Have you located your targets as we discussed?"

Fuzen received nods from both Zai-Aku and Arocoth. "Is there a problem, Kai-Een?"

"No," Kai-Een responded with only a hint of petulance, "it's just that it would have made our choices much easier if it weren't for those other Chosen. That one, Kaji, is too close."

"I admit that due to their proximity to the one we are here for, they would have made ideal candidates," Fuzen agreed, having had thoughts along similar lines himself. "Yes, it is a shame, but we must deal with the situation before us. Claim your hosts We will contact our master tonight and then we will deal with the Chosen of Sapphiros."

"And so we did," Fuzen continued his narration, speaking to a larger audience now that Hotaru, Kaji, and Yue had gathered around partway through, leaving Masaru to keep watch over those we had rescued. "As you can see, we had been sent to Earth to retrieve the one you call Shuzhue, who is now Lady Akuma to us. We chose hosts among her fellows so that when she came back with us as she must do, then she would at least be surrounded by those familiar to her."

"So what happened, then?" Hotaru asked, leaning in, thoroughly engrossed in the story.

"We contacted our master through the Ruby Splitter and informed him of our progress. We believed you four to be a threat to our mission and so we set about to lay a false trail so you would not think to come after us…"

The Chosen of Rubia had been successfully transported through the Splitter. Their mission was now complete, only there was one last detail to take care of before they could return home with their new bodies and they would have to be particularly careful tangling with not just one Chosen, but four.

Fuzen tore a few strips of cloth from the girl's — no, his lady's — school uniform and let it fall into the hole he had dug in the box of sand before him, kicking the dirt with his boot to cover it.

Hopefully this, combined with the other articles of her clothing he had left behind in the places she had visited this day, would be enough to convince the Chosen that the girl they had known had fallen victim to some haphazard crime common to this world and, after seeing the evidence, they would look no further.

It was, of course, possible that they would see through his ruse, or use their power in some way to uncover the truth of the matter, but there was a backup plan in place should it become necessary...

"It was a trap, then," Kaji stated, his expression dark and his eyes darker, remembering that awful night and the pain he had felt upon finding his girlfriend's belongings scattered in that lonely sandbox and wondering what had become of her, "and her phone?"

"To lure you," Fuzen answered with no indication he felt any remorse. "We chose a location we were certain you would pass and called the device ourselves so you would find the clues we had laid."

"You bastard —" Kaji began, but I put a hand up to forestall him. I still wanted to hear what else Fuzen could tell us.

"We had no other choice," Fuzen stated. "We studied our targets closely. We knew how close the four of you were to Lady Akuma and we couldn't risk you following after her. But you did it anyway, though I cannot claim to understand how that was possible without access to your own Splitter."

"Yuko Seig took control of the Splitter the Vile Emperor was using long enough to allow us to pass through," I explained, remembering the way the pillar of light behind the Vile Emperor had turned from red to blue.

But Fuzen only shook his head. "Whether she did or not, you would have needed two Splitters to make the passage between worlds. It should not have been possible."

"But if that's true, then how did the Vile Emperor show up in the park?" Hotaru asked. "Wouldn't he have had to be using two Splitters to do that and to kidnap Shuzhue in the first place?"

"Lady Akuma has always had a way with the Splitters, and Ruby in general," Fuzen responded. "Perhaps her power made it possible for her, I do not know, but as for the Emperor he was never actually on your planet. Consider his appearance to have been a reflection of sorts cast by the Splitter."

"A projection?" I questioned, aghast, remembering how the Vile Emperor had summoned lava to destroy us — had it all been an image, then, only as real as a mirage? "Do you mean to say that he wasn't really there?"

"He was and he wasn't." Fuzen shrugged. "Certainly he was not fully present and therefore not at his full power. It was a gamble taking on the four of you."

"We didn't have our power then," Hotaru pointed out, "at least we didn't know that we did."

"I know that now, but at the time we thought that you were simply concealing your strength, so we took what precautions we felt were necessary."

I spent some time mulling over this and everything else Fuzen had told me. Some time later, Goji's voice interrupted my thoughts.

"So, do you believe me, then?"

I sighed, glancing his way and subconsciously examining his face for a sign that Fuzen was there too, watching and listening. "I believe you."

"But?"

"But it's going to take some getting used to. I don't trust Fuzen," I stated, figuring that it was no secret, "and it's a hard thing to consider you an enemy or him a friend. You're both now, whether I like it or not."

"I see." Goji nodded. "Regardless, as a friend, can I ask a favour?" I nodded. "Please don't tell Mifa any of this until I've had a chance to speak to her myself. I don't know if she'd be able to accept me like this, so for now it's best if she doesn't even know I'm even alive."

CH. 12 – THE GREAT RED WAVE

66 It seems that the Stirr are perhaps being lied to," I informed Ao Kouen, speaking into the softly gurgling fountain, "but they've agreed to give us warning should Lady Lilyth threaten us here and due to their forthcoming nature, there is no reason to doubt their word."

"So you'll be staying there for now, then?" he asked, sounding tired beyond belief.

"Yes, though I'm sure we'll be coming and going from here, rather than staying put."

"Yukari!" Masaru called my name

"Go on," Ao Kouen suggested. "I think I've got the gist of it now and you can always get Hotaru to contact me again if you need to."

"Thanks," I answered and stood as Ao Kouen's image faded from the water's surface to Hotaru's goodbye.

"I didn't mean to interrupt ye, but I thought maybe ye should have a look at this," Masaru said as I reached him, indicating what lay at his feet.

I stared at the robotic Binoid for a full minute, wondering how I possibly could have missed him – or it, I suppose – on my first examination of those we had brought here and then I remembered how distracted I had been by thoughts of the Goji/Fuzen situation.

"Is that what I think it is?" Goji asked, coming over to join us.

I nodded. "It's a Binoid, I recognize it from the reinforcements Lord Hex sent. I'm not sure why or how it was imprisoned in an egg, but we're somewhat fortunate that it was. It's got long range communication in it, I'm certain of it. If we can get it working, we should be able to contact Hex in a way that even Lady Lilyth can't sense or track."

"Lord Hex is the one you have connections with, right?" Goji asked. "The one with the outpost nearest to the city of Taiyou?" I nodded in agreement. "All right then, what are we waiting for?"

Goji knelt to inspect the robot and after a moment's hesitation I did the same, as Masaru watched over the both of us with curiosity. Knowing who else occupied Goji's body, being in my friend's presence made me a bit on edge, but after pulling off the Binoid's chest plate with the help of one of Masaru's knives and a few minutes of tinkering, I lost myself in the task and the easy camaraderie that I could find with someone from my own world. It was refreshing to work with someone who understood some things from the same perspective I did.

"Good work, you two," Masaru commented as the Binoid whirred to life and its eyes came alight with a consciousness of sorts.

"Name and status?" I requested.

"Unit 232, operating at eighty-five percent capacity," the Binoid responded in a tinny, metallic voice, speaking with brisk precision. "Full capacity to be reached in approximately one minute and seventeen seconds. Awaiting instruction, Yukari Namikoya."

"That was thoughtful of Hex to have them recognize ye," Masaru noted.

"Very," I agreed, "and useful, too. Unit 232, can you open a communication channel with Hex, please?"

"Searching," the Binoid responded and the three of us waited with baited breath. "Connection established, transferring…"

"Identify yourself," a familiar, lightly-accented voice instructed, the sound coming from the Binoid's speakers.

"X-En," I acknowledged Hex's Binoid assistant. "It's me, Yukari."

"Activating voice recognition software," X-En replied. "Verified, Yukari Namikoya, Chosen of Sapphiros. Yukari, it is good to hear from you, my master sends his regards."

"It's good to hear from you too, X-En," I told the Binoid honestly. "And send my regards to Lord Hex as well. I hope all is well with you?"

"As well as can be expected," X-En answered. "Yukari, my master bids me to ask if you are perhaps able to reach us, as we have something which might be of interest to you and it would be best if we spoke in person."

"I'll be there momentarily," I answered without hesitation.

"Go and come back quickly," Masaru told me. "I'll be waiting."

I nodded and allowed my head to slump to my shoulders, reaching out with my mind to find the unique life force that belonged to Hex and sending myself to him. I expected to find myself in a familiar outpost when I opened my eyes, but instead I landed in the middle of an open Sand Lake with the sun low on the horizon and bathing the sand around me with a golden glow.

"Hello?" I asked, somewhat tentatively, a little surprised to find myself alone. I had never sent myself to anyone before and not found them there when I arrived.

But all that greeted me was empty sand, and it wasn't until I had turned about fully that I saw the half-finished stone wall I remembered from the last time I had been here, and then I realized that as strange as it seemed, I was in the right spot even though no outpost building was in sight. Hex's outpost should have been directly behind me when I faced that rough stone wall the Roughlanders had built to keep the Lillem at bay during those first awful periods of darkness.

"Activating voice recognition software," a familiar voice spoke, causing me to whirl about and search for the source. "Verified: Yukari Namikoya, Chosen of Sapphiros."

The ground opened unexpectedly at my feet, revealing a ramp that had until now been concealed by a layer of sand. Somewhat bemused, I stepped forward and began my descent, crossing the threshold from the brightness of day into the blackness of underground, and the hidden entrance sealed shut behind me, no doubt powered by Hex's advanced technology.

"Welcome back," X-En greeted me at the bottom of the ramp. "Prompt as always, I see."

"This is the outpost, isn't it?" I asked, somewhat awed by the realization.

"Indeed. It has merely been relocated to a more secure position beneath the surface of the sand."

"What is it that you wanted to show me?

"Come, let me take you to my master."

I followed X-En through a stone door and deeper into the Roughlander-style outpost, marveling at the metal shutters that kept the sand out of the windows that I remembered being open to the sky. A metal door whooshed aside to reveal a room on the topmost floor of the outpost building and the massive, vulture-like Hex sat in a chair constructed to support his bulky form. Across from him sat another winged individual, her blonde hair tied back off her neck and every visible inch of her skin covered in puffy red welts in the form of archaic-looking markings.

"Yukari, I believe you are acquainted with my guest?" Lord Hex rumbled softly.

"Lady Arashi?!" I exclaimed, looking past the painful-looking markings and charred, formerly-white wings to the woman beneath and seeing the Espearian Head Priestess for the first time since the fall of Taiyou.

She nodded, her musical southern accent confirming her identity even more than her words. "I'm afraid it's true, my beauty has been irrevocably altered, but it's a small price to pay for my freedom."

"What happened to you?" I asked. "Where have you been?"

"To hell and back," Arashi replied with a pained frown, abruptly reminding me of her impossible age and familiarity with Earth's culture through the extensive library the sisters kept in Espearia. "I wouldn't want to relive it again even to tell it to you, but I can tell you that I will not rest until that woman – no, that vile creature – is punished for all of her crimes. She used her repulsive magic to control me and make me her pet. I was simply lucky I was able to break free just long enough to send a call for help through that remarkable machine y'all left in pieces in the courtyard outside the palace of Taiyou."

"Gin-Kouteki?" I asked, thinking of the giant Binoid that had served me faithfully as long as it had been able to in defending Taiyou. It had fallen victim to an intense electrical storm, which had reduced it to little more than scrap metal.

"The very same," Arashi agreed. "I didn't think there was any hope that it might still be able to hear me, but the miracle I had been wishin' for was granted and Hex heard my call, sending more of his 'men' to save me."

"Binoids," I corrected her absently, recalling the Espearian aversion to all things mechanical and taking note that this experience had obviously resulted in Arashi having a change of heart. "That's quite the story."

"I'm sure that yours would be just as fascinatin'," Arashi commented, "and I'd love to hear it, but for now I have a favour to ask you. Would it be at all possible for you to take me home to my daughter? I can get there on my own, but Hex suggested that I go with an escort so I don't risk getting captured again or bringing trouble down on Espearia, and I must say that I respect his advice after everything he's done for me."

"I'm not sure that's wise at the moment," I noted, feeling bad for refusing her request. "It seems that the Chosen of Sapphiros aren't much welcome in Espearia at present."

"Why ever not?" Arashi questioned.

"The last time we were there things did not go well with the Sisters of Metal and Bone," I told her honestly, leaving out the part about us smuggling Rubian survivors in and out of the country. "More so Bone than Metal, but we were given a day to leave Espearia's borders with all of our refugees and we took it, and though none of us wanted to leave Chikara behind your daughter insisted on staying where you'd left her."

Arashi frowned. "All the more reason why I need to return home."

I found myself nodding. "Come back with me to the others and we can all go to Espearia together."

"I shall do so, Yukari, thank you."

"You'll be heading back to the Mountain of Blue Moon, then?" Hex asked.

"Blue Moon? Uh, yes, unless there was anything else? I don't mean for my visit to be so short, but…"

"Yukari, do not worry yourself about proper decorum in times like these. I am not so lonely that I would try and keep you here when you have important things to be doing. No, what I am concerned about is that we try to establish a reliable means of communication. Lilyth has not found me yet, though she's tried, and until she does I am staying put, but you, as I understand, will be going everywhere and it would be good for us to stay in touch with one another." I nodded my agreement. "Do you still have your communicator?"

"Yes, I do, actually," I answered, taking the object in question out of my medic kit. "I didn't think it would be much use without Gin-Kouteki. Sorry about that, by the way. I know you lent him to me to help protect Taiyou and I should have taken better care of him."

"I managed to salvage his program," Hex said with a wave of his hand. "There will be other Gin-Koutekis and I will improve the model so that they are not so easily destroyed. This box, however," he noted, taking it from me and opening its lid to fiddle with its contents for a moment, "has remarkable range for such a small device and now it is tuned to X-En, so you should be able to speak to me whenever you wish, unless you go somewhere that might interrupt the signal."

"Interrupt the signal? Like far underground, or near a strong electrical current or something?"

"Or the Ruby City," he said meaningfully, and I noticed Arashi's eyes widen. "I hear you've recently become acquainted with the Vile Emperor."

I swallowed hard. "It's not like that, Hex. The four of us did go to the Ruby City, but it was to find a way to eliminate the Lillem threat. The Rubians aren't the enemies we've always thought they were, or at least we all have much more pressing concerns than fighting each other right now. Lady Lilyth is an enemy to us all."

"I'm not mad, Yukari," Hex assured me. "I'm only glad to know that you four are safe. I've never cared much about the Rubian people one way or the other. It was always the Vile Emperor and his vile creation that concerned me."

"Creation?"

"You did not know? Verasheen created Lilyth. At least that's how the story goes. All I know is that she's always hated me. She hunted me before, back when she used to rule the majority of this world, but technology has always been beyond her ability to understand and so I've managed to stay hidden."

"You'll have to tell me everything sometime, Hex," I told him seriously. "I need to hear it, the whole story of this world. If you've been here as long as I think you have, then you might be the best person to explain it all to me."

"It's a long and bloody tale," he warned, "and we certainly don't have time for it now."

"No, we don't, but I will be back for it. What you can tell me might just be the key to understanding all of this, and if we can understand it then we might be able to unravel it enough to know just what it is we're fighting for."

Arashi and I took our leave of Hex, and I used my power to send us both back to the mountain of Blue Moon.

The small, abandoned village took on a new meaning now that I knew what I was looking at. This was where once, long ago, my mother, Fuun, and Sabien had grown up together. It was also the village I might have been raised in, had my family decided to stay on this world. I shook my head, staring beyond the fountain to the small stone buildings and trying to see what might have been, but not getting very far with it. I couldn't see this mountain village as home, no matter how hard I tried.

"So we're going to Espearia, then?" Hotaru asked, stepping into my field of vision.

"I suppose we are," I answered, smiling at my friend's obvious relief at the fact that Arashi was alive and well.

"Good, I've been worried about Chikara ever since we left, and I can't wait to see her face when she gets her mom back."

I nodded, even as I realized that it might be a sadder occasion than Hotaru was expecting after everything both mother and daughter had been through. "Is everyone ready to go, then?"

Hotaru nodded and together we rejoined Kaji who was over by the fountain. He was watching over Arashi as she spoke softly with the two Espearian women we had rescued from the eggs. They had evidently woken up before the humans, who were all still just as immobile as before.

"The two priestesses have decided to return home with Arashi and I've decided that I'm going to stay back with Masaru this time," Kaji informed us as we approached. "I know we have the agreement of the Stirr, but I would feel better with one of us here to defend these people in case anything should happen. Between Goji, Masaru, myself, and the Binoid, we should have everything covered."

I nodded, seeing the sense in this.

"Make sure the unconscious get water every so often," I instructed, as Hotaru headed past us to let Yue know that it was time to go. "We shouldn't be gone long, but in case this takes longer than I think it will I want someone to be taking good care of them."

Kaji nodded. "I will, but Yukari, I've been doing some thinking lately…"

"And?" I questioned, wondering where he was going with this.

"What if we're wrong?"

"About what, exactly?"

"Lilyth."

"What?!"

"Just hear me out," he insisted. "I was talking to Adel before, and others since, and from what anyone who was alive then could tell me, the society that Lady Lilyth built was as close to perfect as could be."

"What are you talking about? There was a civil war at the time."

"That was afterwards, when the Vile Emperor was trying to take power, but from all accounts the land was peaceful under Lady Lilyth's reign. She ruled from the Ruby City through her provincial lords and though there were the odd uprisings, the majority of people were happy and well taken care of – certainly not the chaos we see in the world today."

"So what are you saying? That we should just let Lady Lilyth take over again and then everything will be fine?"

"No, it's just that…"

"Just what?"

"I met her," he stated finally. "It was after I was hit by Hound-fire that first time. I know that Adel said that what I saw was likely a hallucination, but it seemed real to me. I met her in the Temple of Ruby and she made me an offer."

I narrowed my eyes in sudden suspicion. "Don't tell me that you're considering…"

I trailed off, but Kaji's answering silence was condemnation enough.

"Kaji," I said his name firmly, "no matter what she told you, no matter how perfect her society may have seemed to those who lived in it, she is still a tyrant who has killed a lot of innocent people and is going to continue to kill a lot more unless we stop her."

"It's not like I'm thinking of joining her side or anything, I'm not stupid. I've just been having some doubts and I want to make sure that we are doing the right thing."

"Kaji, she hates humans. Whatever she may think of the other races, once she has complete control she is going to wipe out an entire race simply because she thinks she has the right to, and no matter how perfect the world might be after that, a society based on mass genocide is not okay in my books."

"You're right." Kaji hung his head. "I know you're right. How is it so easy for you? Is it always so black and white?"

"No," I answered truthfully, thinking of all the hard decisions I'd had to make and how many more I would have to face. "It's never really black and white and that's the hard part. Sometimes there is no right answer, but we have to stand up for what we believe in, don't we?"

With the Espearians to my left and Hotaru and Yue to my right, we sat in a loose circle before the fountain. I took hold of the people I wanted and my power brought us all swiftly to Espearia. We became solid around Chikara in a dark room.

"Mama?" Chikara questioned, her eyes lighting up as she straightened.

"No!" Hotaru screamed, looking beyond the group of us to a sudden movement in the shadows.

A shield of thin blue light appeared around the group of us as Hotaru threw her hands up and I heard the object strike the shield before I even saw what it was. Arashi gasped in shock as I identified the object as a sharp bit of bone and realized that it must have been thrown by one of the two dark haired Espearian women on the opposite side of the room.

"Y'all will stop this at once," Arashi commanded the two Sisters of Bone. "The Chosen of Sapphiros are our allies and our friends."

The Sisters of Bone declined to respond, choosing instead to advance menacingly toward Hotaru's shield. I took the split second to take in the room we were in. The lack of windows or doors and decidedly rough stone walls suggested that we were beneath, or at least within, the temple that the priestesses controlled.

"What is the meaning of this?" Arashi demanded, as the two sisters simultaneously seemed to reach into their own arms to draw out another sliver of bone; this time, the little weapons dripped dark red with their blood.

"Go!" Hotaru commanded. "Get Chikara and Arashi out of here!"

I quickly took hold of everyone I had brought here as well as Chikara, and willed us back to Masaru and Kaji before the Sisters of Bone could attack again and overcome Hotaru's defenses.

"Where's Hotaru?" Yue questioned.

Seeing the space in our circle where she had been seated caused me to understand what had happened – Hotaru had pit her will against my own and resisted my power; she had chosen to stay behind.

"We have to go back," I announced, preparing to do just as I proposed and taking hold of everyone again.

"Now hold on a minute," Arashi interjected. "I know you're worried about Hotaru, and so am I, but I know the Sisters of Bone a lot better than you do and I can guarantee you that they've already got her in their custody, shield or no shield. They are experts when it comes to handling Chosen and it will do us no good to hand the rest of you over to them."

"But what about Hotaru, Mama?" Chikara asked. "She came to rescue me, we can't just leave her there."

"I agree," Arashi conceded, "but I am also certain that they will not end Hotaru's life. They might try to use her, or simply torture her, but they will not kill her outright. It is not the Espearian way."

"Torture?" I questioned, horrified at the thought.

"I say we leave her there," Yue suggested, "let her learn her lesson."

"Yue!"

"What?" Yue demanded. "She stayed on her own, didn't she? I know that you never would have left her behind if given a choice."

"You're right, I wouldn't have," I told her, "and I won't now." I turned to Arashi and Chikara. "Where will they take her and how do we go about getting her back?"

"I'm not sure," Arashi admitted, "I've never been in this position before. I was gone such a short time, I'm surprised that my sisters have turned against me so easily."

"Can't you make them listen to you, Mama?" Chikara asked.

"If I had the rest of Priestesses of Air to back me, then maybe yes, but unfortunately right now there are far more Sisters of Bone in Espearia than I have Sisters of any other Order, and I'm not sure where the Sisters of Metal stand."

"Is there another way?" Yue asked.

"The only thing I can think of," Arashi answered, "is to bring in the one person that the Sisters fear enough to listen to: Jeth. With his brother Goron dead, Jeth is as good as King of Espearia, even if his powers are still locked away."

Silence met Arashi's words. "Don't tell me you've lost Jeth."

"He went underground after you, Mama," Chikara explained. "Hotaru told me that Uncle Jeth challenged the Hounds to get you back."

Arashi pursed her lips in a frown. "That foolish man."

"Then we'll just have to get him back," Yue decided. "If you and Jeth disappeared together and we've got you back now, then we should be able to get him back as well."

"I was exceptionally lucky to make it out of Taiyou alive, Yue," Arashi told her.

"Well, we have to try," Yue countered. "We can't just leave him there."

"If it can be done then it is certainly worth doing," I agreed, willing to do whatever it took to find another of the lost souls on my list. "Any ideas on where he might be, though? I've tried to find him with my power, but so far I haven't had any success."

"Well, we'll just have to do it my way, then. Hold onto your hats everyone, I'm getting Jeth back!" And with that confident statement, Yue promptly closed her eyes and manifested that familiar cyan-coloured bird with her power. The bird didn't waste any time at all before leaping into a dive and descending into the ground beneath us.

Somewhat surprised by Yue's leap into action, it took me a moment to catch up to her, but I was determined that I was going to help if I could. I locked onto her and in my mind's eye I rode along with her through rock and dirt, deeper and deeper into the bowels of this planet. I couldn't see but I could feel the distance, and it was a long ways away when her faster-than-sound speed finally slowed.

Finally she stopped and, at a complete loss to what I might find, I sent myself across the distance as mist, appearing somewhere deep within the earth, perhaps almost as far as to be on the other side of the planet altogether. It was hot and although I was only mist – or perhaps because of it – the searing heat hurt and told me immediately that I could not linger here long, wherever here truly was.

"Yukari? And Yue, is that you in there?" Jeth spoke hoarsely from where he sat, crouched in a small metal cage suspended cruelly above a pool of lava. "Now I know I'm dreaming, because only I would imagine Yue as a blue bird."

"You're not dreaming Jeth," I told him, frowning at the state he was in. "We're really here and we've come to free you."

His demon arm was crusted with blood, and a large number of the scales seemed to have been pried off individually. The rest of him hadn't been spared either; his body was covered with evidence of having been mercilessly tortured these past weeks. Despite that, Jeth's spirits seemed as high as ever, though perhaps it was only that he was happy to see us.

"Really?" he asked, sounding hopeful. "You came for me?"

"Of course we did," I answered briskly, examining the cage and wondering how best to go about getting him out of it. "We'd have come sooner if we'd been able to sense you, but she had you well hidden, Jeth."

"Shhhppthhh..." An all too familiar hissing came from behind me and I whirled about to take note of a group of Stirr gesturing at us from the far bank of the lava pool in this subterranean cavern. *"Stop them! They are attempting to interfere with the Lady's acquisition."*

The Stirr! But these ones were marked, and so not the same as the ones we had dealt with at the Mountain of the Blue Moon. They were more like the ones I had encountered at the Temple of Ruby, only even at a glance I could tell that these markings were different. They weren't natural formations or tattoos, but rather they were carved into the Stirr's flesh – like Arashi's markings had been.

Either the Stirr had lied to us about the depth of their devotion to the Lady Lilyth, or perhaps the Stirr were not as united as they believed themselves to be. Either way, we had to get Jeth out of here before they found a way to stop us.

The bars of the cage were thick and hot, the welts all over Jeth's body from making contact with them proof enough of that, and I wondered at how Jeth was coping with the state his feet must be in from squatting on the cage's hot metal floor. It would hurt like hell, but from where I floated I could see little choice but to drift into the cage with him and become solid just long enough to take us both back to the surface with my power. I was all set to try it, hoping that the cage wouldn't prevent my power from working somehow, but I hadn't accounted for Yue.

The cyan bird landed gracefully on a bar of the cage and dove its head into the cage with a quick pecking motion, much like it had done with the Ruby eggs. After the briefest touch of its beak on Jeth's shoulder, he disappeared.

Yue's bird swiveled its head to look at me and with that she disappeared, leaving me no choice but to follow, fading from the view of Lilyth's loyal Stirr and returning to the Mountains of Sapphire.

Jeth appeared before me as I became aware of my surroundings once more and, as soon as she had released him, Yue caused her cyan bird to disappear and opened her eyes much like I had done after returning from our unorthodox journey to the center of the planet.

"Jeth!" Arashi exclaimed, checking him over quickly with emotion thick in her voice.

"I'm okay, really," Jeth protested, feebly waving her off.

"How dare you come after me like that!" Arashi abruptly changed her tone to scolding. "What a noble, yet foolish thing to do!"

"I'll remember that for next time," Jeth answered dryly and although he always sounded tired, for once he actually seemed that way. "Where's Ris? I could really use her blue bubble right now. Speaking of which, where exactly are we? Hey, wait, I know this place."

"The Mountains of Sapphire," Yue clarified. "Everyone else is at the Roughlander Children's Outpost, but Ao Kouen's got his wall up so for now we're here."

"And Jeth, we have a problem that we're going to need your help with just as soon as you're feeling up to it," Arashi began and then proceeded to fill Jeth in on how matters stood in Espearia, including what had happened to Hotaru.

"And there's more," Chikara added unexpectedly from where she had wriggled herself under her uncle Jeth's less-damaged human arm. "I didn't have a chance to tell y'all about it yet, but things haven't been quite right in Espearia since you left. People have been going missing. I was payin' real close attention and people were going missing all over the city. There were some rumours of people seeing giant dogs that weren't really there, or at least I never saw any."

"Hounds?" Kaji asked, approaching with Masaru.

"I don't know, but it might be," Chikara admitted. "If they were sneakin' about. The Sisters, when they were talkin' to me, said that they hadn't seen anything either."

"This could be a much bigger problem than just a few rebel priestesses," I pointed out. "We knew that Lilyth would come to Espearia eventually. Maybe she's trying a different approach than she did with Taiyou."

"Espearia would be tough to defeat directly with the power of the Espearian Priestesses on their own land," Kaji agreed. "It's possible."

"Then we need to be in Espearia," Yue stated. "We can't let her take them too."

Yue was right, but we also had survivors here to protect, my father among them.

"Well, I have the feeling that we're pretty safe here," Masaru noted. "If it's anything like what Yukari's told me about when we woke up from the eggs, it's going to be some time before these people are ready to go anywhere. I think as long as we let the Stirr here know, we can likely leave everyone here with the Binoid to look after them, especially if it's only for a day or two."

"I'll stay as well," Goji offered. "I've been looking after these people this long, it makes sense that I continue to do so. Besides, I'm not sure how well received I'll be anywhere else."

I wasn't completely comfortable with the idea, but it made the most sense. If matters were as dire in Espearia as it seemed, then we would need all the help we could get to foil Lady Lilyth's plans and get the Espearian Priestesses to cooperate with one another again.

It was time that we made a stand.

CH. 13 – ...SO THEY FEAR WHAT MAKES YOU STRONG

Arashi had not been in any way exaggerating when she had claimed that she could get back to Espearia on her own. It seemed that all full-blooded Espearians shared a peculiar ability that allowed them to return home whenever they wished, no matter how far away from it they had gotten. And so, between Arashi, Chikara, and Jeth, three admittedly powerful Espearians, we were all instantly transported from where we stood to Arashi's office in the temple that was home to the priestesses we had come to confront.

The large, round office with its vaulted ceilings and open archways was dimly lit by a few candles and sealed from the outside. We found it empty, save for the walls of books and the stacks of paper upon Arashi's desk.

"We must do what we can to get the Sisters of Metal and Bone in line," Arashi announced in a whisper that carried throughout the otherwise silent room. "If we can impress upon them the danger we suspect, then perhaps we will gain their help in defending Espearia. I do not want to see them go unpunished for what they have done in my absence, especially to my daughter, but I will be lenient if it means getting a chance to spit in Lilyth's eye."

"Come on," Jeth said, his expression uncharacteristically severe, "let's get this over with. The rest of you should stay here and make sure they don't come after Chikara again."

"I'm coming with you," Yue announced, flashing quickly to Jeth's side. "I have a word or two for those priestesses myself."

"Suit yourself," Jeth replied, frowning, "just don't expect them to listen to you."

"You'll get Hotaru back?" I asked, addressing Arashi.

"It'll be the first thing I do, you have my word. Just keep my daughter safe."

"Be careful, Mama," Chikara added, giving her mother a quick hug, "and you too, Uncle Jeth."

"Stay safe, kiddo," Jeth told her and followed behind Arashi as he and Yue left, shutting the large double doors behind them.

The three of them were not gone long when the unthinkable happened. A whistling sound followed by a crashing boom shook the building.

"What was that?" Kaji asked, looking up at the sky through the openings in the arched ceiling.

I followed his gaze, and although I didn't see anything, my instincts were screaming that something was wrong. Taking heed of them, I let my wings form at my back again and I took to the air.

Espearia, with its structures uniquely constructed of a blend of grey stone and ancient wood, fanned out before me in what, under any other circumstance, would have been a breathtaking view, given the lights that adorned the city to repel the mystery of night. As it was I scanned the city in a state of shocked horror, having trouble believing what I was seeing.

It was just like Taiyou – or at least what Taiyou might have looked like as it was overrun by Hounds.

There were Hounds everywhere within sight of the temple. Some spewed fire and others simply smashed what they could with their massive paws. Terrified citizens of Espearia fled in all directions, while others tried rather unsuccessfully to defend themselves, their homes, and their businesses.

"Kaji! Masaru!" I called down to them.

"I'm on it," Kaji replied, as one of his clones appeared below me on the street.

"Yukari, I could use a lift!" Masaru called back and without tearing my eyes away from the horrific scene before me, I turned Masaru to mist and brought him up to the window ledge.

Reforming him to stand on the ledge, I held my hand out to him. "I'll need your knife again."

With a knife in each hand, I threw them with force enough to stick into the wooden ledge of the window sill. Ten knives landed where there had been two. I stared at the knives before me a moment, deliberating what would be the best way to use them. There were too many Hounds here for what I had done in the Temple of Ruby to be as effective.

I could do it. I could multiply this knife as many times as I needed to strike every Hound and only the Hounds. I could feel them; the Hounds were so different from the humans and the Espearians that their life forces were now a simple matter for me to identify – and that meant that I could target them while leaving everyone else unscathed.

Feeling the weight of the knife in my hand, I looked up toward the sky and willed my power to give me a target. Out of nowhere, dark clouds spiraled and covered the stars, gathering in the open sky above Espearia like a storm was coming – only in this case, the storm was mine to control and I would decide who it struck.

Pulling back my arm, I threw the knife with every bit of force I could muster and let my power guide it to the center of where the storm clouds had gathered at my command. Lightning flashed as the knife struck and from the clouds above a flurry of identical knives began to fall, not straight down like rain, but every which way like a blizzard, only infinitely more deadly. The knives sought out their targets and hundreds of them rained down upon the Hounds, seeking them out no matter how they dodged and weaved. Canine whining filled the air of Espearia.

As soon as he realized what I had done and that the knives weren't going to fall upon innocent Espearians, Masaru began calling and waving to those who could see and hear him to usher them into the safety of the temple where they could be defended.

Kaji, on the other hand, surged forward, picking up a knife and creating yet another clone beside him to do the same. There were a handful of Kaji-clones already, facing Hounds and fighting simultaneously, but still Kaji created more, walking forwards and summoning another of his doubles for each available knife he came across. The effect was staggering as a virtual army of Kajis armed with black-bladed combat knives filled the streets of Espearia.

Unfortunately, it wasn't going to be enough. No matter how much Kaji and I could throw at the Hounds, we were still only two people against an army of supernatural creatures. My storm of knives, though effective, had not defeated any Hounds and had only managed to slow a few down at best. A number of Kajis clones were already being reduced to puddles all over the place, the power-created duplicates of a Chosen not being nearly as sturdy as the real thing.

We put on a good show and we weren't defeated yet, but it was clear, to me at least, that we had no chance of protecting Espearia by ourselves.

"Hey!" a familiar voice called from within Arashi's office and I looked down to see Yue looking at me pointedly with a crumpled form lying at her feet – Hotaru!

I turned to fly back down to see what I could do for my injured friend when I felt a hand inexplicably tap me on the shoulder and I whirled about to find that Ris was perching in the window opening where I had left the remainder of Masaru's knives, ready for use.

"Ris?!"

She nodded, her expression serious, and mimed quickly to explain the situation. *Ao Kouen brought us with his explosive travelling methods. We're here to help.*

I wanted to ask about the state of the outpost, or how they had known to come to Espearia, but having said her piece, Ris gestured me aside and dropped down into the room, opening her wings to slow her descent and make her way down to Hotaru. Yue, I noticed, was already gone again at her usual speed and with Ris present, I could rest assured that both Hotaru and Chikara were in capable hands, which meant that I could return my attention to the fight in the streets of Espearia.

I watched Pine bound off between buildings and Sabien form from a puddle beneath a Hound, impaling it with his sword. Aysel was there too, sword in her Sapphire hand whirling about while she held her shield high in front of her to defend against the Hound she was facing – the Knights of Sapphiros had arrived just in time.

I caught a flash of light out of the corner of my eye and I snapped to attention as a swath of red energy exploded into the city from the west, destroying everything in its path and lighting a beacon that stretched for miles.

The destructive blast could have been caused by Lady Lilyth herself, or another of her servants or unnatural creatures, but, as much as I wanted to I couldn't deny that I recognized this particular method of attack and the devastation it caused, even if I had never seen in it on such a scale as this. Adel was here, and unlike the other Knights she hadn't come to help the people.

Even if she was possessed or being controlled somehow, this was my chance to get Adel back and I wasn't going to waste it. Focusing westward, I let my eyes adjust so I could see as far as I needed to and within seconds I had located her.

She was at the forefront of a Lillem army – standing tall and proud – and she looked much the same as I remembered her, with no disfiguring markings like the ones that had marred Arashi. Adel's skin was flawless, her expression proud, and the red fire in her once blue eyes matched the colour of her hair. She faced me head on, as if she knew somehow that I was using my powers to watch her and she had been waiting for me to do so – whatever else she had come here to do, she had come here in challenge.

I watched her ready another blast, intent on Espearia. I didn't want to hurt her – whatever had happened to her in the last few weeks, Adel was still my Knight and my friend – but she had to be stopped.

I drew back an arrow and had the foresight to make it invisible. Just one should do it, as long as Adel couldn't see it coming. I let the arrow go, and watched Adel closely for the moment that my arrow made its way across the impossible distance of the city to strike her full in the chest.

She staggered as my invisible netting took hold of her and pinned her to the ground. I had her and now was my chance to reach her before she managed to set herself free.

It took mere minutes for me to cross the entirety of the city of Espearia, and soon I was flying above the darkened wastelands and quickly approaching the army of Lillem. Though the Lillem twitched and shuffled impatiently, as a whole they stood still, making no move to advance and join the Hounds already in the city. I scanned the crowd of Lillem as I flew over top of them, feeling a growing sense of unease – Adel wasn't here, if she had ever been. What was going on?

Shaking my head to clear it, I decided I'd better focus on the problem before me, which was something I could affect. There were less than five hundred Lillem here, not much of an army if this was what Adel was supposed to use to attack Espearia. Regardless, these five hundred Lillem had once been people – Taiyouns, from their dress – and if it could be done I would free them all from the curse of what they had become.

I willed myself to turn to mist, then forced myself to drop down among the crowd of waiting monsters and drift through them, spreading myself out as thin as possible to reach them all. It was the oddest of sensations, passing through so much living matter, but as my particles came in contact with the Lillem my power sought out the black flecks of Ruby I knew to be within them and destroyed each and every one, effectively removing the curse or disease that had turned these humans into mindless savages.

I reformed with effort on the far end of the group of Lillem, drawing myself back together to inspect my handiwork and was shocked to discover that it hadn't worked.

"What's going on? Where am I?"

Or had it? I was staring at a crowd of creatures with Lillem talons protruding from their shoulders and hips, but they were all confused and disoriented. Their expressions were no longer distorted in savagery, though some retained the elongated jaw that was a part of the Lillem evolution.

By this time some of them had taken notice of their talons, or those of their fellows, and panic was beginning to rise in the group. If I didn't do something soon it was possible that they might turn on each other, seeing monsters where there were only confused victims.

I let my glowing cyan wings out to draw their attention and lend credibility to my position. "I ask that everyone try to remain calm. I know that you're confused, but you're safe now."

No sooner than I had finished speaking, everyone began asking questions at once, demanding to know where they were and what had happened to them. I heard whispers of 'Chosen of Sapphiros' within the crowd, and after a moment a handful of men dressed in battered Taiyoun legionnaire armour stepped forward to represent the group, some of which were surprised to find how easily they propelled themselves forward on new limbs.

"You're one of the Chosen of Sapphiros, aren't you?"

"Yes, I am. I was in Taiyou when it fell, and I am sorry for what happened to you."

"Taiyou fell?" The legionnaire sounded shocked by this revelation.

"Yes," I answered hesitantly, wondering at what point this man's memories stopped. "There was little we could do. It was over too quickly." I noticed that the crowd had quieted to listen to what I had to say, so I raised my voice slightly to ensure that everyone could hear me, "All of you were infected by the Lillem curse when the armies of Lady Lilyth surged into Taiyou. Since then you have been under her control and most recently were sent here to Espearia to do here what was done to Taiyou. As some of you know, I am one of the Chosen of Sapphiros and my power has freed you from Lady Lilyth's control, but there is little I can do about your altered states. I'm sorry, but this is what you are now. But you will not be alone. Many were altered as you were, and I intend to free as many of you as I can."

"But we're monsters now, freaks!" someone protested.

"You don't have to be," I countered. "You have weapons that are a part of you now, yes, but you are still human in your hearts and still Taiyoun. The King lives and I can take you to him. If you'd like to put your new weapons to good use, you can help take back your country and the lives that were stolen from you by the Lady Lilyth. It's your choice."

"Nicely said," a familiar voice spoke beside me.

"Jeth, what are you doing here?"

"The sisters are all sorted out now. They're fighting off the Hounds under Arashi's direction. I came out here to deal with the Lillem problem, but I see that you've got things under control."

"Yeah, I guess, but Jeth, the reason I came out here is that I found Adel."

"You did?! Where is she?"

I grimaced. "That's just it. She was leading this army, but I lost track of her."

"That's all right, kiddo. We'll get her back."

I shook my head. "I'm not going to let it end like this. I'm getting her back, now."

Not waiting for a response from Jeth, I closed my eyes and felt for the Knight in question, knowing that if she was here my power would find her. Sure enough, I felt her nearby immediately.

"Come on, Jeth," I told him, reaching for his hand.

"Nah," Jeth responded, surprisingly nonchalant. "You go ahead and get her. I'll look after these people. They'll need someone like me to lead 'em back to Ao Kouen."

I nodded, not wanting to lose Adel a second time, and took off. I flew north a short way and came across a most unexpected scene.

The curved ridge hung over a deep valley that may have, at one time, contained a body of water. The former beauty of the hidden grove was still evident, even if now the water was gone and had left only desiccated plant life, clinging tenaciously to clefts in the dry and rocky ground. Within the valley was the woman I had come to find, only she wasn't alone. She stood facing Yue, each of them daring the other to be the one to make the first move.

Part of me wanted to be down there with them, perhaps to take Yue's place in facing Adel, or simply to throw my hands up to try and stop this foolishness all together, but some instinct told me to watch and wait. As far as I could tell neither had noticed me yet and so, causing my cyan wings to disappear, I crouched quickly behind a rock where I could observe them both without being seen.

"I'm all yours, Adel," Yue spoke at last from her defensive crouch, her tone bitter. "This is what you've come for, isn't it? To challenge us?"

"I'm not an idiot, Yue," Adel responded scathingly, balancing her shield carefully with her left arm and gripping her Deathsquad-issued sword in her right. "I'll fight you if I have to, but I know a Knight's chances against a Chosen in direct combat."

"So you'd rather hide behind Lilyth's army than face one of us fairly? I thought better of you, Adel. I thought you had a sense of honour, but I suppose if that were true then you wouldn't have turned on us in the first place."

Adel's mouth thinned to a line, but she didn't refute Yue's words. My mind was reeling – Adel, betray us? That was certainly what it looked like, but I had a hard time believing it was true. It was more likely that Adel had fallen into some trap of Lilyth's, or had been possessed by her to attack us against her will.

"You were dead," Adel stated, "all was lost. What else was I to do?"

"Who told you that?" Yue retorted. "Lilyth?"

"I saw you in eggs. No one gets out of the eggs alive unless the Lady chooses to free them, Yue, no one."

"We did."

Adel shook her head "I couldn't possibly have foreseen that. I did what I had to do and I would do it again. The Lady has won, can't you see that? There is no point in resisting her further."

No point? Wasn't the fact that we were alive and well today proof that the Lady Lilyth hadn't yet won anything? We were resisting her now in Espearia and would continue to do so all over the world. This was far from over; surely Adel could see that, knowing now that we were still alive and still fighting.

"Well, you can make your own decisions, Adel," Yue said, "but you want to know what I think?"

"I'm sure you're going to tell me anyway."

"You're afraid, Adel. You thought that you had escaped Lilyth forever, but now she's back and you've gone right back to being her lapdog, because you're too afraid to stand up for what you believe in. You're pathetic. Aysel would be ashamed to call you sister if she could see you like this."

I saw the warning fire ignite in Adel's eyes before an answering red glow began in the sword she gripped tightly in her fist, and then she fired a devastating beam of red power, so like the power used by the Deathsquad soldiers to destroy their enemies, only more intense.

But Yue simply cart-wheeled to the side. "Is that the best you've got? It's a wonder Lady Lilyth lets you work for her. Seems to me like you've gotten a little rusty."

Adel surged forward, enraged, and I held my breath as I watched a Knight of Sapphiros attack one of those she was meant to protect, for real this time and not under any pretense of 'training'.

Adel's sword blade flashed in the harsh light of the desert as she flung it this way and that – faster than the heavy blade should be able to move – but still Yue stayed effortlessly out of her reach. Yue had come so far with her power after all the trials we had faced in recent months that it was clear, at least to me, that Adel had little chance of getting the better of her. But enraged or not, Adel was a highly trained and effective fighter; she had to know that this was a contest she could not win.

Yue paused for a moment in her movements and, upon seeing her opening Adel brought her sword down with enough force to crack the rock at their feet. Yue waited until the last possible second before leaping into the air, propelling herself off of Adel's shield and vaulting over the lady Knight.

"Or maybe," Yue ventured, ducking as Adel whirled about with her sword to take Yue's head, "your heart's just not in it."

"I'll kill you," Adel threatened and took another stab, which Yue side-stepped.

"I don't think so, Adel," Yue replied, her voice calm as she placed a hand atop Adel's gauntleted one and caused Adel's sword to disappear. "You don't want to hurt me any more than you would want to hurt Aysel. We keep your sister safe from her. If we lose, there's nothing keeping Lady Lilyth from getting to Aysel – and that's the last thing in the world you want."

"She had Aysel already, Yue!" Adel protested, emotion showing through her usually stoic expression as she gripped Yue's arm in turn and drew her in close. "She had her in her grasp and it was only my defection from you that spared her life!"

Yue didn't flinch, but instead met Adel stare for stare. "And has it made Aysel any safer, joining her side? Now you actively hunt her down, helping your 'Lady' take away every safe place until there's nowhere left for Aysel to hide. Are you protecting her, or yourself?"

"Damn you, Yue," Adel hissed, twisting Yue's arm until she cried out in pain, but still neither of them let go.

With neither willing to back down, the two of them struggled on the floor of the valley, rolling this way and that, for now all words forgotten in the desperate physical battle of wills, until they were both so tangled that neither could break loose without hurting themselves or each other.

"Just answer me one question, Adel," Yue spoke once they were both panting and facing each other over Adel's shield, having come to a standstill in their wrestling match, "why?"

"You were dead."

Yue met Adel with a scathing look. "It takes a lot more than a cheap trick to kill a Chosen," she commented wryly. "There was still a chance we would survive and we did. So, I repeat my question: why, Adel?"

Adel let out a breath, "I already told you, she had Aysel. My sister was in an egg, only she hadn't been whisked off like the rest of you. Lady Lilyth had her and joining her side was the only way to guarantee Aysel's release."

"Okay, but that still doesn't explain why you're here now, still working for her. We're alive. Aysel's alive. Why attack Espearia? Why attack us?"

Adel stiffened. "It was my Lady's will."

"Your Lady's…Adel, this is outrageous! Have you joined her side for good, then?"

"I didn't have a choice, Yue."

"There's always a choice. You just made the wrong one."

"She's stronger than us all," Adel protested, her voice wavering now in the face of Yue's scorn. "How many times do I have to tell you? You'll never win this."

"There was a time you believed otherwise," Yue stated, reminding me of a time when things hadn't been quite so complicated and when we had all stood together against everything that sought to destroy us, "and some small part of you must still believe it because you sent Aysel to us. You wouldn't have done that if you thought we would be so easily defeated."

"I was buying her what time I could. You will lose and the world will once again go back to the way it was. Even the sun has returned to its normal course. It is the same with Lilyth. She will rule this world once more."

"This isn't about winning and losing, Adel. It's not about some ideal of the perfect society and who would rule it. You're afraid, aren't you? The great Adel Kusabana is really nothing more than a coward, too used to following in a greater shadow to stand up on her own for a cause she believes in. Well, I'll tell you something, Adel: Aysel may have come to Knighthood a lot later than you did, but she's a better Knight than you'll ever be because she makes her own decisions."

I winced, expecting a backlash, but Adel just dropped her gaze. "You're right."

"What?"

"I said you're right, Yue. Aysel is the better Knight. My sister's never been afraid of anything in her life, but I'm terrified. Terrified of the hold Lilyth has over me, terrified of losing to her, but she's so powerful and she knows my weakness. Aysel is everything to me, everything. Without her, without at least knowing that she is alive and out there somewhere…I've got nothing to live for."

"You don't have to be afraid, Adel. You're stronger than this. You've stood up to her once before, remember? You left Lilyth when she threatened Aysel and you can do it again. You don't need to be anyone's slave and neither does Aysel."

"But…"

"We're still here and Aysel is with us. You don't have to be alone, you just have to fight to protect your freedom and that is something I know you can do."

Adel seemed to consider Yue's words for a moment. Yue, with her insults, her banter, and finally her inspiration, had ripped away the illusions Adel had convinced herself were real, finally allowing her to see the thin ray of hope that waited for her on the other side.

"I'll do it for Aysel," Adel said finally, "but not only that…I'll do it for myself."

Yue smiled and let go of her hold on Adel as the Knight did the same. The two of them struggled for a brief moment, trying to disentangle themselves from the awkward position they had gotten themselves in. Eventually they gave up trying, falling backwards to lay on the ravine floor and breaking apart at the last second.

Yue, lithe as ever, was the first to climb to her feet and she offered Adel her hand. Adel took it with a determined nod and got to her feet once more with Yue's help.

"I suppose you can have this back now," Yue said, causing Adel's sword to appear in her hand and holding it out, hilt first.

"Keep it," Adel stated. "It's a Deathsquad weapon and that's simply not who I want to be any longer." With deliberate motions, Adel reached around and unhooked her shield from her arm, dropping it onto the ground before her. "You can have that as well. I've hidden behind that thing for far too long and the time for hiding is past."

"But what about your power, the one with the sword? There's no sense giving that up."

"And I haven't," Adel replied, drawing her battered wooden mace from the straps on her back and hefting it in her hands. "Jeth gave me this," she commented, regarding the mace fondly, "when I left with him to join Sapphiros. It's served me better than that sword ever has."

"Won't losing the sword and shield change your fighting style and leave you at a disadvantage?"

"Let them think me weak, Yue," Adel stated, lifting her heavy mace one-handed and leveling it at a rock on the other side of the valley, "so they can learn to fear what makes me strong."

Adel's eyes lit with blue fire and a matching blue light fired from the tip of her mace, pulsing outwards. The rock she had set in her sights exploded with a resounding crash, leaving nothing but debris in its place.

Silence fell over them both and I stood to reveal myself when there was a rumble and a distant, yet familiar cry. I whirled around and my eyes adjusted automatically to see across the open desert, only to realize that what I was seeing was the largest sand cloud I could possibly imagine, stretching across miles of the barren landscape and rapidly approaching the direction of Espearia. There were few things that could kick up that much sand, but the sounds I was hearing left no doubt in my mind as to what was coming for us, though it was awful to contemplate. Sandcrawlers, a whole herd of them barreling toward the city of Espearia.

"Yue, Adel!" I yelled. "There's a herd of sandcrawlers headed this way!"

"No!" Adel gasped.

I turned back to try and calculate how much time we had before the beasts reached Espearia only to find that it was gone. The high-walled city of Espearia simply wasn't there anymore and there was no rational explanation for it.

"It's gone." I whispered.

"Gone, what's gone?" Adel asked, reaching my side.

Yue pointed and after a moment Adel's jaw dropped, taking notice of what we'd already realized. I admit that by her reaction my mind immediately supplied me with the logical leap that the disappearance of Espearia, like the sudden appearance of the herd of sandcrawlers, was something else that wasn't of Lady Lilyth's doing, or just part of the plan that Adel hadn't been privy to. She was on our side again now, or so she said, but when would my suspicion of her fade?

I realized I was angry, angry with Adel for doubting us and for not having faith that we could survive, that we would fight to our last breaths for her, her sister, and everyone else that needed protection from the Lady Lilyth. I had always believed in Adel. I had trusted her and relied on her, in battle and out of it, but it seemed that the sentiment wasn't returned like I had thought.

I wanted to yell at her and let her know how I felt. I wanted to tell her how I had considered her and Aysel like family, and let her know how much her betrayal hurt, but I realized that now was not exactly the time. Knowing our lives, it was also likely that there might never be the time to say what I wanted to, and not only that but Yue had already said everything that needed to be said – I didn't think that Adel needed to hear it twice.

Speaking of Yue, I turned to ask her what she thought we should do about Espearia or the sandcrawlers, only to discover that she was already gone, to where I had no idea.

"Come on, we have to try and warn them, or at the very least take cover," I told Adel, my voice controlled enough not to reveal my tumultuous emotions. "That many sandcrawlers will level any structures they come across."

I didn't give Adel the chance to respond or protest before I turned her to mist and took to the air. I wasn't sure I was quite ready to talk to her, but more importantly I had work to do. Flying upwards quickly, I angled my wings to take Adel and I in the direction of Espearia – or at least where it had been.

CH. 1 – A CHANCE TO REST

As impossible as it seemed, there was a crater in the place where Espearia had once stood, yet as I was to discover, the country that had crash landed here from another planet centuries ago was still somehow in exactly the same spot it had always been – and still virtually unchanged.

"We're safe now," Chikara insisted, speaking to those who had gathered in Arashi's office as morning came after the miraculous end to the battle in the streets of Espearia. "Espearia is now as safe as I can make it."

The office was more populated now than I had yet seen it but the spacious room was far from crowded, even if there were few chairs and most people were leaning against the various bookshelves that lined the curved walls. All the Knights had gathered, including some I hadn't even known had come to Espearia with the others, and now everyone was accounted for.

"Pardon if I may seem skeptical," The Head, who must have returned to Espearia with the Knights, spoke in his usual exuberant fashion and with his thick Espearian accent. "I know you Chosen-types have vast power that normal folk like me can hardly comprehend, but what exactly is it that you did? How'd you make all them Hounds disappear like that?"

"Well, I don't know, exactly," Chikara answered shyly from where she stood before her mother's desk, "but I felt the sandcrawlers comin' so I took Espearia away from where it could be harmed. Only I didn't want to move it like I did the last time, so it's still in the same place but it can only be reached by those who belong here."

The Head's face went white, and I could imagine a little of what he must be feeling. The 'last time' that Chikara so casually referred to was over a thousand years ago when she had single-handedly moved what was now considered Espearia from the planet where it originated. Back then she had been rescuing a country from being destroyed along with the rest of the planet, and now she had found a way to do it again. Despite still being young by her race's perspective, the girl had access to more power than I could fathom even after all I had witnessed.

"All that matters is that she succeeded," Sir Sabien interjected before anyone else could question Chikara's miracle. "Chikara has given us some temporary respite. As long as her power holds, Espearia can be a haven for the resistance. Chikara, how long do you think the effect you created will last?"

"Well, I can't leave Espearia like this forever and there are some resources that we'd need to bring in from the countryside," Chikara admitted. "Not too long, I don't think, but maybe…six or seven years?"

Sabien smiled indulgently in Chikara's direction. "Well then, I'm sure that will be more than sufficient. We'll post guards, just in case something should figure a way past what Chikara has done, but I think that it would be a good idea for everyone to get some rest while we have the opportunity."

"But isn't that exactly what she'd expect us to do?" Yue spoke, somewhat unexpectedly. "Hide where we think we're safe and lick our wounds until she finds a way to get at us? Isn't that what we did in Taiyou and then in the Ruby City? We're not going to win if we keep doing what she expects us to do."

"What do you have in mind, Yue?" Masaru asked. "I don't think Sabien's wrong in saying that we're all in need of a rest, but I don't think we should just hide behind Chikara's power either. No offense, Chikara."

"That's all right," she allowed.

"I don't know," Yue admitted, "but we won't get anything done sitting here. What about the people that are still out there? The Croatins, for one, or the town of Sresh? They're all alone out there and they don't have a Chosen like Chikara or Ao Kouen to protect them."

"And we all know how that turns out," Adel added with a frown. "I believe you were right when you called it a…what was the word? 'A fish-bowl'? Even with protection like this, or Ao Kouen's flame wall, or even the Ruby City's barrier, it's still only a way to delay the inevitable. She will find a way to bring the walls down and then we will all be at her mercy."

"So better no walls at all?" I questioned Adel a tad more sharply than I intended; then to soften my words, I turned to address everyone at once. "Yue is right, though. There are people out there who need our help, especially if they've managed to survive this far. If she can't attack us directly, she'll go after those she can reach: our allies and the remaining Roughlander outposts. She wants to eradicate all humans, or at least have them where she can control them."

"That makes sense for all the humans out there, but we still don't know anything about what happened to the Croatins," Kaji interjected. "The only Croatin any of us have seen since the fall of Taiyou is Pine."

"Yes," Pine agreed in his customary whisper, speaking from the corner of the room where he had quietly stationed himself in his dark cloak, "and I'm rather worried about my brothers."

"And I'm sure Dahlia would want to know what happened to Krox," Masaru added.

"I think I can answer –" Adel and Arashi began at once, speaking from opposite sides of the room. Stopping, Arashi gestured for Adel to continue.

"The Croatins are still in Taiyou," Adel explained. "They were of the Lady's creation and, like the Hounds, it seems that she has some sort of hold over them. They cannot disobey her will. Pine may be an exception because of his Knighting, I don't know, but the Croatins are lost to us. They are now a part of Lady Lilyth's army."

"So why haven't we seen any of them, then?" Kaji questioned. "Why not use them as weapons when the Lillem failed?"

"She keeps them in Taiyou to keep order there," Adel answered. "Matters in Taiyou are not as stable as she would like. There is still much of the country that she has not brought under her control, such as the Raman province. And as far as I know there is a resistance force in the city itself. I don't know much about it, though. I had only begun to investigate it when I…left."

I narrowed my eyes, regarding Adel closely. What she had neglected to clarify was that she had no doubt been trying to uncover the resistance for Lady Lilyth's benefit, and not as a means of helping the ravaged citizens of Taiyou. In addition to that, when she said 'left' she likely meant when she was ordered to go and spearhead the attack on Espearia. None, other than Yue and I, knew what had really happened to Adel and that until convinced otherwise she had been serving her 'Lady' quite willingly. Adel still had a lot to answer for.

"But we have other possible allies too," Hotaru mentioned, and I was glad to see that she seemed in good enough spirits after being healed by Ris. "It's not just the Croatins, or the free Taiyouns, there's the Kumori. They're out there somewhere and I'm sure they don't like Lady Lilyth either."

"And perhaps the Stirr as well," Sabien added. "The Stirr have been instrumental in the defense of the Children's Outpost since we explained to them that the compound exists to guard our young ones. I believe it is possible that their way of thinking could be brought around to see that Lady Lilyth is not the friend of the Stirr that she pretends to be."

"And don't forget Hex," I mentioned, since we were on the topic of allies. "He's still out there with his Binoids and he's managed to evade Lady Lilyth so far. He is a powerful ally whom we can certainly rely on."

"Indeed," Sabien agreed. "He's been in contact with us at the outpost through radio relay and he's even sent us another Gin-Kouteki unit."

"So we've established that we have the ability to hold for a few more days, maybe even longer," I pointed out, "so why don't we use this opportunity to take the offensive?"

"What?!" Adel questioned.

"It's simple," I stated. "We make a show of strength and remind Lilyth that we are still here, that she hasn't managed to defeat us yet and we can strike back at any time."

"You're talking about guerilla warfare, aren't you?" Kaji asked.

"Ye mean like baiting a sandcrawler?" Masaru asked.

"Kind of, I suppose," I answered both of them. "We know we can't attack her outright, especially not in Taiyou while she's got her army stationed there, but as Kaji's pointed out before – she's spread too thin. She's desperate to regain control of this world and if we shake that control it might enrage her enough to do something stupid, like come out of Taiyou, and then we'd have our chance."

"I don't think she's leaving Taiyou, Yukari," Adel countered. "She's sitting on the throne there because she needs its power. Whatever happened to her before, she's greatly weakened, but she's using Jedeite's power to supplement her own and with it she's invincible. She won't lose that advantage willingly."

"Either way, it'll prove that we're a force to be reckoned with and that we're not just going to give up," Kaji stated. "We'll be a thorn in her side until she deals with us herself, or until we win back what she's taken from us."

"That's all well and good," Aysel spoke up, startling us all as she had been silent before now, "but how are we going to get her attention if she won't leave Taiyou and we can't attack there?"

"A worldwide demonstration," I announced and the room as a whole turned to look at me. "We split up and contact each and every one of our established and possible allies, then we set up a disturbance of some sort in every part of the world, by doing something as ostentatious as possible. She'll think it's a distraction for something else, something bigger, and she'll think twice before attacking any one group, for fear that the others will converge on Taiyou while her defenses are down.

"Think about it," I urged, taking note of some dubious expressions, "Espearia disappears and she thinks we're hiding within it. Then, all of a sudden, Chosen pop up all over the map, causing disturbances and making nuisances of themselves. We prove that we can attack wherever and whenever we wish, and just when she thinks we're going to take a risk and end up in her hands, we disappear and return here where she can't get us."

"It's certainly a bold plan," Adel admitted. "I can't decide if it's brilliant or foolish."

"It may be both," Yue answered her.

"I think Yukari's on to something," Masaru said with a proud grin. "It's exactly how a Roughlander would take down something as large and vicious as a bull sandcrawler. Harass it until ye've got it cornered right where ye want it, then go in for the kill."

"Just answer me one question, Adel," I said as I met her stare for stare, when until now I had mostly avoided her gaze, "is it something Lady Lilyth would ever see coming?"

"No. it certainly isn't...which is why I think it just might be crazy enough to work."

"So we split up, inform any and all allies we can reach, and get into position. Once we've made contact we can take our chance to rest. Then, the day after tomorrow, we attack just before dawn," I told them all in a no-nonsense tone, "and by the time the sun comes back up, we'll be nowhere to be found."

"So, like she used the return of night to bring her army, you will use the return of day to bring yours?" Fuun spoke unexpectedly, stepping out of the shadowed doorway. "Fitting. Come morning, I will do what I can to help you 'go to ground'. The Temple of Machalite is also hidden from her and through it I can quickly transport those of you who require my assistance."

"So we'll need teams and destinations." Sabien nodded to Fuun before continuing the discussion at hand. "I suggest we keep to our policy of a Knight to every Chosen, unless there are any objections?"

"I believe I should visit Hex," I volunteered, deciding that since I had broached the plan I had best state my intentions first. "I've much to discuss with him and going there would put me close enough to Taiyou that I just might be able to see how matters stand there."

"I'd like to accompany you, if you'll have me," Adel ventured, somewhat tentively. "Hex and I have some unfinished business that I'd like cleared up."

"Masaru, will you come with me to the Children's Outpost?" Kaji asked unexpectedly, speaking before I had the chance to. "I have a plan that I think I'll need your help with."

"I'm not sure I'm going to like whatever it is ye have in mind, Kaji, but ye know I've got yer back."

"Thank you, Masaru."

"Well, I'm going to Taiyou," Yue announced.

"Yue, I'm not certain that's wise," Sabien cautioned.

"Don't get your panties in a bunch," she told him. "I'm only going to see Lord Rama. Someone's got to make contact with the people who are still holding out against her."

"If you're going to Taiyou," Pine spoke up, "I'd like to come with you to see for myself what has happened to my brothers. Also, the Croatin base is nearby and if possible, I'd like to visit it and see if the Third Spawn who were left behind to guard it are still free."

Yue nodded. "I can drop you off."

"Well, I'd like to see about the Kumori," Hotaru ventured. "Hex told me a long time ago that they might be willing to ally with us. Ris, would you know where to find them?"

Ris nodded and signed, *I will go with you to translate.*

"You do?" Hotaru questioned. "Can you tell me where to find them?"

Sabien smiled. "Even better than that, Hotaru, she's offering to come with you."

"Oh! That's wonderful. Thank you, Ris."

"What about me?" Chikara asked. "Do I get some mission to accomplish?"

"I think it best if you stay here, darling," Arashi told her. "It's not that I think you wouldn't be able to handle yourself out there, but rather that I wouldn't want Espearia to suffer in your absence. However, I did hear Yue mention Sresh, and I fear that she is right in sayin' that is a place that needs to be dealt with, though not for the reasons one might think.

"Sresh is being used as Lady Lilyth's barracks for the remainin' Lillem. She's turned the whole town into Lillem, and as far as I understand it she's using the city as a place to rebuild her army with fresh troops after what y'all did to the Lillem Heart."

"But what about the Preservation Squad?" Yue asked. "Their only job is to protect the people of Sresh. Surely Lady Anaeth wouldn't have –"

"The Lady Anaeth is far older than I'm sure you knew, Yue," Arashi informed her. "She was once one of Lady Lilyth's Generals before the civil war. Now she might not have rejoined her Lady except for one thing, Lady Lilyth has threatened the life of the woman's only daughter if she does not do as she is told. As a mother myself, I know exactly how effective such a method is. Lady Anaeth is very much under the Lady's control for the time bein'."

"What do you propose to do about it?" I asked, genuinely curious. "If it would be more effective I could accompany you to Sresh and help cleanse the Lillem taint there instead of visiting Hex."

"It's quite all right, Yukari," Arashi ensured me. "Once Jeth returns to Espearia, he and I will make a special visit to Sresh. Lady Anaeth should listen to me. Failing that, I'll have Jeth with me to make her listen," Arashi informed us with a dimpled smile. "It never hurts to have some muscle at one's disposal."

Sabien nodded. "Well, that takes care of all the Chosen and if Fuun will help bring people to and from the various locations, that leaves only Aysel and myself. Aysel, will you accompany me to the Mountains of Sapphire? I believe it is time we speak to the Stirr."

Aysel nodded her assent as Masaru spoke up once more. "There's still Rama," he pointed out. "If we can get a message to him he's with Lady Akuma and I'm sure the Ruby City would join in, if we let them know what we're planning."

"I still have the mirror," Kaji offered. "When we get to the outpost I can give her a call. Speaking of which, how are we getting to the Children's outpost? Fuun's method of traveling is all well and good, but it won't get us inside Ao Kouen's barrier if he's got it up."

"I'll take you," I offered. "I can bring you both straight to Ao Kouen's side, and from there Adel and I can go to Hex's."

I said my goodbyes to Masaru in the sunny yard of the outpost building. The Children's Outpost was so unlike the others I had visited; being built into a pre-existing mountain gave it access to natural reserves of water enough to allow it to have a spring that gurgled into a rocky pool, kept shady by overhanging melon plants.

"It's only a couple of days and it'll be over before ye know it," Masaru assured me.

"I know, but it's risky what we're doing. I have to take responsibility for that since it was my suggestion that led to this plan."

"No matter what plan we decided upon, each would have had its own set of risks, Yukari. We've all decided to do this on our own and it won't be your fault if anything goes wrong. In fact, I think ye've come up with a pretty clever plan, if I say so myself."

I smiled at his attempt to flatter me and was going to tell him to be careful, to make sure that he and Kaji both got back to Espearia in one piece, when Masaru pre-empted all that by kissing me full on the lips.

"Now go on," he told me. "The sooner ye get going, the sooner ye'll be getting back."

Rejoining with Adel, I willed us both to Hex's outpost as mist and took it in stride when we appeared in the middle of the wide open desert and were greeted by X-En's pleasant tones requesting verification of our identities. It wasn't long before I was leading a bemused Adel down a long ramp, heading under the sand to Hex's hidden bunker.

"So this is how he's been hiding from her. Very clever."

Hex met us at the foot of the stairs, his massive bulk filling the metal doorway. "Come in. I have something to show you and then we must talk."

We followed Hex deeper into the outpost and stopped in the familiar room that was his office, though it had been altered somewhat since my last visit. It now contained a large screen along one wall and a bank of consoles to complement the usual wires draped here and there along the walls and floor. Binaris was present, the red-painted female Binoid plugged into one of the consoles at its base and her bright cyan eyes staring blankly ahead.

"I've hooked Binaris up to the system, so she can monitor for incoming transmissions while X-En and I are occupied," Hex explained, "but recently a disturbing transmission has come to my attention and I think it's one you should see. Binaris, play back the most recent transmission from Unit 232."

That was the Binoid that we had left to watch over those under the protection of the Stirr at the Mountain of Blue Moon. I felt my heart thump in my chest as the screen lit up with the view of a familiar cave. My father and Goji were with that Binoid – had something gone wrong?

Moonlight streamed into the cave entrance Unit 232 had set itself to guard. Wind whistled calmly over the rocks, until bit by bit that sound was joined by another less innocuous one, a hissing so low as to be incomprehensible.

"The Stirr?" I questioned.

"Just watch," Hex replied, his own attention focused on the screen as if it would show him something different from the last time he had watched it.

"There you are, Mr. Namikoya," Goji's voice was heard through Unit 232's speakers. "You'll be just fine."

I felt my heart skip a beat. My father – was he awake? Had the others also awoken – and were they still safe? I forced myself to pay strict attention to the Binoid's recording, as it might just be able to give me the answers to my questions.

By now Unit 232 had become aware of the rising hissing noise that came across as little more than a disturbance in the sound quality of the transmission. The Binoid turned its head to view within the cave, turning on its night-vision as it did so.

The recording showed only a small glimpse of Goji leaning over my father with a canteen in his hands. By all appearances my father was still very much unconscious like the others lying in orderly rows around him. Behind Goji loomed a multi-limbed shadow, which Unit 232 could identify as a Stirr, thanks to its night vision, but which Goji had no chance of noticing unless the thing made a sound to alert him to its presence.

Unit 232 surged forward as the Stirr rose up on its back legs, a curved bladed weapon held in its hands. At the last possible second, Goji's head snapped upwards, his expression hardening into that of Fuzen's and when he spoke it was with those dreaded European tones, "Look out!"

Long fingers covered Unit 232's vision for a split-second before all turned to static, as the Binoid's camera went dead and the transmission was terminated.

"I have to go," I spoke, belatedly catching a glimpse of myself in the darkened screen and realizing that my wings had appeared at my back with my need to be on my way. "When did this happen?"

"Yukari, rest easy," Hex instructed me. "I received this transmission during the night and have already sent Binoids to deal with the situation. There were no casualties, save Unit 232, and by now those who were present should have arrived safely at the outpost with the rest of your companions. Your father and the others are unharmed. I simply felt that you should know what almost happened."

I found that I could breathe again, Hex's words bringing me back from the brink of panic.

"So the Stirr betrayed us," I stated, coming to terms with the facts that had been presented.

"I don't think so," Hex replied. "Look."

Hex had Binaris rewind the transmission and pause it when the Stirr behind Goji was most visible in the green tinge of the night vision camera. It was the moment the Stirr had its knife held high and I cringed watching such violence suspended.

"Just there, see the markings on the Stirr's face and arms?" Hex pointed a massive clawed finger at the screen. "They are similar to those Lady Lilyth had carved into Lady Arashi. I was able to study them at some length while she was here, so I have little trouble recognizing them."

Hex was right. This Stirr was marked, like the one in the Temple of Ruby had been and like Arashi, but unlike the ones that we had dealt with. Were there, in fact, divisions among the Stirr?

"Are they simply sworn to her, or is she controlling them in some way?" I asked, thinking aloud.

"I've never seen such creatures before," Adel answered "but either is possible, I suppose."

"The Stirr have been around since the beginning," Hex informed us. "They are one of the four original races of this planet. But whether these marked Stirr have joined Lady Lilyth, or whether they are controlled by her, this is still an indication that the Stirr are divided like they have never been in their entire history that I know of."

"The unmarked Stirr don't know," I realized. "The Stirr don't lie and the ones we spoke to believe themselves still whole. This could be the proof we need to show them that Lady Lilyth is lying to them and causing some Stirr to act against the word of the rest. Wait, you said the four original races. How long have you been on this planet, Hex?"

"A long, long time," he answered ambiguously.

"You promised me the story," I reminded him, "and now that I've got some time I think I'd like to finally hear it from the beginning."

"And I'd like to tell it to you, but first I have some matters that require my attention and you both look like you could use some rest. I'll have X-En show you to your chambers and when you wake I'll begin the lengthy tale."

There was little use debating the delay. I could see from looking at her that Adel was emotionally and physically exhausted, and I wasn't much better. I numbly followed after Adel and X-En to the round metal door, which led into the sparse yet functional chamber that Hex had set aside for us. The room's walls were a mixture of sandstone and metal with bunk beds built into one wall, and a small round table with two chairs set up in the center contained a small platter of food in the Roughlander style.

X-En left us after ensuring that we had everything we could possibly need, and then Adel and I found ourselves alone for the first time since her rather uncelebrated return. She pulled out a chair for herself and our eyes met as I shut the door and turned into the room.

"Yukari, I —" Adel began somewhat awkwardly.

"Hm?" I questioned, heading past her for the beds and using the excuse of climbing to the top bunk to avoid giving her my full attention. I knew I was being rude, but somehow I couldn't find it in me to face her just yet. I also knew that if we tried to hash this out now, it would be a very long and uncomfortable wait in this tiny room until the time when Hex came back for us.

"I was hoping we could talk."

"I'm afraid I've got quite a bit to do."

"Do?"

I winced, trying to find something to make my statement true. To cover up my lie, I reached into the medic kit I wore strapped to my chest and pulled out whatever was on the top, which incidentally was the silver-worked scroll case that used to contain the 'Blue Moon Scroll'.

"What is that?"

"It's the Blue Moon Scroll," I answered. "I managed to open it, but I never did figure out how I did it. I'm almost certain that this case contains more secrets than I've managed to unravel."

"Is there anything I can do to help?"

"No, not really," I answered truthfully, more caught up in the renewed puzzle in my hands than I had originally intended to be.

Putting Adel out of my mind for the moment, I fumbled with the case's two lids in my hands, trying without success to re-attach them to the ornate metal tube. Try as I might the case would not seal back together, but just before I gave up one of the lids slipped in my hands and flipped around until the Sapphire end of it was facing inwards and something odd happened. The lid seemed to float in place about an inch from the case, as if repelled and attracted simultaneously by a magnetic force. Taken aback, I held the case carefully with one hand and reached into my lap for the other lid, flipping it and positioning it like the first. It, too, began to float in place.

I held it up and was amazed to see that the floating lids remained secure, though they twirled in place with a growing speed, and an inner glow began in the Sapphire ends of the lids that was matched by a glow coming from the case itself.

"What the…?"

But Adel didn't seem to share my confusion.. "That reminds me of the Splitter."

"So when Sapphiros wrote 'the key to understanding the Splitter' he was being literal. This, whatever this is, is how to use the Sapphire Splitter."

"Well, that's wonderful news, I'm sure," Adel commented wryly. "Only the Sapphire Splitter is on Earth, so I hardly see how that bit of information is going to be of much use to you right now."

Adel's words reminded me of the fact that I was trying to avoid speaking to her. "Yes, well, now that that is solved I guess it's time we got some sleep."

"Indeed."

Following my own suggestion, I lay down on the bunk and felt more than heard Adel climb into the one below me. In the tense silence that followed, I'm certain it was some time before either of us got to sleep.

◊

It was much later in the day when we awoke but Hex was still occupied, which left Adel and I no choice but to wait for him. Unfortunately, 'waiting for Hex' meant staring at each other across the tiny round table in the room, which didn't seem to help the tension between us.

"So, I must have missed a lot," Adel ventured. "We could use this time to get me up to speed."

"I suppose you're right," I agreed, thinking back to those awful first moments when we had awoken in the Temple of Machalite and how best to sum up all that had happened since then.

"Fuun brought as many of us as he could to the Temple of Machalite," I began. "Most of us were in eggs, but we discovered that the eggs can't hold Chosen for long and we were able to break free on our own. Once free, we discovered where we were and that the only people who weren't in eggs were Aysel, Ris, Ao Kouen, and Leon –"

"Leon?"

"Sir Rama," I clarified.

"I know what his name is, but when did that happen? You've always called him by his title before."

"Yes, well, as you said you've missed a lot. Leon and I became a lot closer during our stay in the Ruby City."

"The Ruby City?!".

I smiled at her reaction, knowing that had our positions been reversed and I was hearing this story for the first time, mine would have been identical. "Yes, but I'm getting ahead of myself."

"Okay, but before you continue, answer me one question. You…" she said hesitantly, pointing at me and then away, "and Leon Rama are…together now?"

My jaw dropped. Leon and I? Together? "No, no! We're just friends." I stopped, realizing something. "Oh my god, you don't know, do you?"

"Know what?" Adel asked, her eyes wide.

"You might be the only person in this world that I actually get to tell before Dahlia does. Adel, Masaru and I are a match," I used the Roughlander term for it before I noticed Adel's confusion and added, "we're getting married."

Adel spluttered visibly for a moment before settling on, "Well, congratulations! I knew you both had feelings for one another, but I was hardly expecting – either way, I'm proud of you and happy for you both. I hope it's not too much of a presumption to ask if I'm invited?"

"Of course you're invited, Adel," I replied. "It wouldn't be the same without you."

I noticed tears welling in the Knight's eyes before she hastily wiped them away. "Thank you."

"Don't mention it," I murmured in response and in that moment I realized that I wasn't mad at Adel. I had simply been worried for her and in some ways mad at myself for ever having doubted her. In her heart she was loyal to us, her friends, but life had forced her to make difficult choices and sometimes, due to our own failings as human beings if nothing else, making the right choice, the choice our heart cries out for, is not always possible.

Adel had a great many questions about the coming wedding and how it had come about, and before long the two of us were laughing as I told her of all the antics Dahlia had gotten up to in her quest to tell every single person she knew. So when Hex finally came for us, he found us both lost to peals of laughter, the tension between us completely forgotten.

"That's more like it," Hex commented. "I had begun to wonder."

Adel sobered immediately and I tried to do the same. "We've got a lot to tell you, and a bit of planning to do."

He nodded. "So I hear from Dahlia. Is it true that you and Masaru are going to be Joined in the Roughlander fashion?"

This evidence of Dahlia's continued mission almost sent Adel and I back into a fit of hysterics, but I recovered quickly enough to nod in agreement.

"Congratulations," Hex continued as if nothing was amiss. "Come, let me give you a tour of the facility and you can explain everything to me."

'The facility', as Hex called it, was more than simply the outpost as I remembered it. It was a massive underground factory operated solely by Binoids of all shapes and sizes and the sheer amount of Binoids the factory had already produced was staggering.

"How do you power this?" I asked, amazed by what I was seeing. Hex had a veritable army here, one that he had been growing in secret for centuries.

"Underground volcano," he answered. "It's primitive, but it suits my needs."

Touring the rest of the facility, Adel and I explained to Hex the plan that had been concocted in Espearia, and together the three of us managed to develop what would become our contribution to the worldwide demonstration. Provided I could uphold my end of things, it had the possibility of being a very successful ploy, while hopefully accomplishing more than I had dreamed would be possible.

"And now I think it's time you told us the history of this planet," I informed Hex as we finished the tour and returned to the room where Binaris sat immobile, monitoring for any transmissions. "We have hours before it will be time to put things into motion."

"Very well," Hex agreed, taking a seat in the only chair large enough to fit his bulk, "but I will warn you that the story is not a pleasant one. This world's history is long and bloody."

"I expected as much, considering the present," I told him with a frown, "but I feel that it's something I need to hear, so I have a better chance of understanding why things are the way they are now."

Hex nodded. "Well, the story begins well before I arrived here, but I can only tell you what I know…

In the vast and chaotic universe, there have always been warlike races who, for whatever reason, develop the belief that they should have the right to rule over planetary bodies other than their own. The Aldanians were one such race, and their confederation laid claim to a sizeable piece of what had yet been charted around their home galaxy.

The Aldanians were not a fierce race on their own, especially when compared to others with more physical advantages, but they had something that most did not: a unique grasp of technology coupled with an unrelenting ambition, causing them as a race to always strive for more than what they had.

It was this that had brought the Aldanians to prominence, but this set of qualities was also what had made them so many enemies, including some who were bent on their complete annihilation.

Aware of these tensions, Hex had skirted wide around Aldanian territory in his exploratory vessel, headed for a solar system that had yet to be charted. What he didn't know was there was something the Aldanians and their enemies wanted from a particular planet in that solar system, and unfortunately by the time he arrived there it was already too late to escape the skirmish that had broken out on the edge of charted space.

Hex's ship barely escaped intact, having been caught in the middle, and had no other choice but to flee further into uncharted space as quickly as its damaged engines could manage. By the time the ship's power source finally failed, Hex was far out of reach of any relay and there was no hope of a distress signal being heard or investigated.

He drifted, lost in space until he finally managed to locate a planet that according to his scans might have what he needed to re-power his ship. Having no other options, he used what reserve power he had to land.

So far from where such things were important, the planet in question had no name and was simply home to four native races: the aquatics, the air-walkers, the cave-dwellers, and the plains-runners.

These names, though relatively uncreative, were given to the native races by a fifth race – humans – who had come from who-knows-where to colonize this planet for their own reasons.

Humans, physically so like the Aldanians that Hex had good reason to be wary of, seemed friendly enough and greeted him with open arms, despite his very alien appearance even by this world's standards. But as it turned out, the power source Hex had scanned from space ended up being no more than the remnants of whatever space-faring equipment the humans had used to arrive here and was no longer in any state to be salvaged, even if the humans were of a mind to let him try.

Soon Hex had to face the fact that he may never see his home again, but even in the face of this knowledge he did not give up hope entirely. In the years that followed he faded into relative anonymity, watching the planet's development from a distance as he searched for an alternative power source for his ship. During that time, the humans tried their best to forget their pasts and blend in with the cultures that were already present on the planet they had chosen to call home. Five tribes soon developed around the planet's five gods and temples were erected in their honour to serve as communal centers.

"Today, you would recognize these five tribes under very different names, though the gods they once followed exclusively remain the same," Hex explained. "The aquatic ones are now the

Croatins. Their ancestors followed Jedeite and made their home in the marshes and swamps we now call Taiyou."

"That would be why the Croatins consider Taiyou theirs by right," Adel noted.

"Indeed," Hex agreed. "The air-walkers, or Kumori as you know them, settled into the volcanic region of Rubia, and the cave-dwellers, now Stirr, settled underground, where they built the Temple of Machalite. The plains-runners were unfortunately so altered by Lady Lilyth that they aren't recognizable today, but they used to live in the sprawling grasslands and followed the ideals of Damos."

"The Hounds," I said, recalling the display in the Ruby City museum.

"Yes, though I'm afraid that the plains-runners fell for Lilyth's promises to improve them. You might call it forced evolution – but I'm getting ahead of myself. The fifth tribe, the tribe of Sapphiros, was made up of the various groups of humans, some who remained nomadic and others who settled across the world, living with and studying the ways of the other races.

"Hundreds of years passed, the humans settling in and all but forgetting that they weren't native themselves, and all seemed relatively peaceful until the unfortunate arrival of the Aldanians…

They landed far from where Hex had established himself and so he was able to observe them before their inevitable meeting took place. It became obvious that these Aldanians were not much like those that Hex had previously encountered. It seemed they had not come to this planet to conquer it, but much like Hex himself they had somehow found themselves stranded here. Their leader was called only the 'Yaboun Tenchi' and after much time spent delaying the inevitable, Hex finally went to see him to discover his true intentions.

Their meeting went well, so well in fact that they had the potential to become friends. As it turned out, the Yaboun Tenchi was one of the fabled Chosen of Aldania and had vast power granted to him by his god. Despite this, the Yaboun Tenchi found himself and his people unable to return home.

"Perhaps," the Yaboun Tenchi claimed, "it is for the best. There is civil war amongst factions of the Aldanian confederation and this planet can be a fresh start for us."

Having hope for the future, but determined to keep an eye on the newcomers, Hex returned to the remains of his ship and the home he had built himself from the scraps of his former life.

The Yaboun Tenchi, a Chosen of the gem god Damos, was pleased to discover that his god was represented on this planet and so, doing much like the humans had done, the Aldanians built a temple to the gem god of their choice and developed their society around it.

Then, one day, she came and all hopes for a peaceful future were dashed. She arrived in the form of a meteor, crash landing into the side of the volcano that is the Temple of Rubia.

The take-over began immediately.

Lady Lilyth's conquest began with the region of Rubia, claiming power there as she deemed her right as a Chosen of Rubia. To look at her no one could doubt her affiliation with the gem god, as her chest openly displayed a large glittering Ruby some claim was there in place of a heart.

The Kumori fell in line, accepting Lady Lilyth as the Chosen one of the gem god they worshipped. The plains-runners were next. With the fierce plains-runners and the magically powerful winged Kumori as her army, she swept across the land and conquered everything in her path, paying little attention to the devastation she was causing to the delicate balance the planet's cultures had achieved before her arrival.

Lady Lilyth surrounded the Croatins and eventually she emerged victorious. Their leader, a Croatin Chosen of Jedeite, wisely sided with her in order to spare the slaughter of his brothers. In a few short years, Lady Lilyth gained control of over a good percentage of the planet, establishing her seat of power in the Temple of Ruby, while she plotted how best to use her new Croatin army to conquer the remaining territory, that which belonged to the Yaboun Tenchi and his Aldanians.

But the Yaboun Tenchi had not been idle during this time. No stranger to war, the Aldanians rose up to rid the world of this tyrant. As one, the humans, Aldanians, and remaining plains-runners true to Damos marched to the Temple of Ruby to confront Lilyth and defeat her once and for all.

The battle was fierce, and no one, save the Stirr – who remained apart in their hidden underground homes – was spared the hardships of war. Hex, beseeched by his friend the Yaboun Tenchi, also did what he could to help them.

There were heavy losses on both sides, but at long last the battle had been pushed to the Valley of Ruby and Lady Lilyth found herself cornered in the very place where her conquest had first begun. Many thought then that the war would be over soon and Lady Lilyth dead, but that wasn't to be the case.

Just like she had arrived, two more meteors fell on that fated day when the war should have ended. Those meteors turned out to be a Chosen and his Knight, two brothers named Verasheen and Venon.

The brothers, Aldanian themselves with powers granted to them by the gem god Rubia, joined the Lady Lilyth and together the three of them turned the tides of battle and pushed back the combined forces of Damos. It was all the Yaboun Tenchi could do to help his army flee when faced with two such powerful Chosen, so close to their seat of power.

So the forces of Damos retreated back to the territory they had claimed and did what they could to prepare themselves for the onslaught they knew would come. And come it did, but being forewarned, the Yaboun Tenchi was able to successfully repel the advance and hold onto his lands.

Lady Lilyth was furious. With the added help of Verasheen and Venon, she had managed to reclaim the territories she had held before, and even convince the Stirr of her right to rule, but the territory of Damos continued to elude her. Over the centuries that passed she tried repeatedly to conquer or destroy the Yaboun Tenchi, but he held strong and defended his borders, growing more and more adept at doing so.

Meanwhile, Hex remained hidden, considering it prudent to do so rather than involve himself further in another Aldanian war, while the world around him changed and shifted, becoming two distinct kingdoms or empires rather than a loose conglomeration of tribes.

Under Lady Lilyth's rule, the tribal territories became no more than provinces of the Ruby City and their leaders became Generals of the Ruby City's army called 'Provincial Lords'. Taiyou, or the Land of Jade as it was called then, was one such province, ruled by the Chosen of Jedeite. Others included the Mountains of Sapphire, ruled by Yuko Seig, and Espearia, ruled by Venon, who by then was known simply as the Lava Lord.

To Verasheen, or as the people began to call him, the Vile Emperor, Lilyth gave the honour of ruling over the newly constructed Ruby City, leaving her free to look after larger concerns, like the problem of the Yaboun Tenchi and his continued defiance…

"And that's how things remained for some time," Hex explained. "Lilyth couldn't break the defense of Damos, and the Yaboun Tenchi was too busy defending his borders and training Knights and soldiers to launch another campaign against her."

"But what led Verasheen, I mean the Vile Emperor," I corrected myself, "to rebel against her? He seemed to be well taken care of and firmly seated as Emperor. Did he just want more power?"

"Not exactly." Hex gave a sidelong glance in Adel's direction before continuing, "She did eventually place one of her Knights above him in status, but it was what she did to his brother that really started the civil war…

CH. 1 – FALSE DAWN

*I*t was a public spectacle.

Verasheen was forced to drag his brother across the public square and bring the traitor to justice before the Lady. The Lava Lord had been badly treated, showing bruises and worse all over his naked body as he was paraded in shame, his legs dragging uselessly across the cobblestones.

"You have betrayed me," Lilyth proclaimed, "and in so doing you have betrayed us all. You will pay for your treachery. Now," she commanded the Vile Emperor, "do it, or I will."

"...Brother..." the Lava Lord managed, "you promised..."

"I promised," he agreed, and within his hands the Vile Emperor gathered his power as a Chosen of Rubia.

Lava formed and rippled, heat billowing outwards, and then the Vile Emperor smote his brother, pouring lava over the place where he knelt before him and causing the assembled to shy back from the heat of it...

"In less than a moment it was over," Adel finished, telling her part of the lengthy tale of the reign of Lady Lilyth. "He turned the lava to rock and when he did there was no more trace that the Lava Lord had ever existed, save for a misshapen lump. It was the worst possible fate I could even imagine, for him to destroy his own brother like that, it was nearly too much."

I was thoroughly disgusted, but it fit with what I knew of the man who called himself the Vile Emperor and I couldn't say that I was shocked by any of it.

"What happened then?" I asked.

"Verasheen turned on Lilyth," Hex replied. "Some say he'd been plotting against her the whole time with his traitorous brother, others that he simply snapped after what Lilyth had made him do. Either way, the civil war dragged on for some time before he fought her and she lost – or so it was said. After that, he took over the Ruby City and has ruled there ever since.

"Now, that took longer than I thought it was going to, and I'm afraid it's nearly time for us to begin the operation."

"What time is it?" I asked.

"Two hours before dawn. The sky will begin to lighten soon. False dawn, I believe it is called."

"Perfect," I answered, my expression severe as I anticipated what was to come. "Let's get going, there's no more time to waste."

On a high ridge in the darkened desert, three forms appeared, two human and one the altered shape of a cloaked Croatin. Moments later, all three headed off in separate directions, vanishing after only a step...

Yue raced across the sand toward Taiyou. She had been told not to go there by more than one person, and likely no one would be pleased she was going alone, but none of that mattered. Taiyou was where Lady Lilyth was and she had to see how matters stood there for herself.

The Raman keep was a beacon in the darkness, drawing Yue directly to the bridge she needed to cross into Taiyou. The bridge and the courtyard beyond it were well guarded, but Yue blew past all the soldiers and at the speed she was going they didn't even know she was there apart from the gust of wind created by her passage.

At last she came to a stop in the dead center of the keep's common room, which was bustling with all the signs of a late night feast coming to a close. Startled, the stately man seated upon a raised dais at the far end of the room was the first to notice her unorthodox arrival and he surged to his feet.

"Don't stand on my account," Yue told him, looking the man up and down and noting the features he shared with his son, white hair included. "You must be Lord Rama."

"And who are you?" he demanded.

"That's Yue Noh, one of the Chosen of Sapphiros," Lady Rhine answered the Lord's question, the Taiyoun councilwoman composed as she strode forward to greet Yue formally. "Welcome to the Raman Province, but I must ask: why have you come?"

Other than Lady Rhine, one of Ao Kouen's advisors, there were also several sorceresses from the Temple of Jade and a few regular Taiyoun legionnaires, as well as members of the Lion Brigade, Lord Rama's personal force.

"What is everyone doing here?" Yue found herself asking, instead of answering Lady Rhine's question.

"Those who were able to do so fled the city, or were smuggled out and brought here," Lady Rhine answered cautiously. "We have a strong force and we're holding strong."

"That's good," Yue agreed, "and I'm certainly glad to hear it, but I've come to warn you that you might want to evacuate Taiyou."

There were shocked expressions around the room. "But we can't leave," someone spoke from the crowd. "The Lillem are out there in the sand," another said and yet another asked, "Where would we even go?"

Yue shook her head. "The sand Lillem are gone now. They've been destroyed and the Sand Lakes will be a far safer place than here, especially once we're through riling the Lady Lilyth. The last thing we want is for her to turn on you when she can't find us. Leave Taiyou," she urged them, "leave now, and go over the bridge and south to take shelter at Hex's outpost. It's the nearest place and well defended. Or better yet, go visit the Croatins in their underground base. I can arrange someone to show you the way."

"We're not leaving Taiyou in that woman's hands," Lord Rama stated. "Unless we are defeated and have no other options, we will stand in defiance. The Lion Brigade is strong and with help we can repel the witch's dogs. You're a Chosen, aren't you? Stay and help defend us, and together we may be strong enough to take the offensive."

"I'd love to, but I'm afraid there's a much bigger world out there that needs defending," Yue answered. "Since you're not going to take my advice, all I can do is try to give her another target to take out her frustrations on. Good luck to you all and be prepared for some backlash, because we're about to make our move."

"So where exactly is it we're going, Kaji?" Masaru asked. "And what's the purpose of bringing a whole army with ye, if ye're just going to walk by all those Hounds?"

"The Hounds think we're leaving the outpost undefended. They're wrong, of course, but it'll be interesting to see how they react to us simply walking out of the place we have defended so fiercely. But no, what we're doing is not just to confuse the Hounds. We're going on a sandcrawler hunt."

"That's why ye wanted me on yer team? Ye want to bait a sandcrawler?!"

Kaji nodded. "You're the one who gave me the idea, actually, at the meeting. You called what we're all doing 'baiting a sandcrawler', so I thought why not? It gives us a reason to be out here and it'll certainly attract attention because the Hounds will wonder what the hell we're doing."

"Ye mean I'll wonder what the hell we're doing. It's a foolish plan, Kaji, but I suppose that's exactly what we're supposed to be doing."

"Exactly, that's the spirit."

The 'army', such as it was, consisted of every able-bodied Roughlander, refugee, and even the Japanese men and women of our parents' squad. The Hounds, who had kept a careful watch on the outpost these last weeks, were currently nowhere to be seen, and their sudden absence during this momentous event was more worrisome than their presence had ever been.

The ruins of the Roughlander outpost once ruled by Lady Kichigai were the perfect choice of location from which to stage a long-ranged attack. It was near enough to Taiyou without being far from Hex's outpost, and it had lain empty and abandoned since it had been overrun by the Hounds and Lillem in the first handful of dark periods.

"Can you really strike Taiyou from all the way out here?" Adel asked. "I know you can see a lot further than most people, but that's over a day's march from where we stand."

I nodded while standing atop the toppled outpost building and looking outwards. "I may not be able to aim precisely, but I can guarantee my arrows will rain down over Taiyou."

"What about the people held prisoner there? Can you strike simply the Hounds or the Lillem?"

"That's the tricky part," I answered, still peering through the darkness and wishing that I was just a little bit closer, so that I could really see what was going on in the city of Taiyou. From here my power allowed me to make out the shape of it, but little else. It would have to do. "I could strike only the Hounds, but that would leave the Lillem, or I could strike the Lillem, but that would leave the Hounds. Not to mention the fact that the Lillem are people and I want to save them, not destroy them.

"Neither of those answers are really good ones and I have no way of knowing if I'll get another shot off after the first," I continued, reasoning aloud for Adel's sake. "If they manage to trace where the arrows are coming from, they'll be here in no time."

"So what is your plan then? Hounds first?"

"No, I'm going to fire a new kind of arrow, one that won't hurt anyone but will cause quite a stir when all the Lillem that are struck by it return to their right minds. There will be chaos in Taiyou and hopefully I will free as many Lillem as possible, which should give the Taiyouns a chance to take back their city themselves."

"That's brilliant. And while you're busy with Taiyou, I'll watch your back."

I heard the familiar whine of engines before I saw the fleet of Hex's Binoids hurtling through the sky towards Taiyou in the soft light of pre-dawn. False dawn was here and all over the world the teams we had put into position would be beginning their demonstrations. It was time that I began mine.

The cavern was dimly lit by the light glow of Aysel's power-wrought arm, but even still the sight was atrocious. Stirr limbs and even a severed head lay discarded on the cavern floor, and dark stains marred the rock walls.

Sabien took a step forward and gestured for Aysel to do the same, as he knelt down to inspect the body before him. It was cold to the touch, which was expected given the length of time the corpse had lain here, but what wasn't expected was the strong scent of rot after only twenty-four hours.

By the light of Aysel's arm, Sabien continued his investigation and sure enough, the torso was covered in carved tattoos in an intricate design – Hex was right that these were no ordinary Stirr.

"Shhhphhhthhshh..." a sharp, hissed warning came from deeper in the cave and Sabien stood, slowly raising his arms in a peaceful gesture.

"We've come to talk," he informed the Stirr, whom he could not see in the cave shadows.

There was an answering hiss and then a moment later the Stirr stepped into the dim light, followed cautiously by two of its fellows. The first Stirr offered its hand and two baby spiders crawled forward, one for each of them.

"Humans did this," the Stirr spoke almost before the tiny spiders were in place.

"The human in question was defending his charges," Sabien replied as diplomatically as possible, "and though I would need Yukari, or perhaps Yue, to verify this for me, I am of the opinion that the creatures that were killed here were not exactly Stirr."

This seemed to get the Stirr's attention, but they were still wary. *"Humans lie."*

"Yes," Sabien agreed, meeting the Stirr's eyes directly, "humans can and do lie, but with a little trust we can show you proof that our words are true."

The home of the winged Kumori was the hollowed-out inside of the tallest mountain this world had to offer. Far to the north of the Ruby City, it would have been impossible to reach in time for the operation without Fuun's help. As it was, Ris and Hotaru found themselves with little time and little to offer the Kumori to convince them that they should risk their lives to help the rest of the world.

"Lady Lilyth," Hotaru mimed as she spoke, having picked up the gesture from watching Ris translate her words so far, "is not 'coming back'," she told them. "She's already here and all over the world people are suffering because of her."

The Kumori leader, one of the few male Kumori Hotaru had ever seen, interrupted her with a series of gestures she had no hope of comprehending. Smiling awkwardly in her nervousness – Hotaru desperately wanted this mission to succeed – she turned to Ris for help.

Ris looked a combination of frazzled and exasperated, but she made sure Hotaru was paying close attention before she began signing in the simplest gestures she could think of.

"The Kumori are not dead?" Hotaru translated, but Ris shook her head at the last word. "Oh! The Kumori are not suffering!"

"Oh," Hotaru repeated, realizing her mistake and turning to address the assembled Kumori once more. "I'm glad, but it's only a matter of time before the war reaches here too. Right now we desperately need your help, especially if you can heal or have other abilities like Ris." She mimed the gesture Ris always used when she activated her power to heal somebody, running her fingers together before separating them and holding her hands out before her. "If you don't help us now, then there might not be anyone left to help you when the Lady Lilyth," she mimed the one gesture she knew again, followed by curling her fingers into claws and miming a vicious attack, "comes after you too."

"How did you get in here?" Lady Anaeth demanded.

"I have my ways," Arashi informed her, fully stepping out from behind Lady Anaeth's bedroom curtain with a flourish.

"You and I need to have a little talk," Arashi continued, "and I'm in no mood to take no for an answer."

"What is it, what do you want?"

The tell-tale markings inflicted by Lady Lilyth were having the desired effect on her audience. She had Anaeth scared, not knowing whether her unexpected visitor was a messenger from Lady Lilyth or a free agent.

"Why, what I want is exactly what you want, the only difference between you and I is that I'm in the position to give you what you want."

"What are you talking about?"

"Your daughter."

"Excuse me?"

"You want your daughter to remain free of Lilyth and you want to protect the people of Sresh – is that not so?"

"Of course it is, but…"

"No buts, it's a simple matter. If you do what I want, I can guarantee your daughter's safety and what I want you to do is no different from what you want done anyway. Free Sresh and defy Lilyth."

Lady Anaeth seemed to consider Arashi's words a moment before her face fell, at last showing all the fear and worry that had only been leaking through her careful control until now. "I can't…" she whispered. "You know I can't."

Arashi frowned. She had been expecting this sort of response, but it was still unfortunate. "I'm truly sorry to hear you say that, but you leave me no other choice."

At these warning words and the sudden change in Arashi's tone, Lady Anaeth remarkably managed to bring her features under control in an instant, raising her head to shout at the top of her voice, "Guards!"

"So I gather this isn't exactly what ye had in mind?" Masaru asked, indicating the veritable wall of Stirr that had the entire force brought out from the Children's Outpost surrounded.

"Not exactly, no," Kaji answered, deceptively calm.

"What do they want?" Kaji heard his father ask from somewhere to his left, the darkness making it hard to tell who stood where.

He couldn't see the Stirr's expressions, but the way they stood rigidly in a circle surrounding them was odd in and of itself. From what he understood ever since their conversation in the Mountains of Sapphire, the Stirr had been willingly guarding the Children's Outpost, as they had learned that it was where the human Roughlanders were hiding their children from the dangers of war. This unanticipated help from the Stirr had set Ao Kouen free of the need of constantly drawing upon his power to maintain a barrier around the place, allowing him to finally catch up on his rest.

Kaji would have loved to believe that these Stirr were here to guard them or even to politely suggest that they turn back to avoid any bloodshed, but by the silhouettes of the curved scythe-like weapons in their hands and the angry hissing sounds, he knew in his heart that the Stirr's intentions were not in the humans' favour.

"Brace yourselves!" Kaji used his power to enhance his voice so all could hear him. "No one is to attack first, but we will defend ourselves if necessary."

Yue raced across the Taiyoun countryside, running faster than she had ever run before. If this was going to work she needed to be undetected until it was too late for anyone to stop her.

The greenery blurred by, but she didn't need landmarks to tell her where she was going. Ao Kouen had told her that the Hounds had destroyed a number of the Leyins, but Yue knew that if she just kept running straight from Lord Rama's lands to the city of Taiyou then she would cross one of the remaining ones eventually. Those lines of power fuelled the magic of Taiyou and were exactly what she needed to make a suitable demonstration for today's festivities.

Aha! She felt the surge of sudden power as she crossed an active Leyin and skidded to a stop, flashing backwards until she was standing within the pulsing line of power and could feel it in every fiber of her being.

She took a moment to consider the force beneath her feet. She knew she could direct energy, even energy such as this; she'd done it before. The problem she faced now was determining how to store it, but Yue threw herself into the task with her usual gusto and began drawing as much power as she could physically hold.

"Look out, Taiyou, here I come!"

Centered directly between Taiyou in the northwest and the Ruby City in the northeast was the neutral city of Middleton. It welcomed all and had no real affiliation, despite any attempts by the Ruby City, among others, to claim it. It was there that Lady Akuma, Bastion, and his Deathsquad decided to make their stand on this momentous night.

"It's worse than we thought, my Lady," Bastion informed Akuma.

Akuma just nodded while looking ahead to the darkened town, her lips pursed. "Can you get me to the center of the town and hold a defensible position?"

"Yes, my Lady."

"Do it, then. That's the only way we're going to make a difference here."

Bastion nodded and, gesturing to the Deathsquad around him, he sent them moving forward into the Lillem-infested streets of Middleton.

Straining my power to its limits, I thought I could just make out the shape of the distant palace spires. Taking aim to the sky above them, I pulled back my first arrow, manifesting its cyan glow between my hands. Centering myself, I took a deep breath and shut out the sounds of the wind rushing in my ears, focusing only on the sky above Taiyou and drawing on my power. This arrow would be special; it would do exactly what I needed it to and yet harm no one, passing through all organic matter and removing the Lillem curse, just as I had learned to do with my mist.

I watched the clouds gather impossibly far away in the skies over Taiyou. They spiraled in the dark sky, giving those in Taiyou a subtle warning of what was to come if they chanced to look upwards.

Sure of my power, I loosed the arrow and watched it arc upwards into the night sky toward the point I had designated. I followed the cyan arrow long after it would cease to be visible for anyone else, until it sunk into the dark patch of clouds above Taiyou and winked out of existence.

That was when the storm began.

Yue ran, her speed making her invisible to the naked eye, and all around her there were Hounds, Lillem, and even some regular folk who seemed to be trying to avoid the notice of the former. The city of Taiyou was well populated, though not necessarily with the same races and people that had lived there before.

"Whoa!" Yue had to swerve suddenly to avoid a sudden deluge of cyan arrows that fell with a vengeance from an angry sky.

The Hounds ran for cover and all around her arrows stuck into the ground as they landed, creating glowing beacons and announcing that the power of Sapphiros was in Taiyou once again. At first Yue followed the lead of the Hounds, but then she realized what was actually occurring.

A man running for cover stopped suddenly as he watched an arrow pass right through his hand. Moments later a Hound did the same and stopped to look upwards at the sky in confusion, an arrow passing harmlessly through its nose.

The Hound that first came to the realization that the arrows were an illusion howled to its fellows to show them the truth, but then the real purpose of the arrows suddenly became evident.

The Lillem, too stupid to run when even the sky was falling on them such as it was now, had each been pelted with the illusionary arrows, which by their nature passed through them to stick into the cobblestones below. The Lillem continued to stare up at the sky as they had been doing before, but then something strange happened as they began to react like people lost and confused, rather than mindless savages.

Realizing what was happening, the Hounds barked orders to one another they leapt forward as one to engage the freed Lillem-people, who were still too disoriented to react properly to their circumstance. Thankfully, Yue was there, and although she hadn't wanted to use her power in this way she now found herself with no choice.

Stopping suddenly and becoming visible before the Hounds, she raised her arms and fired out a burst of the power she had stored.

A ribbon of energy, a curious mix of green and cyan, surged out of her and writhed in the air like a snake looking for a target before it twisted downwards to the Hounds, exploding with the impact and leaving nothing in its wake.

"Guess you can't deflect that kind of power, huh?" she asked of the Hounds she'd killed, before she saw more of them lurking in the shadows of other nearby buildings.

"Come on! What are we waiting for?!" A new voice startled Yue as the freed Lilliem surged past her and scattered into the city after the Hounds. Yue turned from them, dashing away at her usual speed to continue the mission she had come here to complete. She wasn't certain what the outcome of this battle between Lillem and Hounds would bring, other than chaos, but those Lillem were Taiyoun and this was their city; if they wanted to fight for it, then more power to them.

True to his word, Bastion had granted his lady her request and before long they found themselves in the open sand patch that served as the city square in Middleton, still fighting for their lives against an angry horde of Lillem.

"Whatever you've come here to do, my Lady," he commented, "I strongly suggest you do it now."

The Lillem pressed in all around them, and while the Deathsquad did their best to keep them at bay, they were tiring quickly.

"Yes, Bastion," Akuma agreed, her voice calm despite their circumstance. "I think we've drawn enough of them to us now."

Closing her eyes and lifting her head, she summoned her power and the symbol of Rubia on her chest lit up with an inner fire, matched by the glow that came from behind her closed eyelids. From where her hand was pressed into the sand before her, a lick of flame sprouted and then quickly grew as it spiraled outwards, fueled by her power. Faster and faster the spiral grew, staying low to the ground but claiming the sand and eventually the surrounding cobblestones. When the fire had spread as far as she wished, Akuma held it there a moment, taking a deep breath before exhaling and sending the flames upwards to engulf the attacking Lillem.

Bastion expected screams, loud and unnatural. He expected faces contorted in pain, or even the unlikely result of the Lillem simply turning to ash or sand, but none of these things happened. The Lillem simply stopped fighting, their contorted inhuman expressions relaxing.

A few more Lillem died before he thought to stop his men. "Defensive positions! Hold!"

Bastion caught Akuma as she swayed, exhausted from her efforts. "I think I got them all, but Bastion, send scouts to see if there are others further out. I will have this place free of taint before we leave it."

"Yes, my Lady."

Annalise, daughter of Lady Anaeth, found herself once more alone in her secret garden. The pale moonlight was enough to see by, even while still being odd after so many long years of sun. She had spent much time in this garden since the trouble had begun in Sresh, because her mother was overprotective of her. On the one hand she resented it, but on the other she'd rather be in here with the flowers than out there with those nasty looking Lillem...

"Oh!" she exclaimed, startled by unexpected movement in the garden before the creature that had been stirring the plants revealed itself. "What do we have here? You're a dog, aren't you?"

"Woof!" The dog, black all over except for red tufts here and there and a red poof to the tip of his tail, seemed to respond to her question in the affirmative.

"Well aren't you just something else."

"He certainly is," a voice responded and Annalise snapped her head up to find a stranger in her garden.

"Is he yours?" she asked cautiously, rising to her feet.

There were no extra limbs that she could see and the young man before her didn't seem threatening. He wasn't tall, but nevertheless gave off a quiet air of authority. His eyes seemed tired but kind and they were a vibrant green she'd never seen before. He was a Roughlander by his dress, if not his accent, and she found herself wondering if he was smiling or serious behind the shadow of his scarf embroidered with leaves.

"He's a friend," he answered ambiguously, as he got a far away sort of expression, "and it's time to be going now."

"Woof!" the dog agreed, sidling up next to Annalise and putting the soft fur of his head innocuously under her hand.

"Oh," she replied, somewhat at a loss and petting the dog absently, "but you've only just arrived. Surely you could stay a little while."

"I'm afraid not," he answered, "but you can come with us."

Something about the way he said it gave the implication that it wasn't a polite request for her company. "N-No –" she stammered. "I think I'll stay here."

"I'm afraid that's not an option." The strange young man frowned before looking past her to address the dog, "Jeth?"

"On it," the dog spoke, its voice gravelly. "Espearia, here we come!"

There was a slight feeling of disorientation, and when it passed Annalise found that she was no longer in her garden but somewhere else, somewhere she felt in her bones to be very far away from Sresh.

Yue was in the halls of the palace now and still no one had stopped her. If the Hounds or anyone else could sense her coming, they gave her no sign. She could feel the power of Taiyou pulsing within her and she knew that even after the attack she had fired on the Hounds outside there was still at least one good shot left in her. Yue would like nothing more than to fire that shot on Lady Lilyth herself, but there was something she had to do first.

She found them by chance and she was glad she did.

"Get the eggs," Yue heard a Croatin voice whisper. "This diversion may be our only chance."

She rounded the corner and stopped, staring at an old friend who was standing before an opening in the palace walls she hadn't known to be there. "The First of the Second Spawn," she greeted the hooded, yet unmistakable, short purple frog-person, "fancy meeting you here."

"Yue! I suppose I should have known that the Chosen would be behind something like this."

"I suppose I should have known the Croatins hadn't defected and joined Lilyth," she responded in kind.

"Shh, we don't speak her name unless we want her wrath brought down upon us. What you've heard about the Croatins is true, the First of the Firsts is being controlled by Lady Lilyth and does what he is told. The rest of us are not so sanguine about our circumstances, especially we of the Second spawn."

"The resistance," she guessed.

The First of the Second spawn scanned the hallway in each direction before cautiously nodding.

"Good, then you're exactly the person I needed to see. I have a bit of advice for you and I hope you'll take it to heart more than the fools in the Raman province did. Get your people out of here, now. This palace won't be standing much longer if I have anything to say about it."

He swallowed visibly before nodding. "Can you give me a few minutes?"

"That's all you have," she answered grimly.

"Let's see how you like it, you spoiled little child. You think you're so special just because you've managed to sit in someone else's chair. Well, I can do that too! You can't be everywhere at once, even if you do have a million legs, and while you're resting your lazy bottom in Taiyou I'm sitting on your throne. Do you hear me, Lilyth?! There's a human in your chair and there's nothing you can do about it!"

"What are you doing?" Oka asked, watching Leon Rama wriggle around on the Emperor's obsidian throne shouting anything that came to his head.

"Sass-talking Lilyth," Leon answered promptly. "How am I doing so far?"

"You really think she can hear you?"

Leon grinned, showing teeth. "If she can, just think of the frustration it would cause her. Besides, it's wonderfully therapeutic. You should try it."

"I'll pass, but you have fun."

"Oh, I will. Where were we? Oh yes, humans! Not only is there one in your chair right now, but we're also all over the world you thought was yours…"

Curved blades flashed in the moonlight and the enemy Stirr started forward, closing in on the humans. Kaji watched them come, his dread mounting but unwilling to make the first strike, lest he be the one to break the Stirr's mandate and bring their wrath down upon the rest of humankind. But perhaps, that was what was already occurring.

"On my mark!" Kaji yelled to the Roughlanders and to the Japanese who held their weapons at the ready.

"Hold your fire," a familiar voice called out and Kaji turned to identify Sir Sabien, riding on the back of a Stirr of all things. "The Stirr will handle their own."

True to his words more Stirr began appearing, seemingly coming out of the night itself, to strike down those who had them surrounded. They were brutally efficient and within moments a circle of Stirr lay headless around them while the newcomer Stirr took up a guard around them.

"Sabien, what's going on?" Masaru asked, looking askance at the Stirr the Knight Commander rode and at Aysel beyond him, atop another.

"Lady Lilyth has been animating her own army of Stirr," Sabien informed them, "likely from the Stirr's burial grounds. They're like the Lillem that rose from the sand and controlled by her in the same way. Once we showed this to the Stirr, they realized that Lilyth has been lying to them. They have broken ties with her and have sided with us. We are fortunate as the Stirr are a powerful ally to have."

"I can see that," Masaru noted, glancing once more at the corpses all around them.

"Thank you," Kaji said to the nearest Stirr. "Your help is much appreciated."

"*Shhhptthhhshhh…shthhhshh,*" the Stirr responded.

"He says," Sabien translated, and Kaji noted the tiny spider sitting in the man's ear, "'You are welcome…Human.'"

I was readying my third arrow when I became aware of the sounds of fighting below me.

"Adel, are you all right?"

"Never better," Adel answered as she dodged out of the way of a blast of Hound-fire while simultaneously bashing another Hound soundly with her mace. "Only I should warn you," she noted, staring down the remaining Hound as if daring it to attack, "that if more than this show up then it will be time for us to depart."

"One more, then," I answered, turning from her to ready my last shot and send it after the others into the sky above Taiyou. "After that, I've done what I can for them and it'll be up to those in Taiyou to do the rest."

There was a hole straight through the walls of the palace, through two hallways and clear to the outside. This hole, however it had been originally created, had stemmed from within the throne room itself, and it was in the hallway furthest from the throne room that Yue now found herself looking inwards, debating whether her strike was going to be enough.

"Seize her!"

Hounds leapt forward to obey their Lady's command, leaping through the holes in the walls, bent on reaching her and tearing her to shreds. Yue didn't fear the Hounds, not even this many of them, but that voice had confirmed one thing: Lilyth was indeed still in that throne room and this was her chance.

Ignoring the Hounds entirely, she unleashed the power she had brought with her from the Leyin, sending it rippling through the intervening space between herself and the throne room. The stone walls crumbled, the tapestries burned, and Hounds fell, whining in pain, but it wasn't going to be enough.

Yue could see her now; Lilyth herself filled the hole in the throne room's wall. She was terrifying, tall, and powerful, with a surreal sort of beauty despite unnatural features and spider-like bone limbs fanning out around her.

The ribbon came for her, sure of its target, but Lilyth simply raised her hand and the power exploded in mid-air, filling Yue's view with fire and debris.

She didn't wait to find out if by some miracle the blast had succeeded. Before the dust could clear she was gone, racing southward toward where she would meet Fuun for the return journey to Espearia. She had failed, but the message was sent.

As the soft light of dawn began to show over the tips of the easternmost mountains, the sky was filled with the flapping wings of the Kumori as the ancient race migrated southward to join the rest of the world once more.

Hotaru beamed over at Ris before looking down at the sand rushing by far below. She was being carried in a litter of sorts, kept aloft by four Kumori who flew above her, but she didn't mind the odd method of transport in the least. She could see the lights of the Ruby City ahead and the familiar plume of smoke that constantly rose from the active volcano that was the Temple of Ruby. The city would be their first stop; it was too far to make it to Espearia in one night and it was best they go to ground where it was safe. Whether the Ruby City or Espearia, both countries were her allies and now the Kumori were as well.

This flight was the first step and a long way from taking back Taiyou or defeating the Lady Lilyth, but Hotaru had to believe things were finally going to start turning around soon.

CH. 16 – RETALIATION

The sun came up slowly over the mountains to bathe the Sand Lakes in the golden light of dawn. It lit the cities and the villages, and spilled in through outpost windows. The sun's light covered everywhere from Espearia to Sresh, illuminating a quiet world where the chaos of the pre-dawn was already fading into memory.

There were no armies to be seen on the Sand Lakes, no wars or battles waging in the cities, no weapons firing, and no blasts of energy or shows of a Chosen's power.

All was quiet, perhaps too quiet.

"Is everyone accounted for?" I asked, having sent myself as mist to Chikara in Espearia.

"Well, if you've got Lady Adel, Kaji, Masaru, Sabien, and Aysel there with you, then yes," she answered. "Everyone else is here in Espearia, except for Hotaru and Ris, but Lady Akuma already contacted Ao Kouen through Kaji's Ruby mirror and told him that they brought all the Kumori to the Ruby City, so we've sent Fuun to go and pick them up."

I let out a breath. "Good. Don't bother sending Fuun this way, I'll bring the rest of us back to Espearia soon. There are just a few matters I have to see to first."

Chikara nodded. "All right, but there's just one thing you ought to know. Annalise of Sresh is here in Espearia."

"Who?"

"Lady Anaeth's daughter. Uncle Jeth brought her here and she's real unhappy about it, but Mama says we have no choice, we've got to keep her here until this is over."

"I'll talk to her when I get there, Chikara. In the meantime, just try and be her friend. She probably needs one right now."

"All right, I will."

I faded out from Chikara's view and returned to my body, which was seated in the sunny yard of the Children's Outpost, to find Masaru beside me. He was waiting patiently, but it was obvious he was happy to see me.

I climbed to my feet, a smile filling my face, and before I knew it I was in his arms.

"Ye seem pleased," he noted after a moment. "I take it that yer mission went a little better than ours?"

I smiled ruefully. "I heard about what happened with the undead Stirr. There was no predicting that, but at least now we have the Stirr officially on our side."

"Aye, but that's hardly thanks to Kaji and I. Hex's transmission was what really convinced them and that wouldn't have been possible without Sabien and Aysel."

"Don't be too hard on yourself. We all more or less accomplished what we set out to do and we've all come back safely. That's all the victory I need for the moment."

"Ye're right, of course. Oh, I almost forgot, there've been people who've been askin' after ye and there's good news to tell ye also."

"If it's about Neva and her baby I already know that I have to check in on her and I intend to do so."

"Well, Neva's one of them, yes, but yer mother's also anxious to see ye and tell ye the happy news."

"News?"

"It's yer father," Masaru replied, smiling in anticipation of my reaction. "He's awake."

I should have probably felt elated at the news, but instead I found my relief was mixed with a sense of trepidation – my father didn't yet know about the plans that Masaru and I had made and I was at a loss to predict what his reaction might be. I smiled anyway for Masaru's benefit as I didn't want to give him cause to worry.

"So did ye want to go see him then or did ye want to find yer mum or Neva first?"

"Hmm?" I was busy running through the various ways the conversation with my father could go. "Oh, well, I should make sure he's okay first and we'll likely find my mother with him, or at least nearby."

"Ye're probably right about that. Come on then, I'll show ye the way."

My father was in the infirmary on one of the upper floors of the Children's Outpost. We found Razor waiting outside the infirmary door and no sooner had he laid eyes on me than he rushed forward to scoop me up into his arms and hold me aloft.

"Razor!" I protested, laughing despite myself.

He put me down as suddenly as he had picked me up, with a roguish grin and a quick ruffle of my blue curls. "I'd heard you were here and I figured that this was the first place you would come."

"You guessed right," I told him with a smile; worries aside, it was good to see Razor again. "Did you need me for something, or did you just miss my company?"

"Both, actually," Razor admitted and his cheerful expression faltered. "I'm worried about the baby."

"I'm on my way to see Neva, just as soon as I've seen my father."

"It's just that it's not normal, Yukari. No one's ever seen or heard of anything like it and I'm afraid that what comes out of Neva might not be what we're all expecting."

I didn't like the sound of what Razor was saying, but I could only reasonably deal with one problem and Neva wasn't here for me to examine, so all I had to go on was Razor's fears and conjectures.

"Razor, go find Neva and bring her here so I can have a look at her. In the meantime, I'm going to talk to my father."

Razor nodded, a sly grin returning to his face. "Good luck to you both," he added rather unexpectedly, "and remember, if you don't tell him while you have the chance, my sister certainly will."

"Oh, go on with ye," Masaru told him, giving Razor a little shove to get him moving. "Can't ye tell she's worried enough about tellin' him as it is?"

Still grinning, Razor left Masaru and I alone before the closed infirmary door. It had been silly of me to think that Masaru hadn't noticed my distress and the reason for it.

"So are ye going to be the one to open it, or should I?"

I was being silly. This was my father, the person I'd been so desperate to rescue ever since the moment I learned he was missing. Of course I wanted to see him and confirm for myself that he was alive and well; the rest of it, including the subject I was dreading to bring up, could wait.

"No, it's all right," I informed Masaru, pushing open the heavy metal door in question. "I've got it."

My father was propped up on the bed with my mother on a stool beside him. They were facing the door from across the room and he lit up as he took sight of me. The dark circles under his eyes and the pain in his expression gave evidence to the ordeal he had lived through, but his hand was on my mother's and he looked as if he was trying to make the best of his situation. My mother was smiling, either glad to see me, glad my father was awake, or simply glad that we were all in the same room again.

I made myself focus on her happy expression and put one foot in front of the other, intent on crossing the room to reunite my family once more, when I realized belatedly that Masaru wasn't following me and I turned my head back to look at him.

He was frozen in the doorway, unable to do what I had already done by taking those first few steps into the room. Apparently he was just as nervous about facing my father's response to our announcement as I was, no matter how well he pretended otherwise.

"We're in this together now, remember?" I whispered back at him, holding out my hand.

He nodded, swallowing somewhat apprehensively, before stepping forward and taking hold of my outstretched hand, his tanned face nearly as white as a sheet.

My mother was on her feet and putting her arms around me before I even made it to my father's bedside. "I'm so happy you're safe. You don't know how worried I was when those robots dropped your father off and you were nowhere to be seen."

"I've been really busy…" I began somewhat lamely.

"Let her be, Hana," my father interjected. "I'm sure Yukari has had her hands full keeping us and everyone else safe." He turned to me, holding out his arms for a hug. "It's good to see you, Honey."

"You too, Daddy," I replied, my voice thick with emotion as I buried my face in his shoulder.

"Masaru," my father acknowledged him with a nod after I had pulled away, "I'm also glad to see you safe, son."

Masaru's complexion shifted from white to red. "Thank ye, sir," he said with some difficulty. "The same goes for ye as well and Yukari's mum. It was such a relief when Yukari finally found ye."

"As to that," my father replied, shifting his gaze to me, "it seems as if I've been gone quite a while, though it felt like no more than a few hours. I know I must have missed a few things…"

I felt my throat dry up; it was true that he'd missed a lot, especially concerning the war effort, but the most important thing he'd missed was the one thing I wasn't quite sure if I could bring myself to tell him about. My mother was giving me a pointed look and by now my father had taken notice of the awkward silence and my pained expression.

"What is it, Yukari? You can tell me."

Masaru took my hand and squeezed it in wordless support, and I realized that I had little choice in the matter now that the subject had been broached. It was either I tell him now myself, or watch as matters fell to pieces if I let Dahlia do it for me – I had to tell him.

"I should have told you on the day Taiyou fell," I began, struggling for every word. "I've been waiting for my chance ever since. I wanted you to be the first to know, but…Masaru and I have decided to be Joined according to Roughlander custom."

"'Joined,'" my father repeated, his tone and expression betraying nothing, "is that like–"

"They're getting married, Dear," Mother explained. "I had a little trouble with the terminology myself, at first."

"You knew about this?" he questioned, his voice rising dangerously.

"You said it yourself," Mother retorted, "you've been gone a while."

Masaru cleared his throat audibly from behind me. "If I may," he began, "I'd like to tell ye that I love your daughter very much and I'd be extremely thankful if ye'd give us yer blessing to be Joined."

"It's a little late for that, isn't it?" my father retorted.

"Daddy!" I exclaimed, just as my mother said, "Seijiro!"

Father smiled suddenly, contrary to all my expectations, and he shook his head while trying to keep from laughing out loud. "I'm sorry," he said, "but you should have seen the look on your faces. No, but honestly," he said as he sobered immediately, "I'm proud of you, Yukari, and I know that you wouldn't have made this decision lightly. Of course, you have my blessing," he added, taking my hand in his and looking past me to Masaru. "I would never try to stand in the way of my daughter's happiness. Welcome to the family, Masaru."

Masaru's relief was palpable and I felt the tension drain out of me, as well. "Thank ye, sir. Ye won't regret it!"

"See that I don't, young man," Father responded with a smile, "though I can't say I wasn't expecting something like this. You never do anything halfway, do you, Honey?"

I shook my head, smiling in genuine relief.

"Oh, come here, both of you," Mother ordered us, beaming, and for the first time in memory I was pulled into a family hug.

"Ahem," someone cleared their throat from the doorway and we broke apart to see Razor waiting there with Neva in his shadow, though I almost wasn't sure it was her by the unbelievable size of her pregnant belly.

"I have to go," I said, standing abruptly.

Father looked confused, but Mother nodded knowingly. "Yes, go on, Dear. Masaru and I can fill your father in on the details. Just do me a favour, would you, and have Razor lead you and Neva down to the common area when you're done with her."

I nodded in absent agreement, with my gaze focused on Neva's midsection and Razor's barely-concealed worry. Squeezing Masaru's hand one last time, I left him alone with my parents as I joined Neva and Razor out in the hallway.

"Is there somewhere private we can go to talk?" I asked Razor, trying to avoid staring at Neva.

"I figured you'd say that, so I found an empty room down the hall. Follow me."

The three of us – Neva with some difficulty due to her bulk – made our way down the hall to a door that Razor had thoughtfully propped open with a stool.

"Have a seat," I instructed Neva, pulling the stool over to the middle of the small, empty room and letting the door close behind us. "How have you been?" I asked, once she'd seated herself and Razor took up position by the small circular window carved out of the rock wall.

"Mostly okay," Neva answered. "I've been eating and drinking a lot more – anything I can get my hands on, really – but other than that things have been okay."

"Any pain or discomfort?" I asked, examining the shape of her belly with my eyes, without using my power to see inside her. I wasn't sure yet that I wanted to know what I would find.

"No," she answered, shaking her head. "I kept thinking that there ought to be. All the ladies give me polite smiles, but I can tell they're worried. This is far from normal, isn't it, Yukari?"

From all appearances she looked normal and healthy – for someone who was maybe seven or eight months along – but as far as I knew Neva had been pregnant for no longer than a month and a half, and that was maybe an exaggeration. Had we been in the eggs longer than I had initially thought, or was it possible that the stasis within the eggs worked differently than time outside of it?

But no, I had examined Neva the same day we had all emerged from the Ruby eggs and she'd not been so far along as to suggest either possibility. This simply wasn't a normal phenomenon, at least by my world's standards, and likely this one's as well, if the Roughlander reaction was anything to go by.

"Well, I've certainly never heard of anything like it," I told her honestly, "but if there's one thing I've learned since coming here, it's that nothing is impossible."

"So my baby is just different, then?"

I took a deep breath. "Let's have a look and find out, shall we?"

With the memory of the tiny fetus I had witnessed there before fresh in my mind, I twisted my vision to see into Neva's womb. The baby was so much larger than it had been before, but it bore a strong resemblance to the pictures of developed fetuses I had seen in my biology textbooks back on Earth, with some very obvious exceptions.

Curled up over its shoulders were tiny, talon-like limbs, matched by two more below, one on either hip. However it had happened, Neva's baby wasn't exactly human, or at least not fully so; the little girl growing inside of this Roughlander woman was a Lillem.

I peered farther, scanning within the baby. She had an extra kidney, and I couldn't be certain but she also seemed to have more rib bones than normal, as well as a slightly elongated jaw, which reinforced her Lillem appearance. Most importantly, though, is what I didn't find; try as I might, I didn't find any trace of the little black flecks that animated the Lillem. There was no indication that this little baby girl, Lillem or not, would be a mindless savage, controlled by the Lady Lilyth.

"What is it?" Neva asked, unable to stay silent any longer. "What do ye see?"

"Well, it's a girl," I told her the good news first, aiming for enthusiastic and falling just shy of it.

A glimmer of a smile crossed Neva's features at the news and she tilted her head to share the moment with Razor behind her before turning back to me. "That's it, then?"

"The baby looks healthy, and by all indications it shouldn't be too long before it's ready to come out, but I think it's also safe to say that this pregnancy isn't normal. The baby isn't exactly human…"

Razor stood up straight at the words, alarm filling his posture, but Neva simply locked her eyes on mine with a determined expression and a serious tone in her voice. "What do ye mean, 'not exactly human'?"

"Physically, the baby is a Lillem."

"How is that possible?" Neva asked once she was able to form words.

I shook my head. "I don't know exactly. It's possible that you were infected in some way during the really early stages of your pregnancy, or that something happened to you while you were in the egg, but there's no way to be sure."

"You said physically," Razor noted, picking up on my deliberate use of the word, "what about in other ways?"

I turned to Razor. "I didn't find any trace of the magic that makes the Lillem act the way they do. My best guess is that she'll be like the people who've been infected and then freed. She'll have the Lillem appendages and the physical differences, but her mind will be her own."

"Then, even if she looks different, she can be raised just like any other Roughlander child?" Neva asked.

"I don't see why not, though she will have natural weapons and would have to learn right away how to be careful with them."

"The Lillem parts, they aren't going to make this more difficult, are they? Another thing all the ladies keep telling me about is how much it's going to hurt when the baby wants to come out."

I frowned, considering her question. The Lillem talons were curled up now, but who knew what would happen during labour, or even just when the baby started becoming more active. My biggest concern at this point was Neva's safety, but perhaps there was a solution for that. "I'm pretty sure getting her out won't be a problem, especially if I can find a way to use my power to help. We'd just need to determine when she'll be ready, but I think I'll consult a friend of mine in the Ruby City first anyway. If anyone might know something about Lillem births, it would be him."

It was a measure of their trust in me, or perhaps their concern for the baby's welfare, that neither Razor nor Neva questioned my contacts in the Ruby City. Regardless of what the Roughlanders might think of him, I could honestly think of no one better than General Oka to help me with such a sensitive and unusual circumstance.

"Surprise!"

The common room was filled with women of varying ages all seated along the two long tables, though everyone stood at our entrance. I certainly didn't know everybody, but I was surprised at the number of people I at least recognized. A number of these people, Roughlanders and Taiyouns alike, were among those that had been with us since the Temple of Machalite.

My mother met Neva at the door and whisked her away from Razor, leading her over to an empty chair that had been arranged for her at the head of one table. Seated around that table were some Roughlander women, including Dahlia, as well as Yue and Kaji's mothers. I was somewhat surprised to see Hotaru's mother, Hatsumuya-san, come out of the kitchen area beyond with a platter full of food, followed by Mifa, doing the same.

As soon as Neva was seated, my mother came back for me. "It's a baby shower," she whispered in my ear. "We wanted to show our support for Neva with all that she's going through and it's certainly been nice to have something to celebrate. What do you think?"

"I think it's a wonderful idea."

Mother beamed and shooed Razor out the door with a quick, "Women only, Dear, but thanks for bringing them by," and then she took my arm to lead me to a chair near to her own.

The food was excellent, if a strange combination of Roughlander, Taiyoun, and even pseudo-Japanese dishes, and it was so wonderfully novel to be surrounded by so many people in such good humour that I almost forgot that I had promised to return to Espearia as soon as possible. It wasn't until Masaru and Kaji finally tracked me down that I realized it was past time to be going.

Espearia was nowhere near as lively as the bright and sunny Children's Outpost, which had been filled with Roughlander good spirits. In contrast, the atmosphere in Arashi's office where we gathered was tense and the topic of conversation was war. After we'd all been briefed on one another's exploits, the talk turned to the results of this morning's efforts and what they might mean to us now.

"It simply doesn't follow that she would take what we did last night calmly," Adel postulated, pacing the length of the room. "The Lilyth I knew would be livid and would have already reacted accordingly."

"But so far no one has reported any kind of retaliation," Arashi pointed out from where she sat calmly behind her desk. "All's quiet here and everywhere else."

"Maybe too quiet," Kaji suggested, his expression serious.

"How can too quiet be a bad thing?" Hotaru asked from her seat next to Ris. "Isn't this what we want?"

"Not if she's just trying to lull us into a false sense of security so we make a mistake," Aysel pointed out.

"I think we'd all better assume that she's preparing her next move and be prepared for whatever comes next," Sabien suggested.

"He's right," Fuun agreed from his place against the far wall. "A predator is always silent before it strikes."

"I still say this waiting is unlike her after she's been riled," Adel insisted.

"Maybe she's learned a thing or two since the last time she was defeated," I commented before deliberately changing the subject. We could conjecture all we'd like, but we wouldn't know what Lady

Lilyth was planning until she chose to make her move. "Since we have some time, could someone tell me where I can find Chikara?"

"She's upstairs keeping our guest entertained," Arashi told me with a frown, pointing above her to the office's balcony, "though I can tell you from experience that it's a thankless job."

I nodded to her and, letting myself past Jeth seated on the bottom step, I climbed the spiral staircase to the second floor to meet the young woman we had kidnapped.

"Annalise, I know how you must feel–" Chikara's voice came from the open doorway ahead.

"How can you possibly know anything?" Annalise protested. "My mother is in danger and I'm stuck here with you, unable to do anything to help."

"Actually," I interjected, "Chikara would know better than anyone what it's like to have her responsibilities outweigh her need to see her mother safe. That aside, though it may not look like it from your perspective, you being here is probably the best thing for your mother and Sresh."

"What do you mean?" she asked, pinning me with an intense look. "And who are you, anyway?"

"My name is Yukari," I said, pulling out a chair and taking a seat beside her and across the table from Chikara, "and to answer your question, you being here means that you can't be used against your mother. Because we took you, your mom can't be blamed for the fact that you're missing. She's actually in a better position to do something about freeing herself and Sresh than she was before."

"That's why I'm here?" she asked, her expression incredulous. "You're trying to help my mother?"

"That's what I've been trying to tell you," Chikara began. "You're not our prisoner but our guest, I just can't let you go home until it's safe."

Hearing this, Annalise decided that she wanted to know more about what was actually going on in the world. It seemed that she had been deliberately kept in the dark until now, which had probably been her mother's way of keeping her safe from the horrors that besieged Sresh and the rest of the world. Between Chikara and I, we took turns explaining the state of affairs in Sresh and elsewhere, trying to set Annalise a little more at ease with her circumstance.

But then, between one breath and the next, Yue appeared in the doorway and everything changed.

"The Hounds are attacking the rest of the Leyins," she announced. "Ao Kouen can feel it and it's tearing him apart. He can't tell us much more than that, but something tells me the Leyins aren't the worst of it. Something awful is happening in Taiyou."

This was the bad news we had been waiting for. Everyone in Arashi's office below was on their feet and looking alarmed, except for Ao Kouen, who was slumped in Sabien's arms and holding his head with both hands.

"Chikara, can you stay here with Ao Kouen and Annalise?" I asked her.

Chikara nodded mutely, her eyes wide.

"I'm staying as well," Arashi called up. "I might be needed here in case Taiyou is only a distraction for something else."

"Anyone else?" I asked, climbing down the stairs after Yue who had simply used her power to leap down to the ground. "All right, let's go."

"I'm coming," Ao Kouen stated, struggling to stand on his own.

"No," Yue stated.

"It's my country and they're my people, Yue."

"And they aren't going to lose you to Lilyth's trap. You're staying here unless you're well enough to get there on your own."

Ao Kouen's expression was mutinous, but he couldn't deny that Yue was right and he wasn't given further chance to protest, as I took hold of everyone else in the room and sent us to Lady Rhine. Thanks to Yue's report, she was the one person I knew who was in the Raman province.

It was worse than any of us could have imagined. The Raman Keep was shaking; the ground itself in Taiyou was unstable.

"It's not an earthquake," Masaru informed us with his hand to the ground as he used his power to sense what was far beneath us. "I know how crazy it sounds but there are sandcrawlers coming, a whole herd of them."

"Sandcrawlers?" The Raman keep, which had presumably stood for centuries, was threatening to break apart from the force of the disturbance. "Do they ever leave the Sand Lakes or travel in herds like this?"

"They've moved in force before, though only the once that I know of," he answered my question, "but even at the massacre of Marble Ridge there weren't anywhere near this many."

"sandcrawlers have never come anywhere near Taiyou," Lady Rhine stated, aghast. "Never."

"Well, we don't have time to figure out what has made them change their mind," Adel stated.

I nodded. "No, we don't, and unless anyone can think of a way to stop a herd of sandcrawlers, then we need to get everyone out of here, now."

"How do we do that?" Hotaru asked.

"Get them to the Leyins," Yue answered. "All we have to do is stop the Hounds from destroying the Leyins and Ao Kouen will do the rest."

It was easier said than done.

The wailing of the approaching herd drowned out all sounds other than the rumbling beneath our feet and the grating of the stones of the Raman Keep as they began to crumble. I didn't want to look, but the towering cloud of sand the massive beasts kicked up was soon visible east of Taiyou's border even without my power. At the speed the sandcrawlers were moving, they would soon be upon us.

We split up; the Raman province was more than just the keep and its outbuildings. It wasn't lost on me or anyone else that if we couldn't stop the sandcrawlers here, then the all of Taiyou might face the same fate as the former Roughlander settlement of Marble Ridge, the same fate that had left Ao Kouen the sole survivor of a senseless tragedy years ago.

As I took to the air and angled my flight to take me over the battlements of the keep, so I could see what was coming for us, I found myself wondering why this was happening. Was this Lady Lilyth's retaliation for our show of defiance, or simply a freak occurrence? The literal wall of sand blowing toward Taiyou was as expected, but by focusing on the ground my power allowed me to make out what others would soon see. The sandcrawlers, some taller than even the building upon which I stood, dove in and out of the ground in a wave-like pattern. Their movements, which were perfectly synchronized with one another as they moved in a row, could only be described as organized – this was an attack, and with the last holdouts in Taiyou as the intended victims there could be little doubt as to who was behind it.

I heard footfalls behind me and whirled about to see the Lion Brigade's archers lining the battlements with efficiency and drawing their bows."Are you all looking to die?!" I yelled to make myself heard. I better than anyone knew how ineffective a swarm of arrows would be even against one sandcrawler, let alone this many. "Your arrows will do nothing to slow them down, if they even feel them through their thick hides!"

"We will defend our keep," one of them protested.

"No. The keep will fall, but you can defend your people. Get them to the northern border, it's your only chance."

"Get below and escort the women and children out!" Their captain, a man who knew to trust my words from when we had travelled together before, began shouting orders to his men. "Go north as quickly as you can."

"Get as many people as you can to the Leyin," I told him, as the last of the archers disappeared back into the keep. "Your king will do the rest."

"Take the north side, I've got the west!" Adel called out to her sister, veering sharply left to engage the Hound in her path.

"You don't have to take them all on alone," Sabien reminded her, having reformed from a puddle on the far side of the Leyin to leap upon an unsuspecting Hound.

He drove his two swords into the beast's neck as Adel sent her adversary flying backwards with a powerful blow of her heavy wooden mace.

"I'm grateful for the help, believe me," she told him, offering Sabien a hand up out of the hole in the ground that the Hound had dug in the place where the Leyin ran through the land, "and I'll be even more grateful for it once they get here."

Adel pointed out three more Hounds racing toward them in the long grass. Taking up defensive positions shoulder to shoulder, Sabien and Adel prepared to face the onslaught.

Jeth dealt a powerful blow to the head of the Hound nearest him, his scaled demon arm punching through the tough hide of the creature and resulting in a crunching sound as the Hound's skull caved in from the impact. Greenish yellow light shot out in beams from Pine's elongated fingers, the ten individual beams honing in on two of the Hounds and the unique Second Spawn ability filling the air with the smell of seared flesh. Fuun simply summoned his katana and with it in hand he began to dance, and the Hounds died.

The sandcrawlers, however, were another matter altogether.

I peppered their hides with arrows from hundreds of feet in the air, calling down storms of the kind that exploded on impact. Beside me Ris used her powers to direct the wind to increase the speed of my arrows and even tried raining down sheets of ice over the beasts, but they didn't even slow.

Sensing beneath me, I turned every person I could feel into mist as the line of sandcrawlers dove across the border into Taiyou and through the stronghold itself. I held my breath as the small cloud of mist that constituted those I had saved floated up to me and I watched the keep crumble.

"This way!" Aysel called, funneling as many people as possible toward the invisible Leyin located north of the Raman Keep.

To her left, multiple Kajis were fighting off Hounds, new Kajis appearing as older ones fell to the creatures' attacks. To Aysel's right was much of the same, only there was only one of Yue, but she moved quickly enough to make it appear that she was in more than one place at once.

The people disappeared as they reached the Leyin, Ao Kouen's power transporting them to the safety of Espearia, but the line of people fleeing kept getting longer. Worse than even that, the Hounds stopped focusing their attacks on the magical lines themselves or the Knights defending them, and suddenly decided to turn their attention to the refugees instead. Quite a few of them fell before anyone realized what was happening.

"I've got 'em!" Hotaru declared and moments later people began to disappear, a massive puddle forming in their place, which grew larger as it absorbed more people and transformed them as well. The puddle was in no real danger from the Hounds so it surged forward, weaving to absorb everyone in its path before rushing for the Leyin Aysel was guarding.

Ris and I flew overhead, and I turned those I came across to mist as we went.

"It's a herd of sandcrawlers!" Masaru called out to farmers and soldiers alike as he headed away from the ruins of the keep. "Go on with ye if ye want to live!"

"Need a lift?" I called down to him.

"If ye don't mind," he called back flippantly and I didn't waste time with a response before turning him to mist with the others.

I climbed higher to ensure that the sandcrawlers wouldn't reach us before I angled for the Leyin ahead, gesturing for Ris to do the same.

Ris and I found Adel and Sabien before the Leyin, looking tired and battered, but with a scattering of Hound corpses around them and no live enemies to be seen. We landed, Ris running forward to make sure the two of them were okay, as I directed my trailing cloud of mist into the Leyin, sending all those I gathered to Ao Kouen.

"Good work," I noted, turning to the Knights, "but I'm afraid there's no stopping the sandcrawlers. We're going to have to get out of here now or they'll be on top of us soon enough."

I took hold of Adel, Sabien, and Ris first, as they were nearest to me and easiest to sense. Then I felt for Aysel, Kaji, Jeth, Pine, and Fuun. I knew Masaru had gone already, but I couldn't find Hotaru or Yue.

I strained my power, trying harder...there – Yue and Hotaru were both very far away, in Espearia, then, with Masaru. Satisfied, I located one last person, Chikara, and sent them all to her, deliberately leaving myself exactly where I was. I hadn't been sure that I could do it, but I could sense them all now, far away to the east where Espearia was located and I was still in Taiyou.

I could feel the shaking beneath my feet, stronger than ever; I didn't have much time now, but I wasn't through yet. The rumbling grew in intensity as I wracked my brain for who might still be in the city. My frantic search was interrupted by a loud booming sound to the south and I looked up to see a massive pillar of fire and dark-coloured smoke where the city of Taiyou should be.

No – was I too late? Belatedly, my mind supplied me with one of the last names on my list of people that I had promised to find: Yuge.

The father of Neva's baby and the second in command of the Roughlanders I had led from Hex's outpost to Taiyou, Yuge was someone that I hadn't been able to find since I'd first tried in the Temple of Machalite. If he had been a Lillem like Razor, then he might still be in Taiyou where I'd last seen him.

And, miraculously, he was.

Rather than stay by the Leyin to be eaten or crushed by the sandcrawlers, I sent myself to him.

"Yuge, Yuge!"

I became fully solid some ways out on the lengthy bridge of Taiyou, between the corpse of a Hound and the half-mauled form of the friend I'd been looking for. He was still alive; he had to be, since I had been able to find him, but he certainly didn't have much life left in him.

"Yukari," Yuge coughed my name. "I tried...tried to warn...she knows now."

"Shh, it's all right," I told him, even though it was a lie. I didn't think that even my powers could keep him whole enough to send to Ris in Espearia and hers wouldn't be enough to rebuild what was left of him.

Yuge grabbed hold of my arm and drew me in close with surprising strength. "She used me, she knows everything. 'Bout Lord 'Ex, the outpost, and even the Binoids. You'll tell 'im, won't you? Tell 'im I 'ad no choice and I'm sorry."

The implications of this were not lost on me. Yuge knew full well where Hex's outpost was hidden and far more of its secrets than even I did, and Lady Lilyth had been searching for Hex for some time now. His technology had been the one thing to keep him hidden, but if Yuge had been forced to talk then Hex might have lost the one advantage he'd always had.

"I'll tell him," I agreed, as Yuge's grip on my arm slowly went limp.

I was holding back tears, for Yuge's sake and for Neva's, when another explosion reminded me of where I was standing and what was still happening all around me. Ash fell thickly like grey snow, covering Yuge on the bridge and resting on top of the still water that marked the border of Taiyou. I stood and faced the land that I had once sworn to protect, and I saw in its place a veritable pool of lava stemming from a geyser that had erupted in the very place where the palace once stood.

The buildings closer to the bridge – the storehouses, the guardhouse, and the Roughlander Sanctioned Outpost – were intact for now, but lava coursed through the streets, fanning further and further out from the source. It was, if anything, worse than the destruction that the sandcrawlers had caused, and in this case there was no warning anyone; the worst had already happened and I didn't see any fleeing survivors.

I stood there for some time, watching and hoping that somehow what I was seeing wasn't true, but soon enough the molten lava reached the bank and set the legendary bridge of Taiyou aflame as it flowed into the water surrounding Taiyou. I closed my eyes, but I could still feel the heat of it and knew that the sight would be forever burned into my memory.

CH. 17 – STONE TABLE ALLIANCE

"**E**verything's nice and quiet here," Dahlia told us, her voice coming through Hotaru's canteen, which she held out so everyone in Arashi's office could hear what the Roughlander Corporal had to say. "However, I did receive an emergency transmission from Hex. Lady Lilyth found him. He says to tell ye that he's lost much, but he's on his way to join ye in Espearia."

"But he's all right?" I asked.

"Seemed like it, but it was a recorded message," Dahlia answered. "Either way, I'm sure ye'll find out yerselves soon enough. He said he'd be there in under an hour."

Only an hour to cross from one side of the map to the other? Whatever method Hex was using to flee to Espearia, it wasn't a long trek on foot across the sand lakes.

"If he contacts you again," Arashi told Dahlia through the canteen, "make sure you tell him that he's certainly welcome in Espearia and we'll be glad to see him safe."

Hotaru said her goodbyes to Dahlia, snapping the lid of her canteen shut before addressing the rest of us. "I know Dahlia said everything is okay there, but were Taiyou and Hex's outpost the only places attacked today? Has anyone heard from Leon or Akuma?"

"I've been trying to contact them ever since we got back, but Akuma isn't answering the mirror," Kaji answered.

"That's strange, isn't it?" I asked. "I thought those Ruby mirrors were tied into her power somehow, like my arrows, or Hotaru and her water communication."

"Well can ye sense her, ye know, like ye find other people?" Masaru asked.

"I can't sense anything beyond the Ruby City's barrier," I answered, "and even after the Vile Emperor disappeared the barrier is still there."

"We should go," Yue decided.

"Well, we don't all need to go," Kaji noted, "but I'd like to make sure they don't need our help. It's not like Akuma not to answer, especially now."

"I'll come with you," Hotaru offered. "That way if it's bad I can call back here and Fuun can bring help – or Ao Kouen, if he's awake and feeling up to it."

"I'm coming too," I announced. "I have some things I have to take care of in the Ruby City and I should be there too if they are in trouble. But I have a request: Kaji, can you tether the three of us to Yue as she runs? I'd rather see what we're getting into."

"I can," Kaji agreed.

"I know I don't need to say it," Sabien began, "but I'm going to anyways: be careful, all of you."

There was no second guessing our decision to go; once Yue decided to do something she didn't often wait around for anyone. Kaji used his power to leash us all to her somehow and she was off as soon as he gave her the go ahead.

It was the strangest sensation to move at the speed that Yue could reach, now that her powers had grown stronger. We could see each other as we floated along behind Yue, a few feet safely above the ground whizzing by below, but everything else around us was a complete blur the same colour of the sand and sky of the open desert.

The mountain range was no more than a blip on the radar as we passed through it, and soon Yue's speed began to slow as the volcano that was the Temple of Ruby came into view before us.

"I don't sense the barrier," Yue informed us, sounding worried.

"It's not there," Kaji seconded, confirming Yue's words with his ability to see magic in a way we couldn't.

"What does that mean?" Hotaru asked.

"I guess we're about to find out," Yue told her, leaping forward at full speed and taking the rest of us along with her.

It happened so quickly that the effect was jarring.

I felt like I had left my stomach beyond the borders of the Ruby City, as the world faded to a red blur around me. I was struck with a wave of disorienting nausea and then, just as quickly as the feeling came, it passed, and Yue was slowing once more in the empty city streets.

"Where is everyone?" Hotaru asked.

It was eerily quiet in the streets of the Ruby City. Walking now, Yue headed determinately toward the ramp that led up to the palace on the side of the volcano and as Kaji's power still held us to her, I had no choice but to float along after her. Not having much else to do, I closed my eyes and felt the area around me for whomever might be hiding in the homes and businesses that lined the city streets.

"There's no one here," I whispered, feeling awed.

Where did they all go and how did a city full of people simply disappear? I concentrated harder, fanning outward with my power, but other than the four of us there was simply no one nearby enough to sense.

"What do you mean 'no one here'?" Hotaru asked. "They can't just be gone and it doesn't look like they were attacked. There are no bodies or destroyed buildings."

"I know how impossible it sounds," I told her, "but I don't sense anyone other than the four of us."

"What about the temple, then?" Kaji suggested. "Maybe there are people in there and the magic of the place is blocking Yukari from sensing them."

"It's as good a theory as we've got," I agreed, feeling uncertain.

Yue wordlessly veered to the left and altered her path to head for the temple's large double doors instead of continuing on to the palace. Before long we reached the top of the ramp and Kaji dismissed the power that held us to Yue.

Between the four of us we managed to pry the giant doors open, but the inside of the temple was just as silent.

"Hello?" Hotaru called out as we entered the temple's forbidding halls.

My last memory of this place was of the great battle that had been fought here to cleanse this place of the Lady Lilyth's taint. The rough stone walls and platforms surrounding pools of molten lava still bore the traces of that battle, but where before the temple had been filled with the screams of the dying and the clashing of swords, now it was as silent and still as an ancient tomb.

"We don't have time to search everywhere," I told them, my voice echoing in the empty cavernous space, "but I think it's fairly obvious that there's no one here."

"But what happened to everyone?" Hotaru asked.

First Taiyou, then Hex's outpost, and now the Ruby City; each place had been attacked in a different way but all had been virtually eradicated, or at least had had the residents forced out. Was this Lady Lilyth's response to our demonstration and was this all of it, or was there still more to come?

"I'm checking the palace," Yue announced. "I'll be right back."

What was left for her to target? Espearia, as far as I knew, was untouchable as long as Chikara guarded it with her power, but that left the Children's Outpost. Many people I cared about, including my own family, were staying there with the Stirr – who were once loyal to Lilyth – as their only protection.

"I know they said everything was fine, but I've got a bad feeling and I'm going to check on the outpost," I announced.

"You go ahead," Kaji replied, "I know my way around here pretty well and if Akuma has hidden her people here, I'll find them."

I watched him multiply himself and head off in various directions before settling myself down on some cooler stone near the entrance.

"Hotaru, would you mind keeping watch over me while I go check on them?" I asked. "Don't be alarmed if I disappear – I'll let you know if I need help, okay?"

Hotaru nodded, then I shut my eyes and felt for Dahlia. She'd been in charge of the relay station since it had been set up and was the most likely to know if anything was happening at the Children's Outpost, or any of the other places that Hex had connected through her.

"Yukari!" Dahlia stood, surprised by my sudden appearance.

The small, round relay station was a room I didn't recognize, but it looked much the way I expected it to, with assorted wires draped across the floor and a bank of consoles along one wall.

"What are ye doing here?" Dahlia continued. "It's not that I'm not happy to see ye, but ye shouldn't have come. It's not safe."

Not safe? It was what I had feared, then; something was happening here too, except this time I might be in time to stop it. I brought myself fully here, leaving the Temple of Ruby behind for the time being.

"That's why I'm here," I told her, stepping forward, angling for a view of what danger the monitor showed. "What's happening?"

"Well that's just it, I don't know," she answered at a loss. "I haven't been able to get a hold of anybody –"

"I'll tell you what's going on," a new voice interjected and I whirled around to see Adel filling the doorway with her sword drawn and ready for action. "Back away, Yukari," Adel said as she gestured to Dahlia with her sword, "that's a Hound."

"What?!" I exclaimed, flabbergasted. "What would make you say such a thing? It's Dahlia."

"I can see them, Yukari, plain as day," Adel answered, keeping a sharp eye on Dahlia even as she spoke to me. "Whatever that Hound has told you, that's not Dahlia any more than I'm Lady Lilyth."

"You're certain?" I looked from Adel to Dahlia, wondering what the hell was really going on here.

"Now, wait just a minute," Dahlia protested, offended. "I'm not sure how ye got here, or what ye think ye're seeing, but this is what I've been tryin' to tell ye about. Things aren't what they seem here and ye can't trust anybody."

"I thought you said that I'm the first person you've managed to contact," I noted, meeting Dahlia's gaze and holding it.

I concentrated, twisting my vision to see past what lay before me. If Dahlia really was Dahlia, my power would show me the truth. Then I could work on discovering what was really going on here, because the only thing I knew for sure was that something wasn't right. Dahlia's familiar form shimmered and faded, showing a Hound's red fur beneath. I didn't force myself to look any further; that was all the proof I needed.

"Go!" I yelled to Adel, throwing the door shut behind her as soon as she cleared it, and deliberately turning myself to mist, knowing I wouldn't have the time to escape.

As I phased through the door to the other side, I felt the Hound that had masqueraded as Dahlia strike the metal door, denting it with the force of its leap. I reformed and whirled around to check the damage – the door wouldn't last long at this rate.

"Get behind me," Adel ordered, focused on the door which heaved with the Hound's every attempt to break free.

"There's no time," I answered, moving down the hall. "One Hound is likely the least of our problems. Something's happening here." I stopped, studying Adel a moment. "Wait, Dahlia was right about something, how did you get here?"

Adel hurried to join me, then continued down the hall, tugging me by the hand. "I'm not a Hound, if that's what you're thinking, though I'm sure you have some way of confirming that for yourself."

I was tempted to check, but she'd been defending me so far and there was no reason to believe that she wasn't who she appeared to be – then again, the same could have been said for Dahlia.

"Then how?" I pressed, as we raced down the hallway and I tried desperately to get my bearings.

"You're not going to like the answer," she told me, veering left and taking us down a stairway to another floor. "The thing is, I don't know. There was fire all around me and then I was here. I thought I was perhaps hallucinating because of Hound-fire, but then I found you and now I'm not so certain anymore."

I forced Adel to stop with me, as she still had me by the hand. The sense of wrongness had, if anything, gotten stronger. It was true that this outpost was not the easiest place to navigate and neither Adel nor I knew our way around very well, but we'd been running for some time now and we hadn't come across anywhere I recognized.

"Adel, do you know where we are?" I asked, studying the walls around me and thinking back to all the hallways we had passed.

"The Children's Outpost."

"No, I mean where in the outpost we are," I clarified. "I don't recognize it."

"Now that you mention it…"

The outpost weaved in and out of the mountain it was built inside, but what I remembered most from my last visit here was the remarkable amount of sunlight through open archways and window holes. Since leaving the relay station, Adel and I had run down endless hallways, turned left and right, and taken more than one staircase, but we still hadn't seen the outside, or any of the numerous people that should be here.

"Someone's coming," Adel announced, turning her attention to the corner up ahead of us and holding her sword out before her.

Was it another Hound, or an innocent bystander? I had to know. Closing my eyes, I felt out with my power…

"Yukari!"

It hadn't been Neva that I'd heard distantly calling my name – that voice was male – but I could sense her and the child within her just ahead of us.

"Are you sure it's her?" the voice spoke again from nowhere in particular and I recognized it as Leon's, even if I couldn't explain why I was hearing his voice when I knew him to be in the Ruby City.

"As sure as I'm going to be," another voice answered the first, the familiar nasal tones sounding displeased. *"No one's actually done this before, you know…"*

Oka?

"Yukari," Adel said my name, bringing my attention back to the situation at hand, "any ideas?"

Neva rounded the corner and stopped when she saw us. Her face was flushed red and she was having trouble walking, gripping her monstrously large belly with one hand and using the other to support herself by leaning against the stone wall.

"Yukari, I think something's wrong. It hurts…the baby…do ye think it wants to come out now?"

"That's not Neva," Adel warned. "That's another Hound. I'm sure of it."

This Hound's disguise was convincing, just as Dahlia's had been. I didn't want to believe it was true, but Adel had been right before. Still, I couldn't leave Neva like this if I even had a measure of doubt; I'd promised to be there for her when she needed me. I twisted my vision once more and stared in her direction, dreading what my power might tell me.

The air between Neva and myself shimmered and waved, as if there was some sort of wall there that no one else could see, and before my eyes a hand reached through that wall, fingers grasping.

"Just a little further." That was Leon again, his accent unmistakable. *"I think you've almost got her."*

The hand reached out and as strange as it seemed, its every motion seemed to beg me to trust in it and take hold. Neva cried out beyond the shimmering wall, clutching her belly as she fell to the ground. I heard a tearing sound followed immediately by a pained scream and I knew that the unthinkable must be happening – the Lillem baby was clawing its way out and Neva wouldn't survive the birth without my powers to help her.

However, if Adel was right, Neva might very well be a Hound in disguise and attempting to help her might only serve in getting myself killed. It wasn't supposed to happen this way; it was as if every fear I had harbored within the deepest corners of my mind were all coming true at once – it was a nightmare made real.

Desperate to look anywhere but at the horror before me, my eyes focused on the abnormality that was the floating disembodied hand. It was the one thing that didn't fit in all this. It was strange, yes, but not frightening or menacing in any way. But what did it mean?

I forced myself to look up, to see the horrors unfolding, but all of a sudden everything seemed muted and somehow distant. Neva was screaming and Adel was gesturing with her sword, as if asking me if she should take the Hound out now while it was distracted with its charade of being human, but all I could see was the hand as it slowly began to limply withdraw, as if it had given up trying to get me to take notice of it.

I couldn't let it simply disappear; I reached for it.

It was nearly the hardest thing I ever did, dismissing what I saw before me and focusing solely on the one thing that shouldn't exist, but as the hand gripped mine it felt more real than anything else had so far.

It was like coming up for air. I took a deep breath as I became aware of the sound of cracking glass – or Ruby, I realized – as my sight filled with the red blur of the world viewed through red stone.

"It was an egg, wasn't it?!" I asked sharply as soon as I was able. "How long?"

"It's been three days since the Skyraider patrol found you and brought you in," Oka answered.

"Thank heavens you're all right," Leon caught me in a hug. "I figured you'd make your own way out of there eventually, but it's a relief to know that there's a faster way."

I quickly sensed the room around me and felt three other presences, although they were muted, in addition to Oka, Leon, and somewhat surprisingly, Lady Akuma. So, I was in the Ruby City now, Oka's lab specifically.

"You'll want to tackle that egg next." I pointed across the room. "It's Yue's, and once she's free she can easily release Hotaru and Kaji."

Leon nodded and gave me a reassuring smile before standing. Meanwhile, I pushed a few of the egg shards that surrounded me out of my way, as I slid a little ways across the floor to rest my back against the operating table in the center of the room.

"It's Kaji, isn't it," I said softly, knowing that she was near enough to hear me, even if she was on the other side of the table, "that's why you're here."

Akuma didn't answer, but she came over and slowly lowered herself to sit on the floor beside me.

"Did I ever tell you how I came to be here?" she asked, her voice barely above a whisper. "I wasn't kidnapped so much as I was coerced. I had just come from arguing with my mother. I don't remember the exact reason, but I do remember that she was tense over my grandmother being in the hospital. I was on my way to see Kaji – the last thing my mother would have wanted me to do, especially on a school night – when *he* found me, crying in that park."

"You must have been frightened," I noted, recalling my own encounter with the Vile Emperor in that very same park.

"Not at first. But, you see, he didn't appear to me in his armour. He came as a man, albeit a strange one, who was looking for my help…

Tall and imposing, well-muscled, and with long flowing black hair tinted red underneath, he looked like the male hero of a romance novel come to life. His clothes, an archaic loose white shirt and tight leather pants, didn't help the impression, and neither did his enigmatic demeanor and inscrutable expression.

"You must come with me," he stated, holding out his hand to her. "There is not much time."

"Come with you?" Shuzhue's tears stopped abruptly and she practically jumped off the park bench. "No." She shook her head, taking a few steps backwards. "No, I was just leaving..."

"I need your help," the man continued as if she had not spoken. "Your people need your help."

"My people?" she repeated, confused, and looked around to see if there was anyone else in the park she could turn to, but the place was empty – save for the mysterious stranger.

"You're a Chosen of Rubia, as I am," he said, as though that statement explained everything. "Your world and your people are waiting for you to lead them."

"I'm sorry, I can't help you..." Shuzhue protested. "I have to go, my boyfriend is waiting –"

"I wish I could grant you the chance to say goodbye, but there isn't enough time." As he spoke the image of him began to fade until he was almost transparent, before becoming solid once more. "The connection isn't strong enough."

Shuzhue felt her jaw drop staring at him, suddenly convinced that perhaps at least one small part of this man's story was true. People didn't just fade in and out of existence; maybe he really was from another world.

"Who are you?"

"My name is Verasheen," he answered, his eyes intense as they met hers, "and this is your destiny. You will come with me, now, and you will never return."

She turned to flee but he grabbed hold of her wrist; he was more solid than he appeared.

"I'm sorry, but one day you will understand why this is necessary."

"I screamed and I cried and I fought, but none of it mattered," Akuma continued. "Verasheen got his way in the end and I left everything I ever knew behind without even the littlest goodbye, not even to Kaji. The world he took me to was a place of horrors, with beasts and creatures from nightmares and the wildest weather – the planet was already shifting into its new orbit then – but I hardly noticed any of it.

"We arrived somewhere south of the Ruby City, maybe half the distance to Espearia, I'm not sure. He let go of my arm then, there was nowhere for me to run." Her expression was distant now, pained. "I refused to go anywhere with him. Somehow I knew just how far we had travelled, and that true to his words to me in the park I would never be able to go home. I collapsed at the base of a large rock sitting in the middle of a grassy clearing, then I cried and cried until there was nothing left.

"My power was a storm around me and was my only comfort at the time, not that I knew then what it truly was. Sometimes I would cry or rage and it would grow strong enough to block out the world around me. Other times I would pass out from exhaustion and it would leave me for a time until I recovered.

"It was in those quiet times between sleep and heartbroken rage that he would come. Verasheen never pushed me, never tried to force me to leave the large rock that had become my world. He would simply leave me water and food, and speak gently to me, though I never answered him that I recall.

"I drank the water – I was thirsty, but I never seemed to have need for more than that. My power kept me alive, of course, but I didn't think to question it then. I simply cried, wailed my heart out, and screamed until I was hoarse every moment that I was not asleep. Nearly two hundred years passed before I became aware of the world around me once more, and on that day, when there was nothing left of me and at last I was silent, he was there.

"The rest, I'm sure you know or have at least pieced together," she noted, looking my way at last and raising an eyebrow. "I finally gave up on who I used to be – or so I thought at the time. I accepted my destiny and my people, and eventually I accepted him as well. He was always kind to me and patient. No one knew me better, save perhaps the Talons whom he had made choose bodies among those I had known on Earth, so that I would have some small piece of home. Our relationship was far from perfect, but it was all I had. So you can see why I can't just give up on him, even if the life I thought I had lost has suddenly come back for me."

"I just have one question. If the Vile Emperor – I mean Verasheen," I corrected myself, belatedly realizing that she might not appreciate the name.

"Call him what you will," she allowed. "I know that he means something quite different to you than he does to me."

"All right, if he cared for you, why didn't he leave you some sort of instructions or warning? He knew Lilyth would come back. He had to have known, since he was the one who allegedly defeated her. Did he ever mention her or what happened back then?"

"No. I knew of Lilyth, of course, from the histories. Everyone was told of the 'great power that would return someday and destroy the world', but Verasheen never spoke to me about any of it. We didn't talk much and never about the past."

"But don't you find it odd that he would just leave us, and more particularly you, without a clue as to how to finish this without him? I mean, he had eight hundred years to plan. I don't think he would have simply hoped that this day would never come."

"You're right," Akuma agreed with a sigh, "but if he did leave some sort of clue he didn't leave it with me. He said he needed my help, but I can't think it was simply to rule the Ruby City as his queen. Perhaps this was what he meant, but he never told me. He never prepared me for the day when he would just disappear."

"I'm sorry if I'm overstepping, but that doesn't sound to me like someone who loves you or thinks of you in any way as his equal."

"It wasn't always like it is now," Akuma insisted. "I know he loved me once, but things have been difficult between us for some time now. It's like at times he was two different people. One of whom I knew, the other distant and cold. He would sometimes sit for hours in that armour and not move a muscle, or even seem like he was alive at all. And that armour…it got to the point where he would hardly ever take it off. How could anyone try to love someone who is hardly even present in his own body anymore?"

"He must have known we were coming here, though," I mentioned, thinking about the inconsistencies in Akuma's tale. "The Vile Emperor and Yuko Seig were both responsible for our journey here and somehow for the disturbance that caused us to spend eight hundred years in transit. He knew Kaji was coming," I realized, there being little doubt in my mind that the Vile Emperor knew our identities and our relations to Shuzhue through the reports of his Talons, "and he never told you."

I watched as realization – and then slowly rage – settled over Akuma's features.

"You know, I want to believe that whatever he's done, it was for my good or for the good of our people, but if he ever returns he's going to have to tell me everything."

There was a sudden commotion from the other room and then an exclamation and the sound of Ruby shattering. "That's probably Yue," I told Akuma, "and if it is, Kaji and Hotaru will be out any minute now."

"Thank you, Yukari," she responded, getting to her feet, and I gathered it wasn't what I had just said that she was thanking me for. "You and I were never close on Earth, or even since, but I've always respected how smart you are. I don't just mean book smart, you see into the heart of matters."

With that Akuma left me, intent on going to the room where Oka and Leon were working to free the others. "Excuse me," she said, sidestepping out of the way of someone she encountered in the doorway.

I didn't recognize him at first. Tall and broad-shouldered with a square jaw, he had wild fiery orange hair that fanned out around his head like a halo. "You," I said, catching his attention, and as his red eyes locked on my blue ones I suddenly realized who I was looking at, "you're the one from the egg we found in the museum. Who are you?"

I suppose I owe you thanks for finding me and setting me free," he noted with a slight smile. He bowed almost mockingly. "The Lava Lord, at your service."

"Venon," the name escaped me as I put two and two together – I was looking at Verasheen's long-lost brother, the man whose egg he had kept hidden in the museum tower for centuries.

"Where did you hear that name?" Suddenly serious, the Lava Lord straightened and regarded me intently. "Who are you?"

"Yukari Namikoya, Chosen of Sapphiros," I informed him, giving him a smile of my own, "and let's just say that we both have quite a bit of catching up to do. I think we can be of assistance to one another."

"I assume you want to know the details surrounding my somewhat exaggerated demise," he guessed, kneeling down so we could speak face to face.

His gaze was intense, but his eyes were kind. "Among other things, yes," I answered without looking away. Brother of the Vile

Emperor or no, ancient powerful being or not, I wanted answers and I was determined to get them at last.

The Lava Lord nodded after a moment. "I'll talk, but call everyone together, because I'm only going to tell my story once."

"A wise choice," Akuma stated, rejoining us. "Everyone should probably hear what you have to say, only I cannot think that the Espearians would come here, nor would they welcome us with open arms."

"Then we'll just have to change their minds," Kaji stated, following Akuma through the door.

Yue also entered the room and the conversation. "It's about time we put aside our old rivalries and realize that we're all on the same side in this. The whole world is threatened by Lady Lilyth and we'll have to stand together if we want to defeat her."

"I can talk to Chikara," Hotaru called from beyond the doorway where everyone stood. "I'm sure I can get her to understand."

"And I'll talk to Arashi," Kaji added.

"I'll take you two back with me, then," Yue offered. "When everything's set Kaji can contact Akuma and Yukari can bring those who want to come to Espearia for the meeting. Maybe if we're all finally in one place we can get this sorted out once and for all."

And so it was set; provided Kaji and Hotaru could convince Arashi and Chikara to allow the Rubians to enter Espearia, all that was left to determine was who would attend the meeting to hear what Venon could tell us about the past.

"Yukari," Akuma caught my attention after Yue had disappeared with both Kaji and Hotaru tucked away in her Noh-space, "I have a request."

"What is it?"

"If we're going to be meeting in Espearia I'll be taking Bastion with me of course, but I think that Oka would also be beneficial to have along. The only problem is that he can be a little difficult at times and I was hoping you could try to convince him to come. He seems to respect you."

"You're his Empress, wouldn't he listen to you if you told him he was going to Espearia?"

Akuma frowned. "Oka hasn't left the Ruby City in the entire time that I've known him. You see, he's got a problem with germs.

He wouldn't even leave his lab if his duties as a General and a doctor didn't require it from time to time."

"Ah," I nodded; knowing what I did about Oka, this particular character flaw was not really unexpected. "I'll get him there."

"Good luck. You'll need it."

Knowing Yue's travel speed, I might not have much time, so I climbed to my feet and set off in search of Oka.

"Hand me that, would you?" Oka gestured vaguely behind himself, as he studied the console before him.

The room was spotlessly clean, except for the shards of Ruby scattered all over the floor. Picking up a sizeable hunk, I brought it over to him to see what he was working on.

"This?"

He nodded, taking the Ruby from me. "I'm this close to having a reliable way to crack these things open."

"That's great," I told him and I meant it – there were likely still people trapped in eggs out there that would need to be set free, once we could get a hold of them. "Oka, you've been in the Ruby City a long time, haven't you?"

"I suppose you could say that," he answered absently. "Why?"

"You were here when the Lava Lord was 'executed'…"

"So?" he questioned, putting the egg shard down on a convenient countertop before turning to give me his full attention. "What's this about?"

"I want you to attend the meeting in Espearia."

"No."

"Why not? What you know could be of great use to us, not to mention that your unique perspective might shed more light on the situation."

"I was one of the people who helped bring the Lava Lord to justice," Oka stated, leveling his gaze at me. "I hardly think that it would be appropriate for me to corroborate his story in this instance."

"So, what you're saying is that you worked for Lady Lilyth?"

"We all did, back then," he answered with a shrug.

"And now?" I asked softly. "Is she still your Lady?"

"Of course not, all I care about is my lab and having a place to practice what I do best. Being a General gives me access to my own staff, but I don't really care who rules the Ruby City as long as I'm still free to do my own thing."

"Are you sure I can't convince you?"

"Nope, I'm staying here," he answered, already having turned back to examining the Ruby shard from before.

"Oh, well that's too bad," I told him as innocently as possible. "I was hoping to introduce you to my friend Neva."

"Oh, a friend of yours, how nice," he mumbled distractedly.

"You see, she has a little problem…Lady Lilyth somehow infected her with the Lillem curse – only it didn't affect her, but her unborn child instead."

I watched carefully as Oka's back straightened and his hands lowered the Ruby shard back to the table – good, I had his attention.

"I was hoping you might be able to help me with her case, since she's asked me to be her midwife and –"

"Okay, okay, you win. I'll go to your meeting."

"Perfect," I said with a smile. "I'll take you there and back personally to ensure your complete safety."

"Oh, and can you defend me against all the contaminants that I'll be picking up by visiting a foreign area inhabited by another race?"

"Yes, actually, I can."

Oka grumbled something unpleasant about Chosen, but I was pleased with my success and I decided to leave him to his work until it was time to take us all to Espearia.

We met not in Espearia proper, but within its borders in the mostly barren countryside. A very large stone slab had been erected as a sort of table and an assortment of stones had been placed around it as impromptu seating. It would not be the most comfortable of gatherings, but perhaps the thinly-veiled intention was to keep the meeting short and the arguments minimal.

It was an assorted bunch, but the attendees included a number of this world's leaders gathered here as never before and ready at least to communicate with one another, if nothing else. The momentous nature of this event was not lost on me, nor was the fact that without the four of us from Earth none of this would have been possible.

I saw Yue sitting at the far side of the table. She was conversing softly with Pine, who had his dark hood up. Next to them stood Ris, waving her arms deep in conversation with a tall male Kumori I assumed must be the leader of her people. Hotaru darted past me to greet Leon with a hug. Beyond them, Akuma and Ao Kouen were conversing amiably with Bastion standing not too far away.

After speaking to Oka, who was by and large attempting to keep to himself away from everyone else, Arashi had finished greeting the various officials from the Ruby City and now headed over to rejoin her daughter who seemed to be fascinated with X-En, Hex's robot assistant. Venon was inexplicably speaking with young Annalise of Sresh, who had already taken her seat at the stone table, and to their right sat my father and Corporal Zukatoro, with Kaji and Sir Sabien beside them. Jeth was also present and for him there were no boundaries; he said hello to everyone he came across, wandering through those assembled like he was the host at a party. Adel and Aysel stuck together and chose their seats accordingly, having not seen much of each other since Adel's return.

Lastly, my eyes fell upon Dahlia and Masaru, another pair of people who cared deeply for one another who had been mostly separate during the recent ordeals, and upon seeing me they waved me over to join them.

In the end Oka's squad members had to stand behind him, but we were all seated along one side of the stone table. Oka was to my left and Masaru to my right, with Dahlia next to him and the rest of the Rubians arrayed beyond Oka.

Surprisingly it was Chikara who stood and spoke up to begin the proceedings and not her mother, who sat quietly on a stone beside her daughter. "If I could have everyone's attention, y'all are here by my invitation. My mother and all of Espearia welcomes you as guests. We're here to discuss the war effort in hopes that we can all be allies in freein' this world that we share from one who would claim it as her own.

"To that end," Chikara's youthful voice spoke with wisdom and authority beyond her apparent years and her silver-eyed gaze swept over everyone assembled, "I would like to ensure this gathering remain as civil as possible. As my friend Yue often reminds us, we're all on the same side now, no matter what has happened between us or our homelands in the past.

"And I believe to start off there's somethin' that one of our guests is here to tell us. It's my pleasure to introduce the Lava Lord."

"I'm here to tell you my story, as some of you believe it might be of use to you in your current crisis. My name is Venon," he began, addressing us all in a voice that carried well across the open space. "My brother is Verasheen, known to most of you as the Vile Emperor. We arrived here a long time ago, following an Aldanian distress signal originating from this planet. When we first picked up the signal we'd been on a research mission, searching for hospitable planets suitable for colonization. However, when we landed on the planet's moon we discovered that the call had been placed by the leader of the ruling house with which we were currently at war. For this reason we decided to keep our presence hidden, but this planet, lush and plentiful at the time, was too good of an opportunity to pass up, so we built ourselves a laboratory on the moon and set about doing what we had originally set out to do.

"In the course of our research we journeyed to the planet's surface many times, and sometimes we would take subjects back with us for study. It was on one such journey that I fell in love. Her name was Alyrria and she was Espearian, a Priestess of Fire, and I begged my brother to let her come back with us to the lab. She took quite naturally to the life of a scientist and it wasn't long after she came to live with me on the moon that she and I were married.

"Verasheen changed after that and even more so after our child was born. He envied what we had and seeing me with a family made him feel alone. Watching my daughter grow, he soon became obsessed with the idea of being a father to a child of his own. I didn't know it at the time, but Verasheen began experimenting, trying to devise a way to create a child with his DNA and his powers as a Chosen."

"Why didn't he just find himself a nice woman and have himself a baby the old fashioned way?" Dahlia asked.

"You don't know? Chosen cannot procreate. Something about the power, or the way it interferes with the aging process prevents it. Surely, you must have noticed…"

I hadn't had my powers all that long, especially when compared to Akuma, or even Venon and Verasheen, but just like I had realized slowly that Sapphiros' power meant I didn't have to eat and wouldn't truly age, I suppose I had known, somewhere deep down, that my body had changed in other ways, too. I had said it before that our powers made us something other than what we had been and now it seemed I had proof.

"Either way," Venon continued, "Verasheen was well aware of his own infertility and he tried everything he could think of to overcome it in search of his ultimate goal – a daughter…

CH. 18 – BODY AND SOUL

"Lilyth was born of a human woman," Venon stated. "Or, more accurately, she clawed her way out of the woman's womb, ending the life of her human host."

"A human?" Hotaru questioned, appalled.

"As I mentioned, we had taken subjects back to the moon with us for study," he reminded us. "Verasheen chose a human subject as the vessel for his experiment, but as you can tell by looking at her, Lilyth is made up of more than simply human and Aldanian DNA. She's a combination of all the best aspects of every race on this planet. My brother called her the 'ideal being'.

"She grew quickly, both her mind and body, but she tired often. She was a voracious reader and went quickly through every book or scrap of information she could get her hands on. Due to the nature of our mission this mostly concerned science, colonization, and occasionally books on history and warfare.

"It was a happy time for my brother. He was so proud of what he had created, but it soon became evident that Lilyth wasn't growing stronger as she developed. It was like she was wilting, unable to sustain her growth rate with her own energy. Verasheen performed every test he could think of, but in the end we learned that it was simply that Lilyth did not have the ability to recharge herself. Her life force was like a battery, draining away with even the simple task of existing – in short, Lilyth was dying.

"Obviously, he couldn't let that happen. Many temporary solutions were tested, but the true success came when my brother happened upon a sizeable piece of Ruby and tested it as a means of storing power. The precious stone needed no machines to help it function, no wires or devices to transfer the power it contained to Lilyth, and once installed she could draw upon it at will.

"And she did. The stone allowed Lilyth to live and to recharge what powers she had inherited from my brother's DNA. However he had done it, my brother had created a Chosen and given her access to a continual power source – us.

"The Ruby heart he had given her allowed her to absorb energy, more specifically that borne of a gem god. Soon after the heart was implanted into her chest and she discovered its ability, Lilyth drained me, my brother, my wife, and even my daughter of every last drop of power we had. Then she left us for dead in the lab she set to self-destruct.

"Fortunately, a Chosen's store of power is vast, and even against such an ability as Lilyth now possessed Verasheen was able to recover quickly enough to shield us from the worst of the blast. Only, when the moment passed, I realized that my wife and daughter hadn't survived. In Alyrria's case it was debris from the blast that killed her, but Mikura, my daughter, had simply been drained of everything she had."

There was a collective gasp as Venon revealed the name of his daughter.

"That's not the same Mikura that we knew, is it?" Masaru asked from beside me.

"It is, yes," he answered, "and before you think to break the news to me, I know what has happened. In fact, she was in a similar state then as she is now. Salvaging some of the lab's equipment and using some of my brother's research on Lilyth, I was able to revive Mikura then, and I hope to be able to do it again. Though, it was the use of Lilyth's altered DNA that restored Mikura and at the same time made her especially vulnerable to Lilyth's abilities.

"After that, it took us some time to salvage what we could and get the remaining transport pods to a functional state. By the time we journeyed to the planet's surface, we discovered that Lilyth had already made her presence known and had provoked a war between not only the various races on the planet, but also the other Aldanians we had been attempting to conceal ourselves from.

"Lilyth was losing by the time we reached her. The Yaboun Tenchi, a Chosen of Damos and the leader of an opposing Aldanian house, had her cornered, and he would have destroyed her and the inhabitants of this planet she had gathered to her side. My brother chose to side with his daughter and the Yaboun Tenchi was driven back.

"Things settled into a sort of routine after that. Lilyth established her rule with her father's help, while I used what I had brought with me from the moon to construct a new lab within the Ruby palace that my brother had built and spent as much time as possible with my daughter. Nominally, I was named Provincial Lord over the territory of Espearia, but other than visiting the land my wife had treasured and showing it to my half-Espearian daughter, I largely left Espearia to govern itself.

"But my reputation of non-interference was not enough to shield me from Lilyth's suspicions. She had always known that I had never really forgiven her for what she had done to my family, and so when she became aware that there were certain plots against her she immediately blamed me."

"Were you responsible?" I asked.

"Yes," he answered, "but I wasn't the only one and by no means was I her most dangerous adversary. No, I was a convenient scapegoat and punishing someone in my position meant she could send a powerful message to everyone that she wouldn't tolerate anyone working against her.

"She didn't come for me herself – it wasn't her style – but when the time came that I was taken to be dragged before her, I have to admit that I wasn't completely surprised. I had recently returned from a covert mission into the Yaboun Tenchi's territory by my brother's request and so I knew that there was a possibility that she might have found out about it. I left Mikura in Oka's care," Venon said as he gestured to the scientist in question, turning all of our attention in his direction, "much like she still is today."

Oka waved his hand to try and deflect attention from himself. "Yes, well, go on with your story."

"So when Oka came to get me following Lilyth's orders, I went willingly," Venon continued. "My brother and I had planned for this eventuality and so I thought myself prepared for what was to come, but of course things didn't go exactly as planned. We thought she would order me executed, and we even expected that she would make Verasheen be the one to do it after personally draining my powers so that I could not resist his attack, but we never anticipated she would delay my execution by storing me in an egg."

"So it was all a show, then?" Adel asked. "Your death – all of it?"

"Time stopped for me before the lava hit," Venon answered. "I can only presume that she used the power she had pulled from me to create the egg she trapped me in and perhaps used some sort of illusion to conceal it from the rest of you, and maybe even Verasheen as well."

"And she never tried to get any information out of you?" Kaji questioned. "She didn't want to know the details of the plots against her?"

"She thought she knew everything there was to know already," Venon explained, "and anything she didn't wasn't worth knowing about. She sent her message with my execution and expected everyone to fall back in line because of fear. She was always arrogant, believing herself beyond reproach.

"The rest, you know," he finished. "I can only assume that my brother managed to take possession of my egg and then, centuries later, you found me and learned the secret of cracking open my prison."

"We don't know everything," I countered. "Recent events, yes, but after you were imprisoned all we know is that the civil war began in earnest and the Vile Emperor is said to have defeated Lilyth."

"Which either he didn't do, or didn't do well enough," Kaji added.

"And then after that, he took over ruling the Ruby City, but there was still civil unrest," I continued, "resulting in the Vile Emperor raiding the Temple of Sapphire some five years after he came to Earth looking for Shuzhue."

"Raid the Temple of Sapphire?" Venon questioned. "Why would he do that? The Sapphiros Province was my brother's secret hideaway, his training grounds and the seat of the revolution."

"It was?" Hotaru asked.

"Yes. It was Yuko Seig's province and she was one of the leaders of the civil war. She worked closely with my brother for many years."

I looked to Sabien for confirmation of this, my mind whirling.

"It's true that Verasheen visited the temple often in the years before and after you were born," Sabien answered,. "but after Yuko Seig left and the civil war tore the land apart, relations between the mountains of Sapphire and the Ruby City became strained. Matters escalated from there, resulting in the attack on the temple where we followed emergency protocol and entered the cryogenic bay."

"War was everywhere and matters were tense between the Ruby City and the Temple of Sapphire when we left with the four of you to Earth," my father added. "Lilyth ruled in the Ruby City at that time, but it was Verasheen who allowed us to use the Ruby Splitter to go home."

"So the Vile Emperor defeats Lady Lilyth and then attacks the Temple of Sapphire after Sapphiros is dead and Yuko Seig doesn't rule there anymore," I pieced together. "Why would he do that?"

"That doesn't seem to make any sense," Dahlia agreed, "but that's what Yuko Seig's messages tell us."

"Unless Yuko Seig was in on it all along," I suggested.

"Ye think Yuko Seig was lying to ye?" Masaru asked.

"From what we've figured out, Yuko Seig was already dead and her spirit locked in the Splitter before she sent those messages," I explained. "The Vile Emperor put her there using his own Splitter, so it stands to reason that he could communicate with her spirit whenever he chose to, just like the Knights could from the temple's computers. It's more than possible that she didn't wrestle control of the Splitter to rescue us from the Vile Emperor like we've always assumed. We know from Fuzen's story that the Vile Emperor wasn't fully in the park that night. He was a projection of some kind, which Yuko Seig would have known, being a part of the Splitter herself. She told us she was saving us from the Vile Emperor, but it's quite possible that she set us up – for him."

"But why?" Hotaru asked. "Why would the Vile Emperor want us here? He tried to kill us."

"No, he didn't. He only made us think that he wanted us dead," Yue countered. "I've said it all along that if the Vile Emperor wanted us dead, then we'd be dead already. He's got thousands of years on us in both experience and power."

"To push us?" Kaji suggested. "To drive us to be better and stronger? Strong enough to do what he couldn't and kill his daughter for him?"

"You could be right, Kaji," Adel agreed. "If Verasheen knew that he had not succeeded in fully eliminating Lilyth, then he would have done the logical thing and sent for reinforcements."

"He could have just asked," I muttered.

"No, he couldn't have," Kaji disagreed. "I can't say I agree with him personally, but seeing him as the enemy made us into who we are today, and without that we would never have been able to face Lilyth."

"But where is he now?" Hotaru asked. "If he wanted us to come here to help him, then why isn't he working with us to stop Lilyth?"

"Venon," Akuma interjected, "you wouldn't happen to have any theories on where your brother might have gone, would you?"

"None," he answered. "Oka told me about the Lillem Heart, but the Lillem were still in development when I...left. As far as I understand it, Lilyth was trying to discover a way to improve on the human race, like she had already done to the plains-runners."

"The Hounds," I clarified for everyone else's benefit.

"Exactly," Venon agreed. "I don't know where the Lillem Heart would lead or what it might do to someone who dove into it because I didn't know, until now that is, that it existed."

Understandably, Akuma was disappointed by his answer. "So that's it, then, we're at a dead end."

"Not exactly," Yue interjected, "we now know what Lilyth is and a little more about her."

"That's not what I meant, Yue," Akuma clarified. "Venon has told us all he can and now the only person who can tell us the rest of what we need to know is out of reach. We need answers and I think that it's past time that we got them."

"All's not lost," Yue replied. "The Vile Emperor told me he'd return when 'the body and soul are reunited', which means he's coming back."

"Why didn't you tell me this earlier?" Akuma demanded.

"Because I didn't know what it meant," Yue answered.

"And you do now?"

"Not exactly." Yue frowned. "Have any of you wondered about the part Little Lilyth plays in all of this?"

"She said she was Lady Lilyth's daughter, right?" Hotaru offered. "Wait – can she even be Lilyth's daughter, or would Lilyth have to have made her too?"

"That's not the point I'm getting at," Yue clarified. "Lilyth went to a lot of trouble to get to that little girl and afterwards, as far as we know, Lilyth possessed her daughter's body and used it to rule from the throne of Taiyou."

"That's right," Arashi agreed. "She projected an image of herself over the little girl somehow, but after she'd use her power in some way she would tire and the image would fade."

"And she never did leave that chair," Adel added, "not to go more than ten feet from it."

"So we know that she's weak," Kaji supplied, "and whatever Verasheen did to her, she doesn't seem to have a body of her own, or at least not one that she's using."

"Do you think she's trapped somewhere," I questioned, "or that she's a bodiless spirit now, like the Talons?"

"So 'body and soul' refers to Lilyth?" Akuma asked.

"Could be," Yue answered with a shrug. "Either that or he meant his own body and soul, but we don't know where either of those are, so that's less likely."

"This little girl you're talking about – Little Lilyth? I've never heard of Lilyth having a daughter, but if you want my professional opinion," Venon interjected, "I wouldn't necessarily classify Lilyth as having a soul, exactly. If anything, that Ruby in her chest is the closest thing she has to a soul or a heart."

"So 'the body and soul' could refer to her body and her Ruby heart being separated?" I ventured. "Like when Verasheen and Lilyth fought, he took her power supply so that she would die of natural causes like she was meant to, only somehow she's survived?"

"It's possible," Venon agreed. "It would be the kindest way to end the life of the daughter he'd worked so hard to attain. Without the heart, or a constant source of power to sustain her, she would drain her power completely over time."

"So the question is – where would he have hidden her heart?" Yue asked.

"I think the better question is why didn't he leave us any clues, or tell anybody what he had done to Lilyth," I countered. "If he did steal her heart and hide it from her, then she would have spent every minute of the past eight hundred years searching for it. It would have had to be the most hidden thing on this world. We'd have no hope of finding it if she couldn't in eight centuries."

"What if she did find it?" Hotaru suggested. "Maybe that's why she's back after all this time."

"No, if Lilyth was whole and strong again, however she accomplished it, she would be back in strength as herself, not in her daughter's body," Adel responded. "Whether she's missing the Ruby or looking for it doesn't matter. As weak as she is right now, she needs a power source and the only thing we know is that she's left Taiyou and is no longer sustaining herself with Jedeite's throne."

"Then where is she?" Kaji asked. "She's not in the Ruby City on the throne there and she's not in Espearia."

"Could she be gaining power anywhere else?" Yue asked.

"If she was in the Temple of Machalite, I would know it," Fuun stated, "and I can guarantee that she has no welcome there."

"There is no reason for her to go to the Temple of Sapphire," Sabien added. "The Sapphire Splitter and the source of its power are on Earth. There would be nothing at the temple for her to draw upon."

"That leaves Damos, doesn't it?" Chikara asked. "I know she's not here in Espearia, but is there a Temple of Damos, like there's a temple to every other gem god?"

"Yes," Venon answered, "but on the other side of the world."

"Wait," I said, reaching into my medic kit, "I have a map that shows where all the temples are."

"Where did you get that?" Fuun asked, leaning toward me from where he sat near Sabien.

"It's a long story," I answered, unfolding the map to lay it out on the table before me, "but my friend Mifa drew it following the coded message on the moon."

"Can I see that?" Venon asked.

"Sure." I shrugged and stood to walk around the table to him. "We never did find out who sent it or what it was for, though I guess it could be a part of the distress signal that brought you here."

"This is Aldanian," Venon stated, "but it's not the distress signal we received. You said your friend translated this?"

"Yes," I answered. "She noticed a light blinking out a pattern on the moon every six and a half minutes. When she copied it out she got this."

"You see this part here?" Venon pointed. "Under each temple there's a descriptor in Aldanian: 'Strength and Power' for Jedeite and 'Passion and Fate' for Rubia. Where exactly did your friend see this light?"

"I saw it too," I informed him, "on the bottom of the moon where it looks like a bit was broken off."

"That's the lab," Venon answered, "or at least where it was and the part of the moon that was destroyed when it exploded. This message, or blinking light, wasn't there before I was imprisoned. Somehow Verasheen made it back to the moon, this has to be his work."

I only barely registered what Venon was saying, I was too busy studying the map. Now the lines and dashes that I had interpreted to simply be a part of Mifa working out the code seemed to take on new meaning.

"Passion and Fate, Despair and Loneliness," I said as I ran my finger over the Temple of Ruby in the northeast and the Temple of Machalite in the center.

"You can read it?" Venon looked surprised.

"It describes the Temple of Sapphire as 'Balance and Enlightenment'," I stated, "and there's even a blank space marking where Espearia is, but what are these other markings? 'Right by two', 'down by three'…'Begin third on right from middle'?"

"Sounds like directions," Kaji suggested, standing and coming over to join us. "Where does it say the Temple of Damos is?"

"'Honour and Defence'," I quoted. "It's directly underneath the Temple of Machalite, but it's drawn as an outline, so I presume that to mean that it's on the other side of the world like Venon said."

"So he did leave us a clue," Akuma noted after coming to stand over Venon's shoulder to look at the map.

"Maybe even more than that," Kaji added, pulling something out of his pocket. "Remember the disk I found in the library inside that Japanese book, *Requirements for Interlocking Door Mechanisms*?"

"You think he left you a key of some kind?" Leon asked.

"Hey, that's kind of clever," Jeth noted. "The book's title, I mean, hiding a key inside of it."

"And if the book was in Japanese, then he obviously expected one of you to find it," Sabien added.

"Or me," Akuma said quietly. "I have an idea as to where we might start with this. Maybe we can find some answers after all."

"I'll go with you," Kaji offered. "I think I can help."

"I think perhaps that we're all in agreement that we need more information before we can proceed," Hex spoke through X-En. "If we can find some way to ascertain if Lilyth is seeking the Temple of Damos or searching for her lost heart, it would help us to predict what she's going to do next and prevent her if we can."

"I can get to the Temple of Damos," Yue stated, "and take a look around without anyone seeing me."

"As can I," Fuun seconded.

"Good," Sabien noted. "I think some of us should go back to the Children's Outpost to keep watch in case Lilyth tries something we're not expecting, but is there anything else we can do to gather more information?"

"Little Lilyth's valley," I said, realization dawning. "It was hidden and protected by Lillem-like guardians. She kept her daughter there for some purpose and even if that purpose was just to use Little Lilyth as a spare body, we have to investigate to see if we can't find any other clues about what she intended."

"You make a good point, Yukari," Sabien agreed. "Why don't you and Masaru check it out? You can stop by the Children's Outpost on your way and take Ticket. He'd make a good guide after living there with Little Lilyth for a time and there may be other things he can tell you about her. Oh, and take Jeth with you, just in case."

"Jeth?" I questioned, wondering why Sabien would mention him in particular.

"Hey, how's it goin'?" Jeth spoke up, realizing he was being included.

"He's got a way with rocks, and as I hear it the tunnel access into Lilyth's valley has been blocked off."

"Oh, right," I amended, seeing Sabien's wisdom.

"It's not information exactly," Pine ventured, his whispered voice causing everyone to pay close attention to what the usually taciturn Croatin Knight had to say, "but I'm curious as to where the survivors of Taiyou are now. We know that some were able to leave before it was completely destroyed. My brothers were among those who left. They may have gone to the Croatin base, but I would like to track them down."

"I can go with you and help you find them," Ao Kouen, who had been mostly silent during this meeting, spoke up rather unexpectedly. "Between the Knights and the Stirr, the Children's Outpost is well guarded. The Croatins are powerful allies to have, so if we can find them, or any more of my people who have fled the city, we would be better for it."

"I would be glad for the help," Pine said as he bowed slightly to the King of Taiyou, "and the transportation," he added with a sly smile.

So it was settled. We said a temporary goodbye to the Rubians and those like Leon and Kaji, who were going back to the city with them to investigate the possible clues that the Vile Emperor had left behind. The unspoken agreement was that once we had all followed our leads through we would meet back here, then convene another meeting to discuss the findings and decide our next move.

Masaru set off with Jeth back to the city of Espearia to pick up what supplies he thought we might need, leaving me to wait for their return before we could set off. Curiously finding myself with spare time on my hands, I wandered back over to the stone table, only to see Hotaru sitting somewhat dejectedly next to Aysel and Adel.

"Isn't there anywhere you wanted to go?"

"I wanted to go to the Temple of Damos and see it with my own eyes," she answered, looking down at her hands.

"It's not a sightseeing trip, Hotaru," I cautioned. "Yue is best equipped to get there and back on her own. She's proved it with how many times she's gotten into the Ruby City undetected."

"It's not the temple I want to see," she met my eyes defiantly. "I want to know what's going on and I know I can be of help there."

"I have witnessed you in combat," Fuun's voice came unexpectedly from behind me, causing both Hotaru and I to whirl to face him. "I would take you with me, if that is what you wish."

Hope surged across Hotaru's features momentarily before fading once more. "Yue wouldn't want me there," she objected. "She's hardly spoken to me since Taiyou. I think she hates me."

"I don't think she hates you, Hotaru," Adel interjected, "but regardless, I suddenly have an urge to see the other side of the world myself. If you'll have me, Fuun, I'd love to accompany the both of you."

Fuun nodded his acquiescence as Aysel got to her feet, looking beyond us. "Looks like Ao Kouen's ready to go, and Sabien's waving me over. I'll go tell him that you two aren't coming back to the Children's Outpost with us."

"But what about Yue?" Hotaru began.

"You'll have both my sister and Fuun with you, there's none better to have on your side," Aysel told her, "and Yue won't dare argue with that. Now get ready, you've got an important mission ahead of you."

Smiling at the by-play, I watched Aysel hurry over to where Sabien had gathered with Ao Kouen and those he would take back to the Children's Outpost, before going off to find the Croatins and any other Taiyoun refugees.

"Do you require my assistance in reaching the valley?" Fuun asked me.

"No, I should be able to get us there," I told him. "The guardians have a life force signature of their own and I can sense them, which means I can reach them, but thank you for the offer."

"Then we should be going," Fuun stated. "Time is of the essence."

"Ready, Hotaru?" Adel stood and waited for Hotaru to do the same, before the two of them went with Fuun to join up with Yue and let her know who would be accompanying her to the Temple of Damos.

Truly, it hadn't taken them very long, but nearly everyone else had departed by the time Jeth and Masaru returned.

"Ready?" I asked.

"I got ye an extra canteen," Masaru mentioned, "some more belts, and some rope. I don't think we'll have as much trouble as the last time we were there, but ye never know."

"Thanks," I said sincerely, taking one of the belts from him and fastening it around my waist before attaching the spare canteen to it. "All right, let's go get Ticket, then."

"The throne room?" Leon asked as they opened the large ornate doors. "What do you think you'll find in here? We've been in this room a dozen times since we first got here and Lady Akuma many more times than that."

Without pause for the gravity of his actions, Kaji slid himself past Leon and General Oka to join Akuma at the throne and promptly sat himself down in the Vile Emperor's seat of power. Akuma pursed her lips but said nothing as she leaned over him and placed her hand on a panel embedded into the throne's arm rest. The panel responded to her touch as she took her hand away, flipping open to reveal a small square touch screen, unlabeled, but with a grid overlay.

"Aha!" Kaji exclaimed. "It's just as I thought!"

"What's as you thought?" Leon questioned, coming to stand behind Akuma so he could see what they were both looking at.

"It's a control panel," Oka explained. "It controls the Ruby City's monitors and defense system, and some of the automatic locks in the palace. It's hardly a clue to whatever it is you're searching for."

"No, Oka, look," Akuma directed him, pointing to the control pad. "It's a seven by seven grid. I had Venon write out the translations of the writing on the Aldanian map and the highest number mentioned is six."

"I hardly see how that means you need to consult this device," Oka countered.

"'Begin third on right from middle'," Akuma read from the translation on the map in her hands. "Do you think it means middle of the first line, or the middle of the grid itself?"

Kaji shrugged. "We'll start with one and if that doesn't work, try the other."

"We also don't know which order to use on these directions," Akuma pointed out. "Venon never thought to mention which direction Aldanian script commonly follows."

"Aldanian script is somewhat fluid," Oka answered unexpectedly, earning surprised glances and a raised eyebrow from Leon. "What? Some of the older documents in the lab are written in Aldanian. I can't read it, but I can at least recognize it."

"Great," Akuma muttered. "So we have a set of instructions with no indication of how to follow them."

"Not necessarily," Kaji disagreed. "We have a map which has directions interspersed between each of the labeled temples. Maybe that's a clue on how to read them."

"Right, well the starting point is fairly clear," Akuma noted. "'Begin third on right from middle'."

Kaji counted three over from the center of the grid and touched the screen, seeming pleased when the square under his finger lit up with an inner light.

"Then, presuming we're going around on a tour of the temples, you can either go down to the Temple of Sapphire or up to the Temple of Jade," Akuma continued. "There doesn't seem to be any numbers near the Temple of Damos, but it would make sense to go there last as it's on the other side of the world."

"Sapphiros, then," Kaji suggested. "That's where we started, so maybe it's where this starts too."

"Okay," Akuma didn't sound convinced, but she read out the translated line on the map beneath the Temple of Sapphiros, "'down by one' and then continuing that direction would be Espearia which is 'down by three'."

Kaji shook his head. "No, that can't be right, that takes us off the grid. How do I clear the screen to start over?"

"I don't know," Akuma admitted. "I was lucky that it opened for me. I was only doing what I'd seen him do a thousand times."

"Okay, what's in the other direction under the Temple of Jade. That's the temple we went to next."

"'Six left'," Akuma read. "Why would your journey matter?"

Kaji counted six squares to the left and pressed his finger down to light up the corresponding grid tile. "I don't know, call it a hunch," he said. "Machalite next."

"'Up by one'," she directed. "That doesn't follow, Kaji."

"I disagree," Leon spoke up. "I think that even Yukari would say that it follows logically. If this message was indeed somehow intended for the Chosen of Sapphiros to follow, it would have to be a path they could recognize."

Kaji nodded. "That's if the message was for us. It is written in Aldanian, after all. Espearia next, please."

"'Right by two'," Leon answered, reading over Akuma's shoulder. "Aldanian characters which Yukari managed to learn to read."

"Verasheen couldn't possible have known that Yukari or anyone else would figure it out," Akuma pointed out. "'Down by three' is next, you came here after Espearia."

"How better to hide something you don't want anyone else to know, except for the one person you know is the right person to unravel it all?" Leon proposed.

"That's it," Kaji stated as he pulled his finger away from the last square and the whole grid lit up before the lights winked off, followed by a grinding sound coming from behind the throne.

"Is that the door to the temple?" Leon asked, whirling around only to find that the passage the Vile Emperor had used to allow them access to the Ruby Temple was still sealed shut.

"No, it's something completely different," Oka answered, pointing, "look."

The floor behind the ancient obsidian throne had parted, metal panels disguised with stone coverings sliding aside to reveal a rough stone stairway leading downwards into black shadowy depths.

"We're going to need torches," Leon suggested.

"I can do better than that," Akuma stated, raising her hand and forming a controlled flame, floating in the air above it. "I won't wait any longer, there are answers down there."

Akuma went first, with Kaji trailing after and Leon taking up the rear behind Oka, and they filed into the revealed passage, taking the ancient hewn steps with care until at last they reached what appeared to be a short hallway with only two doors, one on each side.

"Left or right?" Leon asked.

"This one." Akuma gestured to the door on the right.

The doors were both metal, their shiny modern appearance at odds with the dungeon-like surroundings. There were no openings or markings anywhere on the door. It was almost as if the metal panel wasn't made to open.

"This is where I come in," Kaji spoke from the base of the stairs, holding something small and rectangular aloft in his hand. "'*Requirements for Interlocking Door Mechanisms'.*"

With an elaborate gesture, he inserted the device into a socket on the wall. The ceiling lit up, panels coming to life and lighting the dark corridor, as both metal doors simultaneously slid to the side to reveal two well-lit, mid-size rooms.

"After you." Taking the odd phenomena in stride, Oka gestured for Akuma to precede them into the room she had chosen to inspect first.

The room had rough-hewn stone walls, much like the hallway they had just left and parts of the throne room above, but it was also well lit by glass panels inset into the ceiling. There was not much in the room itself, except for floor to ceiling shelves covered in what appeared to be dust-covered relics.

Kaji was the first to pick up one of the objects and dust it off with his hands. "This is Ruby. They all are. They look like vases or bottles, but they're all empty and have no lids."

"Talon casings," Oka clarified, picking up one of the ones closest to the entrance where he stood. "I recognize the style and shape of these ones here, I've worked with these before. Those ones over there," he said, pointing, "seem to be of an older and cruder design."

"So we have a museum of empty containers used to contain Talons," Leon summarized, "but to what purpose?"

"There are far too many here," Akuma noted, staring around the room as if it held the answers to all the mysteries that plagued her. "The Talons are spirits. They are immortal within the bodies they possess, until that body dies and then they move on to another. For the past eight hundred years they've had the same bodies and they could tell you that their memories don't go beyond their original lives, which they led no more than a thousand years ago."

"So either the Talons have been through more bodies than they care to admit, or there are more Talons out there somewhere," Kaji proposed.

"I don't think so." Oka shook his head. "It's possible these were test containers. From what I understand, the process of removing a person's soul from their body isn't what you would call an exact science. It's possible that Verasheen spent a long time perfecting the process."

The silence in the room was palpable as everyone considered the amount of souls it would take to fill the empty jars on the shelves.

"There's little more this room can tell us," Akuma announced after a moment before heading for the door. "Let's see what the other room has to offer."

The other room was somewhat larger than the first and, unlike the dusty ancient shelves that decorated the first room, this space was free of all traces of dust or age, and the walls were the same shiny metal as the door.

"This is a lab," Oka supplied. "Look at this stuff, this computer is better than mine!"

There was a bank of consoles in the center of the room and what appeared to be an operating table along the back wall. Oka went straight for the metal chair before the computer monitor, but Leon and the others were drawn to what lay beyond it.

"What is that?" Leon asked.

"Ruby again," Akuma answered, "but that's all I can say for sure."

The Ruby in question was in the shape of a pillar, nearly eight feet tall.

Akuma walked forward to inspect the device and the inexplicably thick cords ran from the base of the Ruby pillar over to the console where Oka sat, as if the pillar was some sort of machine that the computer could operate.

"It's all in Aldanian," Oka complained. "It'd take me weeks to crack this, if I'm lucky."

"Is this device how Verasheen made the Talons?" Leon asked, looking to Oka as the most likely to answer his question.

"It's possible, but I don't think it likely," Oka answered, pointing to the screen before him. "See, there are pictures here. The ones I recognize are the gem god symbols: Sapphiros…"

As he spoke, Oka's finger touched the screen to point out the symbols in question, but when he touched the symbol for Sapphiros it lit up and the Ruby pillar came to life, pulsing with energy.

It was like a magnet, at the same time attracting and repelling, the two sensations so at odds with each other that they left Leon unable to move or even speak. It was like he was frozen in place, but his mind was whirling uncontrollably; the feeling was so disorienting that he felt he was going to be sick.

It was over in less than a second; he heard Oka continue speaking, oblivious to the damage he had caused, "…Jedeite, Damos, and Rubia…"

Akuma had been touching the side of the pillar when Oka touched the symbol of her gem god and she immediately went rigid. Beyond her Kaji was shaking his head, as if trying to shake off the effects of what he had just been through.

"Turn it off, Oka!" Leon yelled.

"What?" Oka looked up from the screen and his eyes widened upon seeing that the pillar was active. "I don't know how!"

Kaji reached for Akuma, trying to pry her away from the stone, but it was like she was stuck there. Leon hurried forward and shoved Oka out of the way, reaching for the first symbol his eyes located on the screen full of Aldanian dashes and lines. He touched the symbol for Damos and Akuma sagged in Kaji's arms, though the Ruby pillar continued to pulse and glow.

"I didn't know it was a touch screen," Oka protested. "It seems to affect powers granted by the gem gods. I'll work at trying to turn it off, but in the meantime you three should get upstairs so I don't accidentally incapacitate you again."

"You're a Knight of Rubia, aren't you?" Leon asked. "Why didn't it affect you?"

"I'm not much of a Knight, I'm afraid," Oka admitted. "My 'powers', as you might call them, are all pure science. Well, except for a few things here or there. I inherited the position when my General died in the civil war," he explained. "Nobody ever bothered to Knight me."

"That is going to change, General Oka," Akuma said weakly, letting Kaji help her to her feet. "I'm going to Knight you myself and then turn on that machine, so you know what it feels like to have your power drained out of you by force."

"That's what it was doing?" Leon asked.

"As near as I could tell," Akuma confirmed. "I couldn't light a candle right now with my power."

"Then it's like the Ruby in her heart," Kaji stated. "It drains power, only it's selective and has settings for each gem god. Was he making her a new heart, then? One that would limit whose power she can drain?"

"Or a way to defeat her," Leon proposed, seeing it from the other angle. "No one could fight back while in the grip of that Ruby's power and if the right setting could be found to target Lilyth's particular power source, then this pillar might be a way of holding her immobile long enough to end her threat."

"Or remove her Ruby heart," Kaji suggested. "This could have been how he did it."

"Good theory," Oka granted, "but you're wrong. This device hasn't left this room, and it's still plugged into this computer and the power source that runs the Ruby City," he said, pointing to where the computer and the pillar were connected to a socket in the wall. "I presume this thing needs a ton of power to keep it going and without modifications it would be absolutely useless outside of this lab."

Akuma frowned. "Whether he was helping her or planning a way to overcome her this device is still an important discovery, even if it creates more questions than it answers."

"Speaking of questions," Oka noted, "why don't you three run along and give me some peace and quiet, so I can see what kind of answers I can wrestle from this Aldanian nonsense, hmm?"

Akuma smiled. "You'll have your quiet Oka and I'll make sure to send you Yukari or Venon when I next see either of them to help you translate everything."

"What I need is a Rubian to Aldanian dictionary and a lifetime of study, but I suppose they'll have to do in the meantime."

CH. 19 – MAY THIS PLACE ALWAYS RESIST YOU

"So Tim's still down there, huh?" Ticket asked, peering over the side of the chasm.

"Tim?" Masaru questioned.

"Oh, yeah," Ticket answered, "Lilyth gave them all names. Tim's the torso."

"Oh, well isn't that…nice," Masaru commented, swallowing uncomfortably.

"Come on, let's get this over with," I suggested, trying to banish images of 'Tim the Torso' from my mind.

I had never thought I would willingly come back to this place. The narrow tunnel that sloped downward into the secret valley complete with its deadly denizens had been one of the first real horrors I had faced on this world. Sabien had taught us to use our powers by channeling our fears and for the longest time the horrific visage of the guardian in the chasm had been the fear I had called upon to spur me into action. Now I hardly needed fear to access my powers – need was enough – but the image of the relentless undead guardian clawing its way toward me in this dark tunnel was still with me and I couldn't help but shudder once as I left the dubious safety of daylight behind.

The last time I had been down this particular length of tunnel it had been with adrenaline and fear driving me, directing me through the darkness. This time, Masaru had thoughtfully included a couple of torches in the supplies he had gathered, so we were able to take our time and look around. Even if my power meant that I didn't need the torches to see by, the firelight was still a comfort.

"Does anybody hear that?" Jeth asked from up ahead, stopping to listen.

"Ye mean the digging?" Masaru asked. "I remember they were doing that last time."

The 'last time' that Masaru referred to had gotten a Roughlander killed and Masaru seriously injured, as they had ventured forward to see what lay ahead of us. That injury had nearly meant Masaru's death as well, since he had started to become one of the guardians himself. If it hadn't been for Little Lilyth, Masaru might have died before I had even gotten the chance to get to know him.

"Oh, that's probably Tommy," Ticket informed us with a wave of his green webbed hand. "He's always digging down there. All the guardians will, if you let 'em anywhere near this tunnel. They're strange creatures, the guardians."

"Let's go see the valley first," I suggested. "We can figure out what the guardians are working on afterwards, if they'll let us."

"Oh, the guardians are harmless if you know how to handle them right," Ticket told us as we bypassed where 'Tommy' was working on his endless task and heard the sound of digging pause as the guardian began to shamble toward us to fulfill his other duty. "It's okay, Tommy, it's just me, Ticket!" A moment later, the guardian turned back to what he was doing and I let out a breath of relief. "See? Nothing to it."

"Ticket," I said, as we emerged out onto the sunlit platform that would lead down into the jungle on the valley floor below, "is there anything about this place that seemed odd to you while staying here, any particular spot that stood out at all?"

"Not really," Ticket answered with a shrug. "There's the sand box that Lilyth built after Yue told her about them and there's the Meep-moop den, but you've been there before."

"What about the spot where the Hounds broke in?" Masaru asked. "Was that the same way we came in by?"

"No," Ticket cringed, "but I can show you where it was."

Ticket led us through the jungle filled with the calls of the native Meep-moops and their food source, the furry, koala-like Moop-meeps, until we came to the north side wall of the valley and a scene of devastation that marred the jungle's otherwise pristine beauty. The rock wall was cracked, the ground below disturbed where the Hounds had burst into the valley to surround Lilyth and Ticket, and the area surrounding their point of entry was charred and blackened by Hound-fire.

"Were ye here, Ticket, when they came through?" Masaru asked.

"We weren't far," Ticket answered. "The sandbox is right through there, and we called the guardians and came over as soon as we heard the rock cracking, though we didn't know what was happening until it was too late."

I looked up to check the sun's progress through the sky to see how much daylight we had left when something else caught my eye – there were marks on the otherwise smooth surface, some ways up the rock wall. Something about those indentations tugged at my memory and before I knew it my wings had formed, carrying me aloft so I could get a better view.

"Did you find something?" Jeth asked.

"There's Aldanian writing up here," I called down. "It says *'may this place always resist you'*."

"Another clue?" Masaru asked, as I lowered myself back down to the ground.

"Maybe," I answered, mulling it over. "We should search the rest of the valley to see if there are any other messages written anywhere."

From where we were we toured the outside of the valley, keeping close to the wall while I scanned for more Aldanian writing. On the eastern wall the message was repeated, only much closer to the ground, and the same on the south side.

"I'm starting to see a pattern here," I commented, "but it's getting late, so I'm going to fly up and quickly check the way we came in."

I took to the air and flew up above the treeline, my cyan wings in contrast with the orange light of the setting sun. I didn't need the light to see what I'd come up here looking for and neither did I need to be any closer to read the Aldanian characters etched into the stone above the cave entrance.

"'*May this place always resist you*'," was carved in an arch over the only way into and out of the valley, and from up here it was clear that this perfectly-shaped valley with the stone plateau and ramp that led into the jungle below was not a natural formation – it had been created.

I spun about in the air, facing east now, and mentally drew a line from the Aldanian message behind me to the one I knew to be before me, down below the tree line. Then, I added in the two identical messages on the north and south sides and imagined them all connected – forming the pattern of an 'X' over this entire place.

If the Aldanian map and the Aldanian clues had been meant to find something, then this place was it, like a hidden treasure at the end of a treasure map. Only, what had this place been built to conceal? Had it been simply the presence of Little Lilyth, or was there something else?

'May this place always resist you'…were the words a warning or a message? Certainly this valley was deadly enough to keep most people out of it, but the personal nature of the message seemed to indicate someone specific. Combine that with the fact that the words were in Aldanian and it became almost obvious that the message was meant for someone who could read it. As for who had left it, the list of people who could read Aldanian was almost as short as those who could write it.

As I flew back down to join the others, I considered the nature of the valley itself. The jungle below was lush and more fertile than even the protected nature of this valley could account for. The Ruby City – which was also in a valley – could in no way match it. These facts, combined with the message and the constructed nature of this place, indicated that the valley was well protected, perhaps even beyond the obvious protection of the mountains and the valley's undead guardians.

The guardians! Their purpose seemed to be to protect, but what if it was more than simply the valley and Little Lilyth that they were guarding? What if it was the secret that this valley existed to contain?

"The guardians are the key to this," I announced as I landed. "We need to know what Tommy is guarding."

The four of us trooped back to the entrance until we were within the cave, studying Tommy.

"See how he carves out a rock from over there and he carries it over to that pile over there?" I pointed. "I don't think he's digging. He's burying something."

"Ye may be right," Masaru agreed. "If he was simply trying to get at whatever is beyond those rocks, he wouldn't need to go so far to put the rocks down."

"Guardians don't think like you and I," Ticket pointed out. "I'm not even sure they think at all."

"Well, there's one way to find out," Jeth announced. "Call off your friend and I'll see about asking those rocks to move."

"Hey, Tommy, come 'ere!" Ticket called out to the guardian, as Jeth hopped over the rocks we'd taken shelter behind to watch the guardian without disturbing him.

"Whoa, buddy," Jeth commented, as he dodged the guardian's attempt to stop him.

"Tommy – no!" Ticket yelled. "Bad guardian!"

While Ticket scolded the guardian, Jeth did his thing and the rock pile Tommy and the others had so carefully built came tumbling down at his request.

"Hey, look what we have here!" Jeth called out.

"What is it?" Masaru asked, hopping over the rocks himself.

"That's an entrance," I stated, coming up behind him with Ticket and Tommy in my wake.

The entrance was no more than a circular metal hatch jutting out of the rock, but it was definitely an indicator we had found something.

"Let's see what's down there, shall we?" Jeth suggested, reaching for the cross-shaped handle and giving it a forceful spin with his powerfully-muscled arms. With a squeal of protest, the latch clicked open and he was able to pull back the metal hatch door.

"It's pitch black down there," I noted, peering into the hole Jeth had revealed. Power or no, I still needed some light to see by.

"And there's no ladder either," Masaru noted, feeling around the inside of the metal hatch, "it could be a long ways down."

"Only one way to find out," Jeth commented and before we could stop him the Knight leapt into the unknown.

"Come on, we're going after him," I informed them, letting my wings out. "Ticket, climb on."

"Tommy, you stay here," Ticket ordered the guardian before doing as I had instructed, and after picking Masaru up I leapt into the hole myself, fluttering my wings to slow our descent.

Masaru was right, it was a long way down, but before we reached the ground I noticed something in the faint cyan glow of my wingtips which caused me to veer to the side. Landing a little ways off from what I had caught a glimpse of, I put Masaru down and let Ticket climb from my shoulders.

"Where's Jeth?" Masaru asked.

"Over here," he answered from across the cavernous space, "and I don't think you guys are going to like this."

"What is it?" Masaru asked, as I formed a glowing arrow with my mind and fired it off to multiply and light the area around us in a rough circle.

The center of this large cavernous space was nothing more than a pile of corpses, curiously preserved by the sealed nature of this place. The bodies in the pile all wore the familiar face of Little Lilyth, the sweet little girl we had come to know as the mistress of this valley.

Ticket let out a cry of anguish for what he was seeing as ahead of us the first one of my arrows unexpectedly winked out of existence, followed quickly by another, and then another. There were three arrows left lighting the room when the first body twitched and only one when the pile of them started to writhe, the bodies rising up like so many Lillem climbing from the sand with the fall of darkness.

Knowing they would likely last no longer than the first, I fired another round of glowing arrows, this time higher up at the walls. The sudden glow revealed a scene more horrific than even the animated corpses of a friend. The bodies were…unfinished. It was as if someone had been trying to create another 'perfect being' in Lady Lilyth's image and these were the discarded experiments that had fallen short of the original goal. There were bodies with Stirr parts, Hound parts, and human parts. Bodies with wings or fur like the Kumori, or Lillem-like talons protruding in every which direction, and even bodies that were missing key features like arms or a lower half, as if they'd been discarded as a failure before their design had even been completed.

And these bodies, in all their misshapen horror, were surging forward with mindless savagery reminiscent of the Lillem or the guardians. These undead, half-finished corpses evidently had instructions to kill anything that came within reach and today, after who knows how many hundreds of years that they had lain dormant, we had awoken that urge to kill.

The arrows winked out once more as the Lilyths surged forward, some leaping and some crawling, but all intent on us, the intruders in their midst. Out of the corner of my eye I caught a cyan flash as Masaru summoned his energy knives and engaged the Stirr-like Lilyth that had leapt forward to attack him.

"They're absorbing our powers somehow," Masaru called out, staring in awe at the Stirr-Lilyth before him as it rose again from what had looked like a fatal blow. "My knives disappear when they make contact!"

"Uh, guys…" Ticket called hesitantly, as he scrambled back from the three malformed Lilyths who had him surrounded, "a little help, please!"

Using the only means I had at my disposal I formed more arrows with my mind, firing them off on the Lilyths around Ticket and Masaru. The arrows struck, forming nets made of real rope, which did not disappear, and although they would not hold the majority of the Lilyths they had struck for long, they allowed Ticket a chance to bounce on powerful Croatin legs over to where Masaru was pulling out his regular knives.

"The torches!" I called, taking to the air as something whooshed past me.

Between the two of them, Ticket and Masaru managed to get a torch lit in short order, causing the Lilyths nearest them to shy back from the sudden light source and illuminating the cavern so we could all see what we were facing.

Now all we needed was a way out.

"Over here!" Jeth called, and I turned to see him standing in the place where the pile of corpses had been the highest while they had lain dormant.

Before him was an open hatchway just like the one in the ceiling above us, only leading deeper into whatever mystery we had stumbled upon. Evidently the Lilyths coming to life had revealed what they were truly guarding and wherever that hatchway led lay the answers we were searching for, which was enough for me to go on.

Grabbing hold of Ticket and Masaru with my mind, I turned the three of us to mist and, pitting my will and power against the draining ability of the Lilyths, I dove for the hatchway Jeth had opened for us. By the time we were safely through, Jeth had fought the Lilyths around him off enough to climb into the hatch himself and I was relieved to hear the sound of the heavy door locking in place as he pulled it shut behind us.

It was dark down here as well, but as soon as we had reformed Masaru tossed the soggy torch aside and lit the remaining one with a deft motion. "So where are we now?" he asked. "And what's here waiting to kill us?"

"Nothing," I answered, pointing to a faint glow ahead, "look."

The corridor was round with metal walls, like the inside of a submarine. Ahead of us, an arch-shaped opening revealed thick cables and wires along the floor, as well as a familiar style of computer monitor. There were also several banks of consoles separated by wall-length glass tubes filled with unknown substances lit somewhat eerily from within.

"What is this place?" Ticket asked. "And what's it doing here under the valley?"

"A lab, maybe," I ventured, looking around, but being careful not to touch anything, "but we won't know for sure unless we can access the files in these computers."

"Whose lab, though?" Masaru questioned. "The Vile Emperor's or Lady Lilyth's?"

"Probably whoever made those little darlings up there," Jeth answered with a frown. "The Lava Lord said Verasheen wanted a daughter, maybe Lilyth wanted the same thing. It gets lonely after a while, being the only one of your kind."

"Lilyth – Little Lilyth, I mean," Ticket corrected himself, "well, she always did say that her mother made this valley and the guardians to protect her."

I was only half listening to the discussion going on around the light of the torch behind me. The flickering light was more than enough for my eyes to read by and my attention was drawn to the Aldanian script below each of the glass canisters hooked up to the computer system.

The combinations of lines and dashes seemed to be referring to a quantity, or perhaps the contents of the compound within the tube. Either way I had no hope of identifying what I was looking at, but perhaps there was someone who could back in Espearia.

Opening my medic kit, I fished out a somewhat crumpled piece of paper and a lead pencil. It was the last of what I had gathered from the abandoned Temple of Sapphire but I was determined to put it to good use. Sketching quickly, I copied the Aldanian characters on each of the labels before turning my attention to the monitor.

Flipping the switch to 'on,' I waited until the computer console hummed to life, only to find the screen filled with information.

"What's it say?" Masaru asked, leaning over my shoulder. "Can ye read it?"

"Yes, but there's a lot here," I answered. "I think this might be the last thing whoever was in here was looking at. Unfortunately, I can't make sense of most of it. There are quite a few series of numbers and what looks to be names of complex compounds that I'm not familiar with. I'd like to take it back with me to Venon, or maybe Hex, but it would take too long and more paper than I have to write it all down."

"What about this?" Jeth pointed to a square-shaped object partially sticking out of the bank of consoles.

"*Portable disk drive,*" I read the Aldanian script just above the slot which held the disk in question before turning to Jeth. "How did you know what to look for?"

"We had something like it at the Temple of Sapphire," Jeth answered. "The control room there was built with a combination of Earth and Rubian technology."

I pushed the disk fully into the drive and turned back to the monitor to see about transferring what I saw before me. Once that was accomplished, I navigated my way back to the main menu to see what other secrets this hidden laboratory might hold.

However, the main menu was like nothing I was expecting. There were only four very specific options and a fifth that simply said, '*Initiate sequence*'. It was as if this computer – and in fact this entire hidden bunker – had been built for a single purpose.

"Now ye've got a funny look on yer face," Masaru noted. "What're those lines and dashes telling ye?"

"I'm not sure," I answered, looking over the four options again. "It seems to be a list of steps in a sequence, but I'm not entirely certain what the sequence is meant to accomplish."

"Steps like what?"

"'Seeding'," I read out, "'Extermination', 'Germination', and 'Infusion'."

"What does that mean?" Ticket asked. "Is it bad?"

With my curiosity overwhelming my caution, I selected the first option and the screen filled with information, much like what I had already downloaded to the disk, but below it all was a simpler description. *Launch and scatter aforementioned native seed types to replenish the natural vegetation and restore the environment's vitality. Initiate sequence?* It asked on the very bottom of the screen, the lines and dashes blinking to catch my attention. *Yes/No?*

I very carefully selected no, even though this particular step in this program's sequence didn't seem so awful by itself. Certainly there was no denying that this planet needed its plant life and environment replenished, but the title of the next step in the sequence, *'Extermination'*, had me concerned.

Back at the main menu I selected *'Extermination'*. The screen filled with text in what was becoming a familiar fashion. *"Release the aforementioned combination of gases into the atmosphere to eliminate living organisms on the planet's surface."* I read aloud and again carefully selected 'no' to the initiate sequence command.

"So she intends to kill everybody, then?" Masaru asked.

"Her or the Vile Emperor," I noted. "We don't know for sure whose program this is. It's likely been here a long time with the way it was hidden, so either Lady Lilyth built it during her reign or the Vile Emperor did in the time since then. They're the only two people who could have programmed it in Aldanian, unless of course it was Venon."

"He didn't strike me as the 'murder everyone' kind of guy," Jeth interjected on Venon's behalf.

"What's next?" Ticket asked. "After everyone's dead, what then?"

"*Germination,*" I read as I selected the third step. "*Induce rapid growth of seedlings and existing vegetation to create a sustainable ecosystem.*"

"Okay, that makes sense," Masaru noted. "That way all the plants and melons and things would grow quickly. But why would ye need all those plants and food if there's not going to be anyone around to eat it all?"

I shrugged in mute answer to his question before backing out of '*Germination*' to select the final step in this strange set of instructions, '*Infusion*'.

The last step was different from the others. Breaking up the wall of text that had greeted me for each of the other steps were diagrams and these I roughly understood, especially with the description at the bottom. *"Infusion: redirect the energies of two or more Splitters to infuse the planet's organic matter with the power of the gem gods."* I studied the diagrams for a moment, unable to tear my eyes away. "She's making herself a continuous power source."

"I thought ye said we couldn't be sure whose idea this all was," Masaru noted.

"We can't," I agreed. "It's still possible that the Vile Emperor was trying to find another way to save his daughter, but either way this process would turn the whole world into a battery for Lilyth. She'd be able to walk through any patch of vegetation and drain the power from it to sustain herself. She wouldn't even need the Ruby heart any longer because there would be power in everything around her."

"But why kill everyone?" Masaru asked. "There'd be nothing left to rule anymore."

"That's true, but maybe she just wants the planet for herself, or maybe the Vile Emperor doesn't want her in charge again after what happened the last time," I hypothesized. "There's no way to know the reasons this program was created, but maybe Hex or Venon can tell us more about exactly how it is supposed to work. I think we've seen enough. I'll just see how much more I can fit onto this disk and then I'll take us back to Espearia."

Four cyan birds flew in a straight line, phasing through the solid rock of the planet's center at an incomprehensible speed, only to emerge moments later in a dark and unfamiliar landscape. They had left Espearia before the last light of day, but here on the other side of the world they found that it was perhaps nearly morning, though still as black as the middle of the night with not a single source of light anywhere to help them see by. Yue's bird, the first in the line, flew forward like she knew where she was going and the rest of them were drawn by her power with no choice but to follow.

Their flight was silent, though a great many questions flitted through Hotaru's mind as she flew behind Yue. Darkened snow and ice raced by below her, the only real indication that they were somewhere very far away from where they had come, although curiously she could not feel the cold of their surroundings as a magic bird made of Yue's power.

They raced on in what felt an endless silence to Hotaru, but was really no more than a little longer than it had taken them to cross through the planet's center from the Temple of Machalite, where they had made their transformations into the forms they now wore. At last Hotaru became aware that what was beneath them had changed. Instead of icy cliffs and snow-covered hills, there was now only a solid sheet of ice with perhaps a light dusting of snow. At first she thought they were flying over a body of water, but then she became aware of the curious flatness of the expanse of ice and what seemed like a faint light below.

Straining the limits of Yue's hold on her, Hotaru managed to dip down closer to the surface as they flew along, only to find that what she was looking at was an impossible scene. Beneath the surface there were people; some were farmers with tools in hand, others were soldiers armed and armoured, but all of them were frozen in the midst of doing whatever it was they were doing before they were trapped in time.

And the strange phenomena continued. She saw ladies in fine dresses out for a walk, men on horses riding towards something, green grass, and trees perfectly preserved. There were even animals like dogs, cats, sheep, and goats, kept perfectly immobile by whatever had done this to them. The strangest part was they all seemed perfectly content, like they hadn't known what was coming for them. It was as if time had suddenly halted for these people, their day to day lives interrupted somehow, and they didn't even know that the world had passed on without them.

Feeling a tug upwards, Hotaru followed reluctantly, drawing herself away from the strange sights below and she almost didn't realize that Yue had come to a stop until the others dropped down beside her to land on…nothing. Whatever surface Yue and the others had landed on was perfectly transparent, but as undeniably real as the people frozen far below.

"May I present to you, the Temple of Damos," Yue's bird announced, surprising Hotaru with its ability to speak. "I'm going to change back, but I suggest that the rest of you stay as you are because it's going to be really cold otherwise."

Hotaru opened her beak to speak as Yue had done when she realized that she couldn't. Obviously Yue had given herself the ability to speak, but hadn't bothered to do so for the rest of them. Flapping her wings peevishly, she desperately wished herself out of this restrictive form and back into her own body, and after a moment of trying she suddenly felt the sharp cold.

"Suit yourself," Yue's bird said as she also dropped her disguise and appeared as herself before them.

Yue didn't seem the least bit bothered by the cold, but Hotaru could feel the needle-like pinpricks of it all over her body, as her somewhat tattered Taiyoun robes had been constructed to keep her cool in Taiyou's warm summer climate and in the desert's heat.

"How…do you…" Hotaru's teeth chattered together dangerously, making speech difficult.

Obviously, this wasn't going to do, so she'd have to do something about it if she could. Just like she'd made heat bearable in the Temple of Ruby, Hotaru wished for a way to do the same thing with cold and thankfully, her power provided. She sighed in relief as the cold melted away. "That's better. You can change Adel and Fuun back now, I can keep them from feeling the cold. By the way, how do you know this is the temple we're looking for?"

After she had asked the question, Hotaru looked around to see what this temple really looked like, but thanks to the darkness she couldn't see much of anything and looking down only reminded her that she appeared to be standing on nothing. "Is it invisible?"

"No, Hotaru, it's Diamond," Yue answered, rolling her eyes as she absently restored Adel and Fuun to their own bodies. "I found it because firstly, I knew where it was on the map and secondly, because I asked Damos and he didn't tell me this wasn't it."

"Damos…spoke…to you?" Adel asked, her teeth chattering together like Hotaru's had before.

"Not exactly," Yue responded, as Hotaru sidled over to Adel's side to activate her power on the Knight's behalf, "but he has before, and if this is indeed his temple then I know I can get him to speak to me again. It's too bad we couldn't have brought Chikara, that would have made things simpler…but, oh well."

"Thank you, Hotaru," Adel said, straightening now that she no longer had to hunch inward against the cold. "So if this is the Temple of Diamond we're standing on, how do we get inside?"

"That's where Damos comes in," Yue informed her, "just give me a second while I ask him to let us in."

Yue settled herself cross-legged on the hard, clear Diamond beneath them and closed her eyes to concentrate. Noticing Fuun for the first time standing unobtrusively beyond Adel, Hotaru made for him, her hand outstretched to do what she had for Adel and herself.

"There is no need," Fuun told her. "I am accustomed to this kind of weather, even if it has been centuries since it was commonplace."

"I'm also used to it," Adel muttered, "but that doesn't mean that a nice, thick cloak wouldn't be appreciated."

"All set!" Yue announced and bounded to her feet, as true to her claims the temple they had been standing upon became visible as the Diamond seemed to turn opaque.

The remarkably tall structure was made entirely of Diamond – an entire mountain of it – only the Diamond wasn't clear all the way through, like it had appeared before Damos' intervention. The four of them were standing on a platform nearly halfway up the mountain-side and ahead of them, beyond a path with sheer drops to either side, was revealed an open archway leading into the opaque center of the temple.

"This place has been hidden for a long time," Yue warned. "I don't know if Damos has made it so that only we can see it, or if it's just visible now."

"You and Hotaru go on inside and be careful, then," Adel told her. "Fuun and I will stay here to keep watch, and one of us will come in and warn you if anything shows up."

Yue nodded and started off, and Hotaru had to hurry to keep up with her, mindful of her footing on the sleek Diamond platform.

"What do you think is in there?" Hotaru asked, reaching Yue's side and falling in step beside her as they entered the temple. "I thought we were here to see if Lady Lilyth or Little Lilyth were over on this side of the world."

"Keep your voice down, Hotaru," Yue warned. "I don't know what we'll find, but chances are that it'll be whatever Lady Lilyth is searching for, because this place was well hidden and protected for a reason."

"You think Damos froze all those people out there to protect them from Lady Lilyth?" Hotaru asked, the possibilities swirling in her mind.

"I don't know, Hotaru," Yue answered. "Now be quiet and let me have a look around."

Despite the many unanswered questions swirling around inside her head, Hotaru complied and kept her thoughts to herself. The corridor they found themselves in was really quite a sight to behold. The walls were made of Diamond like everything else, perfectly cut to be as smooth as a pane of glass, but opaque beyond a few inches so that any rooms beyond the walls were not visible from the hallway.

Yue found a row of heavy wood and iron doors around a corner and set about inspecting them to see if they would open. Hotaru was distracted by what she could only describe as the feeling of a presence deeper within the temple, so she continued onward and left Yue to her own devices.

Deeper and deeper into the silent mountain temple, Hotaru felt tugged along by the unexplained knowledge that there was something waiting for her and she found that with each step forward there became only one real direction to go, only one destination that mattered.

Then, at last, she found what she was looking for. The large double doors at the end of a wide hallway reminded her forcefully of the throne room in Taiyou, even if those doors were silver-plated Jade and these were made of a heavy, dark wood, supported by iron bracings. The door was likely too heavy for Hotaru to move, but it was clear to her that whatever they had come here to discover must lay behind it.

"Hotaru?" Hotaru heard Yue call her name distantly, but she was too focused on the mystery before her to pay much attention.

She reached for the door's heavy iron handle and gave it an experimental tug. To her surprise the door came open with ease, swinging on what must be a perfectly balanced system, preserved by the timelessness of this sealed temple.

"Hotaru, where did you go?" Yue's voice was closer now, but Hotaru ignored it.

Swinging wide the other door, Hotaru gasped and stepped back a few steps involuntarily as the rest of the large room was revealed to show yet another scene frozen in time. On the left was an armoured man larger than any Hotaru had ever seen. At nearly eight feet tall, his hulking form was covered head to toe in metal plating. He held a massive sword in one hand and a large shield in the other. He wore a helmet which showed no hint of a being within except for the eye slits, which were lit with a fierce white that emanated outwards, illuminating the scene with an unearthly glow.

Opposite him there was another soldier – albeit a less ostentatious one – in Deathsquad armour, holding up a Sapphire disk as if it was a shield of some kind. The Deathsquad soldier stood unmoving, but a haze about him drew the eye and when Hotaru focused on the anomaly she realized that there was a sort of inexplicable double image there.

In the center of it all was Lady Lilyth. She was also frozen, but when time had stopped in this room she had been in the process of making a mad dash toward the far end of the room, where there stood a raised dais and a solid chair made from that same opaque Diamond as the rest of the temple.

Hotaru had never seen the part woman, part creature that was the enemy that had hunted them and destroyed so much, but there could be no mistaking who this was. She stood nearly as tall as the man on the left, but despite his glowing eyes her presence was somehow even more imposing than his. The bird-like claws of her feet dug into the floor in an attempt to propel herself faster toward her goal and her lower half was intent on the throne she was trying to reach, but her upper body, with its many Lillem-like talons arrayed like fleshless wings, was turned backwards to look at her two assailants and her expression could only be described as pure panic.

Hotaru certainly didn't know what about these two men had caused Lady Lilyth such fear, but one other fact caught her eye. The Lady Lilyth, having turned about to look in the direction of the door where Hotaru stood, had a gaping hole in her chest where, Hotaru had been told, her Ruby heart should be.

"Hotaru, there you are! Why did you – oh, my…"

Hotaru wanted to turn to Yue, but she found that she could not turn away from the scene. She felt weak, dizzy almost, but the sight of Lilyth at last seemed to fulfill some need that Hotaru hadn't known existed within her until now.

"Hotaru, what are you doing?" Yue asked and Hotaru realized that she had unknowingly closed the distance between herself and the threshold of the large doorway.

The scene beyond was encased in what appeared to be Diamond, just like all the others she had seen frozen outside and just like the magic that had kept this temple sealed away. Compelled by a force beyond herself, she raised a hand and placed it on the smooth Diamond wall, surprised to find it warm to the touch.

"Stop that!" Yue admonished, grabbing Hotaru's outstretched arm and pulling it away. "Do you want to set her free?"

The sound of a large crack filled the temple as if in echo to Yue's words, and the clear Diamond before them suddenly developed a single flaw, a line crossing the room in a jagged fashion from where they stood to the Lady herself.

Hotaru's gaze followed the crack within the Diamond with a look of shocked horror until it reached its ultimate destination, and then she saw that the expression on Lilyth's face had changed from panic and fear to a vicious grin of triumph.

"Run!" Yue yelled and tugged on Hotaru's arm. This time Hotaru did not resist, letting Yue pull her from the vision that would haunt her nightmares forever.

Yue pulled Hotaru onto her back so she could race back the way they had come at top speed propelled by her power, and in less than a second they were back outside with Adel and Fuun who were both looking out into the early light of morning.

"We have a problem," Yue announced, putting Hotaru on her feet.

"Tell me about it," Adel agreed, pointing out beyond the temple. "Look."

From here they looked no larger or more menacing than a horde of ants, but in reality the horizon was teeming with creatures both large and small, made visible by the early light of dawn rising behind them.

"Is that what I think it is?" Hotaru asked.

"Lilyth's army," Fuun stated. "I'd say they found what they've been searching for."

"The Temple of Diamond?" Hotaru asked. "And her body?"

"I'm pretty sure Lady Lilyth knew all along where her body was, Hotaru," Yue pointed out. "It's her heart. I think she's found her Ruby heart and now her army is bringing it here. Come on, we'd better get back and tell the others. They're still a ways off, and I don't think Damos is going to let them in as easily as he did us, but even still we don't have much time."

Whether or not we were the first ones back, the outskirts of Espearia in the place where the stone table had been set up was relatively unpopulated. After leaving Ticket and Jeth to explain our findings to Chikara and Venon, Masaru and I began the trek across the open wastelands to Hex's ship at a normal human pace, enjoying the rarity of a moment where we didn't have to rush.

"It's nice to be back out in the open again," Masaru noted. "Even if it is dark out, it's better here than in that valley with all those trees and rocks on every side of ye."

I smiled at his aversion to greenery, while internally I found myself feeling conflicted about something that had been bothering me since before we had even left for Little Lilyth's valley.

"Masaru," I began, "I know this might seem like it's coming out of nowhere, but there's something I've been meaning to talk to you about and this might be the only chance we get for a while with everything that's hanging over our heads."

"What is it?" he asked, taking my hand to help me over a rocky patch jutting out of the sand and not letting go afterwards. "I can hear in yer voice that ye're worried about it."

I took a deep breath. "It's not something I ever thought about, but Verasheen and maybe even Lilyth obviously went to a lot of trouble to have children, even though they weren't supposed to be able to. Until Venon mentioned it, I didn't know that being what I am now would mean that I couldn't someday have children of my own, but I wouldn't want to repeat the mistakes that the Vile Emperor made by trying to go against nature."

"Ye're nothing like him, Yukari, nor are ye anything like the Lady Lilyth."

"That's just it, I love science and I'm every bit capable of one day reaching the level of knowledge that Verasheen possesses. Even now I can fathom some of the ways that it might have been possible for him to create Lilyth and the fact that knowledge like that might become a temptation scares me.

"More importantly, though, is that I know that having a family is something that you want. I just wanted to tell you," I struggled over the words, even though in my heart I felt them necessary, "that if you wanted..." I couldn't help the catch in my voice or the tears that came with it. "You're a Knight, so it's still possible for you to...with someone else, I mean."

Masaru stopped walking abruptly and put himself in front of me. "Yukari, I think ye already know that it's you I want." He squeezed my hand tightly and pulled me in closer to him. "There's a difference, ye know, between having kids of our own and having a family. Ye know I'd like the first, but you and I will have lots of chances to raise little ones. There's Neva's little girl, for one, and with how long ye and I are supposed to live, I'm sure there'll be many others.

"Ye've already given me more family than I've ever had," he continued, looking into my eyes, "with yer parents, and even the other Knights and Chosen. Ye've even given me back Razor. Before you I only had Krox and Dahlia, and now I've got more people around me than I know what to do with. If not someday having a child of my own is the price to pay for getting to be with ye, then I consider myself the luckiest man in the world."

I was overcome with emotion and found that there was nothing I could say. I couldn't seriously claim that I'd ever thought about having children one way or the other, but nevertheless I felt as if something had been taken away from me before I'd even gotten the chance to know what it was. However, Masaru was right. I had gotten him in the place of this mysterious something that I would never know, and for that I was luckier than I could ever know.

We stood like that for some time, held close in each other's arms, just taking comfort from the fact that we were no longer alone in the universe and as long as we looked out for one another we never truly would be. And what, other than that, was family really all about?

Sometime later we made it to Hex's ship, and after being admitted by X-En I was able to present the Aldanian disk to the most intelligent and technologically advanced alien I knew. And so, by the time the Stone Table Alliance met again with even more people in attendance, Hex had a chance to translate all the information I had brought him from the valley's hidden lab and we were ready to present our findings with conclusive evidence as to whatever the lab's creator intended to accomplish.

"So Adel and Fuun stayed behind," Hotaru concluded her telling of what she and Yue had encountered in the Temple of Diamond on the far side of the world. "Fuun can make it back here almost instantly if the army reaches the temple or if we need to be informed of something, and Adel intends to guard the temple's entrance in the meantime."

Everyone from the first meeting was present for this one, save Oka and his two squad members, and there were quite a few more attendees, including several more Croatins. It seemed that Ao Kouen and Pine had been successful in their mission to find the missing Croatins and Taiyoun refugees who had fled out into the Sand Lakes following the events of the 'false dawn' operation. Now seated with us was the burly First of the First Spawn, his tiny deep purple companion the First of the Second Spawn, and even the heavily armoured half-Croatin, half-Binoid known as the First of the Third Spawn.

Next to those somewhat illustrious leaders sat the formidable Croatin Head-Taker, Krox, with Dahlia having left our side of the table to sit in her mate's lap and looking as pleased as punch to have him returned to her after so much time spent apart.

In her place there now stood a small party of unmarked Stirr who were representatives from the Mountains of Sapphire. They were also some of the ones who were now interacting willingly with humans, having become teachers once more to the children and adults living, even if only temporarily, at the Children's Outpost in the south.

Beyond them sat someone I hadn't expected I'd ever see again, Yuge's best friend and former outpost leader of the Roughlanders of Hex's outpost, Hitachi. The smarmy and somewhat rough-around-the-edges Roughlander had been responsible for the escape of some several hundred Taiyoun citizens and displaced legionnaires when the going had gotten tough in Taiyou. He may not have looked the part but Hitachi had proved himself a hero, and Yuge would have been proud to know what his friend had accomplished.

"We do have some good news," Arashi interjected. "The Lady Anaeth has sent word that she has broken ties with Lady Lilyth. She regrets that it took her so long to realize which side deserved her loyalty, but she's willing to follow whatever instructions we send her and ensure that her forces do the same. She also asks that her daughter, the Lady Annalise, remain in Espearia for the time being to ensure her continued safety."

"That certainly is good news," Ao Kouen agreed, "and so is the safe return of the Croatins and Hitachi's refugees. Sabien and Aysel also have good news they would like to share."

"The Stirr have informed us that they will continue to regulate the otherwise dangerous shifts in the weather as the world tries to re-adjust itself to having both night and day again in equal measure. According to them they've been using their considerable powers for some time now to ensure everyone's safety, even if none of us were aware of their interference."

"In addition to keeping the weather as calm as possible," Aysel added, "the Stirr also promise to aid us in any way they can against Lady Lilyth and her army. They now understand that she has betrayed their trust and such a betrayal cannot go unnoticed. The only condition being that the Stirr will not fight Stirr. If there are living Stirr loyal to Lady Lilyth the Stirr with us will not harm them, so we'll have to make sure that we are prepared to defend ourselves against them."

"So I think we have a fair idea of what we have at our disposal and what is piled up against us," Chikara said, trying her best to sound formal. "Why don't we look at what new facts we have and how they might be able to help us stop Lady Lilyth and her army? Yukari?"

"We found a hidden bunker underneath little Lilyth's valley," I informed everyone. "We can't be entirely certain who designed the valley or its secrets, but we did establish that the valley was created to keep something hidden from someone else who can read Aldanian. In my opinion, that either means Lady Lilyth created the valley to hide her daughter and her work from Verasheen, or Verasheen created it for the same reason."

"Or maybe he made it to hide Lady Lilyth's Ruby heart inside Little Lilyth," Yue suggested. "We now know for certain that her heart is missing and that more than anything she wants it back."

"Either way," I allowed, "beneath the valley in the hidden bunker guarded by…prototypes of Little Lilyth we found a system designed for a very specific purpose. I was able to bring the files I found back to Hex for him to analyze and he's discovered some interesting facts. X-En, if you would?"

"What my master discovered was specifics of the program's purpose and its proposed execution, but also that the four step sequence described by the program had already been initiated once before. As it turns out, the console that Yukari and her companions discovered was actively monitoring the energy levels of the enclosed valley, which was used as a testing ground for the program's effectiveness. I can also accurately report that according to the program's parameters the test on the valley was a success."

"The program is a four step process," I clarified, "created, it seems, to re-seed the planet, fill it with vegetation, and use the Splitters to funnel power inwards and infuse every bit of organic matter with the power of the gem gods. This would create a world which Lady Lilyth and any beings created in her image, like Little Lilyth, could survive indefinitely, feeding off the planet's resources instead of relying on stealing power from powered individuals."

"That doesn't sound so bad," Kaji noted, "provided of course that Lilyth be defeated before any part of the sequence is put into motion."

"I agree," I told Kaji, "except that one of the steps in the process is to eliminate all living things on the planet and then, when the final stage is completed, all of those bodies would be infused with magic and would rise like guardians.

"The valley is an example of what the world would be like afterwards," I elaborated. "The magic infusing everything would mean that no one could ever truly die. If someone dies within the valley they become a guardian, so it's not the guardians that infect people, not like the Lillem, it's the nature of the valley itself."

"What about the other steps, though?" Hotaru questioned. "The plants would be able to live again, now that there's rain and nighttime, right?"

I nodded. "It makes sense to try and disable the steps that are disagreeable to us, but there's nothing wrong with making use of what could very well give this world a head start to recovery."

"Well as to that, we found a hidden lab ourselves," Kaji mentioned. "We're not a hundred percent sure yet that it'll be of any use to us, but it's possible. It seems that it might have been the place where Verasheen created the Talons, among other things."

"Oka's working right now on translating the Aldanian files he found," Akuma added. "Perhaps you, Yukari, or maybe Venon, could be of assistance to him when we're done here. It seems that we don't have as much time as we might have hoped."

"Um guys..." Hotaru ventured, "what happens when Lady Lilyth gets her heart back?"

Most of us turned to Venon for the answer only he might have a chance of knowing. "I presume that if she's frozen in Diamond like you say, then if the heart was charged and got near enough to her that she would be able to draw on its power to break free. Not only that, but she would be able to drain every gifted individual within her reach."

"So if Lilyth's soul is in Little Lilyth's body " Hotaru reasoned, "then Little Lilyth is probably marching with that army to bring her Ruby heart right to her...and that's bad, right?"

CH. 20 – TEMPLE OF DIAMOND

*"I was not certain you would accept my invitation."
The Yaboun Tenchi's voice reverberated through his helmet.*

*Lady Lilyth stepped boldly through the double doors but her
eyes remained alert as she scanned the large open space. Following
behind her was the only escort she had been permitted to bring, a
lone Deathsquad soldier.*

*"I believe you would agree that we have a common enemy,"
she countered, striding past the Yaboun Tenchi, subconsciously
drawn by the pulsing power of the throne on the far end of the room.
"It is in our best interest to determine how we are going to deal with
the usurper."*

*"Leave us," the Yaboun Tenchi commanded his guards and as
one the double doors were swung shut, sealing the three of them into
the temple's throne room.*

*"Now, shall we get down to business?" Lilyth asked, turning
slowly to face the Yaboun Tenchi after completing her initial survey
of the room.*

She didn't even get halfway turned around before the unthinkable happened.

"Now!" the Deathsquad soldier yelled and flipped his shield over in his gauntleted hands to reveal a disk of flawless Sapphire.

Lady Lilyth turned her head sharply over her shoulder to regard her escort, shocked by this sudden betrayal from the most unsuspected of sources, as the Yaboun Tenchi drew and leveled his sword in a smooth motion to aim it at the Sapphire disk. Her eyes widened, as if fully taking in the presence of the Deathsquad soldier for the first time, when his suit of armour began to rattle and shake.

Her fear was instinctual and she began to flee, her body reacting without conscious direction and propelling her forward toward the Diamond throne – the one thing that might have enough power to save her.

A beam of power fired from the tip of the Yaboun Tenchi's sword and reflected off the Sapphire disk. It caught her in the back, freezing her in place and making her powerless as it was intended to do.

The Deathsquad soldier continued to shudder violently in his armour, then his motions became more erratic, as if any moment he would simply shake apart and there would be nothing left of him. Having successfully immobilized the Lady Lilyth, the Yaboun Tenchi turned his head sharply to regard the Deathsquad soldier.

"This was not a part of our agreement."

In response to this an odd thing happened; the Deathsquad soldier seemed to phase out of his armour, as if the spirit inside was trying to flee the trap he had set within the body he'd been wearing and the face that was revealed was that of Verasheen, the Vile Emperor.

The Yaboun Tenchi realized at the last minute that the Vile Emperor, whom he had conspired with against Lilyth, now intended to betray him in turn and so he called down the power of Damos. He froze time for his lands, his people, and most importantly the momentous scene in the throne room, so that Lilyth would never reach the power she craved, the Deathsquad soldier that had been no more than a ticking time bomb would never go off, and Verasheen would never escape the punishment he deserved...

It lacked the specifics of what had led to the moment where the three most powerful beings in the world found themselves trapped in each other's company for eight centuries and was somewhat far-fetched as scenarios go, but it was the only explanation that seemed to fit all of the little details in the memory of the Temple of Diamond that Yue had provided everyone around the stone table.

The inconsistencies were so vivid in my mind; they were little things, really, but when put together they painted a fuller picture of what might have happened eight hundred years ago. The Yaboun Tenchi's obvious active use of power, the thin but unmistakable tunnel through the Diamond that marked the passage of a beam of power from the tip of his sword to the Sapphire disk held by the Deathsquad soldier, and then to a point in Lady Lilyth's back where she arched visibly from the discomfort or shock of it. There was also Lilyth's expression of panic, and Verasheen's soul visibly caught in the process of leaving the body he had obviously been occupying for some purpose more important than simply disguising himself from Lilyth, whom he had angered by stealing the Ruby heart he had once given her.

"That disk in the soldier's hands is something I recognize." Sabien was the first to break the silence, as we all absorbed the new memory that Yue had stuck in our head with her remarkable ability. "That's the Splitter pad. No doubt it was what Verasheen was after when he raided the Temple of Sapphire."

"And the way he's coming out of that suit of armour is very familiar," Aysel noted. "It's just like when the Talons came out of your friend's bodies that time in Taiyou."

"My brother made himself into a Talon?" Venon questioned, seeming surprised. "If that's so, then there's no way that that Deathsquad soldier he chose was any ordinary soldier. It was a Deepstrike soldier, I would bet my life on it. Nothing else would make Lilyth run like that and certainly not the Yaboun Tenchi using his power on her. That would simply allow her to drain him more easily."

"What's a Deepstrike soldier?" Hotaru asked the obvious question.

"The Deepstrike soldiers were another of my brother's pet projects," Venon explained, "though it was Yuko Seig who oversaw their training and implementation. They were created to be the perfect weapon. Designed to infiltrate almost anywhere, they were trained to blend in perfectly and were completely undetectable until they were ready to strike. Then, those around them had maybe thirty seconds of warning before they destroyed everything in their blast radius. I'm not sure exactly how great a distance that was, but I do know that the Deepstrike order was greatly feared. There's a reason that hardly any of them actually had to be used. The threat they posed was usually enough to convince people to cooperate."

"Were they Knights?" Yue asked. "Did they have some sort of power they could use?"

"They were bombs," Venon clarified, "only worse, because they were living bombs who could choose when and where to detonate. There was no way to tell a Deepstrike soldier from anyone else until they were about to go off, and of course by then it was too late."

"Wouldn't that be kind of dangerous?" Hotaru asked. "Having bombs walking around, I mean?"

"Yes," Venon answered, "and that was sort of the point. Though only a handful of them were ever made, they were all selected from people who showed remarkable self-control and who felt that they no longer had any reason to go on living."

"Suicide bombers," Kaji ventured.

"Yes, that's it exactly," Venon agreed.

So the Vile Emperor had made himself a Talon to gain the ability to legitimately be in two places at once. His body was immortal, so he wouldn't simply end up a disembodied spirit like the others. He'd also created the Deepstrike soldiers with Yuko Seig's help and he'd used his own brother, while he was still free, to set up a meeting with the Yaboun Tenchi, so they could plan how he might destroy the daughter he'd also been responsible for creating. Then later, after she was made vulnerable by his theft of her heart, Verasheen raided the Temple of Sapphire to steal the Sapphire Splitter pad and then possessed a Deepstrike soldier to get close enough to Lilyth to be able to kill her, only to fail and get half of himself stuck in solid Diamond for centuries.

Yuko Seig, Priestess of Sapphiros and Verasheen's co-conspirator during the revolution, had also suffered a fate no less uninspiring. She had trained his secret order of assassins, devoted her life to the cause he had set her, and had ended up begging for him to kill her because no one else would. Perhaps they had even loved each other once, but where was she now? Stuck in the Splitter, barely a ghost of the woman she had once been.

Yuko Seig and Verasheen, working together, had orchestrated the elaborate circumstance that had resulted in our being brought to this world so that we would finish the task that they had been unable to accomplish with all of their scheming. Whatever his true goals, Verasheen had wanted us here on this world and he wanted us at full strength. Using himself as the threat was merely a way to spur us on, to make us stronger and effectively to train us, just like he had his Deepstrike soldiers.

Whether our actions benefited Verasheen or not, Lilyth needed to be stopped. I didn't appreciate being manipulated, but this was bigger than the Vile Emperor now.

"We don't have much time," I reminded everyone, "and there are still preparations we must make. Venon, can you come with me to see Oka? I want to see if he can find us a way to speak to Arocoth and Zai-Aku as they are now, and Akuma, if you don't mind, I might need to rely on your authority to get Kai-Een to hear me out."

"Certainly," Akuma answered, "but what about Fuzen? Does your friend Goji still live?"

"He does. I can get him to the Ruby City and it won't be a problem to get him to help us, though what I have in mind for the others likely won't be an option for him."

"I'm beginning to see what your plan might be, Yukari," Venon noted, "and it's very clever. The Talons were always one of the few things that Lilyth couldn't comprehend, which is probably why my brother thought to become one himself. I'll help you in any way that I can. I would like to see this finished once and for all."

"Thank you, Venon. I have another favour to ask." I turned to Yue. "Do you think you could go to the valley and disable the part of the program that would kill everyone and return them as guardians?"

"Sure, I guess," Yue agreed, "but I'd have no idea what I'd be looking at. You said it was all in Aldanian, right?"

"Well, I have an idea about that part," I told her, fishing out the crumpled piece of paper on which I had copied out the Aldanian labels I had found in the hidden lab. "You'd just need to find the containers with the harmful substances in them and make the stuff inside them disappear the way you do. You don't have to mess with the computer program and risk setting it off. I have the Aldanian written out here and I can circle which labels you're looking for. If Masaru's up for it, he can go with you and help you to identify them. Barring that, you could take the information you need from my memories. I don't know if that will let you read Aldanian, but it might help you to recognize what you're looking at."

"I'll do both," she said, hopping up onto the table and holding out her hand for mine. I reached for her hand and in my mind's eye flashed my time in the valley and what we had found beneath it in a most disorienting way. "Got it," Yue announced. "So, Masaru, are you with me?"

"I can do that, aye," Masaru agreed. "I'll just have to get some more torches first, especially if we won't have Yukari's arrows to see by."

"We'll get 'em on the way," Yue told him. "Hop on," she added, indicating her back with a thumb, "there's no time to waste."

Even as Yue and Masaru flashed off at Yue's usual remarkable speed, the meeting continued.

"I propose that my men and I return to the Temple of Sapphire to see if there is anything there worth salvaging," Corporal Zukatoro suggested. "We had quite an arsenal there once and it is possible that Verasheen did not destroy all of it."

"I'll accompany you and ensure you have access to the temple," Sabien offered. "Some of the passcodes may have changed since your last visit."

Corporal Zukatoro nodded as The Head spoke up on the opposite side of the stone table. "Speaking of weapons, I have quite a collection myself, and my people and I can certainly try to get some more together, if it's a fight we're dead set on getting into."

"Do that," I told The Head, "we can certainly use all the help we can get."

"The Third Spawn will assist in your endeavor," an unexpected mechanical-sounding voice came from the massive half-Binoid Croatin seated to the left of the brutish looking First of the First Spawn.

"As will I," Krox noted, "and I will personally examine what weapons you have to offer."

"Hotaru," I addressed her, thinking of something, "do you think that you could take Dahlia back to the Children's Outpost, so she can use the relay station Hex set up to contact the remaining outposts? If we can establish reliable communications it will be easier to rally everyone and keep them advised of what's going on."

"Sure thing," Hotaru agreed, "and if everyone promises to carry water with them at all times, then I can set up my own relay station and keep everyone connected that way."

"Should we be trying to gather everyone together, then?" Akuma asked. "So the troops are all ready to go when we are?"

"That brings me to my next question," I noted without really answering. "Hex," I addressed him through X-En, "I know you were able to get here very quickly with your ship and I've seen your Binoids cross great distances. Would you by any chance have a way to be able to get a large number of troops to the other side of the world quickly?"

"It might take some time to devise, but I believe I may have a solution to that particular problem," Hex answered. "I would need a few volunteers to test my theories."

"I'll stay," Aysel offered.

"I will as well," Pine added. "I have to admit that I'm interested to see the inside of your 'ship', as you call it, Lord Hex."

"My master bids you welcome," X-En concluded on Hex's behalf. "You may both accompany me back to the ship. It's best that we get started as soon as possible."

"Perfect," I said with a nod. "To answer your question, Akuma, yes, it would be best to bring everyone to Espearia, if that's okay with you, Arashi."

"It's all right with me if it's all right with my daughter," Arashi responded.

"I'll have to stay here, of course, to let everyone in," Chikara noted, "but yes, it's all right with me. We've got lots of space out here on the outskirts of the city, so I don't think it'll be a bother to anyone, and Espearia's the safest place there is right now."

"Well, since my daughter seems to have everything under control," Arashi noted, "that leaves me free to go out and meet with Lady Anaeth of Sresh. Jeth, I'd appreciate your company in case she has anything up her sleeve, but if she meant what she said about changin' sides, then perhaps we can escort Anaeth and her troops back here to await transport with everyone else."

"With your permission, my Lady," Bastion addressed Akuma, "I can do the same with the forces of Middleton. They swore their allegiance to us following our assistance during the false dawn operation."

"That's true, Bastion," Akuma agreed. "I will be returning with Yukari to the Ruby City, so there is no need for you to accompany me. Go to Middleton, speak with Captain Gerard, and then bring him and his troops here. I will see to it that the Deathsquads are prepared for transportation. I still have Kichigai in the Ruby City."

"Then I will stay in Espearia to organize the troops as they arrive," Kaji announced. "We'll need to take numbers, get rations, and decide who needs whatever weapons and armour that The Head and the Corporal manage to obtain."

"I'll help you," Ao Kouen offered. "As many of you as you can make, you still can't be everywhere at once, Kaji."

"You'll also need Generals," Leon noted, "and that's where I can help. I can find leaders among the Taiyouns and Hitachi can do the same with the Roughlanders. We already have the First of the First, and we'll be getting this Captain Gerard of Middleton and Lady Anaeth of Sresh. Once everyone else has arrived, a meeting of the leaders among the troops can help us decide strategy and ensure that everyone is prepared to work together."

A hissing broke through the general din of those gathered. *"We will return to our nests and inform the Stirr of what is to come,"* the Stirr spoke, with Sabien translating. *"We can also bring you, Knight Commander Sabien, and your pack of humans to the Temple of Sapphire as you intend."*

The Kumori leader, still silently present, mimed to Ris, *We heard there may be injured among those brought back from the wastes. We may be of assistance in treating them,* and Sabien translated once more for those who did not speak the language of the Kumori.

"Well, that's it, then," I concluded. "Everyone has their orders and anyone who doesn't can report to Kaji for something to do." I looked around the table for Hotaru, who was making her way past the Stirr to join Dahlia. "Hotaru, can you make it your first priority once you get set up to contact Adel and see how they're holding up out there?"

"I'll let you know as soon as I've talked to them," she answered. "Good luck everyone and remember the water. I'll be in touch!

"Oh, Dahlia, one more thing," I added, "can you check in on Neva and let her know that I'll be sending for her as soon as I can?

With the rate that the baby's been developing, I'd feel safer if she was in the Ruby City with Oka and myself."

"I'll tell her," Dahlia answered, as with a quick, "All done!" Hotaru grabbed hold of the Corporal's arm and turned them both into a puddle of water, splashing into the small pool of it she had prepared. Thanks to Hotaru's power, the two of them would arrive nearly instantaneously in the fountain of the Children's Outpost.

"Shall we go, then?" Akuma asked.

I nodded to Venon and Akuma, and without wasting another moment I took the three of us straight to Oka in the Ruby City.

"Don't you people ever knock?!" Oka exclaimed.

"Do I need to remind you of who you're addressing, General Oka?" Akuma questioned.

"No, Lady Akuma," he said, backing down, "but had you arrived a minute earlier, there may have been some problems. I was testing the machine."

I noticed we were in a room I'd never seen and had only heard about through Kaji's retelling of what they had found. The hidden lab was not large or even well appointed; it seemed almost makeshift. The single bank of consoles was lit with a screen filled with Aldanian writing and beyond that stood Oka where he'd been inspecting a large pillar made of pure Ruby.

"It's a machine?" I asked.

"Yes," Oka replied, "and very simple in its function, even as it is complex in its design. It drains power, but not just any power, only that of the gem god selected by the console. The thing is, it's got six settings and I can't quite figure out what the sixth one is for."

"Maybe I can help," Venon offered, leaning in to examine the monitor. "It says here that it had individual settings for each of the gem gods and one that's set to 'all' just in case the other options aren't enough. Likely my brother was referring to the settings of this device not being enough to stop Lilyth, since she isn't really a Chosen or even a Knight. She just uses any power she can get her hands on."

"Perhaps this device is a prototype of what Verasheen ended up using the Sapphire Splitter pad to do," I ventured. "We know that he had to have gone in there with a more elaborate plan than simply using the Deepstrike solider to blow her up."

"It makes sense," Venon allowed. "If this was the lab he'd used to prepare for his confrontation with her, then all the evidence is here."

"Well, that's nice and all, but this machine is of no use to anyone outside of this lab, which is probably why Verasheen would have probably opted for a more portable version," Oka informed us. "This one's powered by the volcano and linked into this bulky console by some pretty heavy cables."

"Either way, it's one of the few real weapons we have," I told him, a plan already forming in my mind for how the Ruby pillar could be put to use. "We'll find a power source."

"Suit yourself," Oka commented, "but now that the experts are here I'm done with this thing. Venon, it's all yours."

Leaving Venon to puzzle over his brother's lab notes, Akuma and I followed Oka out into a dusty corridor and up a flight of rough-hewn stone steps to emerge in a very familiar setting, the Vile Emperor's throne room.

"I have matters that require my attention," Akuma announced, "but I will send Kai-Een to you when I find him, and I will also make sure that the guards know that none but the three of us and Venon are to have access to the throne room for the time being."

"Thank you, Akuma," I told her. "We'll be in the lab if you need us for anything."

"We will?" Oka questioned, before taking one look at my determined expression and quickly amending his statement. "We'll be in the lab, then."

I was lost in thought for the duration of the walk through the familiar palace hallways up to Oka's lab. I was certain he was full of questions, but he left me alone with my thoughts and I was grateful.

My mind was a jumble, thoughts endlessly looping and running together in ways that ceased to make sense. I was tired, I knew that, but even still I felt frustrated by how a thought that seemed clear one moment would swirl away and feel foggy the next. One thing I did know was that I dare not rest, there was too much at stake. This was it – our one chance to make everything right, or die trying.

Either way, there would be losses, and no matter how powerful we had become I knew I had to steel my heart now, because even a Chosen could not be everywhere at once. I had to face the fact that I wouldn't be able to keep everyone safe and still do what was needed.

The problem was, I didn't know if I could separate myself enough to be able to keep going if someone I cared for fell in battle. I had been tested before, almost losing Masaru, my father, and my friends both new and old, and each time it had almost defeated me. I felt a part of myself just wishing that a miracle would occur, allowing us all to come out of this unscathed and free of the violence that had plagued us until now.

I mentally silenced that part of me, putting my strongest hopes and fears in a box of my imagining, keeping them hidden so I didn't have to face them. We were at war whether I liked it or not, or was prepared for it or not, and this war between Lilyth and the free world had been brewing for over a thousand years. The role we were to play in it was inevitable since our births, and the moment the four of us were chosen by Sapphiros and granted his power.

This is what we'd been working towards, consciously or not. This was the moment when we would finally have the chance to fulfill the destinies we'd been set, to triumph or fail, and in so doing decide the fate of this world.

At least that's what I was supposed to believe, right? I was suppose to believe that all of this had a purpose. It was predetermined somehow by the gem gods, or by fate, a war on a distant planet that only I could resolve with powers I had been granted.

Only I didn't feel that way, not really. I felt misled, lied to, and used. The knowledge that Lady Lilyth's very existence was Verasheen's mistake and that both he and Yuko Seig had conspired to orchestrate our involvement in all of this was still fresh in my mind, and that didn't leave me much room for thoughts of duty and purpose.

Which is not to say that I could give up or back down. In the grand scheme of things I hadn't been on this world long, but I'd made a lot of good friends here in that time and some of them had even become family. The people of this world, most of them good, had fought so long and so hard just to get by, but they deserved more than that. They deserved freedom – freedom from war, oppression, and the ability to choose how they wanted to live should be theirs by right, just as it should be mine as well.

I stopped myself from following that line of thought. I knew now what I wanted from life, but I also knew that the weight of responsibility on my shoulders might mean that I wouldn't live long enough to see a time where I might be free of it. My desires for the future hinged on those hopes and fears that I'd already locked away and I'd not consider them until this was over, one way or another.

And if I didn't survive…well, all I could do now was ensure that I'd said everything that needed saying and fulfilled every promise I'd made to date, so I could go to this battle with my conscience clear and my thoughts free of regrets.

And to that end I began as I noticed we had reached the lab's metal doors, "Oka, I know how you don't like visitors in your lab, but I have a few people I need to bring to the Ruby City and one of them you've already okayed."

"You mean the Lillem baby?" Oka questioned, his hand paused above the mechanism that would activate the automatic door.

"Yes, but I don't think you should call it that – the mother's name is Neva," I informed him, "and the baby is a girl."

"Fine, bring them all in," Oka instructed, opening the door. "I can always kick the extras out."

"Thank you, Oka."

I followed Oka into the main lab but left the scientist to his own devices as I settled myself down cross-legged on the operating table in the center of the room, slowing my breathing and closing my eyes. Attuned to my power like this, I had no trouble sensing Oka as he ventured into the next room and I could feel the location of every life force within the palace – and even a little beyond that. Reaching outwards with my power, searching like I did when trying to find a target for my arrows or messages, I felt for Neva. She was far from me, about as far from the Ruby City as one could get, but it made no difference. I felt her in the direction of the Children's Outpost far to the south and Razor was with her, and I locked onto them both.

There was one more person I needed, but try as I might I couldn't find Goji. Realizing my error, I shifted my focus to sense for Fuzen and all of a sudden I felt as if I could point right to him. "Gotcha," I murmured and then instead of sending myself to Fuzen, or even Razor and Neva, I brought all three of them to me.

Clouds of mist formed shapes around me, which quickly solidified into the familiar forms of the people I had summoned. Razor had his arms around Neva, who obviously had been crying and still had tears in her eyes, but she somehow managed to simply look startled. Fuzen/Goji, however, seemed to take his sudden relocation in stride.

"The Ruby City?" Fuzen asked, the European accent giving his current identity away. "You've brought me home?"

"In a manner of speaking, yes," I answered him, "though if, as you said before, you are still willing to help me, it might only be temporary. If you don't mind, I have a few things to see to before you and I can talk."

"Of course," he answered

Hopping down off the table, I dismissed Fuzen/Goji from my mind for the moment and allowed Razor to pull me in closer to him and Neva.

"We're in the Ruby City?" Razor asked in a tense whisper. I nodded and Neva's eyes widened perceptively. "I know we're all supposed to be allies now and everything, but you'd better know what you're doing, Yukari."

"Trust me," I told them both, "Oka is a doctor and a friend. This is his lab and you don't even need to leave it while you're here if you don't want to. You're in good hands."

"What about him?" Neva questioned in a low voice, shrugging one shoulder in Fuzen's direction.

I smiled in an attempt to put her at ease, but found to my surprise that my smile was genuine despite all the worrying I had done. "Goji," I said at a more normal volume, "you remember Razor and Neva, don't you?"

"Of course," Goji responded affably, stepping forward and offering his hand to Razor. "It's good to see you both and congratulations," he added, taking in Neva's condition.

Neva's jaw dropped as she took in the subtle transformation from Talon of the Vile Emperor to former Taiyoun advisor, but Razor recovered quickly enough to take hold of the outstretched hand and give it a shake. "It's good to see a familiar face."

"Likewise," Goji agreed.

"Good," Oka's interrupted further conversation as he stepped back into the main lab, "now that everyone's re-acquainted we can get to business."

He crossed the room, making straight for Neva's belly. I stepped back when I noticed that there was a new addition to our gathering in Oka's lab. Standing beyond Fuzen/Goji was the person I both needed to see and never wanted to see again – Kai-Een.

"You're in good hands, Neva, I promise," I said, turning back to Neva once more. "Oka's the best, but unfortunately I've got to go…"

"It's Chosen stuff, isn't it?" she asked, looking over my shoulder to where Kai-Een glowered in the doorway.

I nodded. "Yes, it is, and it's very important for all our sakes, or I would be here with you. You know that, right?"

"Of course I do," she responded, wincing involuntarily as Oka stuck something cold on the underside of her belly. "Go on and do what ye have to, Razor and I will get by just fine."

I nodded again and went to turn around to face unwanted responsibilities, when Razor stopped me. "I know you can handle yourself," he whispered, "but I still gotta say it. Be careful, Yukari."

"I know, I don't trust him either."

"I'm not talking about Kai-Een. I mean everything. Don't go and get yourself killed out there, whatever it is you're intending. Masaru isn't the only one who'd grieve, remember that."

I wanted to smile to reassure both him and myself, but I couldn't bring myself to do it; Razor's words hit too close to home. "How could I forget?" I told him, barely above a whisper. "I'll come back. I can't promise anything right now, but I will do everything within my power to come back."

"That's all any of us can do." He squeezed my arm before letting go. "Good luck."

"You too," I managed a shaky smile, "both of you."

Having said all that needed saying, it was time to do what I had come to the Ruby City to do. Turning on my heels, I strode with purpose toward Kai-Een and Fuzen, two men I had once considered among my greatest enemies.

"I need your help."

Their resistance was as I expected, but with Fuzen already on my side it was only a matter of time before the rest of the Talons fell in line, including both Arocoth and Zai-Aku, whom Oka placed in temporary bodies so they could be consulted. Truth be told, the Talons had been in chaos since losing the forms they had held for eight hundred years. With the Vile Emperor gone Fuzen was the next best thing they had to a leader and for Goji's sake he took advantage of that to ensure the Talons would be at my disposal.

Preparations were well underway by the time I succumbed to exhaustion and I don't know how long I slept before I became aware that the vase of flowers beside my bed was talking to me.

"Yukari," Hotaru's voice echoed through the water in the vase, "can you hear me?"

"Yes, Hotaru," I answered, sitting up and realizing that for the first time I felt ready to take on the weight of the world – this was it; the end had come.

"It's time."

Taking only what we were absolutely certain we would need, we left as the sun was just beginning to crest the horizon in Espearia and the Ruby City, only to arrive on the other side of the world at nightfall. With me were Kaji, Yue, Hotaru, and Akuma.

The five of us, once friends on Earth, arrived united again here on the far side of a distant planet, ready to face the destinies for which we had been Chosen. We formed out of mist and regained our solidity facing Adel.

Fuun raised an eyebrow at our arrival, but said nothing. Adel, however, was shivering violently and regarding us with obvious incredulity. Hotaru hurried forward and touched Adel, granting her the same immunity to extreme cold she'd already given us.

"Thank you for that," Adel said, standing up straighter, her red hair whipping in the wind she no longer felt the bite of. "I suppose I should have been more clear. Chosen or not, we're going to need more firepower than what the five of you can offer. Look."

We turned about to look out and I realized that we were high upon a platform with sheer edges and a smooth surface. Beneath our feet could only be Diamond, the flawlessness of it too perfect to be ice. The thought of enough Diamond to stand on was staggering, but it paled in comparison to the sheer scope of what surrounded us – Lilyth's army surged inward from every direction, intent on the temple upon which we stood.

There were Hounds, of course, but more than I'd ever believed existed. There were Lillem too, many more than should be left after the timely destruction of that pool of molten Ruby. And perhaps more than thirty feet tall stood Lillem-like creatures like those the imperial army had defeated with great effort in the furthest reaches of the Temple of Ruby. Those Lillem, with their long spider-like legs, had nearly reached the walls of the Temple of Diamond. I could count three of them from where I stood.

There was no sign of Little Lilyth, not that I expected to be able to see her, especially not amongst the approaching chaos, but when peering into the distance I could see a veritable army of enemy Stirr standing in formation, unmoving. Their markings gave them away as Lilyth's followers but I couldn't fathom what their purpose here was, if not to reach the temple as the rest of the army seemed to be doing. Something told me that whatever they were waiting for, it would not bode well for us.

A familiar mechanical whine pulled my attention from the Stirr as two Skyraiders separated from the incoming fleet's formation to arc down in our direction.

"A Skyraider patrol wasn't exactly what I had in mind either," Adel noted, "but it's a start."

"Just wait, Adel," Kaji told her.

We backed up to give Fuzen and Kai-Een room enough to land.

"We made good time," Goji greeted us with a friendly nod, which earned him a displeased stare from Kai-Een. "We followed the sun most of the way, which means the Skyraiders still have full power. Either way, I made sure each pilot is carrying a spare battery so we're well prepared."

"Good," Yue commented, "and now that you're here, there's something else you can help us with. We need to keep an eye on things inside, but the last time we were down there it seemed like Hotaru was feeding Lilyth power just by standing too close. So, it's probably not a good idea for any of *us* to go in there just yet."

"Understood," Goji replied and stepped away from his Skyraider before turning his head over his shoulder to address Kai-Een in Fuzen's deep Rubian tones, "You know what to do?"

Kai-Een nodded, standing up straighter. "Yes, Fuzen."

"Then I suggest you get to it."

"What about the rest of us?" Adel began, as Fuzen headed off toward the temple entrance and Kai-Een boarded his Skyraider once more.

I waited for the whine of Kai-Een's Skyraider to fade as he rose into the air above us before speaking. "We wait."

"What?! If you haven't noticed, we're completely surrounded now and if we don't do something those Hounds will soon be upon us. Not to mention those Ruby monstrosities. Diamond or not, a few good blows from them might just be enough to take this mountain down."

"Let them try," Kaji stated, "because until that scene inside the temple is disturbed, we can't get to Lilyth. They'd be doing us a favour."

"A favour?" Adel repeated. "Are you all mad? With Lilyth free and her army at her disposal she'll tear us apart, if the Hounds don't do it first."

"It'll be all right, Adel," Hotaru told her, "you'll see."

"Well, I will not simply stand idly by," Fuun spoke, drawing his sword and looking down at the Hounds closing in around us. "Death awaits."

Fuun took off, racing down the side of the Diamond mountain nearly faster than I could follow, and as if his departure had been some kind of signal a burning light began in the sky, reminiscent of a falling star intent on the earth below. The star wasn't alone, however; after the first lit the sky, another appeared beside it, and another beyond that. Like a flock of fiery phoenixes, the lights in the sky plummeted and grew larger as they grew nearer.

"What the...?" Adel began but the whines of the Skyraider engines cut her off as Kai-Een directed the fleet to fly over our heads as planned, so they would not be in danger from the coming onslaught.

Then the first star crashed to the ground – or more accurately, the transport pod crashed into one of the giant Lillem, shattering it into a million tiny pieces with the force of its landing. Startled for a moment by the crash landing of what looked like a comet from the sky, the advance of the Hounds paused. That is, until a metal door swung open from the structure within the flames and the true nature of the fiery object from the sky was revealed – the resistance was here.

Two figures emerged from the shadow of the open door and even from here Aysel's cyan arm and Sapphire fist were unmistakable. As she stepped forward, Pine's lime green skin and the metal frame of his lower half became visible. Seeing that their enemies had arrived at last, the Hounds resumed their forward charge and the battle began.

Seeming to take this as some kind of cue, on the other side of the frozen expanse the mass of gathered Stirr began to move as one in an almost wave-like pattern. They leaned first forward, then back, their bodies firmly planted on their many legs, but their arms outstretched as if pulling in the tide. Although I couldn't yet fathom what their purpose was, I knew they had to be stopped before they could fulfill it. Another pod crashed down in the space between the marked Stirr and the temple, but in this case there was no pause in the motions of the enemy. The Stirr simply continued to sway forward and back, unfazed.

In the light of the fire created by the transport pods' re-entry into the atmosphere and thanks to my power-enhanced vision, I caught sight of the first figure to exit from within the blaze and my breath caught as Masaru stepped out, gesturing for those behind him to do the same. Masaru's troops filed out of the transport pod behind him, looking awkward but determined in their mismatched armour and brandishing an array of miscellaneous weapons. Many of the men and women of the town of Middleton and its surrounding area were of Roughlander descent, but until the Lillem attacks Middleton had been a relatively peaceful place caught between the rule of Taiyou and the might of the Ruby City, and was largely left out of the affairs of each. Other than the occasional sandcrawler to scare off, the people of Middleton had never faced anything like this and their inexperience showed.

My heart went out to Masaru at the head of the pack; he faced a veritable army of marked Stirr and seeing his group of amateur warriors, the nearby Hounds had shifted course for easier prey than the Binoids that were emerging behind Pine and Aysel. My Roughlander Knight would not have an easy time ahead of him and the situation was just about to get worse.

A violent eruption of light and sound drew my attention and I whirled about only to find that a new threat had presented itself. Erupting from the rocky crags to the east was an impossibly tall geyser of red-hot molten lava. The sudden eruption couldn't be a coincidence; it had to be the marked Stirr causing it, their power was unparalleled when it came to the subtle control of natural forces.

Several more pods crashed down; they were massive structures, originally constructed by Hex as a method of sending his Binoids across great distances quickly. Since our battle plan had been developed, he had modified the original designs to make the pods safe enough for human transport and had loaded our armies into them in the place of the many Binoid troops he had lost when Lilyth had attacked his facility.

To the northwest, Hitachi's pod landed and the many souls he had rescued from the remains of Taiyou piled out, weapons in hand and ready to take their revenge against the army responsible for destroying their home. To the south and west, respectively, the Kumori and the Japanese landed. The former took flight as soon as they were able and the latter carried pieces of machinery between them, hurriedly setting themselves to the task of assembling whatever it was they had brought with them.

Dahlia landed nearest to us, leading a pod full of battle-ready Roughlanders, and beyond them, closest to the encroaching lava was a pod full of Deathsquad soldiers, led by Lady Kichigai. Bastion emerged from his pod to the north, leading troops from the imperial army of the Ruby City, and Leon Rama emerged from another with his smaller – but no less competent – force of Taiyoun legionnaires and members of his own Lion Brigade. Near the Taiyoun force landed the Croatins, the First and Shird Spawns standing out because of their greater size, but the Second Spawns and the rest were no less present or ready for war.

To the east, the Espearian pod landed with The Head's troops and the formidable Priestesses of Espearia, and with them landed another pod containing Jeth, the Lady Anaeth, and the combined forces of free Lillem from Sresh and elsewhere. The Hounds surged forward with Lillem between them and the war began in earnest, but to us on the platform there was nothing to do but wait and conserve our powers for when the real threat would emerge.

Adel's expression was mutinous at our inaction, but I ignored her and fired a single arrow up into the sky to give Kai-Een the signal he'd been waiting for. The pods had landed and all were accounted for; it was now time for the Skyraiders to move. With a deafening whine, the Skyraider fleet dove for one of the two remaining giant Ruby Lillem.

Each engine whine preceded an explosion, as the Skyraider pilots pulled out of their dive above the massive creature, simultaneously dropping the handheld explosives they'd been issued back in the Ruby City. The concussive force of the bombs cracked the Ruby and damaged the structure of the Lillem, but it was clear right away that at least one more pass would be needed to take it down.

Seeing this, I turned to take note of the other Ruby Lillem and was pleased to note that the Croatins were swarming it, making great leaps and bounds on their powerful legs to close the distance between them and the monstrosity.

Watching the giant Lillem, I caught sight of Fuun as he reappeared briefly to swipe at one the massive Ruby limbs. His sword sliced cleanly through the Ruby, leaving a lengthy mark along the thing's leg. Flashing around, Fuun left similar scoring marks along the other limbs he could reach before he moved on and I lost sight of him.

The whine of the Skyraiders making another pass reminded me of the first Lillem, and I turned to see how that situation was faring when some motion further out caught my eye. The Hounds had converged on Masaru's group from Middleton and the bulk of them were now fighting desperately for their lives. Masaru was lost in the chaos and difficult to spot, but he was there too, facing a Hound of his own.

I felt divided, a part of me insisting that my place was down there with Masaru using my powers to fight the Hounds, or even just to rescue the fallen, while the more rational part of my brain argued that I had to stick to the plan no matter what the cost.

"We have a problem," Akuma noted, pointing northeastward to direct our attention.

Leon and the legionnaires had formed into a tight formation to hold off the Hounds and the Lillem around them. They weren't making what I would call forward progress, but their tactic was certainly allowing them to hold their ground with minimal losses and there was already a dead Hound on the ground beside them, with another one to follow shortly by the way it was listing to one side. However, from the sloping ground to the north and the crags to the east came a wall of savage Lillem, marching with purpose despite their usually uncontrolled natures, their numbers so great as to be uncountable.

Where had she gotten all the Lillem from? Certainly it hadn't seemed a week ago that she had these kinds of numbers to bring to bear against us, yet here they all were. In some ways it helped to explain why we'd been able to make contact with so few outposts – clearly Lilyth had gotten to them before we'd been able to.

The wave of Lillem crashed into the legionnaires and I winced, being unable to stop it. My power, or even Yue's or Akuma's, would be able to free the poor souls that Lilyth had turned into monsters to serve her, but we had to hold back and because of that more people would be lost on both sides – ones that could have been saved.

The Lillem pushed the legionnaires back, but thanks to the intense training those soldiers had received against the sand Lillem that had plagued them in Taiyou before the fall, they were able to hold their formation as the tide rose around them.

Thankfully the legionnaires were not alone. To the north, the wall of Lillem struck the imperial army. On the eastern side, The Head was also able to rally the Espearians and direct them at the new threat. Best of all, Jeth was there, his own tough skin too thick for the Lillem to infect him, and he was surrounded by a horde of Lillem of his own, free Lillem from Sresh who knew exactly how to fight those who were like them but still controlled by the enemy.

The noise in the darkness was agonizing. And no matter how much I willed them to stop or tried to shut them out, the sounds only increased in pitch, louder and louder until I thought even the Diamond temple behind me would shatter with intensity of it all.

As if my thoughts were prophecy, the platform beneath our feet began to rumble and shake. Moments later, a thunderous cracking sound drowned out the cacophony of battle just long enough for the entire structure to shatter like a glass window, exploding outward in a shower of debris.

Ch. 21 – The Coming of the Lady

Seeing her for the first time in his life, the terrifying beauty of the monster that was Lady Lilyth caused a spark of recognition in Goji. *So you've seen her before, then,* he spoke to Fuzen in his mind while keeping a wary eye on the tableau before him.

A long time ago, yes, Fuzen responded in kind, *when I was newly made.*

The figures held in Diamond were perfectly still, though the large crack in the once perfect prison betrayed a weakness that could be exploited. Neither he nor Fuzen recognized the large armoured figure on the left, but they'd been told who he was. Opposite him was the Vile Emperor, Fuzen's master and creator, his spirit caught for centuries in mid-flight from the body of a Deepstrike soldier and exposing him for what he'd made himself into – a Talon, like those he'd ruled over for almost a millennium.

Here, so deep within the temple, the sounds of the battle outside were dim, except when the temple itself shook. Goji, with Fuzen as his ever present companion, settled himself down to wait and to watch as he'd been asked to. Whatever was coming, it wouldn't be long now…

Throwing his flag arm out wide, Kai-Een flashed a brief set of instructions to the pilots behind him. Then he banked sharply to the right and listened to the mirroring squeals as the other pilots followed suit. It had been some time since they'd been able to fly like this, the whole fleet synchronized in perfect harmony under one commander. Traditionally that commander had been Fuzen, but now Kai-Een had been given his time to shine and he wasn't about to waste the shot he'd finally been given.

Circling wide around the high point of the Temple of Diamond, Kai-Een left the Ruby Lillem they'd bombarded alone in favour of the second one that was rapidly approaching the temple on long, spider-like legs. He could see the Croatin brutes, pinpricks of movement highlighted by the fires burning here and there below, racing forward to engage the thing, but strong as they might be their fists and feet weren't going to do much to the rock-hard Ruby unless Kai-Een was able to give them something to work with.

On his signal, the co-pilots readied their explosives and released them as they made their pass over the second Ruby Lillem. The resulting explosions rained down in a satisfying manner and the Lillem began to fall, its legs having given out from below.

A cracking louder than thunder split the air. Almost forgetting to signal his intentions, Kai-Een wheeled his Skyraider about and was taken aback by the shocking sight of the upper half of the Diamond mountain shattering and spraying outward with concussive force.

Fuzen had been assigned to a position within the mountain and all Kai-Een could think about while staring at the wreckage was how Fuzen had told him that neither of them were the same anymore – they were one with their host bodies now. In Fuzen's case, it was because he shared consciousness with his host, but for Kai-Een his host was already dead. If either of them died, they wouldn't simply move on to another body; for the first time in their whole existence they stood to lose everything.

"Goji, Goji! Fuzen? Answer me!"

Having turned to mist by instinct when the explosion hit, I was the first to recover and the first to recall that Goji had been at the core of the blast. Having not yet reformed, my power found him for me and I drifted down into the ruin that was the Temple of Diamond, drawn straight to him.

I was solid now and my knees sliced open on the shards of Diamond that littered the floor around me, but all of my attention was focused on our former school student council president and how it was our fault that he was laying here in a pool of his own blood.

"Is he?" Kaji asked, arriving beside me.

I tried to hold onto his life force, but I felt the moment he slipped away from my grasp. I choked back a sob and upon hearing it, Kaji had his answer.

"Come on, Yukari, there's more to be done."

With the pain in my heart like a stabbing knife, I let Kaji pull me to my feet and tug me away.

Krox unleashed the power behind his bionic leg and leaped clear of a blast of Hound-fire before it could reach him. He leaped again and landed on the creature's back, and the force was enough to drive the beast to the ground. The Hound beneath him struggled to get to its feet, startled by its sudden helpless state, and waved its head from side to side in an effort to locate the adversary it had been facing.

"Up here," Krox called to it, taking a step forward and deliberately planting his metal foot on the base of the beast's neck.

The Hound looked up and it was precisely that motion which cost the creature its life. A razor-sharp metal cord whipped around the Hound's neck and Krox pulled hard on both ends while keeping the Hound steady with his foot. There was no sound until the metal cord reached bone, but by that point there was no one present to hear it. Krox didn't need this head; there were many others like it and no time to waste.

Between myself and where the throne room doors had once stood, I could see another Kaji beyond, supporting Akuma as she limped forward to join us, a gash on her leg bleeding badly. Scanning the area I took note of the Yaboun Tenchi on his back, a stone's throw away to my left. The Lady Lilyth was straight ahead and looking roughed up, with a myriad of little cuts all over her, but she was on her feet and moving quickly away with her back to us.

The Vile Emperor was nowhere to be seen and neither were Hotaru or Adel, who'd been with us outside, but there was no time to dwell on that now. Yue waved her arms in the space before me and Venon appeared, seated between the console we'd had Yue gather from Verasheen's hidden lab, which was attached to a generator Hex had helpfully supplied, and the massive Ruby pillar, its deep red hue so out of place here in this temple built of Diamond.

"My chair! Look what you've done to it!" Like a spoiled child throwing a tantrum, Lady Lilyth's shrill voice demanded to be heard and the chair she no doubt was referring to could only be the throne of Damos that she coveted.

"Now!" Yue called, pointing with force at the frayed end of a cable jutting out of the generator and shooting a bolt of electricity from her outstretched finger to give the machine the boost it needed.

Corporal Zukatoro was in position on the makeshift tower his unit had just finished constructing when Hatsumuya-san gave him the all-clear. He lowered his eye to the sight, which was rigged to the platform where he was stationed.

"Eight degrees right, twenty degrees down – no, better make that ten to the right," he called down to Hatsumuya on the radio and felt the platform move beneath him, as the weapon system was re-oriented following his commands.

"Do we have it in sight, Corporal?" Hatsumuya questioned.

Zukatoro watched the Ruby Lillem for a moment before giving the order. The towering construct had been hit hard by the first Skyraider assault but it showed no sign of slowing. Another Lillem just like it had fallen easily before reaching the tower, but this one doggedly continued to assault what remained of the Temple of Diamond, slamming massive Ruby talons into its base again and again with rhythmic consistency. It wasn't going to move out of their sights; it wasn't going anywhere.

"Fire!"

With thundering force, missiles fired from the tower's base and Corporal Zukatoro hung onto the rails as he watched the results of the command he had given. The shots fired into the night sky arced with precision to rain down upon the Ruby Lillem, striking its spider-like body and reducing it to rubble.

The console lit up and the Ruby pillar followed suit as Venon selected the setting for Rubia as we'd planned. The Ruby pulsed, bathing Yue, the Talons, and the surrounding Diamond with red light, and Venon hunched in on himself, clutching the side of his chair for support as the Ruby pillar locked down the gem god's power to which it was attuned.

To my right, Akuma showed signs of obvious discomfort. She no longer moved forward, her eyes closed tight, and her fist clenched to her heart, but Lady Lilyth, a little further off in the opposite direction, merely seemed to slow, as if a force held her from moving at full speed.

"It's not enough, Venon!" I called out, watching Lilyth struggle against the power of the Ruby Pillar, her face contorting in rage against whatever it was she was feeling as she fought to overcome it.

On the ground, the Priestesses of Espearia, or at least the Sisters of Metal and Bone, which were all that were left of the ancient race after the losses they had suffered in Taiyou, had little trouble holding the line they had established and keeping the Lillem and Hounds at bay. Conversely, from Arashi's vantage point high above the battle raging beneath her, the various dangers that sought to destroy them all were clearer and grander in scope than any of her sisters likely imagined.

Lava coursed in the valleys of the jagged rocks nearby where the priestesses fought and the flow from the geyser that had unexpectedly erupted still had not slowed or stopped. Also, the enemy forces were advancing from all sides. The Hounds were mostly already caught up in battles all over, but the wave of Lillem was only just crashing on the swords of the Taiyoun troops, and there was a whole ocean of them waiting for their chance to infect, maim, and kill.

To her left and right flew her only two remaining Sisters of Air and there being only three of them, there was little they could do against the Lillem horde or the spewing geyser, but perhaps they might have a chance against the lava that, if not stopped or re-routed, would soon spill over to where the battle was taking place.

Signaling to her sisters, she called them in close enough to hear her over the clash of battle. "We've no hope of stopping such a force with only the three of us, but we must make the earth hear us and ask it to wall up the lava and encourage it to flow away from the battle."

As one the Priestesses of Air nodded before flying off in separate directions, their white wings made visible against the night sky by the glow of the fires below. Being Espearian meant that the earth would hear them, so provided they were quick enough and strong enough, the lava was at least one tide that they had a chance of turning back.

Lilyth took a step forward and then another; her many talons, normally fanned out around her like fleshless wings, were now curved forward as if reaching for the Ruby pillar, seeking to destroy it. Raising her face to meet the eyes of her attacker, her gaze slid over the rest of us to lock onto Venon, "You."

But Venon took no notice of her. He was hunched in on himself, one arm wrapped around his own midsection and the other gripping tightly to the side of the chair where he sat. And although Yue called upon the power of Sapphiros and not Rubia, she was in no better of a position. The lightning she had absorbed earlier was now flowing through her to power the machine that was supposed to keep Lilyth at bay and the force of it was holding her relatively immobile for the time being.

There was nothing to be done for it; I rushed forward, racing Lilyth who was closing the gap between her and Venon one step at at time, despite the pillar's influence. Unaffected myself, I reached his side first and leaned forward to do what was necessary — disabling only Rubia's power wasn't going to be enough.

"Fall back!" Masaru called out, whether or not anyone would hear him or listen. "Fall back and regroup!"

Hound-fire flared before him, illuminating the area briefly and revealing a ghastly scene. Bodies lay discarded everywhere and only a disappointing few of them belonged to the enemy. Masaru saw the faces charred beyond recognition by Hound-fire.

He hadn't seen Captain Gerard in quite some time either; for all he knew the man was already dead. The Hounds, densely muscled and thick of hide, were hard to take down and the forces of Middleton weren't prepared enough to handle what had come hunting them.

Still fearsome enough, the Hounds had by now grown complacent. Upon discovering that the forces of Middleton were easy prey, they began taking the time to enjoy themselves and as the soldiers ran or inexpertly fought back, the Hounds trampled them wantonly. Masaru rounded on a nearby Hound and drove his black-bladed knife into the thing's neck, aiming directly for the kill shot. The Hound, not expecting such a bold maneuver from someone who looked just like any other Roughlander in the group, had no chance to retaliate before Masaru was finished with it and he moved onto another target, leaving the Hound to finish dying in its own time.

He could see the Stirr beyond, still swaying back and forth, pulling with some power only they could see or feel. Masaru knew what they were up to now, but the knowing of it didn't give him any piece of mind. Even from here he could feel the warm glow of the lava on his back and he knew that many of their forces were much nearer to the natural disaster that the Stirr were calling upon to destroy them.

Not only that, but there was another group of people entirely who stood to suffer from the actions of Lilyth's Stirr. With no way to know whose side they were on in the battle raging above them, the people of Damos remained frozen beneath their feet, but doubtless the lava, if it reached this far, would be enough to destroy them, too, and they would never even know what had claimed their lives.

As his forces died around him and the Hounds rejoiced, all Masaru knew was that he had to reach those Stirr and stop them before the lava they were unleashing fulfilled Lilyth's goal of wiping out what was left of humankind.

Standing so close to the Ruby pillar while it was active was pure torture. My back arched as I was simultaneously drawn in and repelled by the power I had unleashed with the touch of a button. To my left Yue convulsed as the power she had been channeling through her cut off suddenly at the source. Venon on my right was still lost in the throes of what the rest of us were now feeling along with him.

However, my gambit worked.

Lady Lilyth, her expression contorted as she fought to regain control of her body and her power, was no longer advancing or even moving other than the occasional involuntary twitch of one of her many limbs.

Now we had her immobile as we had planned, only none of us were in a position to take advantage of the situation, not even the Yaboun Tenchi who had succumbed to the power of the Ruby pillar in the act of getting to his feet.

A wall of earth rose at the command of three winged Priestesses of Espearia, rocks shooting upwards to hold back the tide of flowing lava and keep it from running into the valley below where the battle raged on. Arashi turned to call out to her sisters on either side of her and thank them for their help in this when she heard a cracking sound and felt the earth cry out to her in warning.

She drew upon the force of her will and pulled harder on the earth, directing it to shore up the weak point that was developing in the wall before it could burst and make all their efforts wasted. She watched the crack mend itself, reinforced by yet more rock, but then the impossible happened – the lava boiled over as if it had a mind of its own.

Shooting upwards and over the high wall, a stream of lava came right for Arashi, pouring outwards with unexpected force and slamming into her with all its might. Her wings caught fire immediately and she fell from the sky.

I fought the mind-numbing disorientation with everything in me. I knew full well that I'd never be able to summon any of my power like this – in fact, I could feel that energy inside me being slowly sucked away – but I didn't need my power to face Lilyth, and it couldn't help me in this task.

Forcing one arm to move, I tried with every bit of will I could muster to reach behind my head to the quiver of arrows I had strapped there before leaving the Ruby City. A Roughlander-style bow was there too; so close yet so far away, and try as I might I couldn't reach it. Just like Lilyth, every other Chosen, Knight, or Talon within sight of the Ruby pillar, I was well and truly trapped.

That is until Venon shuddered once and then sat up straight.

Slowly and rigidly controlled, Venon's hand left the death grip he had held until now on the edge of the chair and deliberately made its way to the lit screen of the console where he entered the command that would shut the pillar down.

Held in tight formation, the legionnaires of Taiyou formed an impenetrable bubble of order in a raging storm of unending chaos. Shoulder to shoulder, shield to shield, they held their ground, dispatching Lillem one by one, as the mindless once-human creatures threw themselves to the task of breaking their lines.

Leon Rama, in the eye of the storm, gave commands to his men and when there were too many Lillem for them to handle or a legionnaire would fall, he used his own three swords whirling in the air to temporarily fill in the gaps in their ranks and make the necessary strikes to keep the rest of them protected.

Even though they were cut off from the rest of the army, the legionnaires were holding strong, but they couldn't keep up their defense forever; there were simply too many Lillem for them to break free of the continuing onslaught. The Taiyouns were tiring and they needed help – the sooner the better as far as Leon was concerned – because if this continued, despite their every effort, they would eventually be overrun by the Lillem's sheer advantage of numbers.

I was slow to regain control of myself, like an elastic band held taut too long. "Venon?" I questioned as soon as I could speak. "Why did you…? It was working…"

I reached for the controls and Venon struck me with the back of his hand. Pain blossomed across my cheek and I was flung back by the unexpected force. Before I could recover Yue was there, holding Venon by the throat and staring into his eyes, as if daring him to strike her too.

But my attention was not fully on Venon or Yue. Though I was Still feeling disoriented and pulled in every direction at once, my eyes caught Lady Lilyth where she stood facing the Yaboun Tenchi, poised to strike.

Ris swerved in mid-air when she saw what was happening, and flapped her wings as hard as she was able to get close enough before drawing them in for a dive. She struck the winged Priestess of Espearia bodily, sending them both tumbling from the air as she felt the searing pain of the lava.

The resulting collision with the ground hurt, but not as much as the fire eating at her left wing. Ris rolled with the impact instinctively, the remaining priestess she'd risked her own life to rescue held tightly in her arms and still alive, she hoped.

She felt the Espearian woman in her arms move before rough hands grabbed her by the shoulders, causing her to scream soundlessly with the pain of it, as they lifted her to her feet and pulled her back sharply and away from the woman she'd saved.

"Ris! Ris, oh gods, Ris, are ye still with us?" a familiar voice spoke quickly and urgently. "That was a foolish thing ye did, flyin' in there like that! Ye could have been killed!"

Somewhat disoriented, Ris felt the wind rushing by her face and though she was certain that she was not running or flying under her own power, she was certainly moving quickly.

"It may have been foolish, but it was also brave," another voice answered the first and Ris craned her neck to the side to see who was speaking.

Wearing black armour like a Deathsquad soldier, the woman in question wore no helmet and her red hair was held back in a ponytail that streamed behind her as she ran to keep up with Ris and the Roughlander mount she was draped over. Ris hurt all over, but more than anything else she wanted to ask where the priestess she'd rescued had gone to, but Dahlia spoke again, indirectly answering her question.

"Aye, that it was, and just in time too. Captain Grinkin says that the winged girl's going to be all right, provided that the rest of us can get clear of that lava."

"Dahlia," the Deathsquad General spoke again and Ris belatedly put a name to the face; this was Lady Kichigai of the Ruby City. "I think we may have a bigger problem – look."

The Hounds emerged from the roiling pool of lava like it was no warmer than bath water. One step at a time they followed after their prey, stalking them as if they had all the time in the world to catch them. Ahead of them, Ris could hear the sounds of the continuing battle and the howls of the Hounds as they closed in, cutting off all means of escape.

The Yaboun Tenchi faced Lilyth squarely, having gotten to his feet and somehow located his sword even in all of the debris. However, even as he brought his sword up to defend himself she was draining him of any power he could possibly bring to bear against her.

He brought his sword down in a sweeping motion, slicing one of Lilyth's talons clean off, but she hardly seemed to notice the loss, being too absorbed in the taste of his immense power to register any danger to her person. She dodged the next strike half-heartedly as she circled her prey and lost another talon for it, but with each strike his motions grew slower and hers more confident, the balance tipping in Lilyth's favour as the power of Damos flowed from his body to hers.

In the state the rest of us were now in, we couldn't afford to let Lilyth recharge herself like this. The Yaboun Tenchi was, in effect, the largest battery around. When she was finished with him, there would be nothing to stop her from coming after the rest of us and using our combined power to decimate our armies outside – it would be the fall of Taiyou all over again.

Inhuman screams of hunger and uncontrolled savagery filled the air as deadly talons clacked on the frozen landscape. Lilyth's Lillem surged forward, hungrily anticipating their prey and practically tripping over one another in their haste to reach it. None of them could have possibly predicted, even if they had minds enough to do so, that their brothers and sisters, those altered as they had been altered, would turn on them – Lillem facing Lillem and tearing each other apart.

"Hey, not so fast there," Jeth commented, grabbing a Lillem by the talon before it could strike him with it and twisting the offending limb backwards to hold the creature in place. "If you're not going to play nice, then no one is going to want to play with you."

The Lillem Jeth was holding screamed, bringing another talon around to strike him despite the lack of success of its first attempt. "Yeah, that's what I thought," Jeth commented, snapping the talon in his hand effortlessly and using the bone to block the incoming attack.

The creature kept coming at him, not seeming to feel pain, and there were many more just like the one before him all swarming around, intent on turning anyone they could reach. "You're not leaving me any choice," Jeth told it, sincerely regretting what he was about to do, but there were more lives at stake than just this one if he let this creature go on as it was. "I'm sorry," he added, stabbing the Lillem full in the chest with its own talon.

"There's no use trying to reason with them," Lady Anaeth next to him noted, as she removed the head of a Lillem with a single efficient strike of her sword. "They can't hear you like this."

Jeth snorted, blocking the next attack and more quickly dispatching the next Lillem as well as the one behind it. "Doesn't mean they want to die," he muttered mostly to himself before speaking up so Anaeth could hear him. "Come on, the Taiyouns are counting on us."

"No!" I pushed myself to my feet, simultaneously drawing an arrow and retrieving the bow from my back as I drew on my power to pull the two remaining Talons to my location. "Zai-Aku, Arocoth, do it now!"

This was a part of the plan, albeit a part that I'd hoped I wouldn't need to call upon in quite this way, but still among the possibilities I had considered and prepared for. The Talons arrived to either side of me and stepped forward at my command. The new bodies they had been given were built for this specific task by Oka, who had used the cloning technology that Verasheen had inadvertently invented when he'd created Lilyth. Oka had been very specific in only using human DNA so as to avoid creating another hybrid creature like Lilyth or her Lillem, but he hadn't stopped there. He had accessed the ancient technology that had once been used to create the Deepstrike soldiers to build his own human bombs, exactly as I had requested.

Zai-Aku and Arocoth had agreed to the deal I had made with them, which would grant them new and permanent host bodies once their task was completed. Even if they were within a body while it self-destructed, the Talons would live on as spirits, so other than the discomfort of dying they stood to lose a lot less than a real Deepstrike soldier would have. Thanks to Oka's reinvention of Verasheen's technology, they also now had the opportunity to gain a lot more in the form of a body that wasn't already inhabited dand had been built solely for their use.

The Talons were beneath Lady Lilyth's notice, so they could get close enough to activate the bombs within themselves. By the time she realized what was happening, two Deepstrike soldiers would have gone off in her immediate vicinity and it would be too late for her to save herself.

Yue then had thirty seconds from the time the Talons initiated their self-destruct to store the rest of us in her Noh-space and get as far away from the blast radius as she could get.

Unfortunately the thirty second count-down began and came to a screeching halt in the space between one heartbeat and the next when Venon spoke in an authoritative voice, "Talons, I command you to desist."

There was one more transport pod to arrive and when it crashed to the icy plains below like the last star falling out of a dark sky, its single occupant emerged to find the battle in full swing around him. Taking in his surroundings with a sweeping gaze, Lord Hex leapt into action, stretching his large black wings and reveling in the freedom that darkness granted him.

Before him the Roughlanders and the Deathsquads stood shoulder to shoulder, but even their newfound solidarity wasn't going to be enough to save them from the lava that was encroaching on them as they sought to fight their way free of the Hounds who had gathered to effectively block their escape.

To his left, Hex caught sight of the Croatin Knight of Sapphiros in mid-leap before he crashed down onto the back of an unsuspecting Hound. Pine's metal body landed with enough force to crack the Hound's spine, but that wasn't all the Croatin had set out to do. He extended his vibrant green arm from beneath his cloak, thrusting it into the air, and even from here Hex could hear Pine's call, "Engage!"

At the Knight's command, the Binoids surged forward to take on the enemy as they'd been programmed to do. Metal blades attached to metal arms sliced determinedly as each Binoid engaged its respective target. As many Hounds as there were and as fierce as the creatures could be, there were just as many Binoids, and true to the programming Hex had given them they were fiercer and the nearest thing to unstoppable because they had no capacity for pain.

The Hounds fell by the dozens, caught off guard by the living weapons brought to bear against them. Their teeth and claws had little effect on the metal frames of the Binoids and the Binoids' array of weapons were perfectly tailored to cutting through the Hounds' thick hides.

And the Binoids weren't alone, either; the Roughlanders and the Deathsquad soldiers pressed the advantage they had been given, using the distraction to harry the Hounds from all sides, cutting them off from one another and decimating their numbers quickly and efficiently.

Hex felt a smile spreading across his ancient face, and his smile only grew wider as he took note of the sounds of gunfire to the east. Aysel and her contingent of newly remodeled Gin-Kouteki units had engaged the Hounds emerging from the lava and now, thanks to Hex's long years of work, it was Lilyth's forces that would fall to his trap instead of the other way around.

I wouldn't have thought that Venon had any control whatsoever over the Talons, who had seemed to take a liking to their newfound freedom without their Emperor to command them, but at the sound of his voice both Arocoth and Zai-Aku froze in their tracks and turned back to look at the man who had addressed them.

I also turned to regard Venon, belatedly recalling how he'd struck me before to stop me from reactivating the Ruby pillar. The man in question was turned around completely in his chair, his gaze focused beyond us all to one person who stood as far from Lilyth as she could get – Akuma.

The way his gaze locked onto her and the way the Talons had reacted to the sound of his voice finally clued me into what was going on here; Venon wasn't betraying us, this was Verasheen, the Talon – he had taken possession of his brother's body.

Despite the violence in the surrounding area, none had yet challenged the Stirr, their half-human, half-spider bodies still swaying with dark intent and their gazes focused on the lava they'd called forth to be their weapon in this fight. If unchecked, they stood a good chance of undermining everyone's hard work and ending countless lives.

Alone and far from the carnage he'd left behind, Masaru advanced on the crowd of marked Stirr with resolution. The Roughlander Knight was not unscathed from the battle, but he ignored his injuries. It was obvious to Sabien that this was a Knight on a mission, and as the Knight Commander and as his friend, it was up to Sabien to stop Masaru from going through with that mission.

The Knight Commander changed course quickly, angling for Masaru, and reformed from a puddle as he reached him, grabbing for his arm. It was a mark of the young Knight's reflexes and training that Masaru was able to avoid his grasp even with so little warning.

"Sabien…I…" Masaru whirled to face him, startled by Sabien's sudden appearance.

"I know what you're planning, Masaru," Sabien told him, not needing to gesture beyond them to where the Stirr had not yet deigned to notice them, "and I know how important it is, but it's not your day to die."

Masaru's expression grew darker. "I can stop them. Most of them, anyway, and more if ye help me. There are people down there, Sabien. Innocent people are trapped below us and all of them will die if we don't do something about it. Aren't ye the one who said that 'death is a worthy adversary, but sometimes also a necessary one?' I'm only doing as ye taught me to do."

Sabien nodded, his heart heavy in his chest, knowing that at one time he would have done exactly the same as Masaru was planning to do. "You're right, but we've both got something to live for now, don't we?"

Masaru hung his head, the anger and tension that had formed as he watched his men die around him draining out of him with the realization that his death would create more pain and heartache than it might solve. "Aye…we do."

"Then let's get some help," Sabien suggested. "We've still got a little time."

In the dark and empty space that separated the marked Stirr from the chaos of battle, one man melted into a puddle and the other seemed to summon a creature made from the ice and snow at his feet so he could climb atop its back. The two raced off in separate directions, determined to find help powerful enough to match the army of marked Stirr before it was too late.

"Verasheen," Lilyth spoke in a voice that was unexpectedly pure and melodious, but with a tone that suggested that she was used to being obeyed, "so good of you to stick around. Now we can finally see how this all ends."

Turning at the sound of Lilyth's voice, I quickly took note of the inert form of the Yaboun Tenchi lying discarded in the rubble of his Diamond temple. Lilyth was advancing now, her gaze locked on Verasheen in Venon's body. She didn't seem to take any notice of the rest of us – as if we were beneath her – and the Talons were the least of her concerns, even though they stood between her and Venon/Verasheen.

I did a double take as I took in the Talons; despite Verasheen's order to desist, Zai-Aku was trembling now, her body beginning the spasms and convulsions that preceded the explosion that would inevitably follow. I opened my mouth to call out for Yue to take us away from here, but despite her outwardly calm demeanor Lilyth was fast and before I could even draw breath she had already snapped Zai-Aku's neck, putting an end to her life and the threat she posed in a single decisive action.

Zai-Aku crumpled and Arocoth stepped back, but it wasn't enough to save the Talon from the sudden strike of Lilyth's fleshless wing. Four points blossomed red on her back, as the second Talon fell limply to the ground to join her compatriot.

Fuun naturally moved at a speed faster than any Lillem eye could follow; death seemed to follow him like a cloud as he felled those bodies he passed and left only corpses in his wake. Not having any real destination, Fuun continued to speed forward, disposing of any enemies he encountered nearly effortlessly in an attempt to cut back the sheer numbers that Lilyth had spawned to inconvenience them.

That is, until he happened upon something different within the horde.

"Ticket," Fuun said as he paused, making out the tiny Seventh Spawn as he waded against the tide of never-ending Lillem, despite the multiple injuries he'd already sustained for his efforts. "This is no place for you, you should head back."

"I'm trying to find Lilyth," Ticket responded, determination evident in the tiny Croatin's expression and his tone. "She's got to be here somewhere."

It took Fuun a moment to understand who Ticket meant, but he'd heard of this 'Little Lilyth', who apparently was supposed to be Lady Lilyth's long-lost daughter and perhaps the key to understanding the Lady's motives here, if the theories discussed around the stone table in Espearia were accurate.

"I understand," Fuun stated. "I will keep my eyes open for her."

"Thanks, Fuun," Ticket replied, offering a shy smile. "You're not so bad. Scary maybe, but not so bad…"

Fuun nodded, confused by how the little Croatin had made it this far, but then he was off, racing through the Lillem and cutting them down like they were tall grass blowing in the wind. He had a purpose now and a destination: find Little Lilyth to find answers and maybe then, end this.

"Don't do this, Lilyth," Verasheen pleaded. "It doesn't need to be this way."

"Don't do what?" she questioned disdainfully. "Don't do what I was made to do? Don't live? I can no more stop myself from living than you can bring yourself to kill me. You made me this way! You gave me life, gave me power, and now you want to take that away? I have as much right to live as you do. More, even, for I'm as close to perfect as anyone is ever going to get!"

"You're an abomination."

The words came from everywhere at once as a force of innumerable Kajis appeared around Lilyth, surrounding her completely and cutting most of her off from view. As one, the Kajis swarmed inward, attacking any piece of her they could reach and putting as much force behind each blow as they could.

And it was working; hard exoskeleton or no, Kaji's fists were doing damage and as the attacks came from all sides at once, Lady Lilyth hunched in upon herself defensively. She brought her talons in tight to her body and I allowed myself to hope for a moment that maybe she had been weakened enough that physical damage just might do the trick – and then she retaliated.

Striking outwards faster than the eye could follow, her talons were like a multitude of scorpion tails, stabbing each Kaji-clone just once before moving onto the next. Only eight talons facing uncountable Kajis, but one by one they began to fall, splashing into puddles of water and washing away the Diamond rubble at her feet.

Remembering the bow in my hands, I drew an arrow and put the force of my power behind it to multiply it and make the resulting arrows all sharp enough to kill. As I loosed it, Lilyth stiffened in a familiar way, her body now held hostage to the flow of blood within her veins, as Akuma applied her power to the task of eliminating our enemy once and for all.

Outside and blocked from the view of events within the Temple of Diamond by the few remaining walls and towering piles of debris, two people applied themselves to a very different sort of task, but one no less important. High upon the platform where they could oversee the battle below, Adel stood looking out and relaying what she could make out to Hotaru, who was hunched over the lip of her canteen, deep in concentration and speaking as quickly and as precisely as she could.

"I hear you, Bastion, just do what you can and I'll try to contact the Croatins. First of the First Spawn," Hotaru said as she closed one line of communication and opened another one swiftly; she was getting better at this, but the constant use of her power was still taking its toll. "First of the First Spawn?"

There was no answer where she expected one. She'd only just spoken to the chief of the Croatins moments ago, or that been nearer to the start of the battle? She couldn't remember; it was all blurring together now, the drain on her power and her own stamina taxing ever since she'd shielded herself and Adel to save them from the initial explosion that had marked the beginning of all this.

She changed tactics. "Krox?"

"Yes."

"Are you with the Croatins? Has the First of the First fallen?"

"If he has, I wouldn't know about it," Krox replied gruffly. "Try the Second Spawn."

"Forget the Croatins," a voice spoke on the platform, breaking Hotaru's concentration and severing the link she'd established with Krox.

"Sabien!" Adel exclaimed, startled by the Knight Commander's sudden arrival.

"Call the Japanese, or the Roughlanders, whoever's closest to the southwest side," Sabien instructed. "Stopping the marked Stirr needs to be our number one priority."

"On it," Hotaru told him, bending down to her canteen once more and steeling herself against the exhaustion that threatened to overwhelm her. "Hitachi, Corporal Zukatoro, new targets…"

Mere inches from striking their target, five arrows and several dozen Kajis froze in place, as Lilyth ripped free of Akuma's hold on her and let out a blood curdling scream with force enough to shatter the temple of Diamond, had it still stood. I felt the bow fall from my hands but I didn't hear it clatter to the floor, as I instinctively tried to shield my ears from the deafening shriek that split the air.

And it didn't stop there; the power coursing around her was nearly palpable as it pulsed outwards once, destroying the Kaji clones in a single blast and causing my arrows to fall harmlessly to the ground.

The scream reverberated in our ears long after Lilyth had gone silent, the mind-numbing sound of it making thought and action beyond our capabilities. Lilyth, unaffected by her own ability, simply straightened, shook the water from her talons with one sharp motion, and lifted her head high, surveying us all with contempt as she strode past us like this was her throne room and we were her subjects.

Ch. 22 – Chosen

"What was that?" Adel questioned.

Hotaru stood up. She'd managed to keep herself distracted until now with everything that needed doing, but that shriek had forcefully reminded her of the fateful events that were taking place nearby and the sound they'd just heard could only mean one thing – Lady Lilyth was still alive.

Her fears were confirmed when the Lady herself strode from the rubble with her head held high. She was injured – she was missing at least two talons, blood dripped from scratches all over her body – and she still didn't have her Ruby heart, which left a gaping hole in her chest where it had once been.

Hotaru choked back a sob – if Lilyth was here and alive, then what had happened to the others who had gone in there to stop her?

"You..." Lilyth spoke, focusing her attention on Adel the way a snake might turn on its prey – but that was as far as she got before someone pounced on her from behind.

Hotaru let out a relieved breath at seeing Yue alive and well, but her relief didn't last long as she watched her friend dangle from Lilyth's back, trying desperately to grapple with the deadly talons.

Yue was tough, but it was obvious she wasn't risking the use of any of her power to enhance her strength or speed, so when Lady Lilyth simply reached back and took hold of her, she was able to easily rip her loose and toss Yue bodily from the platform atop which they stood. Hotaru had to resist the urge to run to the edge and look down to make sure that Yue would be all right; with Yue temporarily out of the picture – and both Kaji and Yukari unaccounted for – it was up to Hotaru to stop Lilyth from going any further.

"You thought you could get away with betraying me?" Lilyth questioned Adel. "I told you you would pay and now the time has come to own up to your debts."

There was no hesitation or even thoughts of bravery; Hotaru simply couldn't let Lady Lilyth harm Adel. She put herself deliberately in front of the Knight, summoned her swords of water and ice, and held them at the ready. Part of her knew she was being foolish, but she couldn't simply stand by while one of her friends was in danger.

◊

The Japanese had joined up with Hitachi and his Roughlanders who had come down from further north. Thankfully, they had thought to bring an all-terrain vehicle with them from the Temple of Sapphire, so it was a simple matter to load everything up onto it and move it all down to where they were needed.

"All loaded up?" Noh-san asked, checking the straps to make sure that all the equipment was secured.

"I think so," Hana answered. "This is everything Hatsumuya-san gave us, but we've got the back seat mostly full now. I'd fit, but that's about it."

"That's all right," Noh-san answered. "You ladies go on ahead. The Hatsumuyas will likely be there already and I'll follow along behind on foot. Namikoya-san's already told me that he's staying behind with the Corporal in the tower."

"Let's go, then," Hana instructed the other two ladies, climbing up into the available space amidst the last of the weaponry she had just finished strapping down.

"See you on the other side," Mrs. Noh called back to her husband as Zukatoro-san's wife started the engine and before long the three of them were off, racing across the ice to where the Roughlanders were taking up position to face the Stirr.

Noh-san watched the vehicle race off for a moment before grabbing his pack and starting to jog; he would need to start now if he wanted to make it to the battle before it was over.

He heard a sharp cracking sound and instinctively stopped dead before he even registered what it was actually implying. The ground beneath his feet shook as another loud crack filled the air, drowning out even the distant sounds of the fighting still happening to the north and the east.

He scrabbled backwards in the nick of time to avoid the chasm that opened up beneath the place where he'd been standing, but despite his own near brush with death it was not his own safety he suddenly found himself concerned for.

"Yumi!"

Another crack sounded – from ahead this time – and his worst fears proved true as the all-terrain vehicle swerved sharply to the right and then flipped onto its side. He watched a passenger get flung from the moving vehicle before it dropped out of sight, falling into the newly created chasm that had opened up before it.

"YUMI!"

Noh-san ran forward, heart-thumping with fear and adrenaline, the sound of Diamond cracking sharply continuing until it was all he could hear. He had to veer from side to side to find the safest path as the Diamond shelter that had held the people of Damos safe for nearly a thousand years was breaking open.

"If you want Adel, you'll have to go through me," Hotaru stated, standing strong before the terrifying visage of Lady Lilyth in defense of her friend.

"Gladly."

Lilyth reached forward as Hotaru leapt at her, swords outstretched; she wasn't going to waste this moment and let Lilyth gain the upper hand. What she hadn't considered was that her swords were made with her power – and therefore useless against Lady Lilyth – and even worse than that, they were something that Lilyth could use against her.

Hotaru didn't even get close enough to strike before the water sword disappeared. The ice sword followed after, shattering on contact instead of cutting through Lilyth's tough exoskeleton. Suddenly feeling weak and dizzy, Hotaru faltered in her advance and fell to her knees. Lilyth laughed, the malice in her expression shifting subtly to glee, as she took in the sight of a Chosen brought to their knees before her.

With her anger overtaking fear, Hotaru felt something inside her rejoice as Lilyth's laughter was cut short by Sabien's sword being thrust into her gut from the side.

Shock silenced Lilyth for only for a moment before she screamed, whipping her talons about to impale Sabien as he had done to her. However, Sabien had already wisely splashed to a puddle, leaving his sword behind as he took himself out of her reach as quickly as possible.

Lilyth grabbed hold of the sword blade in her bare hands and tugged it free of her side, leaving a gaping wound, red with freely flowing blood.

"You should know better…" Lilyth addressed Hotaru, panting slightly from the pain Sabien had caused her, "than to send Knights against Chosen. Even you…are no match for me…"

"The Diamond is cracking, we don't have much time," Masaru told the Stirr, knowing they could understand him even if he couldn't understand them.

"Shh pthh sshpthh…" the Stirr Masaru was seated upon responded before evidently giving it up as a lost cause and turning to its fellows, *"Shh…Shpthshh sshh Shphssshshhh Sshh ssspthhshhh."*

Several Stirr broke off from the pack, disappearing into the night, as the Stirr Masaru rode reached back a hand to offer him a tiny spider. "Thank ye," Masaru told him gratefully. There was too much at stake for him to not know what was going on and unfortunately for him, he didn't have Yukari's way with languages.

"The Stirr will stop the lava from reaching the tribes of man," the Stirr told him.

"I'm grateful for yer help, but what about the marked Stirr? I know ye said ye don't want to have to fight yer brothers and I hate to say it, but ye're likely the only ones who can."

"It is a momentous day,. Hold on tight, human. This night, Stirr will face Stirr and all will change."

True to his words, the Stirr raced forward as one, their many spider-like legs silent but speedy on the tightly-packed snow and ice. Black as the night itself, the Stirr stalked their brothers. They ran swiftly past the Roughlanders who lowered their guns, surprised to see their unlikely allies, and they continued running without pause until they crashed into their unsuspecting brethren. Terrified inhuman screams split the air, as the Stirr mercilessly began to purge their own kind, tearing the traitors to their race apart limb from limb.

"But I am." Adel's voice came from above Hotaru as the Knight stepped up to defend her, facing her Lady head on for the first time in her life.

Adel whirled her Espearian-wrought mace faster than Hotaru's eyes could follow, forcing even Lady Lilyth to step back and defend herself from the whirlwind attack. Adel kept coming, never stopping her forward motion or the swinging of the heavy wooden mace in her hands, but Lilyth somehow managed to stay just out of reach of the blunt end of the weapon, never letting so much as a glancing blow reach her, despite Adel's relentless assault.

Realizing that her efforts weren't producing results, Adel abruptly changed tactics. She lunged forward, throwing all her strength behind one single blow, and brought the mace down hard onto Lilyth's right shoulder.

Hotaru heard a sickening crunch as the mace connected, but that wasn't what caused her to gasp sharply. Having spent much time training with the formidable Knight, Hotaru immediately realized the fatal error Adel had made – in order to land a hit on Lilyth, she'd left herself wide open.

Hotaru found herself hoping that Lilyth wouldn't take advantage of Adel's mistake, but it seemed that Lilyth knew her protégé well enough to know Adel had overstepped herself. With a wicked grin crossing her face despite the pain she must be feeling from the solid hit she'd just taken, Lilyth reached forward with her multitude of talons, eager for more blood.

Distracted by her quarry, Lilyth had no chance to protect herself as a second Adel appeared beside the first. Lilyth's talons closed in on snow and ice as the clone of Adel she was fighting crumbled lifelessly, and then the real Adel swung her mace as hard as she could to collide with Lilyth's midsection.

The blow sent Lilyth reeling and skidding across the ice toward the cliff edge of the diamond platform. She might have toppled over the edge, her balance shaken by the brutal assault, if it wasn't for her many talons scrabbling for purchase on the slick surface and finding it just soon enough to catch herself.

Lilyth's head snapped up once she had her footing secure once more. "Nice try Adel," she commented, her lip curling upward in a snarl, "but you forget one thing…"

Adel stood tall, facing her former mistress with pride in every inch of her, her mace held steady in her hands. "Oh, and what is that?"

"You may have learned a trick or two from Sapphiros, but you are still mine!"

Hotaru watched, powerless, as Lady Lilyth's eyes flashed red with an inner light and Adel's knees buckled, the Knight drawn to obey her Lady's will despite herself. Adel took one reluctant step forward and then another, as she struggled against the Lady's control.

Hotaru tried to surge to her feet, but she found that despite her every effort she didn't have it in her to move. Her whole body felt heavy and unresponsive, but even if she couldn't stand she could still fight.

"You're stronger than her Adel! You've beaten her will before and I know you can do it now!"

Adel grit her teeth, clenching her mace with both hands as despite her every effort her feet carried her another step closer to Lilyth. However, Adel wasn't the only one struggling; the strain of the invisible battle was written all over Lilyth's face as she fought to control the Knight who'd once sworn to her willingly.

"Betrayal has its price, Adel," Lilyth spat as she pulled the Knight just one step closer, leaning in so that she and Adel were face to face.

"I," Adel spoke with deliberate clarity, facing the monster that had ruled her life for as long as she could remember. "Am. Not. Afraid."

"Then you are a fool," Lilyth stated, finally letting go of the effort to control Adel and in that instant simultaneously striking with every single one of her talons, driving them into her prey and reaching for the Knight's heart from every side at once.

Yue had recovered quickly following her trip down the mountainside. It wasn't precisely the way she'd intended to get herself off Lilyth's radar, but it would do. Once her feet were firmly on the ground, she didn't have to wait long for Kaji to appear beside her as they'd planned.

"Is Ao Kouen in position?" Yue asked.

"Let me check," Kaji replied, his eyes going blank for a moment as he transferred his consciousness to the clone he'd left behind with Ao Kouen. "He says he's been waiting for our signal."

"Good," Yue stated. "Let him know that we're nearly ready."

Blood spurted from Adel's mangled body as the life went out of her and she went limp, supported only by the talons of the woman she had once faithfully served. Lilyth tore her talons free in one sickening motion and let the corpse of the one true Knight she had ever made fall uselessly to the ground.

"Nooo!" I couldn't help the scream that escaped me at seeing Adel fall as I rounded the corner, having finally been able to pull myself together after Lilyth's debilitating attack.

The formidable Knight had always been there; she had always stood strong when the rest of us were weak. Only against Lady Lilyth had she been the one to need protection and now it was too late for us to give it to her.

Kaji surged forward, creating doubles of himself as he went, but Lilyth paid him no mind; having done what she had paused here to do, she went over the side of the Diamond mountain and onward to her next victims. I was unable to stop Lilyth in any case and Adel was beyond any help I might provide, so I went to Hotaru who sat despondently in a heap, though she appeared not to be injured, at least on the surface. As I reached Hotaru's side I heard Fuun's voice come from someplace just beyond her.

"You must be Little Lilyth," Fuun stated tonelessly. "Strange, I expected you to be less human in appearance considering your parentage. Still, though I regret having to end the life of a child, for one such as you I will make an exception…it is time for us to dance."

Hotaru melted unexpectedly into a puddle.

"It's too late, Hotaru, you can't stop this!" I called.

The puddle didn't answer me, of course, and neither did it stop. I knew what she was up to, but I thought the little canteen slowly spilling its contents out onto the ice wasn't enough water and that would be enough to stop her. I was wrong. Hotaru's puddle changed course unexpectedly and went straight for Sabien, who was pulling himself together and reforming a little ways away. Sabien never got the chance to fully become solid before Hotaru splashed into him, leaving nothing but a quivering puddle in his place.

I was used to Sabien and Hotaru both being able to become water at will, just as I could turn myself and others into a cloud of mist, but this was different. Wherever she was now, Hotaru had just ripped through Sabien when he had been almost solid. She had forced him back into this liquid state and now the water seemed agitated, like its molecules were having trouble holding together.

I frowned. Locating Hotaru was the least of my worries, but Fuun, and how he had already decided to solve the problem of Little Lilyth, was higher on the list of priorities. I sent myself after Hotaru as mist, but as it turned out she had already managed to call Fuun off before I appeared behind her.

Little Lilyth was as I remembered; the little girl was completely unchanged by the time she'd spent controlled by her mother's spirit. She still had guileless blue eyes and wore her customary red and white stripes under a black, bell-bottomed jumper, making her look no more than eight years old. Her red hair wavered slightly in the cold wind, starkly contrasting with the Lillem who stood still around her, reminiscent of the way her guardians had once obeyed her.

"Lilyth, we're your friends," Hotaru was pleading with her. "We're here to help you. We don't have to fight…"

"This is who I am. I was made to be this and I don't know how to be anything else," she said in the same sweet and innocent voice I remembered.

"We can help you," Hotaru insisted. "You don't have to be what your mother wanted you to be. You're your own person."

"You mean what my father made me to be," Lilyth said and something about her words struck a chord. *'You made me this way...'* Lilyth had said to Verasheen.

"Hotaru, back away from her," I cautioned, "it's Lilyth."

"She's our friend," Hotaru countered, looking back over her shoulder at me.

"No!" I screamed.

From some place beyond this world a spirit rose like a shadow, darkening the air around Little Lilyth as she brought her power to bear. It was just like the power she had once used to save Masaru's life, but now it was being used to harm – and that made all the difference in the world.

All it took was one touch and Hotaru crumpled, the last remnants of her power drained.

Fuun's sword was at the little girl's throat before Hotaru had even reached the ground.

"I don't think so," Little Lilyth said softly. She touched her fingers to the blade of Fuun's sword and coldly watched as he slowly fell to his knees, also drained of his power. "There's no time for that now," she told him tonelessly, turning the sword about in her hands until she held it point down above him, "mommy's coming."

She drove the sword point down mercilessly and I flinched, unable to react as the lengthy katana pierced Fuun's neck and red blood spurted wetly across his pale skin to blossom in the snow beneath him.

Fuun was dead, but Hotaru just looked…wilted.

Little Lilyth passed right by me like I was beneath her notice and I let her, lost in grief and despair. I fell to my knees in front of Hotaru and felt desperately for some hint that she was still in there. I sobbed, fighting back the wave of emotion that threatened to drown me, knowing that if I let it take me then my power would fail and with it, Hotaru's chances. I simply couldn't let that happen.

"Aahhhhh!" Neva let out another scream, writhing on the metal table and gripping her belly, as if trying to keep the baby from bursting out of it.

"Oka!" Razor called out, trying to hold Neva down as members of Oka's team of assistants – or whatever they were – did their best to fasten belts that would strap her to the table.

"I'm coming, I'm coming!" Oka responded, coming over from the other side of the room. "You don't think I can hear her myself? Hold her still!"

It took three of Oka's assistants to hold Neva in place despite the straps and she still jerked violently under their hands with every contraction, but evidently that was enough for Oka who dove right in – literally.

With his hands up to his elbows through Neva's flesh, Oka used his unique ability to reach past the layers of organic matter between the baby and the outside world.

Razor didn't want to watch, but he held a towel at the ready in one hand like Oka had instructed him to and Neva had a death grip on his arm to keep him close. He found himself unable to look away as he could see the mound that was Oka's hand moving around beneath Neva's skin, doing whatever it was he needed to do.

It only took a moment, but it felt like years before Oka brought his hands back up and with them a tiny baby girl…

She was covered in blood, but she was the most wonderful thing Razor had ever seen. Impossibly tiny – at least in his estimation – she had her eyes squeezed shut against the world, and her Lillem-talons were all furled up and tucked in at her sides and against her back.

As Oka lifted her up and she felt air on her face for the first time, she opened her eyes, revealing yellow irises, bright with surprise. All at once her talons unfurled and she let out a wailing cry, filling the room with sound, as only a newborn baby could.

"Oops, gotta go," Oka mouthed, holding the baby out to Razor.

"What?!" Razor yelled, not understanding.

Looking a little fuzzy around the edges, Oka disappeared, leaving Razor to catch the baby as she fell into his arms. Thankfully, the sudden drop in elevation caught the little girl off guard and her screams cut off abruptly. She didn't even think of using her talons to break her fall, letting Razor cradle her in his arms momentarily before showing her to her mother for the first time.

Riding on Yue's back was the fastest and easiest way to catch up with Lilyth, so that was what Kaji did. The Lillem didn't even react to their passage as they moved too quickly for their simple minds to follow. The closer Yue took him to where they would find Lilyth, the less the Lillem seemed to move at all; they just stood limply, as if waiting for directions.

As soon as he saw her, Kaji realized how little time they truly had left, so he leapt into action and disposed of the clone he left behind on Yue's back. Lilyth was now less than thirty feet from her daughter and presumably the jewel encased within her that she so coveted. She didn't hurry to her destination; she walked slowly, savoring each step closer to her prize because she believed she had already won – that no one worthy was left to challenge her.

Well, Kaji was about to prove her wrong.

"You've lost. It's over."

Lilyth stiffened at his words.

"You've already failed," he stated, another clone appearing before her, its posture relaxed.

"Out of my way," she commanded, lip curling up in distaste as she raised her talons, ready to strike him down.

The clone took a step forward, meeting her stare for stare. "Do you honestly think that getting your heart back is going to be enough to save you?"

She slashed at him with her talons and the Kaji before her splashed to a puddle, with another one appearing to take its place almost before the first was entirely reduced to liquid. "You're a mistake."

And to her left another clone spoke, "Verasheen may have given you a taste of a gem god's power, but you're nobody's Chosen."

Flailing her talons wildly, Lilyth quickly dispatched the clone before her and the one to her left. He caused two more to appear.

"Adel forsook you." Splash. "You force your creatures to obey you." Another clone destroyed, another born. "You aren't loved..."

"You aren't feared or respected," yet another clone chimed in as Lilyth, getting quicker now, destroyed its predecessors. "Nobody wants you…" Splash. "…For their ruler." Splash.

"Nobody even wants you…" Clone after clone splashed to water as Lilyth's strikes grew more frantic, more desperate to silence his words. "…Alive."

"You're an abomination." Several clones were speaking in unison now; she couldn't destroy them all, no matter how hard she tried, and although none of them were the real Kaji, the truth of every word he spoke was undeniable. "You're not human, not a Croatin, a Plains-runner, a Stirr, or a Kumori. You're not the best of anything. You're nothing – you're just pieces. A make-believe thing that acts like a spoiled child in order to feel alive, and who breaks every toy she gets her claws on…"

Oka appeared before me in the flesh, summoned by my power and brought fully here by the force of my will. He appeared facing me, with his hands inexplicably covered in blood and held up before him, and a startled look on his face as he tried to get his bearings.

"Please, Oka, help her," I pleaded, gesturing helplessly to Hotaru's still form.

However, instead of seeing to Hotaru, Oka started forward, intent on something beyond me. I finally saw what I'd been ignoring when I turned around to follow him with my eyes.

Lilyth stood not far beyond where her daughter had stopped to wait for her. She was flailing with a clear lack of control, trying in vain to destroy every last clone that Kaji caused to appear around her, but what really caught my eye was Yue far above, flying through the air in her demon form to intercept a flowing green ribbon of power. I recognized the magic; it was the power of the Leyins in Taiyou, the most powerful weapon this world had to offer.

As it struck Yue, she took it into herself and redirected it, shooting it out again through her mouth like a dragon breathing fire. The ribbon changed to a curious mix of green and cyan as it shot forth from Demon-Yue's mouth and moved in a downward spiral toward its target.

Oka took advantage of Kaji's distraction of Lady Lilyth to sneak right up behind Little Lilyth. Then with a lightning-fast motion he reached forward and into the little girl, pulling his hands back out of her flesh almost instantly, and revealing a glittering Ruby that was large enough to have filled the small girl's chest.

Lilyth straightened suddenly, somehow feeling the pain of losing her heart for a second time, as Little Lilyth, now an empty husk, fell forward. She screamed and the Lillem that had stood motionless all this time went wild, surging inward, intent on Oka.

Surrounded by Lillem, and so closely linked to the faint beat of Hotaru's heart, I felt the moment her heart was impaled by a Lillem Talon and abruptly stopped beating, her life force not slipping away so much as ripped from my grasp. With a gasp of shock my power saved me and I found myself turned to mist to avoid being trampled as well, as the wave of Lillem washed over the patch of blood soaked snow where Hotaru and Fuun had fallen.

However intent Lilyth was upon Oka, something warned her in time of the doom that was about to befall her. Perhaps it was the power itself, or the whistling of the wind created by its passage, but as the greenish cyan ribbon of power came for her, Lilyth turned her head at the last moment and was able to raise her talons and draw on her power to protect herself.

The Ruby Heart in Oka's hands began to glow fiercely. I wasn't thinking clearly, but one thought stood out to me above the rest – if Lilyth managed to counter this strike here and now, then everyone we'd lost here today would have died for nothing.

I became solid with my wings out to keep me aloft, and I summoned an arrow then loosed it without even raising my arms in a gesture to do so. The cyan arrow flew straight to its target and exploded outward, the air itself seeming to ripple as one cyan arrow became five, then twenty, then a hundred. Each arrow did exactly as it was meant to and fanned outward, creating a web of netting, but instead of energy which Lilyth could absorb, or rope which she could easily break free of, my arrows created cables made of steel.

The steel nets stuck Lilyth all at once and formed a latticework, knocking her off guard with the force of the unexpected solidity of the attack and sinking into the ice around her, like so many barbed arrows latching into rock. Lilyth was trapped for just the single moment that was needed, and then the ribbon struck.

When the snow finally settled and the shards of ice finished falling, I reformed from mist once more to find a crater in the place where Lilyth had been standing, one so large that the edge of it reached to where the body of Little Lilyth lay covered in shards of shattered ice and rock.

It was over.

Oka lay dead, the Ruby heart still clutched in his hands, and this, combined with the crater beyond the corpse of the girl Hotaru and I had hoped to save, was too much for me. Even though I was reasonably sure Oka would be reborn thanks to his squad, I was abruptly reminded of the price we had all paid for this victory. I fell to my knees, succumbing to emotion at last.

Back at the Temple of Diamond, all had long since grown quiet; the battle below was distant, if it even still continued. The throne room could hardly even be said to still be standing, the ruins of Diamond walls open now to the starry night sky above, but it wasn't empty. There were those who had been left behind, forgotten in the chaos of this long and violent night.

"All of this is your doing, isn't it?" Akuma questioned as she stepped softly out from behind the shadow of the Ruby pillar, moving slowly and favoring her left leg. "Every last bit of it is because of you..."

Verasheen, regrettably stuck now in the body he'd stolen from the brother he'd always cared so deeply for, looked up slowly, taking in her beauty one more time. "Yes," he answered simply, there being nothing else he could say in his own defense; she knew the truth now, perhaps not all of it, but enough.

"You used me," she stated and he did not deny it. "You used us all," she continued and still he had no words for her.

"I think that after everything," she said, gesturing vaguely to the world around them, "that I, at least, am owed an explanation."

"I owe you a great many things, and an explanation is the least of them. I loved you, I still do, but what I did to you was not kindness. Though I did it out of love, what I did was selfish. It is no more complicated than that."

"What are you talking about?" Akuma demanded.

"You," Verasheen answered. "I know you don't remember it, but I made you a promise once. You begged me to kill you, but I couldn't let you go, so I made you what you are today – a soul divided, like me."

"I'm a...Talon?" Akuma asked, her jaw dropping in disbelief. "But I'm a Chosen..."

"As am I. It makes no difference."

"But..." She struggled, trying to come to terms with what he'd waited so long to tell her. In the end, it was clear by her expression that it all came down to one final question. "Why?"

"Because I was selfish and alone and all I ever wanted was to be loved. Lilyth was my daughter and I wanted her to be enough for me. I wanted her to live and to be happy, and so I gave her the world. But she never loved me, she wasn't truly capable of it.

Akuma's expression hardened, her heart closing on him for good. "You should have killed me then, because I can never love you the way you want me to. What's in my heart can never be enough for a man as cold and lonely as you are."

She turned from him then, and took the first steps to leaving him alone forever when fate intervened. Unbeknownst to them both, Arocoth had not been killed when the monster Verasheen had created had run her through; she had only been mortally wounded. She had lain there since that moment, blood seeping slowly from fatal wounds, as she lived through the agony of dying, wishing and waiting for that final release while working up the strength and resolve necessary to end it all herself.

As the Talon took her last breath, she willfully activated the explosives within the host body she'd been given, sending the body into convulsions in order to escape the torment of the flesh that had become her prison.

EPILOGUE – THE LESSON

66

❶ ❶ ❶ And, as you know, that explosion ended the lives of both Lady Akuma and the Lava Lord, effectively taking away the last two people Verasheen ever loved," I concluded the rather lengthy tale, reaching for the glass of water I'd left on the table beside me.

"But what about him?" a voice asked and I looked up to focus on a dark-haired boy no older than seven, seated near the back of the crowded room. He was a little younger than my usual audience, but had listened quietly and with rapt attention until the very end. "Verasheen, I mean the Vile Emperor, was a Talon. He couldn't die."

"That's right," I clarified, "he couldn't die, and neither could Lady Akuma, as she was a Talon as well."

"So what happened to them?" he pressed and I saw several heads nodding at the question.

"As far as anyone knows Verasheen lived, in a manner of speaking, though no one has seen or heard tell of him since. Arocoth and Zai-Aku both took on new bodies as General Oka promised them, and Lady Akuma died in the blast, the part of her soul that is Yuko Seig is still in the Splitter and I suppose always will be."

I watched a girl in the front row put her hand up just a little faster than the rest and I nodded in her direction.

"But how did you know she was Yuko Seig? I mean, how did you know the parts of the story you weren't there for?"

"Most of what I told you was what I learned from someone who was there when it happened, but the end is a little different," I answered with a smile, thinking of the many times I had told this story and how many times this same question had been asked when I finished. "What I told you is a conclusion based on certain assumptions. Arocoth doesn't remember much beyond being stabbed by Lilyth and the pain of dying, but because Kaji left a clone with her, we know at least that Akuma stayed in the temple and I believe that she would have confronted Verasheen if given the opportunity.

"I'd like to think that in their last moments together Verasheen finally gave Akuma the answers she'd been searching for. It's true that we'll never truly know all of what Verasheen kept secret, just as we can never truly know what another person keeps inside their hearts unless they choose to tell us. What I told you was only what I was able to piece together and what logical leaps I could make from those pieces. You can call it an assumption, but as much as we might try to understand why it all happened the way it did we may never know the truth."

There was a lull while the whole group of them did their best to absorb what had taken me years to learn. I didn't hate Verasheen anymore, not like I had. The man who had once called himself the Vile Emperor had more than paid for all the mistakes he'd made with what he'd lost in the end and if he was really still out there somewhere, unable to die because of what he'd turned himself into, then I felt sorry for him.

It had taken me years to understand, but the truth of the matter likely was that Verasheen had only been doing what we all do. He was not making what he perceived to be errors in judgment, but making the only choices he believed possible with what life had presented him.

A hissing sound broke through the silence that had fallen over the classroom and, despite the alien sound of it, I had no trouble understanding the question the young Stirr posed, *"What happened to the tribe of Damos?"*

"Forget Damos," one of the girls countered instantly with a wave of her hand, and I marveled that she would have one of the Stirr's translator spiders in her ear; by her appearance, she didn't seem the type. "I want to hear about the Joining."

The girl's friends all nodded, as did a few others in the crowd, jumping in with questions about the Joining and what happened after the battle was over.

"I'll answer as many of your questions as I can," I told them, having anticipated this as well. I let my gaze sweep over the eager faces of my audience as I began to speak again, diving back into the painful story of the past that was so vivid for me with the re-telling.

There were few casualties among the people that had been frozen within the Diamond, but as time had stopped for them when the land was peaceful and the weather pleasantly warm, none of them were prepared for the sudden shock of the cold and icy landscape that the world around them had become after eight hundred years.

"Do not panic! Whatever has happened, I have no doubt that the Yaboun Tenchi has everything under control."

I didn't have it in me to correct him with the truth; the Yaboun Tenchi was dead.

There was no saving him or any of the countless others who had fallen to Lilyth. In the end we had beaten her and with the help of the Stirr we scattered what parts of her army remained. Later, when we left this place and washed the blood from our hands, we would call it a victory, but it didn't feel that way now; we had simply lost too much.

All around me was the evidence of the price we had paid. Between the cold and disoriented people of Damos, the bodies of the people who had fought to free them lay as they had fallen. There too, covered in the debris of shattered Diamond, lay the corpses of the enemy, mostly indistinguishable from the former, save for the red-furred forms of the fallen Hounds, their armoured spikes coated in their own purple-hued blood.

My vision was good – perhaps, in this instance, too good – and I could see farther and in more detail than I wanted to. I saw grief and loss on almost every face. From my vantage point I could see clearly all the way to where the Temple of Diamond had stood for thousands of years, with every face between here and there upturned in horror at the hole in the sky where that bastion of strength and power should still be, but was no longer.

The temple, like so much else, was now little more than a pile of rubble and it was that fact, more than anything else, that seemed to be having the worst effect on the people of Damos. Truthfully, they were the least of my concerns; from here I could make out Kaji at the edge of the rubble, digging through the shards with his bare hands like sifting through sand in a sandbox.

His hands were bloody, useless things by the time Leon reached him, but still Kaji did not stop his frantic motions. I knew why he was there and what he was looking for. It was just like the last time, when he had lost Shuzhue in Shinjuku and had thought he might find her remains in the sand. He hadn't found her then, despite his digging, and it wasn't likely he would now either. The ruins of the temple spanned an impossible distance to search, if her body had even survived the blast of the two Deepstrike Talons intact.

Leon took hold of Kaji's arm and I winced, fearing the backlash, but Kaji simply stopped and turned to look at him, his face devoid of expression. Leon said something – I was too far to hear what – but Kaji didn't answer. Leon repeated himself, shaking the arm he held for emphasis, but still Kaji did not react; it was as if he didn't even register that Leon was there.

Akuma's Knight, Bastion, tears rolling unabashedly down his face, approached the two of them and placed a hand on Leon's shoulder, then said something quietly, his lips barely moving. Leon threw his hands up in defeat, before walking away and leaving Bastion to deal with Kaji.

To this day, I do not know what Bastion said to make Kaji hear him, but no more than a word or two from the grieving Knight sent Kaji to his knees to let out a wail of anguish that was loud enough to cross the distance. The heartfelt cry and the tears that followed would never be enough to heal the hole in his heart, but doubtless it was better to begin to feel the pain and work through it than to attempt to inflict more suffering upon himself needlessly.

I tore my gaze away from Kaji; it didn't seem right for me to watch him suffer, but no matter where I looked I saw someone's pain. Ris lay upon her stomach, unconscious and surrounded in a red dome of light created by a small group of Kumori who stood around her, frowning in sympathy for the state of her wings. Blistered and melted beyond recognition, it didn't seem as if her wings were reparable and it would take more than a miracle to see Ris fly again, if she even survived.

Sabien was a puddle beside his mate. He had been unable to reform after what Hotaru's desperate flight had done to him, but even still he had made his way to Ris and it was there he stayed. I found myself hoping that despite her unconsciousness and his lack of solidity that they could still feel one another's presence like they always seemed to, and that despite everything it would give them some comfort.

Not too far away, the Croatins had gathered wordlessly around the lifeless form of the First of the First Spawn. The massive brute of a Croatin hadn't exactly been well liked, but his strength of will had been respected and his loss was a great blow to the Croatin race.

Arashi had also been a devastating loss. With only one winged Priestess of Air remaining after all the fighting, Lilyth had nearly succeeded in her goal of wiping out an entire race and the look on that lone priestess' face nearly tore my heart right out of my chest.

Desperately trying to find somewhere else to look, my eyes locked momentarily on my mother as she cried into my father's chest. Noh-san had just finished laying his own wife's still form on the ice next to Kaji's mother, after having managed to retrieve them from the rubble nearly single-handedly. Out of all of the members of the Japanese military that had followed us here, his grim expression was the most controlled, but it struck me that it would be a long time before anyone saw Noh-san's infectious grin again.

And where was Yue? There was her family, or what remained of it, and she was nowhere to be found. She was able to flit across the world as she chose now, so I could only assume that she had gone back to Taiyou where Ao Kouen had been stationed to fetch him, but it seemed to me that she was back to her usual habits of ignoring what was too painful to deal with and being elsewhere when there were people who needed her.

Blinking to refocus past the tears of frustration, sadness, grief, and who knew what else, I found Ticket nearer to me, within a more normal range of sight. The Seventh Spawn Croatin seemed out of place away from his brethren who had gathered to mourn their fallen together, but perhaps he was with his kind now and mourning one of their own.

The guardians of Lilyth's valley, or what was left of them, stood in a rough semi-circle around the empty husk of a body that had once been the little girl to whom they had sworn their loyalty. In a way of their own, the guardians, and especially Ticket, had loved Little Lilyth; a cruel fate had taken her from them and they had been powerless to stop it.

Nearby, Aysel was inconsolable. Adel's body was lost in the rubble, but the lack of the solid Knight's presence told Aysel that her sister had fallen, even if she didn't yet know how it had come about. With a more serious expression on his face than I'd ever seen from him, the usually affable Jeth wrapped his arms around Aysel, and let her cry and rage into his chest.

I was distracted by motion as Leon made his way toward me, walking with purpose and ignoring the crunching of the debris beneath his feet. I opened my mouth to say something to him, but stopped when I saw his expression and I realized that nothing I could say to him right now could possibly return the light to his eyes.

He got down on one knee as he reached my side, but I knew immediately that it wasn't me he had come here to see. Next to me on the blood-stained ice and snow, Hotaru lay where she had fallen when her life had been cruelly and inadvertently cut short by the unfeeling Lillem, and by my own inability to keep her safe at a time when she had needed me to do so.

I felt like I was intruding upon Leon in a private moment as he said his goodbyes, but I didn't know what else to do. There was no use staying beside Hotaru now and I knew that, but I couldn't bear to leave her like this. I had failed at keeping her safe, first from Lilyth and then from chance as the Lillem had thoughtlessly ended her life. My powers should have been enough to protect her long enough to get help, and if not mine then her own.

We could die, yes, but our powers were supposed to help keep us safe; they weren't supposed to let us die like this. I was still alive, and so were Kaji and Yue. Was it simply that luck hadn't been on Hotaru's side, or was there something else to blame for this?

Leon paid me no mind as he paid his respects, despite the tears on his face. I only realized I was staring when a hand touched my shoulder, snapping me out of my despondency long enough to turn my head away from the heart-wrenching sight of one friend mourning another.

Masaru was smiling sympathetically down at me and I realized how actively I had been watching the actions of everyone else around me to avoid having to live inside my own emotions. I couldn't escape them, however, because everything I saw around me just reminded me of the thoughts and feelings I was trying to avoid.

Despite my desperate desire to be anywhere but here, I hadn't yet made any effort to move and I was still in the spot where I had landed once I had reformed after the defeat of Lilyth. I was still next to Hotaru, who could not and would not ever leave this place under her own power.

"I think he'd probably appreciate a moment alone with her," Masaru noted gently, being careful to keep my gaze locked with his.

He held out his hand to me and I took it, letting him pull me to my feet and take me into his arms. I don't know how long he held me like that, but it was enough just to be in his arms and let him block out the sight of the world around me. No matter how prepared I had thought I would be going into this battle, the reality of the aftermath was something else and it was just too much for me to take in all at once.

The survivors of the desperate battle, the soldiers, the civilians, and the people of Damos would just have to take care of themselves for a while. With the loss of Akuma and Hotaru, Yue's absence, Kaji's grief, and my useless state, there were no Chosen left to help them, no powered individuals around to perform miracles and make this crimson winter any easier to bear.

There were few Knights without injuries of their own, but those that were there had loved ones of their own to take care of, and so it was up to the people to rise to the occasion and protect themselves – and one another – as we all waited in the cold and unforgiving landscape for Hex to bring his ship overland to take us home.

"Now the lands of Damos are hospitable again, or at least more so." I smiled, remembering the last time I'd visited the wintry plains around the temple and hadn't been prepared for how cold it was over there. The Stirr had certainly meant it when they'd promised to allow the world's environments to slowly right themselves. "Many people have settled there once more, but a lot of the *'Tribe of Damos'*," I added that part in Stirr, causing some laughter at seeing a human make the odd hissing sound that usually only a Stirr could produce, "now live in Middleton, Sresh, and in more than a few outposts."

"And the Joining?" a familiar voice cut in, drawing my attention to my left where my friend Mifa had taken up a position against the side wall of her own classroom. She was older now, her brown hair streaked heavily with grey, but she was still the same girl I had known, inside as unchanged by time as I was on the outside.

"The Joining," I said with a smile over at Mifa while speaking for the benefit of my entire audience, "was not too long after we returned and was certainly a day I will never forget.

"As much as any of us wanted to leave the frozen land of Damos behind, including myself, it was difficult to face the thought of going home to more reminders of what we had lost and how much had been taken from us. I'd lost my best friend, others had lost members of their family, their mother or their father, their husband or their wife, or in some cases simply the person that they'd held closest to their hearts, even if they'd never gotten a chance to tell them how they felt.

"When we left we would all have the task of rebuilding, of course, but there were some things that could never be rebuilt or replaced, and there wasn't a person among those of us that had survived that didn't feel this keenly. And so it was that Dahlia believed that a little bit of celebration was just the thing to improve people's spirits and to get us all to focus on what we had gained, rather than what we had lost…

"Dahlia's right, Dear," my Mother insisted, following me to the infirmary at the Children's outpost where I'd been told that there had been a package found with my name on it. "We could all use a little bit of cheering up and a wedding would be just the thing."

"I don't know," I responded noncommittally, thinking of how I hadn't felt in any way like celebrating since we'd been back these past few days.

"You still want to marry him, don't you?" she pressed.

"Of course I do," I answered, not bothering to correct her on the terminology anymore, as she had obviously decided that she was going to call it what she liked. I paused, opening the door to the infirmary and noting that it was still blessedly empty; the wounded had been treated in the field or aboard Hex's ship, and those still recovering had been left in Espearia with the Kumori. "I just don't want it to happen for the wrong reasons. We've got time now and there's no sense in rushing it."

With Mother at my heels, I made for the back room of the infirmary, which was both an office and a supply room in one. I had no clue why there was a package there with my name on it, and no one I'd asked had admitted to knowing anything about it.

"I know that, Dear," Mother continued and I knew I hadn't heard the last of the discussion, not by a long shot. Since she'd started conspiring with Dahlia on the preparations, it had been all the two of them talked about. "I'd just hoped that perhaps you had reconsidered. We're all so excited for you."

I smiled, though behind the expression I felt the sadness that always came with thoughts of the Joining; Hotaru was supposed to have been there, to stand for Masaru and I, and now she would never get the chance. "I'll think about it," I promised her.

"That's all I ask, Yukari. You know I wouldn't push you if you weren't ready."

I saw the package on the corner of the lone desk in the cluttered room. It was bulky and wrapped in brown paper, which was curious enough in itself. Like the trees it was made from, paper was a rarity, especially this far from Taiyou. Had it traveled a long way, then? And if it had then someone had evidently taken great care of it, as the paper was not torn or crumpled in any way besides the folding that had been done to wrap whatever was inside.

There was no note, save the elegant script across the top that read simply, *Yukari*. Taking the package into my hands, I flipped it over to untie the string that held it together.

"What is it?" Mother asked, leaning over my shoulder, the room being far too narrow between the desk and the supply shelves for her to do anything else. "Does it say who it's from?"

I found myself unable to answer her as the paper fell away to reveal the silky fabric of the dress I had believed lost with the palace in Taiyou. Turning to show my mother what I held in my hands, I let the white dress unfold and was surprised to see a small piece of paper flutter to the ground.

My mother caught the note in her hands and stood once more to inspect it. "It's from Fuun," she noted, holding it out to me. "I recognize his handwriting."

Cousin, it read simply, *may this day be as perfect as the eternity that follows it.*

I felt tears well in my eyes, blurring my vision momentarily, and I handed the dress to my mother to free my hands enough to wipe them away. Fuun, who had been the bane of this world for over eight hundred years, had fallen before Lilyth in avenging Hotaru because he cared. Hated and feared for so long, in many ways the 'self-proclaimed' Chosen of Machalite had really been misunderstood. Besides being the cold and calculating force of destruction his reputation painted him as, he was also a brother, a cousin, and a man with his own troubles, his own causes, and most importantly his own emotions. He had given his life in defense of another and I knew in my heart that he would have believed that to be a worthy sacrifice.

"All right, Mother," I told her, recovering a little, "you win. I'll talk to Masaru and if you can manage to get everything together in time we can have the Joining tonight."

Mother beamed, excitement filling her expression. "I knew you'd come around! Come on," she said as she took my hand and draped my dress over one arm, "there's lots to be done and no time to waste!"

My part in everything, I quickly learned, was minimal. I had only to sit still while I was fussed over by my Mother and the team of ladies she had put together for the occasion. Later I was given leave to use my power to summon those people who would want to be present for the festivities but had returned to places other than the Children's Outpost.

Razor and Neva were among those I had to summon but I left them for last, enduring countless congratulations and warm wishes from the others I brought to me as mist. The happy new parents had spent the last few days resting in the well-appointed Ruby City under Oka's close scrutiny, in case there should be any complications following the rather unique birth, but upon hearing the news that my Joining to Masaru was finally taking place, they were more than happy to return home and bring the baby with them.

I felt three familiar life forces when I reached out for them, so I wasn't at all surprised to see the baby in Neva's arms as she and Razor became solid before me, and I was caught up in a hug from Razor.

"Don't wrinkle me or my mother will have a fit," I cautioned him, but hugged him right back, despite my words; it was good to see him and Neva again.

Neva smiled, waiting for her turn, and when I was free she hugged me with one arm before pulling me back to show me the little girl I'd seen many times while she'd been asleep in the womb, but had yet to meet. Her eyes were open, her irises a curious yellow and her expression attentive. Her eyes locked onto mine as if she recognized me, and from within the blanket Neva held wrapped around her a tiny talon unfurled and offered itself to me.

Smiling at the solemnity I wasn't sure I was imagining on her face, I reached for the proffered talon and shook it formally. "I'm pleased to make your acquaintance..." I began and then realized that I hadn't even thought to ask what Neva had named her.

"Tira," Neva supplied before I could form the question. "We named her Tira."

Razor smiled with pride, putting his arm around Neva, and I turned back to Tira, feeling the tears welling up once more as I looked over Masaru's long lost sister's namesake. "Pleased to meet you, Tira," I finished, my voice thick with emotion. "I'm sure your uncle Masaru will be very happy to know you as well."

"Oh, come here," Razor said, pulling me in once more, only this time for a family hug.

By the time all was ready to go it was well into the night, but that didn't seem to matter as far as anyone was concerned, since no one had yet gotten settled into a proper schedule of night and day. I had not seen Masaru since the moment I'd informed him of the plan to go ahead with things tonight and I'd begun to piece together that there must be some sort of silent conspiracy to keep the two of us apart until Dahlia was ready for us.

When that moment came, I wasn't aware of it. My mother only led me outside into the night, telling me she needed my help with something, and then handed me off to my father before sneaking off.

"Honey," my father said, turning me about to face out into the Sand Lake, "I think we could use a little light, and if you could do your best to make it last that'd be nice."

Neither my mother or father could have known how perfect my vision was in the dark, so the surprise they'd evidently planned for me was somewhat ruined. As I raised my arms and loosed a shower of glowing cyan arrows to land in a wide circle, the darkened Sand Lake lightened and revealed a crowd of expectant onlookers made up of all the people I'd met and grown fond of in my time on this world, including those I'd brought with me from Earth.

My father put his arm through mine and I suddenly felt the nervousness I'd somehow managed to avoid until now.

"Are you ready?"

I trembled slightly, the hairs on my bare arms standing on end, even though the desert was only cool at night and never cold. I took in the expectant faces all turned in my direction, clear as day to me in the dim light, no matter how far away I stood from them, but even though they were friends and family members every one, none gave me the confidence I needed to take that first step forward.

Then I saw him, beyond the rest and straining with his eyes to make me out across the distance that separated us. Masaru stood next to Dahlia, who was beaming with anticipation and wearing formal white robes for the occasion. He looked nervous too, but as our eyes met I felt my heart soar and the darkness of the night seemed to visibly lighten around me.

I heard the gasp of the crowd before I realized what had happened; without conscious direction my wings had emerged, my power responding to my heart's desire to take myself directly to Masaru.

Embarrassed, but unwilling to retract them and further embarrass myself by drawing attention to my lack of control, I left my wings out. My father took this as my response to his question, smiled, and led me forward. Together we took one step, then another, to where Masaru waited for me and the crowd parted to let us pass.

I passed many faces, most of them human, but there were also Croatin, Kumori, and even Stirr present. I only had eyes for Masaru and the way his face lit up as I grew near enough for him to fully make me out in the dim light.

I hadn't managed to get a look at myself, there being no mirrors in the outpost beyond those hung in the slits that served as windows to reflect the light further into the mountain, so I wasn't aware of my outward appearance, but I saw the effect it had clearly on Masaru's face.

The dress Fuun had returned to me was the one Masaru had bought me for the coronation ceremony when Ao Kouen had been made King of Taiyou. The white Chinese-style dress with its gold trim and trail of embroidered doves in flight was the finest thing I'd ever owned and my most treasured possession, though I thought for certain that I had lost it in the fall of Taiyou. Evidently, Fuun had risked his life to return it to me, a timely gift and a reminder that our family ties were something he treasured.

I reached Masaru's side and stopped, feeling my father release my arm to take hold of my hand and squeeze it once before passing it to Masaru, who took it gently in his own. It occurred to me then that I hadn't thought to ask what was involved in this ceremony and no one had bothered to prepare me. Evidently, the same didn't hold true for Masaru as he smiled at me, turned to face Dahlia, and held our combined out hands to her.

Dahlia unfastened the rope she wore around the waist of her robe and with deliberate motions she began to tie the braided silk around our wrists to bind the two of us together. "Ye were born apart, two souls with two lives and two families," she intoned formally as she looped the silk rope between our hands. "Ye came to us a matched pair, your two souls having found one another against all odds and recognizing one another as having a likeness." The silk rope got two knots, one below our hands and one above. "And now the two of ye are to be Joined as one. Two souls, two lives and two families, choosing one another and forging a bond that can never be broken. Do ye both agree that this is the reason ye have come before us all?"

"Yes, it is," Masaru answered, looking Dahlia in the eyes.

She turned to me. "Yes," I answered.

"Then may those that would stand for Masaru and Yukari please come forward," Dahlia continued, looking out beyond us.

"I stand for Masaru," Razor's voice spoke from somewhere in the crowd.

Unable to separate, Masaru and I had to spin fully around to face everyone assembled. I belatedly realized that although Razor had already been decided upon to stand for Masaru, with Hotaru gone there was no longer anyone to stand for me and it had been the furthest thing from my mind to try and find someone to take her place.

"And I offer to stand for Yukari," Neva added and the crowd parted to reveal the pair of them, with Neva still holding baby Tira in her arms.

Together, Razor and Neva made their way up to the front where we stood to take up positions beside us, Razor to Masaru's left and Neva to my right.

"Masaru," Razor addressed him with the utmost seriousness,"I vow to you with everything that I am that I will do whatever is within my power to keep you both safe, and should I fail, I promise to protect her and cherish her with all of my heart, just as you will do in this life and whatever lies beyond it. With your permission?"

"I know ye will," Masaru told him, "and yes, ye have my permission."

Razor returned Masaru's amused expression with a grin of his own before stepping forward and taking my free hand in his. "Yukari?"

I didn't know if there was something I was supposed to say or do, but I didn't have much time to think about it before I was pulled into Razor's embrace and kissed soundly. The Roughlanders in the crowd cheered suddenly and loudly, no doubt startling those who were not familiar with this custom, or perhaps it was only Razor's bold interpretation of it.

When the kiss ended, I was red in the face with embarrassment, but I couldn't hold it against him as he leaned into my ear to whisper, "Masaru's a lucky man," before pulling away and returning to his place at Masaru's side, earning himself a jab in the ribs from Masaru for his trouble.

"Yukari," Neva said, "I vow to ye that I'll be a friend to ye both when ye need it, or even when ye don't. I'll look after ye and care for ye, and if ever ye cannot be there for Masaru, I will be there in your place, a shoulder to cry on or an ear to listen, whatever is needed. That is, of course, with your permission?"

Neva looked hopeful and I realized that it was less my permission to kiss Masaru that she was after, but more an acceptance of her offer to stand for me, and with that, her offer for the two of us to become closer as the friends we'd had so much trouble becoming.

"Yes, and thank you, Neva," I told her sincerely. "I don't know what I would do without you."

Neva returned the smile with a relieved nod and passed the baby to Dahlia to hold. Then she stepped up to Masaru to give him a kiss, albeit one much less enthusiastic than the one Razor had given me. Razor reached for the silk rope and tied the length of it on Masaru's side, then Neva took the ends from him to do the same on mine.

Dahlia raised her voice once more. "Two souls, two lives, two families come together and a contract is made. May those who stand as the family of Masaru and Yukari please come forward."

My mother came to stand behind me and Krox did the same for Masaru, as the rest of Masaru's pseudo-family already occupied positions in the ceremony.

"This ring belongs to Dahlia," Krox spoke, holding out a slim gold band made even tinier by his massive fingers. "It was passed down to her by her father and now it belongs to you."

Masaru took the ring from Krox as my mother began to speak, "This ring was the one I gave to your father. He's proud to have me pass it on to you."

Feeling slightly overwhelmed, I took the heavy gold ring my mother held out. I'd been told that an exchange of rings was a traditional part of the Joining ceremony, but I hadn't anticipated anything quite like this.

"Yukari," Masaru said, "the first day I saw ye in the Sand Lake I learned that you were beautiful," he began and I blushed, remembering, "and when I got to know ye, I learned that ye were just as beautiful inside as out. Now I know that I love ye and it feels like the most amazing discovery of all. I promise ye that ye'll always have me by your side. I'll be your Knight, your friend, your husband, and everything in between for as long as you'll have me."

I was overcome with emotion, but very much aware of all the eyes centered on us both when I realized that it was now my turn to speak. "Masaru..." I began and it occurred to me then that I should have prepared for this moment. I had known it was coming; I had been told that we'd exchange vows to one another, but I hadn't put any thought to the matter. Now all I could do was try and speak from the heart.

"I never dreamed this day would come, or that any of this could be possible," I told him, holding his eyes and feeling the world fall away around us, "but now that it is it feels like a dream come true. You mean everything to me and I promise you that my heart will be with yours for the rest of eternity. No matter what challenges arise to face us, I know that together we can be enough to rise above them."

"Let the two souls, two lives, and two families that have come forward this day be joined as one," Dahlia concluded, grinning from ear to ear. "Ye can kiss now, if ye'd like."

It was difficult to place the rings on one another's fingers with our hands bound as they were, but we managed with only minimal fumbling. As the early light of dawn crested the horizon and bathed us in its light, we kissed, and those assembled erupted into cheers and fanfare in celebration.

Following the conclusion of the ceremony, food was served and music began to play from where some talented Roughlanders had gathered with what instruments they either had in their possession or had found within the outpost. Masaru and I were led over to a long table that had been brought outside for the occasion and offered a plate of whatever we wanted from a variety of dishes.

"I knew the two of ye would eventually get around to it!" Dahlia gushed, setting a rather full plate of mostly unidentifiable food items down in front of us. "I guess it paid off for me to be patient. Everything is lovely, if I do say so myself."

"You did a wonderful job, Dahlia," I told her sincerely, "and Mother, too. I only have one complaint," I said as I lifted the arm that was still tied to Masaru's, lifting his in the process, "it's going to be a little difficult to eat unless you let us go."

"Oh, I think ye'll manage..." Dahlia noted cryptically and I noticed Masaru's face redden slightly as Dahlia winked at him before making herself scarce.

"What did she mean by that?" I questioned, figuring that by his reaction he must have some idea.

His blush deepened, but he was saved from having to answer by Sabien who came over to congratulate us and then came one guest after another with congratulatory words of their own.

"I'm so happy for you both," Ris signed, her eyes glistening as she looked us over.

"Ris! You shouldn't be up and about," I told her, taking in her heavily-bandaged wings.

"I'm fine," Ris insisted, *"and I wouldn't have missed this for the world."*

I took note of Yue standing just beyond Ris and looking like she was considering coming over but hadn't decided one way or the other, but at the same time Hitachi sidled up with a sly grin and blocked my view of her. By the time I leaned past him to wave her over, she was gone.

"You've got yourself quite a prize there, eh, Masaru?" Hitachi commented with his usual flair.

"Watch yourself, Hitachi," Leon noted, taking Ris' place as Sabien led her off to a chair he'd found for her to take a seat, "one might begin to think that you were jealous. Yukari, Masaru," he said as he nodded to us, taking my free hand in his and bringing it to his lips, "my best to you both."

"My master and I are pleased at your good fortune," X-En informed us, having politely waited his turn.

"Thank you, X-En," Masaru told him, "and Hex too. I assume he can hear me."

No sooner had X-En moved away than Ao Kouen was there to take his place. "It was a wonderful Joining," the King of Taiyou and Chosen of Jedeite noted, reminding me that despite his titles and powers he was still a Roughlander.

Corporal Zukatoro was next, followed by Noh-san, and even though both men had tragically lost their wives in the recent battle, they still had warm words to spare for Masaru and I. Mifa and Felice were next, Felice exclaiming exuberantly over my dress, while Mifa remained withdrawn. My heart went out to my friend; I had known how she felt about Goji and perhaps they even would have managed despite Fuzen's inevitable presence, but now we would never know.

Ticket stopped by; then Marc, the storehouse keeper, with his daughter Sally who'd been returned safely to him following the tragic events in Taiyou; and Annalise of Sresh, with Chikara by her side, the two having become fast friends in the time they'd spent together in Espearia. Pine gave his regards, as well as Bastion, Captain Grinkin, Kichigai, and even Aysel, who had been less than communicative since she had learned of her sister's death at Lilyth's hands.

"I'm really very happy for you two," Aysel told us, the sadness in her expression at odds with her words as much as she meant them, "and I know Adel would be as well."

I nodded in agreement, taking Aysel's hand in mine. "I know she would be. She told me as much herself."

"I'm glad to know that you and Adel worked out your differences," Aysel noted, emotion making it difficult for her to say everything she wanted to. "I know how difficult she could be, but she really did care for the four of you. You most of all, I think. You had so much in common."

I could see how hard this was for her; Aysel had only just gotten used to being elevated to the same status her sister had nearly always held, and now in Adel's absence she had to be the strong one, as there was no other choice left to her. I squeezed her hand once before letting it go. We would talk again and soon, but we both knew that now was not the time or place to bear our shared sorrows.

However, not long after Aysel's visit, it was apparently time for speeches, whether that was typical of a Roughlander Joining or not. Around where the ceremony had taken place, Jeth instructed the musicians to take a break before clearing his throat and waving his arms. "If I could have everyone's attention," he began, "there are some people who'd like to say a few words. Sabien?"

"Thank you, Jeth." Sabien nodded to the Espearian Knight and took a position at his side, where all eyes were now directed. "First and foremost, I feel that I owe Yukari and Masaru both an apology. I once tried to keep the two of them apart and I have come to see how misguided that was. What the two of them share is not a distraction and can never be a weakness. It is a bond that only makes them both stronger. I suppose," he continued, a rueful smile on his usually stoic features, "that though I never really considered it, I always took time for granted. No matter how long we are destined to live, we really don't ever have enough of it and there's no sense in denying ourselves love or companionship, simply because we feel that the time isn't right.

"So this day I would like to wish happiness upon my cousin and her Knight." There was some surprised murmuring at this revelation, but I found myself smiling; this was the first time that Sabien had openly acknowledged our relation to one another.

"Yukari, may you never hesitate to tell Masaru how much he means to you, and Masaru, I know you don't need me to tell you but I'm trusting in you to keep your Chosen safe. She's important to all of us and worth protecting."

I was a little taken aback by the heartfelt conviction of Sabien's words, but as the Knight Commander gave the focus back to Jeth I watched him cross to where Ris waited for him and I suddenly understood. He had lost his brother, among others, in the battle against Lilyth and nearly lost Ris as well. It was no secret that he loved the silent Kumori Knight, but perhaps it was that he had put off being with her because he had felt that it would distract him from his duties as Knight Commander. Now he recognized the importance and depth of his feelings for her, and that the biggest distraction would be trying to keep her at arm's length, instead of relying upon the strength of the love they had for one another.

Kaji took the floor next and his words were, if anything, more surprising than Sabien's.

"I know what it is to love somebody," he spoke deliberately and his opening words made the crowd fall silent. "It is without a doubt the best thing in this world or any other. It lifts you up and shows you possibilities you would never otherwise imagine. Love is the most wonderful thing two people can share, but the awful truth is that sometimes we don't get forever to enjoy that perfect feeling. Sometimes we only get ten years, ten days, or even ten minutes.

"I think we've all come to realize that life can be hard. It can be unforgiving and it can be cruel. We've all lost people we care about. We've all sacrificed something, especially those people who cannot be here with us today, but we did it so that those who are left behind can have a chance.

"So I urge you all to take charge of your own destiny," Kaji said, his usually controlled voice filled with emotion. "This is what we fought for, this is what we sacrificed for. So don't waste a single moment and don't leave yourself with any regrets. If you only have ten minutes to be happy, then make them the greatest ten minutes of your life."

Kaji's speech left a lull in the proceedings that even Jeth's usual exuberance had trouble filling as he thanked Kaji and asked for any other volunteers. Kaji had effectively reminded everyone of why we were here and through his words he allowed the spirit of those who were missing from our lives to have a voice and a will.

As difficult as his speech had been to hear and no doubt to deliver, ultimately Kaji was right; we did owe it to those friends, family members, and loved ones to live the life they had given us to the fullest, even if it meant living on in their absence.

The Roughlanders among us were not so surprisingly the first ones to break the silence, raising a cheer for Kaji and a toast to the fallen he had spoken so valiantly for. The Roughlanders in particular understood death, understood loss, and most importantly knew what it meant to bounce with the sun and live in the moment; this was, if nothing else, a Roughlander occasion.

I felt Masaru squeeze my hand as the music started up once more, and I turned my head to look at him and see his smile. He was a Roughlander; he understood, and I found that now I did as well. The battle had been long and dark, and friends of ours had gone into the night, but the sun had risen again like it always does. Those of us left would live in the light, cherishing the memory of the ones who'd given us the freedom to walk in the sun.

"Would ye dance with me?" he asked, making the motion to stand while keeping in mind our bound hands.

"I would love to," I answered with a smile of my own and let him lead me out to where other couples were pairing off to do the same.

I danced with Masaru as the sun rose higher, perfectly pleased that none could cut in as we were bound together and unable to move further apart than an arm's length. He held me close, swaying or twirling as the music dictated, until it was nearly noon and I simply couldn't keep up any longer.

We made to leave the floor and return to our seats when Dahlia appeared suddenly before us, Masaru's black-bladed knife held in her hand and pointed rather deliberately at his chest.

I expected any sort of reaction from Masaru but the one he gave. Seeing Dahlia, or the knife in her hands, caused him to blush furiously with embarrassment and upon noting his discomfort, Dahlia smiled wickedly before thrusting the blade's handle into Masaru's free hand.

"I'll leave ye both to it, then," Dahlia noted. "Off ye go, through that door, third floor, second door on the right, and I don't expect to see either of ye until the sun comes back up again, do ye understand me?"

My blush matched Masaru's as her meaning abruptly became clear, and continuing to smile with satisfaction, Dahlia dismissed herself to leave Masaru and I both standing awkwardly in the midst of nearly everyone we knew. Without a word of discussion between us or even a consulting look, we turned about as one and fled for the privacy of the outpost to escape the knowing eyes of our family and friends.

Once in the shadow of the mountain that was the Children's Outpost and realizing that no one, save perhaps Dahlia, had spared enough attention to watch us go, we simultaneously realized our foolishness and erupted into uncontrollable laughter.

"You should have seen your face," I told him, trying unsuccessfully to reign myself in.

"Ye were just as red in the face as I was," he countered, sobering as best he could, "or worse, maybe, because of your blue hair. I'm going to have to have a word with Dahlia later. She was supposed to slip me the knife, not stab me with it."

"Do you think anyone saw us?" I questioned, looking back over at the party which was still going on in our absence.

"So what if they did," Masaru responded unexpectedly, startling me by stepping forward and cupping my face with his hand, "we're Joined now, you and I. It's expected that we slip away together."

I felt my heart race at his words as I realized the truth of them. We were together now and we had the blessing of everyone around us; there was nothing more standing between the two of us. I nodded once and squeezed the hand that was tied to mine, and together we made our way into the darkened outpost where our new lives together would begin.

$$\diamond$$

"That's always been my favorite part," Masaru's voice startled me out of the telling of the story.

The entire class of students whirled about, all of them too startled to see a character from the story arrive suddenly in the flesh to even make a sound. It was one thing to know the story was a true history and another to have the figures of that history be present for the telling of it.

"Mine, too," I admitted, smiling in his direction. "I'm almost done here, would you mind waiting a little longer?"

"I can take it from here," Mifa offered, to the disappointment of the students who didn't want the end of the story to mean a return to regular lessons. "I think I know the rest well enough."

"I suppose you do," I agreed. "Well, in that case," I said and turned my attention back to my audience, looking over the young faces of the children of this world and knowing that they all still had their own stories to live, "I know that it was a lot to take in, but if I've done my job correctly then I hope that you'll all take something away from this and remember the lessons you've learned here today when life faces you with challenges that you feel are insurmountable."

I got a chorus of thanks from Mifa's students as I crossed the room to where Masaru waited for me, and by the time I reached him I could hear Mifa take control of the classroom once more. "Do you all remember how Ku-Roi, who was the Chosen of Machalite, went to Earth when the Japanese people came here?"

I tuned out Mifa's lesson, letting Masaru take my hand and lead me through familiar corridors. I remembered Ku-Roi well, though I had never actually met her. The actual Chosen of Machalite had been a formidable threat, but as we were to discover she was no more than that. She had been someone from Earth, like us, who had simply yearned for the chance to return home.

Following the Joining, it was decided to re-activate the Splitters and re-establish the connection with Earth. I wasn't against the decision, but curiously I found that even with the path open to me I wasn't even the slightest bit tempted to make the journey back to Japan. Perhaps it was because that had always been Hotaru's dream and not my own. Since our arrival here, she had kept the belief in her heart that she would one day return home. Now she never would, but it would fall to others to go in her place and determine what threat Ku-Roi posed to that world or this one.

Yue led the mission, assuring us that she would be careful and that she would return by the Splitters once she had accomplished her task. She was accompanied by Jeth and the remainder of the Japanese military unit that our parents were a part of, except my own parents who chose to stay behind.

Leon also decided to accompany Corporal Zukatoro and Noh-san, in order to attempt peaceful negotiations with the Japanese government, but more than that he went to see the world that Hotaru had always wanted to show him and to bring her spirit home with him if he could.

Hotaru's parents made the journey back to Earth as well, but in their case they firmly decided that they were through with the military. After the death of their daughter, the bereft parents simply wanted to return to a world where they had once been happy together, to try and salvage what was left of their family and truthfully, no one could blame them.

Kaji and I both stayed behind, neither of us having any desire to return to the world we'd given up. In my case it was because I had gained so much and had my family here with me. In Kaji's case it was because he felt there wasn't anything to return home to. With his mother and the love of his life both taken from him by fate, he had lost his sense of purpose and would have likely drifted as lost and as lonely as Verasheen's spirit must be, if it wasn't for Bastion.

Bastion had given Kaji purpose by demanding that he step up and take responsibility for the kingdom that Verasheen and Akuma had left behind. The Rubians were just as lost as Kaji was without the rulers they had known for a millennium and so Kaji found his place among them, leading them, but never ruling over them with an armoured fist and concealed visage as their Emperor once had.

Kaji's first act as ruler of the Ruby City was to pull the plug on the Mikura project, disappointing Oka, perhaps, but ensuring that the little girl would not be re-awoken to a world where she would be faced with the loss of her closest friends and family. Following that pronouncement, Kaji empowered the Generals both new and old and the people to learn to govern themselves. His unorthodox methods took some getting used to for the citizens of the Ruby City, but the change was a necessary one in light of the new worldwide policy of cooperation that took hold in the years following the end of Lilyth.

Chikara returned to lead Espearia, Annalise to Sresh, and Ao Kouen went to rebuild Taiyou with the help of Lord Hex and the Croatins, including Pine. Sabien continued his post as Knight Commander, taking Ris and Aysel with him to the Temple of Sapphire, where he began training new Knights in case a day should ever come where their strength might be needed to keep the world safe.

My mother and father, among others, made the journey overland to the mountain of the Blue Moon at the invitation of the

Stirr for humans to once more inhabit the village from which they had been driven away. That, along with the reparations made to the weather, was the Stirr's way of offering peace between their kind and the tribes of man; since then, that peace has held strong.

As for me, Masaru and I stayed at the Children's Outpost for some time just enjoying being a family with Razor, Neva, Tira, and even Dahlia and Krox. Although never truly leaving that behind, we did eventually set out on our own, wanting to see how the world was getting along and if we could be of any help in rebuilding the communities that had been disrupted by all that had happened.

We spent a lot of time in what had been formerly known as the wastes, now fertile because of the re-seeding program found in Lilyth's valley. The Sand Lakes, in most cases, became real lakes or swamps, filling with water slowly as time passed and the world righted itself. We travelled from outpost to outpost, making friends and establishing contacts with people in each area so that I could return us to those places whenever I wished. For a time it was a solitary life, though never a lonely one as we had each other, and within one breath and another I could bring us back to the people we loved most.

"Penny for yer thoughts?" Masaru interrupted my reminiscing.

"Don't you mean krevel?" I countered with a smile.

"Of course," he said with a grin, "only I wasn't sure ye'd know what I was talking about. Ye had such a far away look on yer face that I thought ye might as well be back on Earth."

"I was thinking about the Joining," I admitted.

"So was I," he informed me with a wink, "only I can tell by your expression that ye were thinking about a different part than I was."

Even after all this time I felt my face heat at the implication in his tone at the same time as I realized where we were – third floor, second door on the right.

"I managed to get our old room back," Masaru informed me with a grin. "I thought maybe ye'd appreciate it, ye know, for old time's sake?"

With Masaru's hands in mine I looked one way and then the other, and with my power to confirm that no one was nearby enough to see us I turned us both to mist. Between one breath and the next we disappeared, slipping away through the door just like we had first done all those years ago.

So much had changed since then, as it always does with time, but so much was also still the same. I knew now what it meant to be what I was and why I had been given the power to do more than those around me.

Being Chosen made me different, just as my choosing him had done the same to Masaru. It wasn't about being more than human, or closer to the divinities whose power had enabled us. The roles and the power we had been given set us apart and left us caught between what we had been and what we could become, leaving it up to us to realize that difference and become who we were meant to.

This message – this lesson, if you will – is one that I felt I needed to share with others. I needed to tell my story and give as many people I can the means and the will to reach their own potential. What I had learned, painfully and with great obstacles in my path, was that the power one wielded didn't make the difference – people did.

The power that I had been given didn't make me who I am any more than the position I was born to – my actions did. And with or without power, strength, or even resources, I know now that one person really can make a difference if they believe in themselves enough to rise to the occasion.

And if there is one other thing that I've learned, it's that there are some things that are worth believing in and fighting for, most importantly the right to choose one's own happiness and the path you take to get there.

A wise man once told me that a good story is one you can hear a thousand times over and never grow tired of it, but in my opinion, a great story is one that never really comes to an end because people keep telling it.

This story, I believe, is both.

The End

About the Author

Justine Alley Dowsett is the author of over ten novels, and one of the founders of Mirror World Publishing. Her books, which she often co-writes with her sister, Murandy Damodred, range from young adult science fiction to dark fantasy/romance. She earned a BA in Drama from the University of Windsor, honed her skills as an entrepreneur by tackling video game production, and now she dedicates her time to writing, publishing, and role-playing with friends.

WHO WE ARE...

Mirror World Publishing is a small independent publishing house based in Windsor, Ontario. We publish quality paperbacks and ebooks that feature other worlds, times and versions of reality. Our novels are for all ages and are creative, unique, imaginative and engaging.

We pride ourselves on our originality and 'outside the box' thinking, while taking a good look at the question, 'what if?' Our stories are never ordinary, the dialogue and action engaging, the characters believable, and there will always be some element of romance, adventure, science or magic. We are dedicated to bring our readers novels that will not only entertain them, but also teach them something about the world they live in by showing them one that mirrors it. We hope you'll consider picking up a novel from our collection today so you can see for yourself what we're all about.

You'll find a wide variety of our wonderful titles in our online bookstore and you can also purchase or review them through most major retailers worldwide.To learn more about our authors and our current projects visit: www.mirrorworldpublishing.com or follow @MirrorWorldPub or like us at www.facebook.com/mirrorworldpublishing